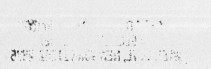

MR. WOLF'S CLASS

FIELD TRIP

ARON NELS STEINKE

AN IMPRINT OF
SCHOLASTIC

For Ariel

Copyright © 2020 by Aron Nels Steinke

All rights reserved. Published by Graphix, an imprint of Scholastic Inc.,
Publishers since 1920. SCHOLASTIC, GRAPHIX, and associated logos are
trademarks and/or registered trademarks of Scholastic Inc.

The publisher does not have any control over and does not assume any
responsibility for author or third-party websites or their content.

Library of Congress Control Number: 2019950318

ISBN 978-1-338-61764-1 (hardcover)
ISBN 978-1-338-61763-4 (paperback)

10 9 8 7 6 5 4 3 2 1   20 21 22 23 24

Printed in Heshan, China   62
First edition, October 2020

Edited by Cassandra Pelham Fulton
Book design by Phil Falco
Publisher: David Saylor

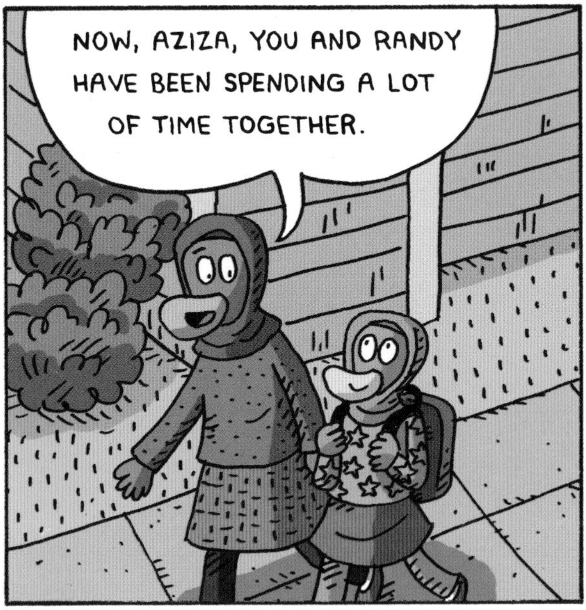
NOW, AZIZA, YOU AND RANDY HAVE BEEN SPENDING A LOT OF TIME TOGETHER.

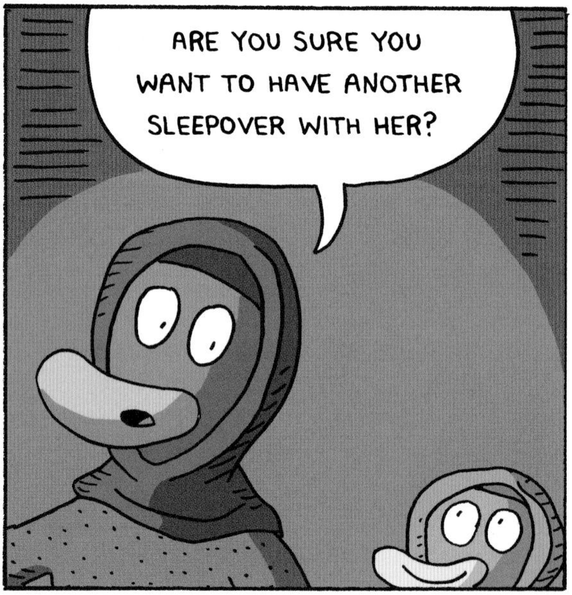
ARE YOU SURE YOU WANT TO HAVE ANOTHER SLEEPOVER WITH HER?

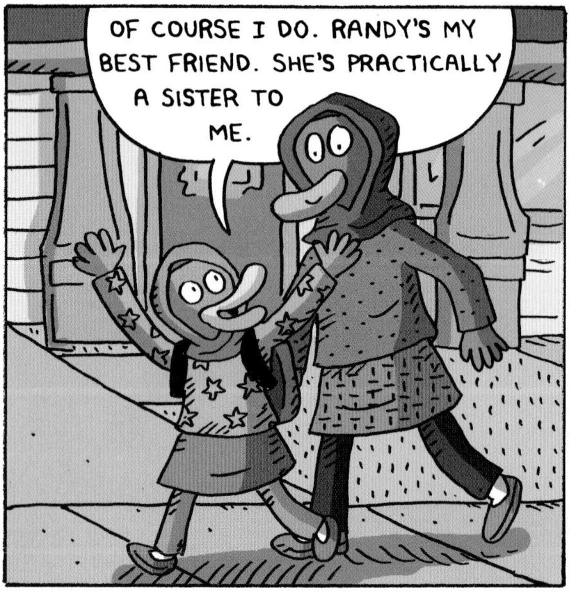
OF COURSE I DO. RANDY'S MY BEST FRIEND. SHE'S PRACTICALLY A SISTER TO ME.

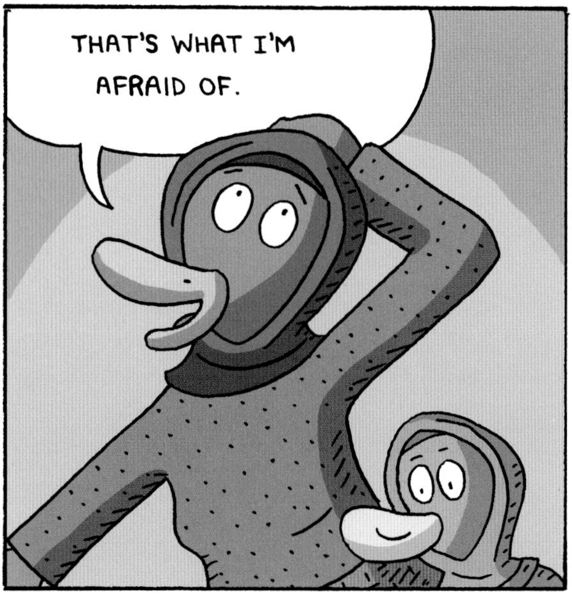
THAT'S WHAT I'M AFRAID OF.

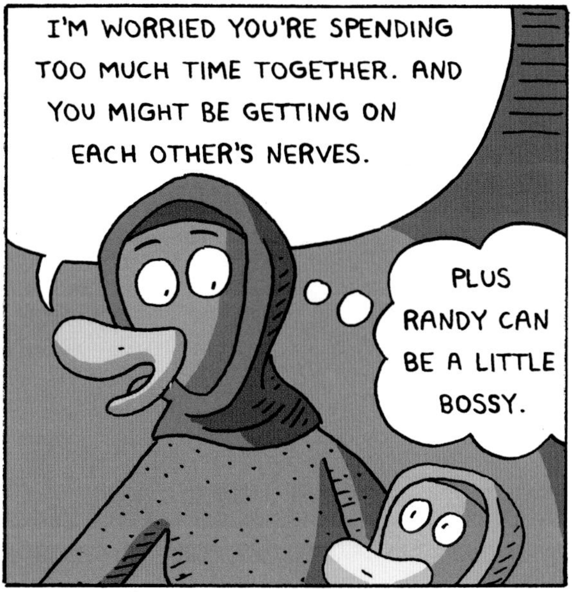
I'M WORRIED YOU'RE SPENDING TOO MUCH TIME TOGETHER. AND YOU MIGHT BE GETTING ON EACH OTHER'S NERVES.
PLUS RANDY CAN BE A LITTLE BOSSY.

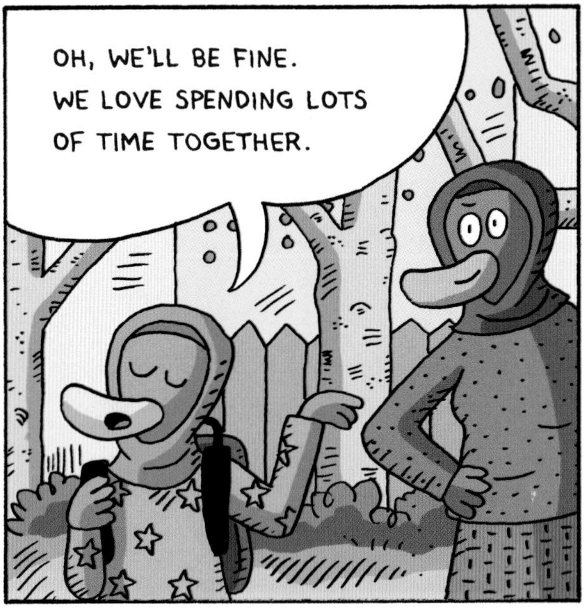
OH, WE'LL BE FINE. WE LOVE SPENDING LOTS OF TIME TOGETHER.

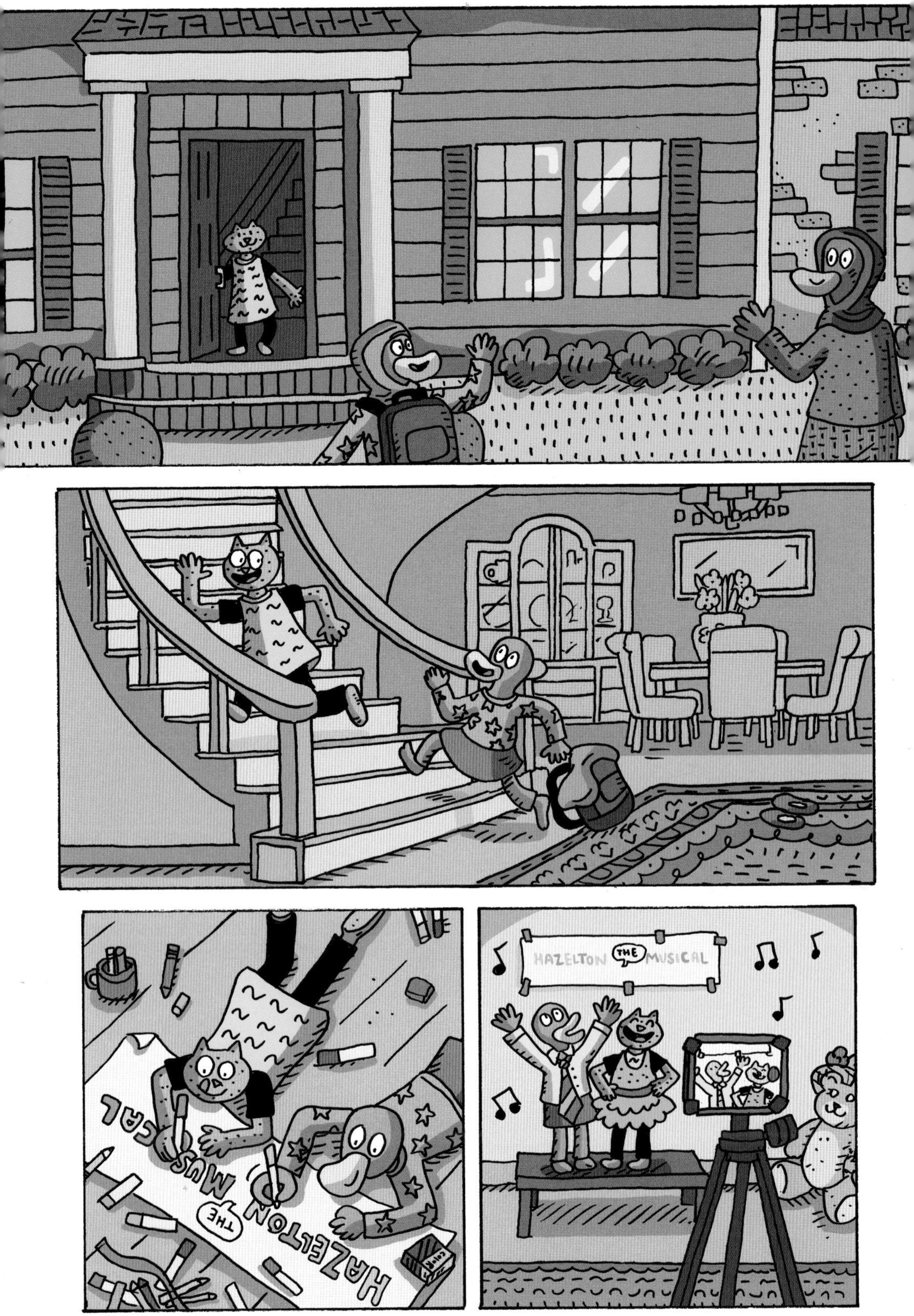
HAZELTON THE MUSICAL
HAZELTON THE MUSICAL

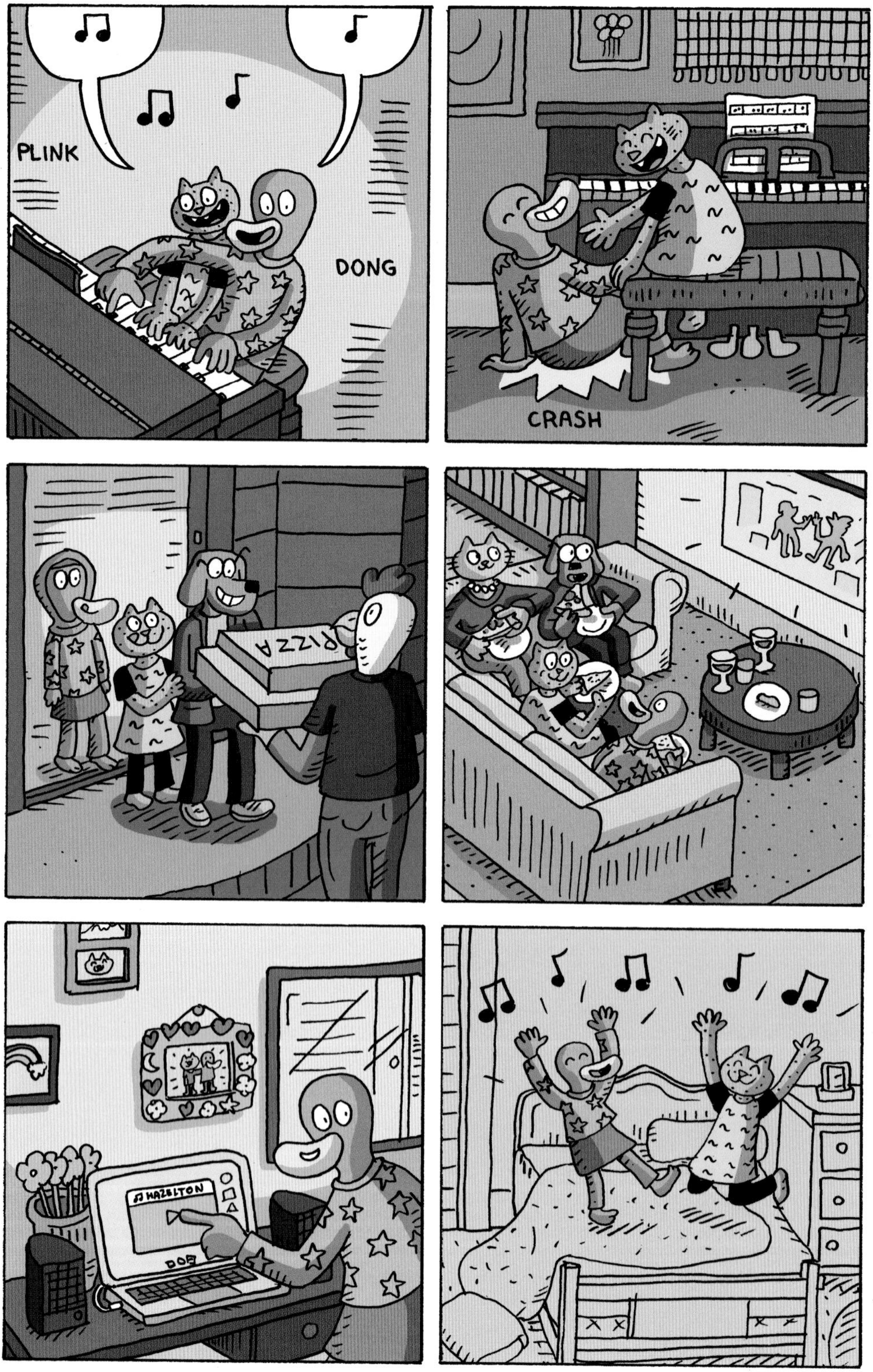
PLINK
DONG
CRASH
PIZZA
HAZELTON

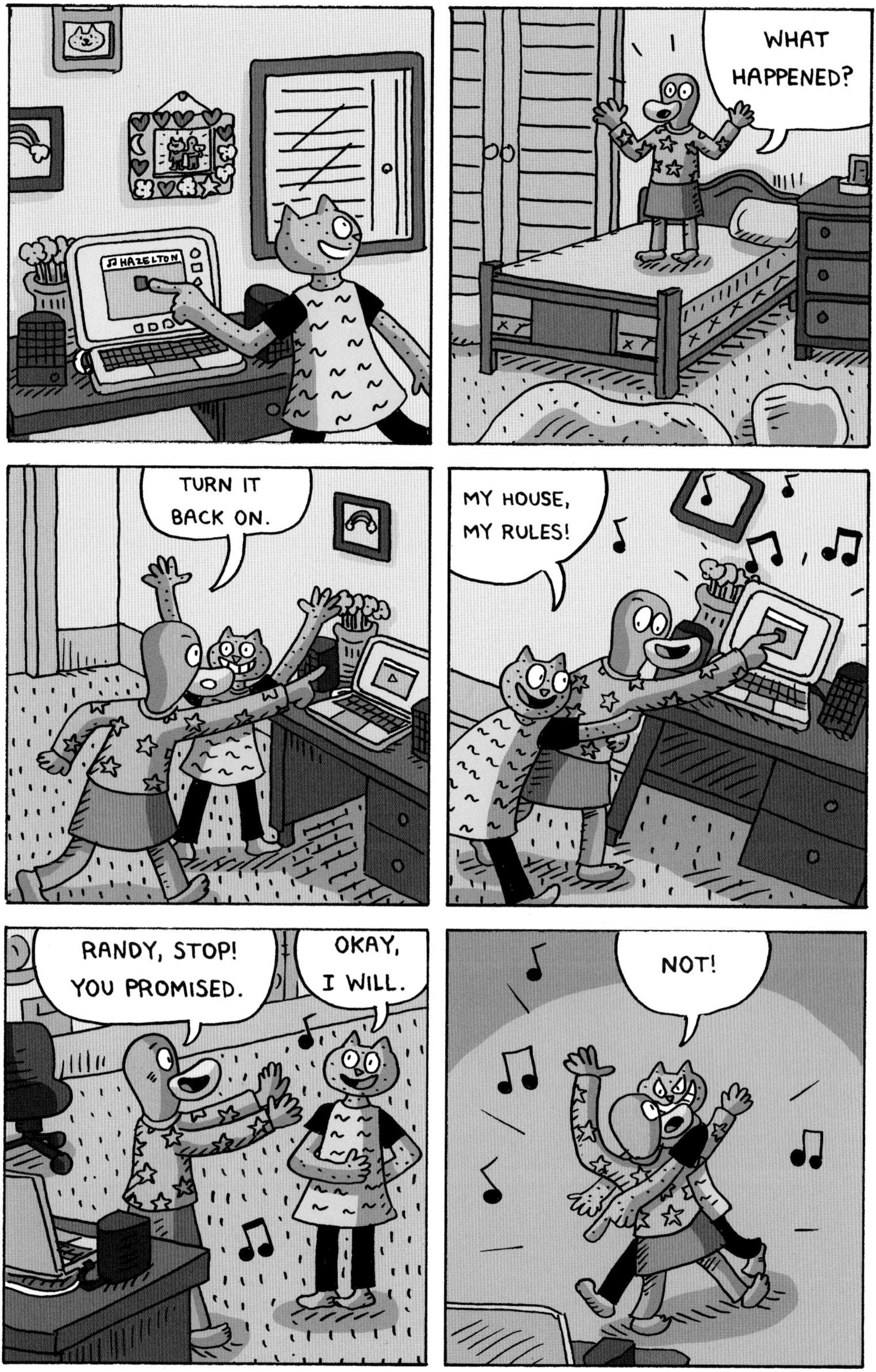
HAZELTON
WHAT HAPPENED?
TURN IT BACK ON.
MY HOUSE, MY RULES!
RANDY, STOP! YOU PROMISED.
OKAY, I WILL.
NOT!

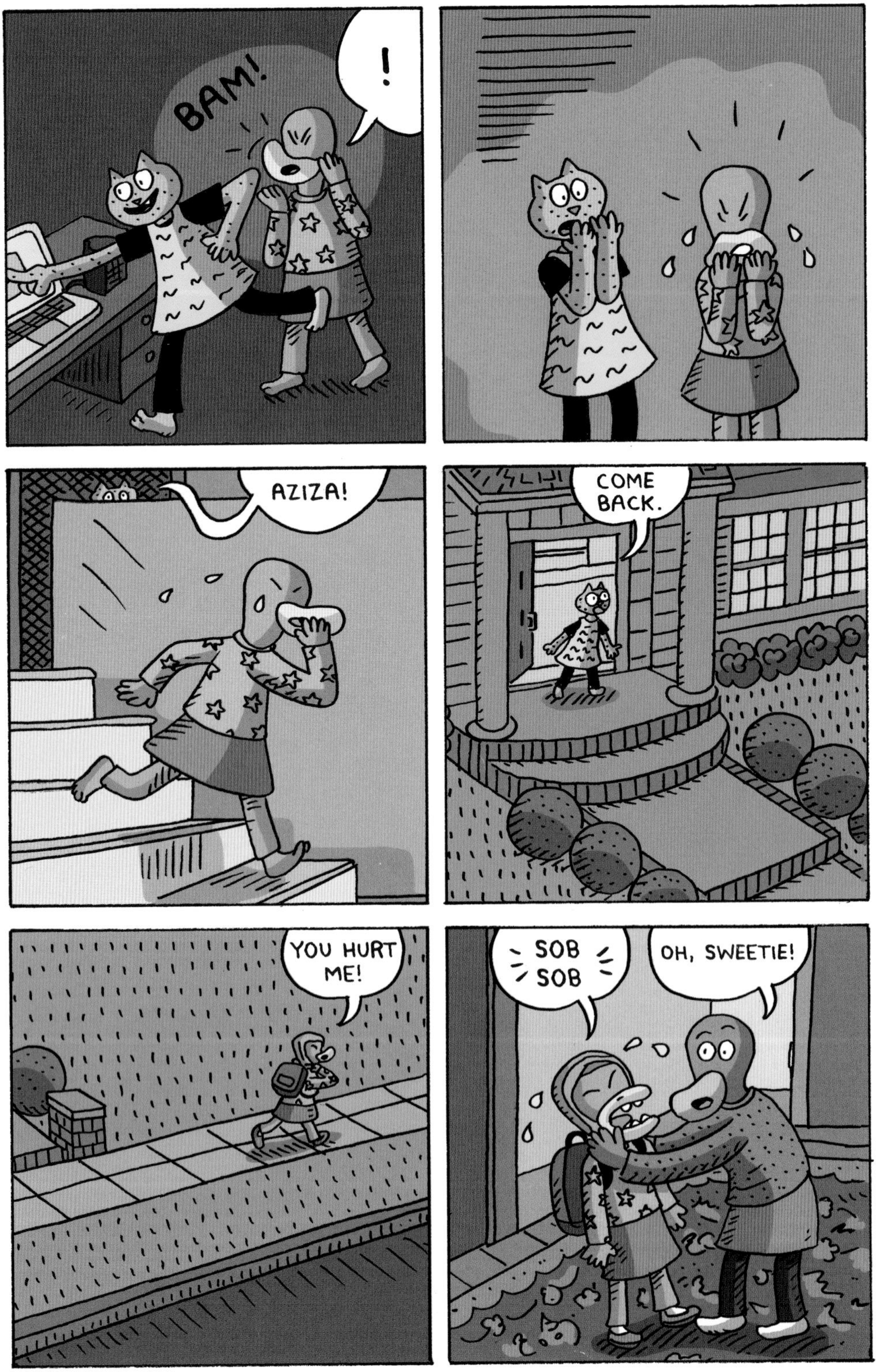
BAM!
!
AZIZA!
COME BACK.
YOU HURT ME!
SOB SOB
OH, SWEETIE!

CHAPTER ONE
The Silent Treatment

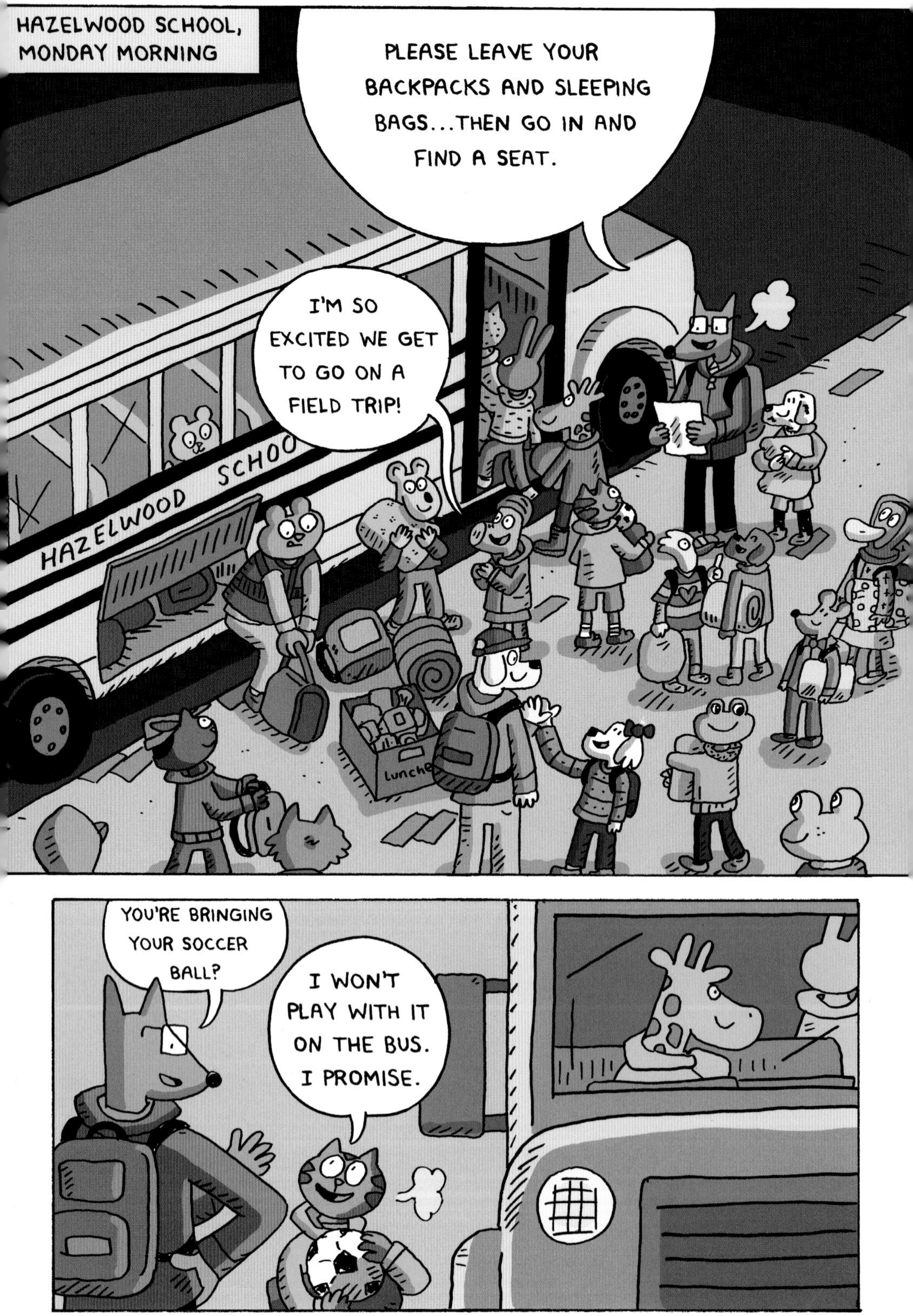
HAZELWOOD SCHOOL, MONDAY MORNING
PLEASE LEAVE YOUR BACKPACKS AND SLEEPING BAGS...THEN GO IN AND FIND A SEAT.
I'M SO EXCITED WE GET TO GO ON A FIELD TRIP!
HAZELWOOD SCHOO
Lunche
YOU'RE BRINGING YOUR SOCCER BALL?
I WON'T PLAY WITH IT ON THE BUS. I PROMISE.

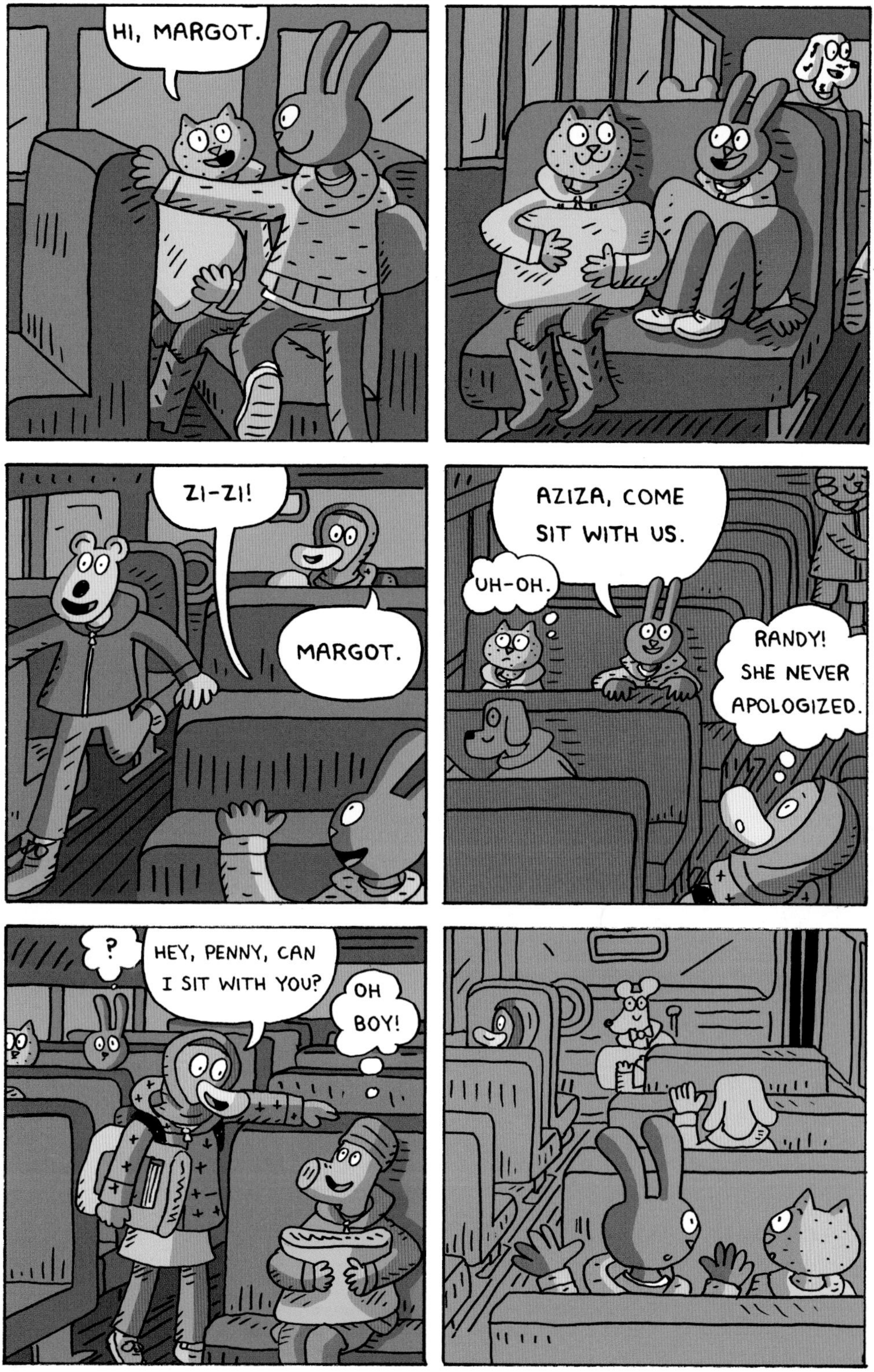
HI, MARGOT.
ZI-ZI!
MARGOT.
AZIZA, COME SIT WITH US.
UH-OH.
RANDY! SHE NEVER APOLOGIZED.
?
HEY, PENNY, CAN I SIT WITH YOU?
OH BOY!

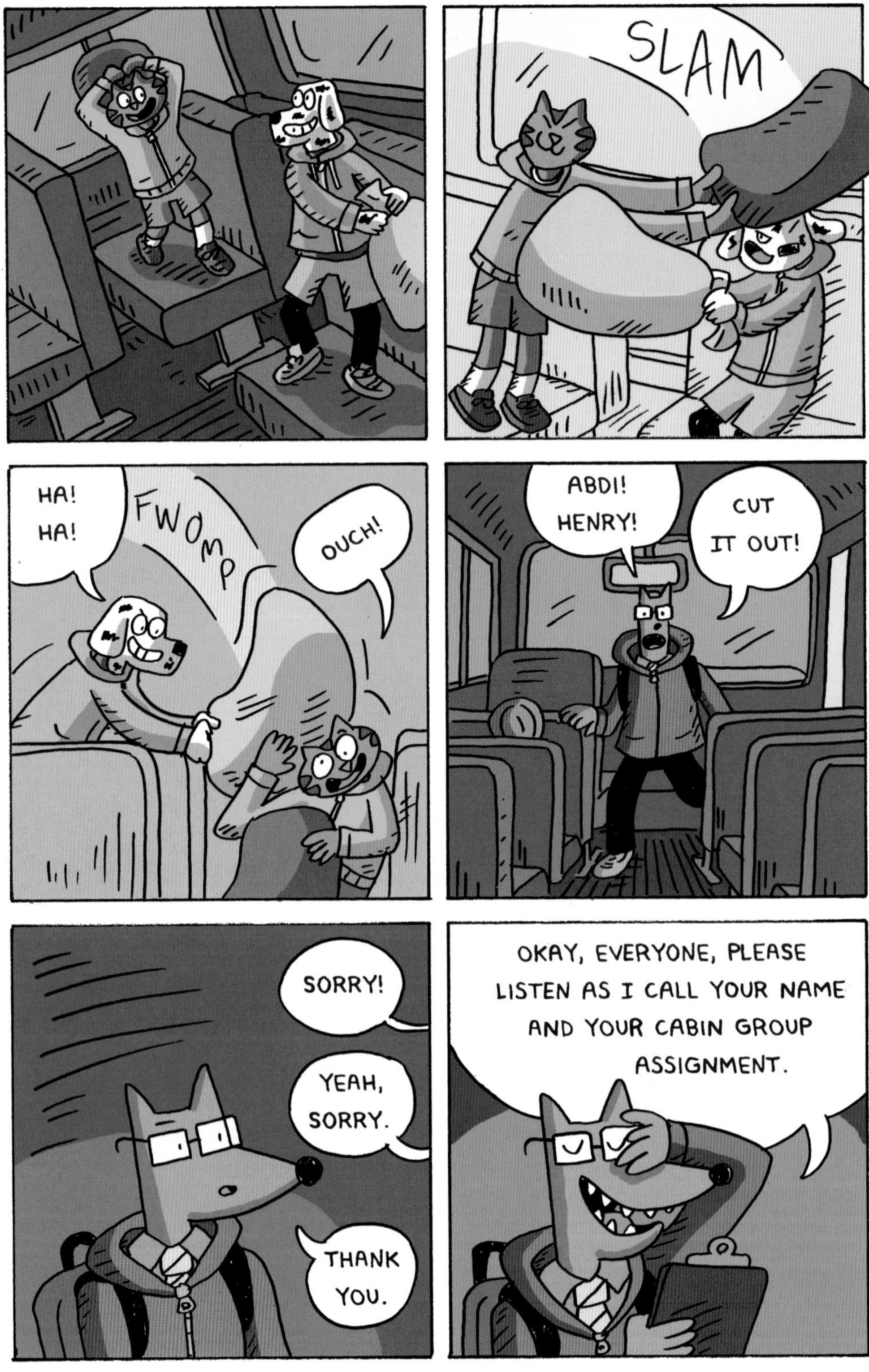
SLAM
HA! HA!
FWOMP
OUCH!
ABDI! HENRY!
CUT IT OUT!
SORRY!
YEAH, SORRY.
THANK YOU.
OKAY, EVERYONE, PLEASE LISTEN AS I CALL YOUR NAME AND YOUR CABIN GROUP ASSIGNMENT.

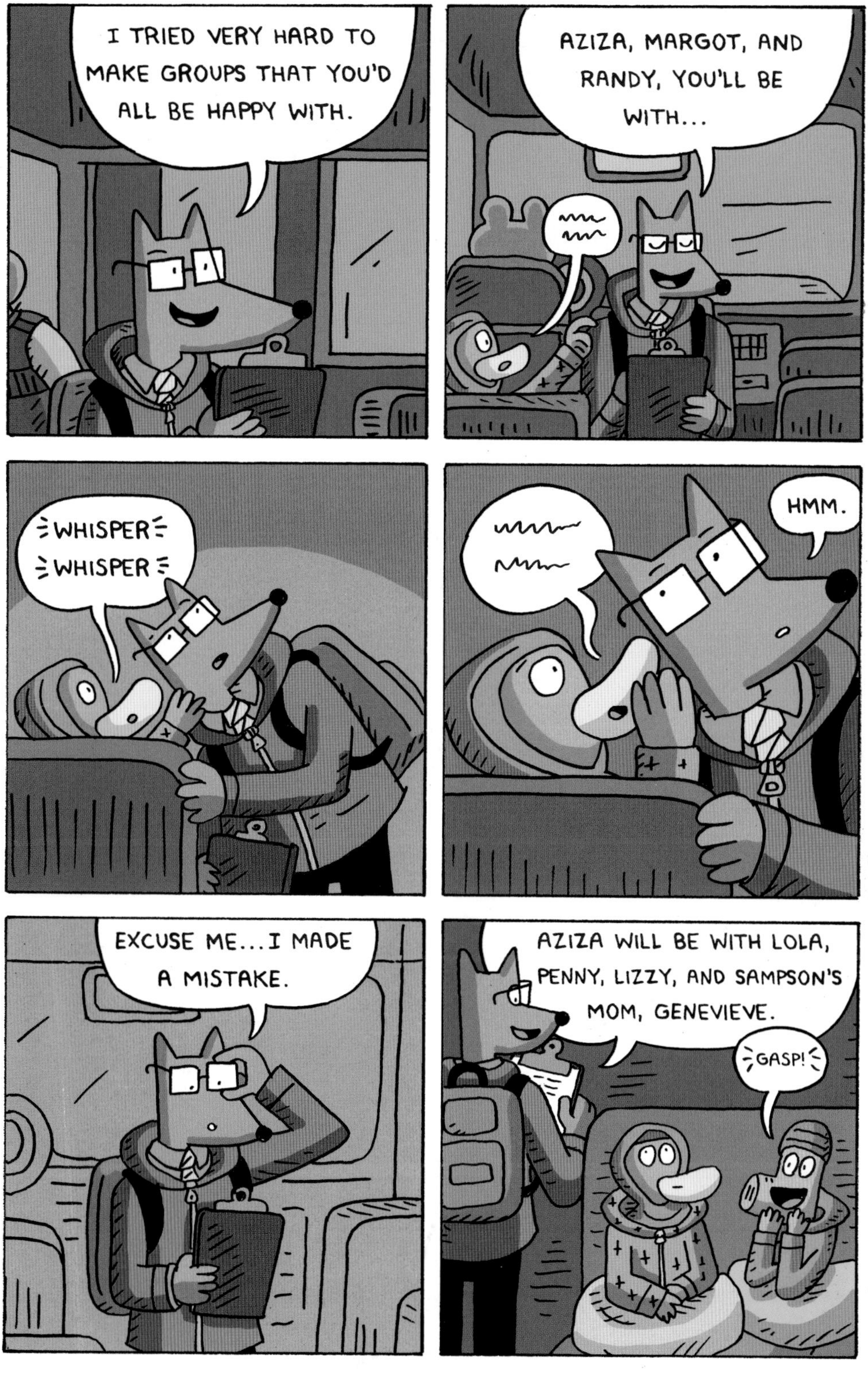
I TRIED VERY HARD TO MAKE GROUPS THAT YOU'D ALL BE HAPPY WITH.
AZIZA, MARGOT, AND RANDY, YOU'LL BE WITH...
WHISPER WHISPER
HMM.
EXCUSE ME...I MADE A MISTAKE.
AZIZA WILL BE WITH LOLA, PENNY, LIZZY, AND SAMPSON'S MOM, GENEVIEVE.
GASP!

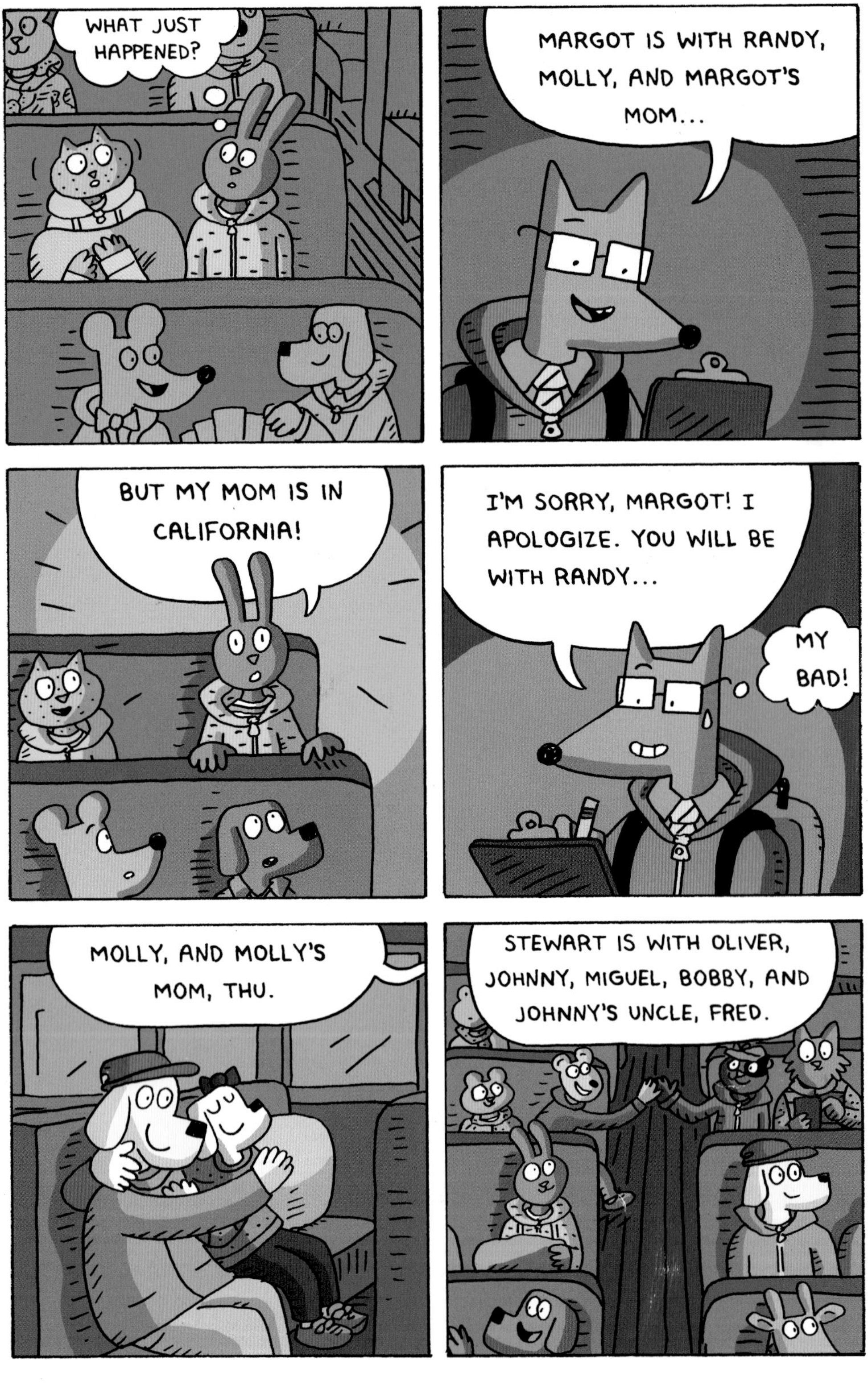
WHAT JUST HAPPENED?
MARGOT IS WITH RANDY, MOLLY, AND MARGOT'S MOM...
BUT MY MOM IS IN CALIFORNIA!
I'M SORRY, MARGOT! I APOLOGIZE. YOU WILL BE WITH RANDY...
MY BAD!
MOLLY, AND MOLLY'S MOM, THU.
STEWART IS WITH OLIVER, JOHNNY, MIGUEL, BOBBY, AND JOHNNY'S UNCLE, FRED.

THE LAST GROUP IS COMPRISED OF ABDI, HENRY, NOAH, ME...

SAMPSON, AND OSCAR.

BUT, MR. WOLF... OSCAR ISN'T HERE YET.

WE'LL GIVE HIM A FEW MORE MINUTES, BUT THEN WE'LL HAVE TO BE ON OUR WAY.

COME SIT WITH ME, PENNY.

SKY WORLD

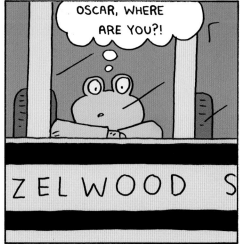

OSCAR, WHERE ARE YOU?!

Z E L W O O D S

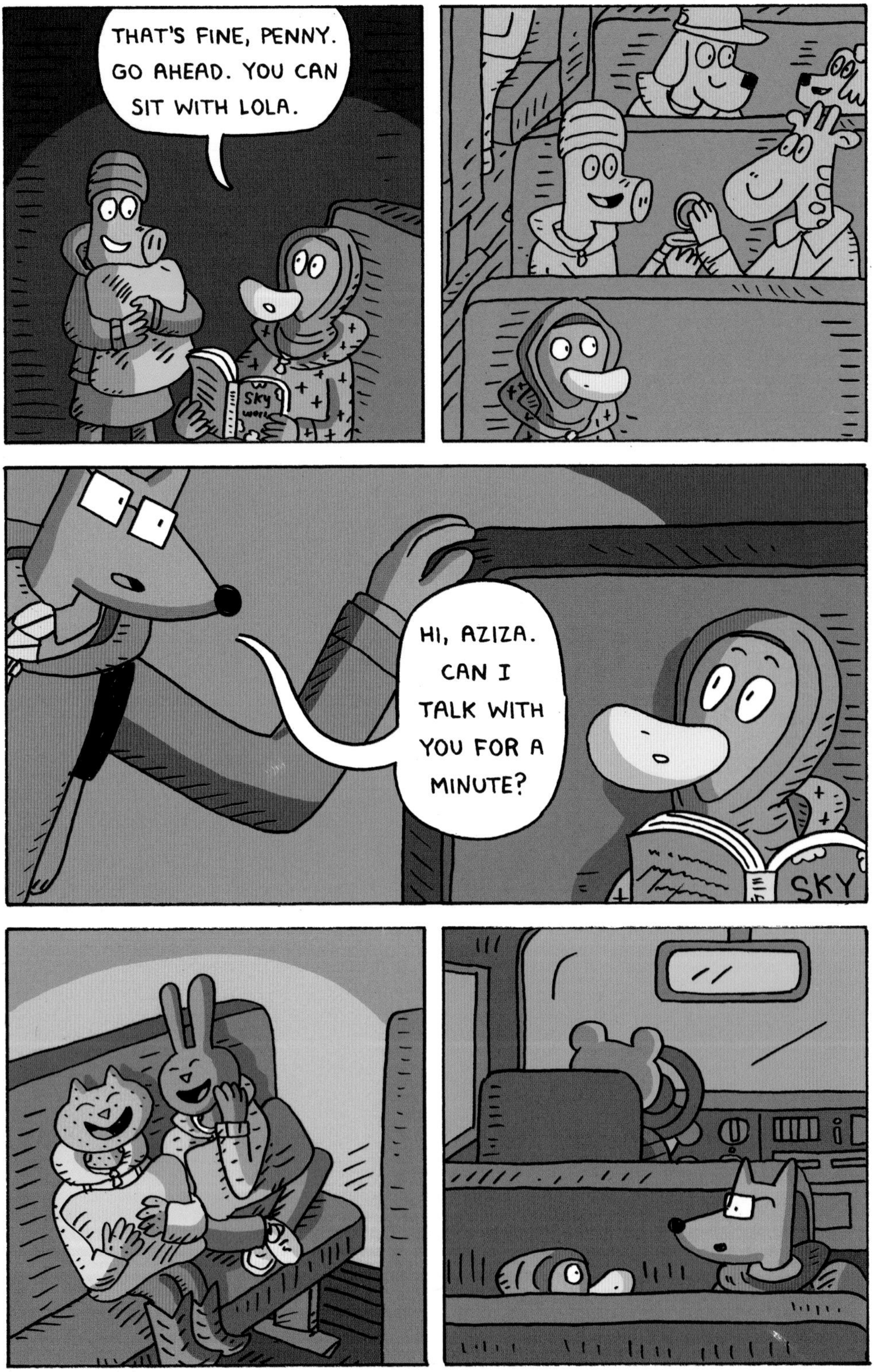
THAT'S FINE, PENNY. GO AHEAD. YOU CAN SIT WITH LOLA.
HI, AZIZA. CAN I TALK WITH YOU FOR A MINUTE?
SKY

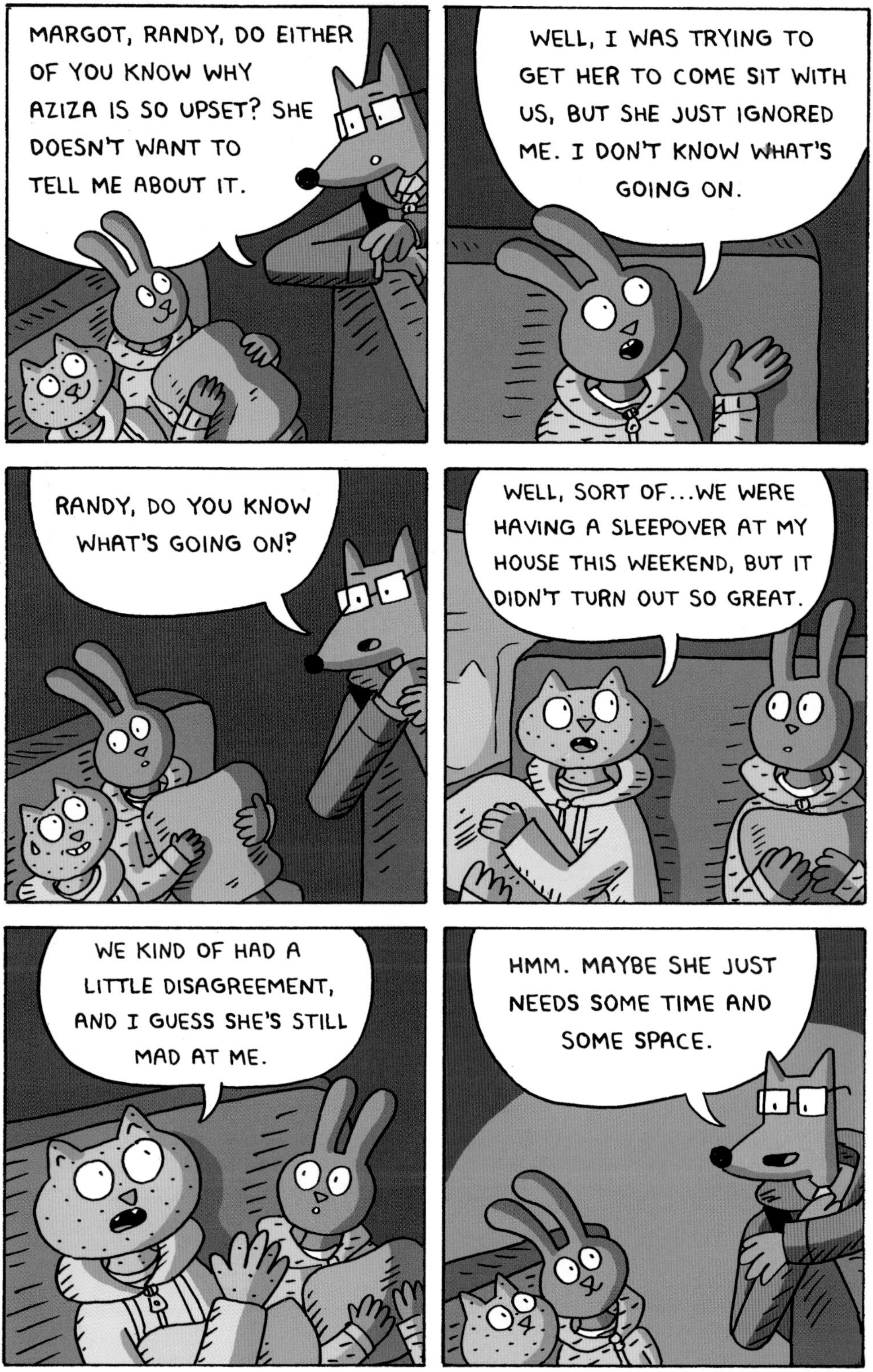
MARGOT, RANDY, DO EITHER OF YOU KNOW WHY AZIZA IS SO UPSET? SHE DOESN'T WANT TO TELL ME ABOUT IT.
WELL, I WAS TRYING TO GET HER TO COME SIT WITH US, BUT SHE JUST IGNORED ME. I DON'T KNOW WHAT'S GOING ON.
RANDY, DO YOU KNOW WHAT'S GOING ON?
WELL, SORT OF...WE WERE HAVING A SLEEPOVER AT MY HOUSE THIS WEEKEND, BUT IT DIDN'T TURN OUT SO GREAT.
WE KIND OF HAD A LITTLE DISAGREEMENT, AND I GUESS SHE'S STILL MAD AT ME.
HMM. MAYBE SHE JUST NEEDS SOME TIME AND SOME SPACE.

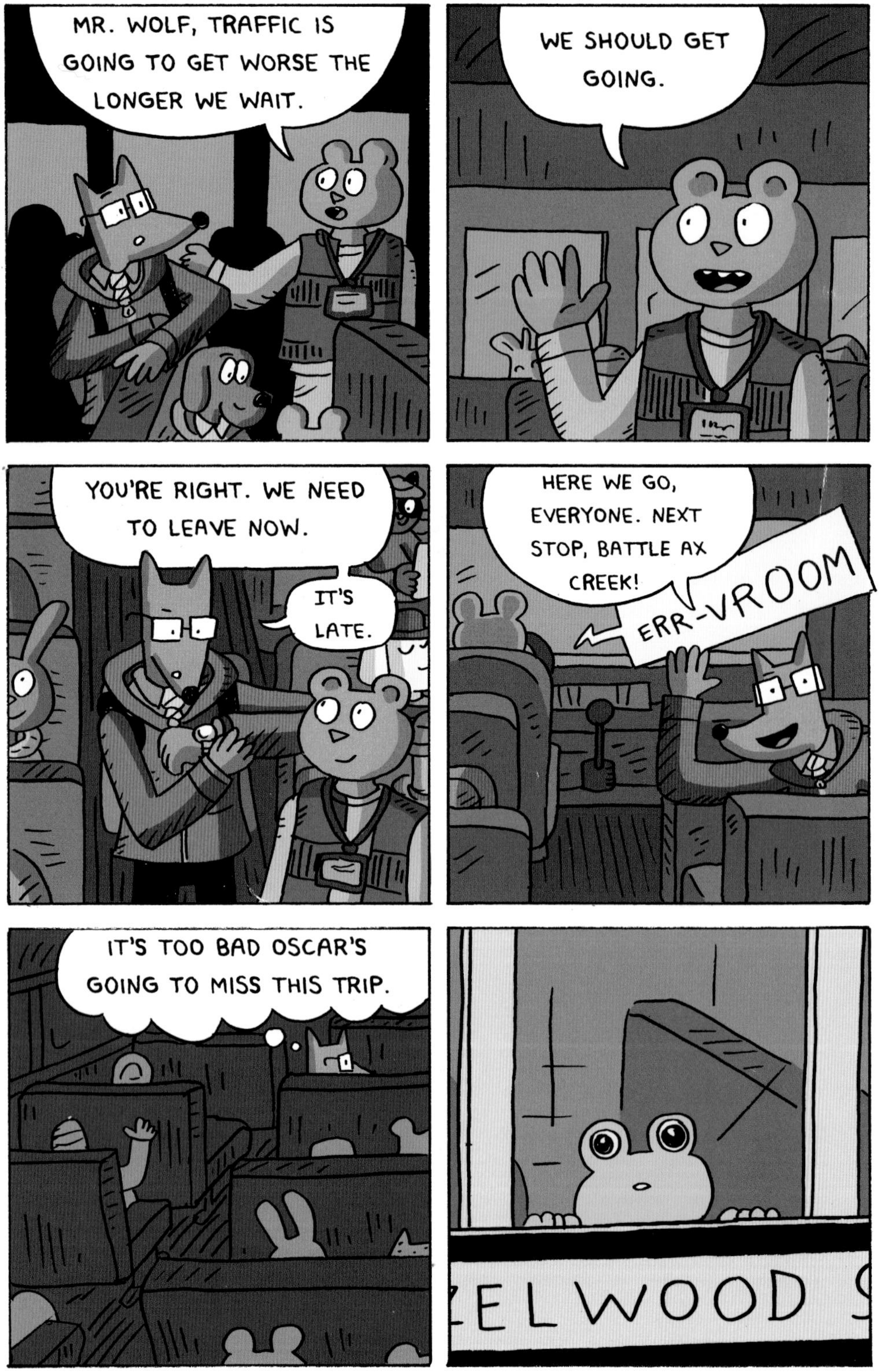
MR. WOLF, TRAFFIC IS GOING TO GET WORSE THE LONGER WE WAIT.
WE SHOULD GET GOING.
YOU'RE RIGHT. WE NEED TO LEAVE NOW.
IT'S LATE.
HERE WE GO, EVERYONE. NEXT STOP, BATTLE AX CREEK!
ERR-VROOM
IT'S TOO BAD OSCAR'S GOING TO MISS THIS TRIP.
ELWOOD

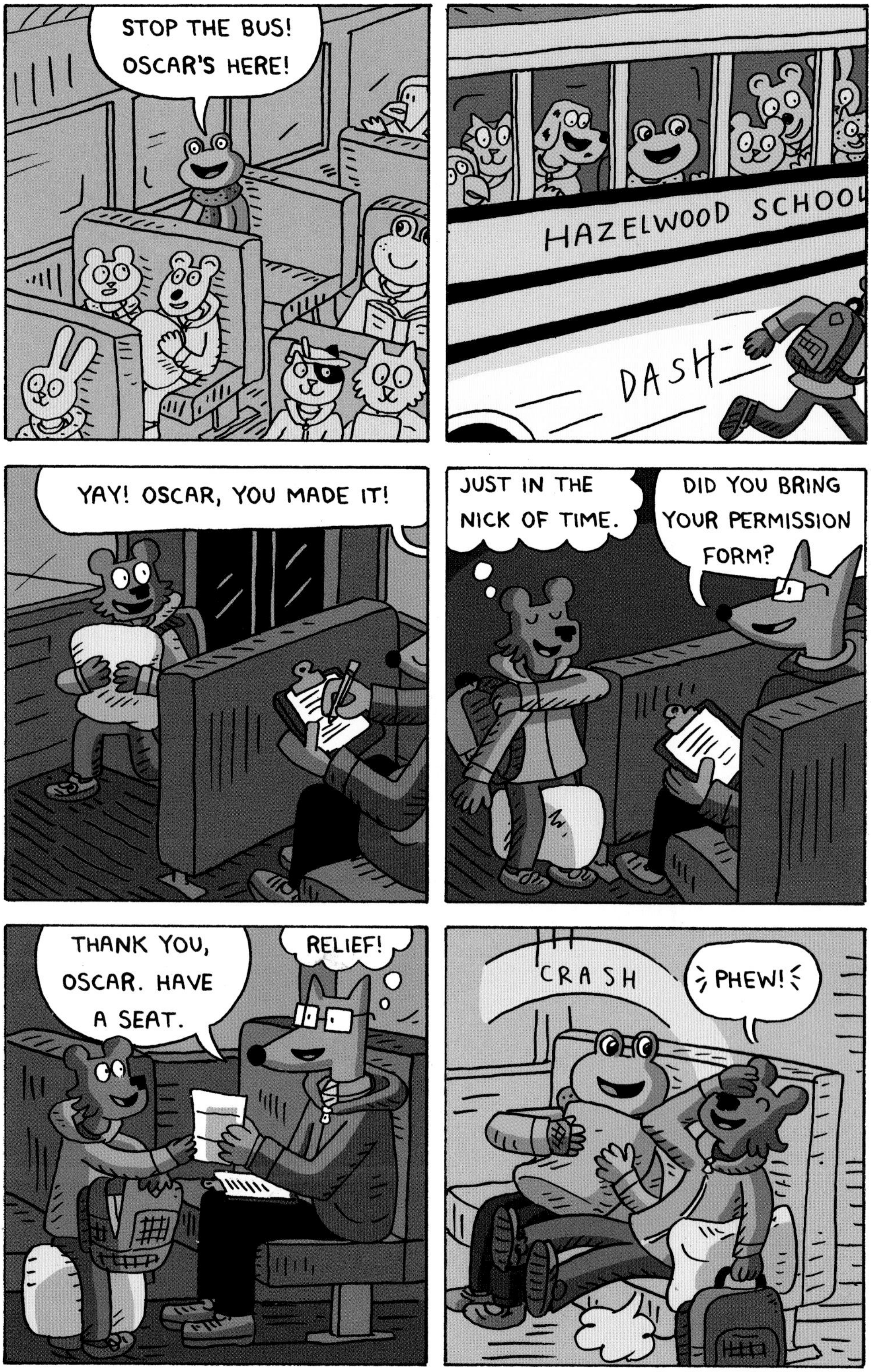
STOP THE BUS! OSCAR'S HERE!
HAZELWOOD SCHOOL
DASH
YAY! OSCAR, YOU MADE IT!
JUST IN THE NICK OF TIME.
DID YOU BRING YOUR PERMISSION FORM?
THANK YOU, OSCAR. HAVE A SEAT.
RELIEF!
CRASH
PHEW!

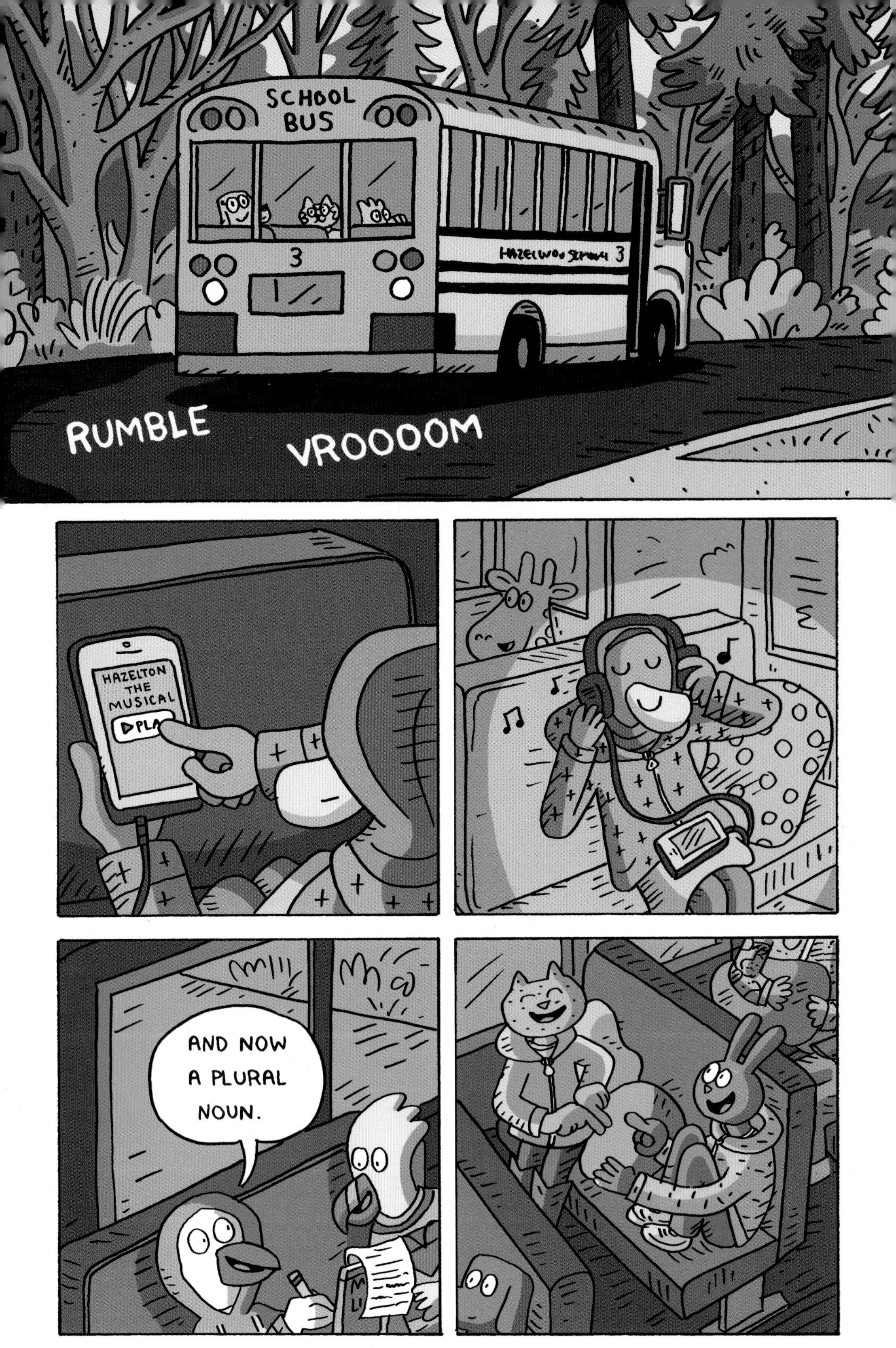
SCHOOL BUS
3
RUMBLE
VROOOOM
HAZELTON THE MUSICAL
AND NOW A PLURAL NOUN.

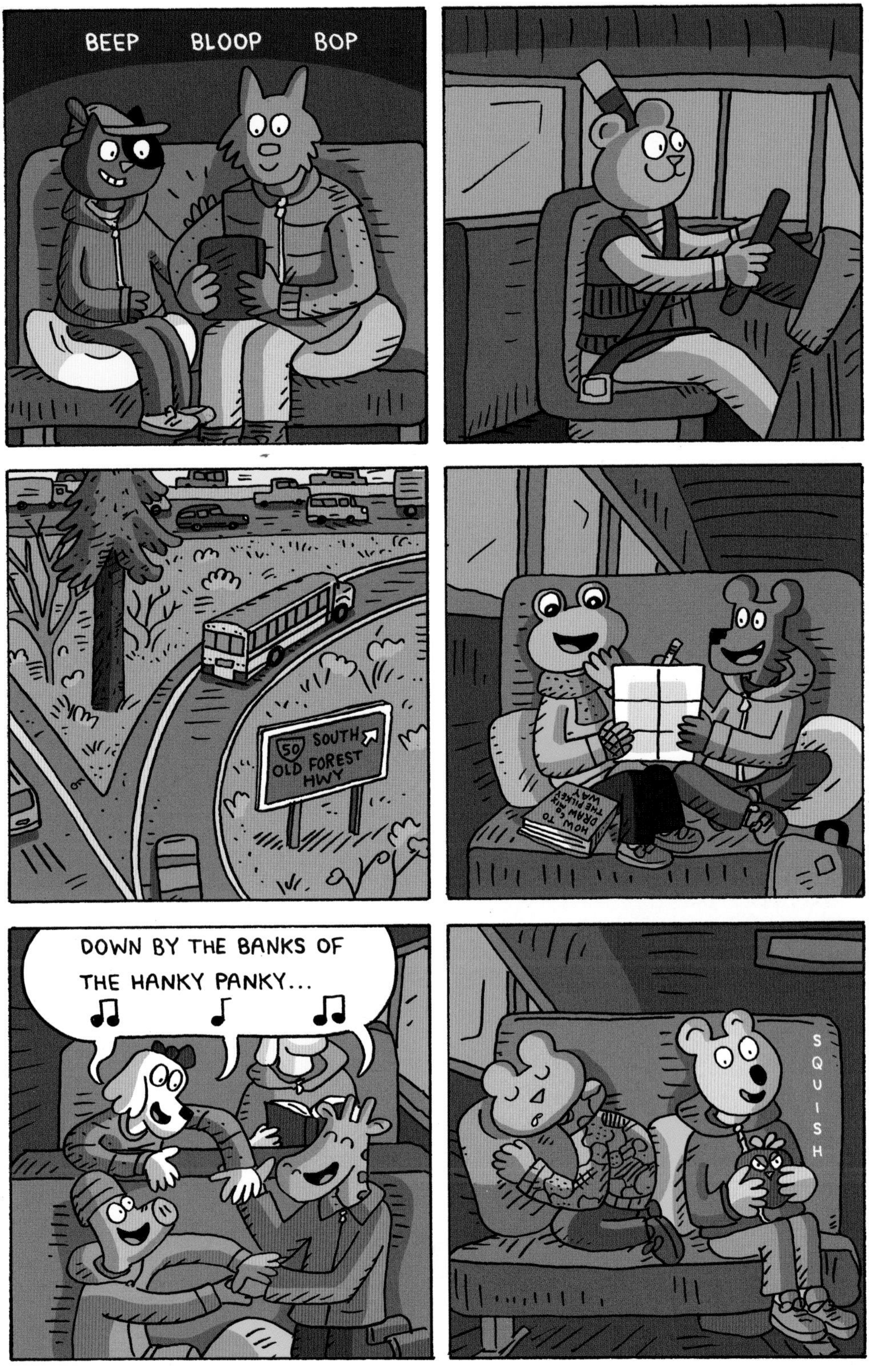
BEEP BLOOP BOP
50 SOUTH
OLD FOREST HWY
HOW TO DRAW COMIX THE PILKEY WAY
DOWN BY THE BANKS OF THE HANKY PANKY...
SQUISH

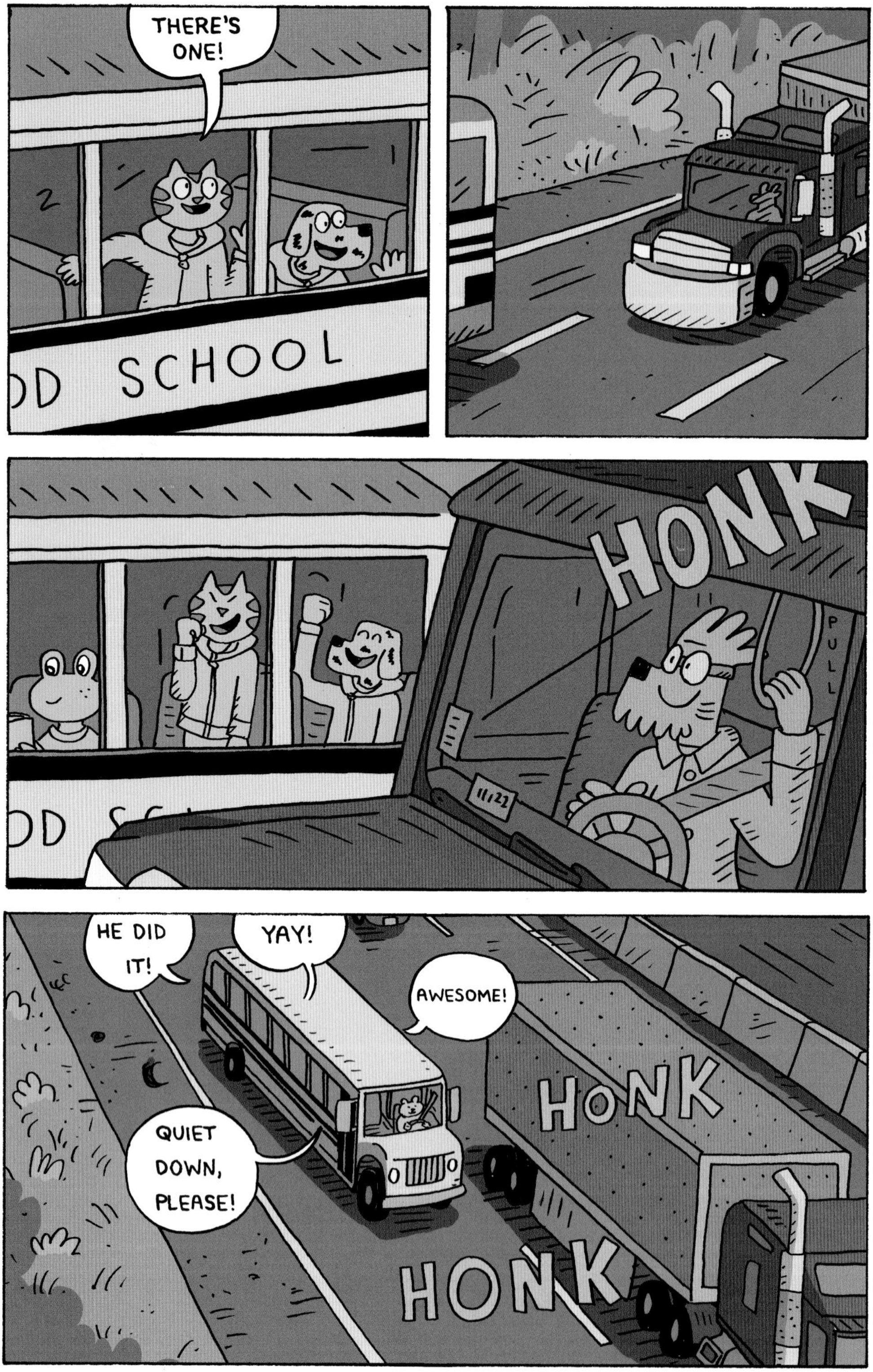
THERE'S ONE!
SCHOOL
HONK
PULL
HE DID IT!
YAY!
AWESOME!
QUIET DOWN, PLEASE!
HONK
HONK

CHAPTER TWO
Are We There Yet?

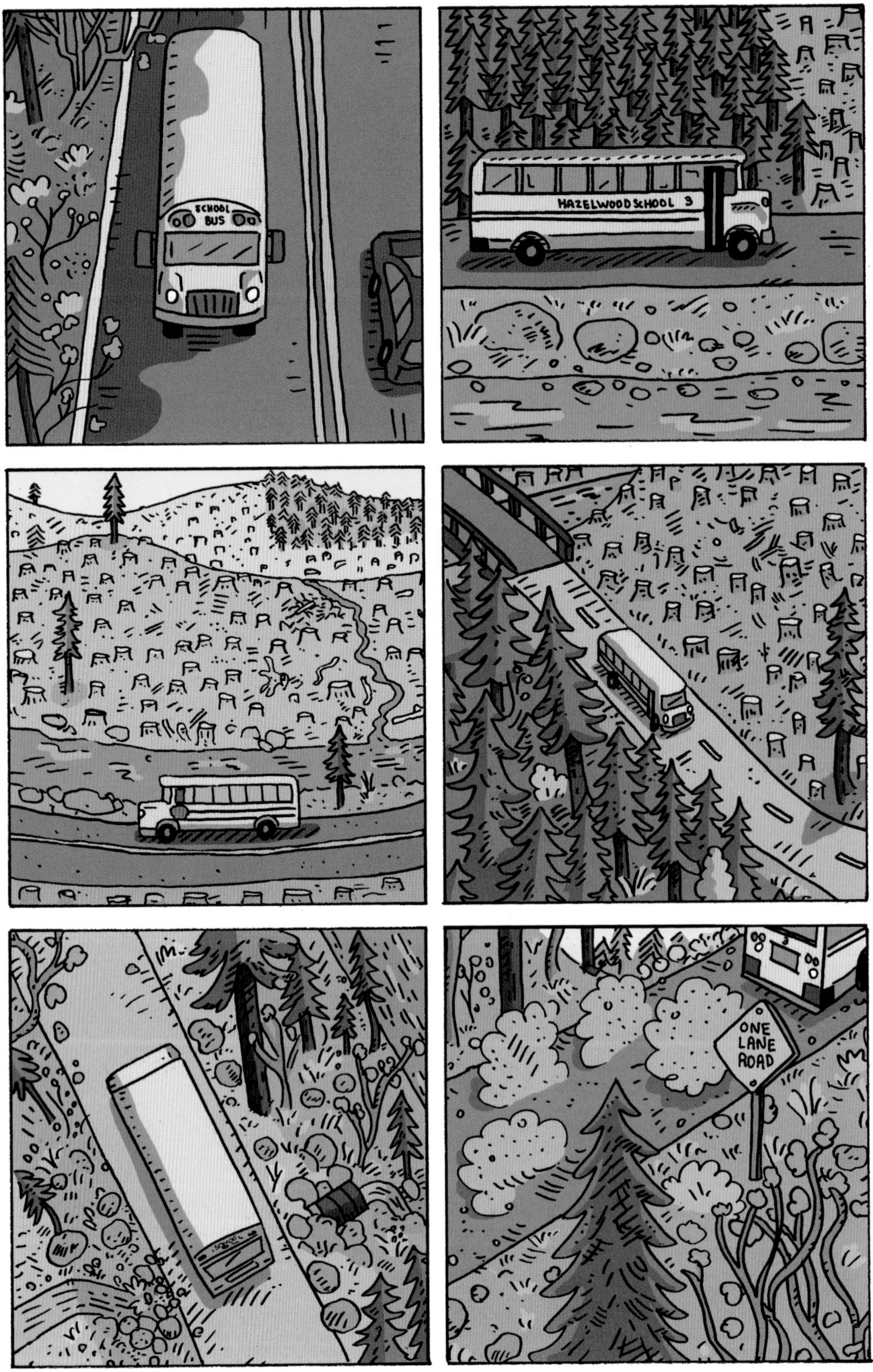
SCHOOL BUS
HAZELWOOD SCHOOL 3
ONE LANE ROAD

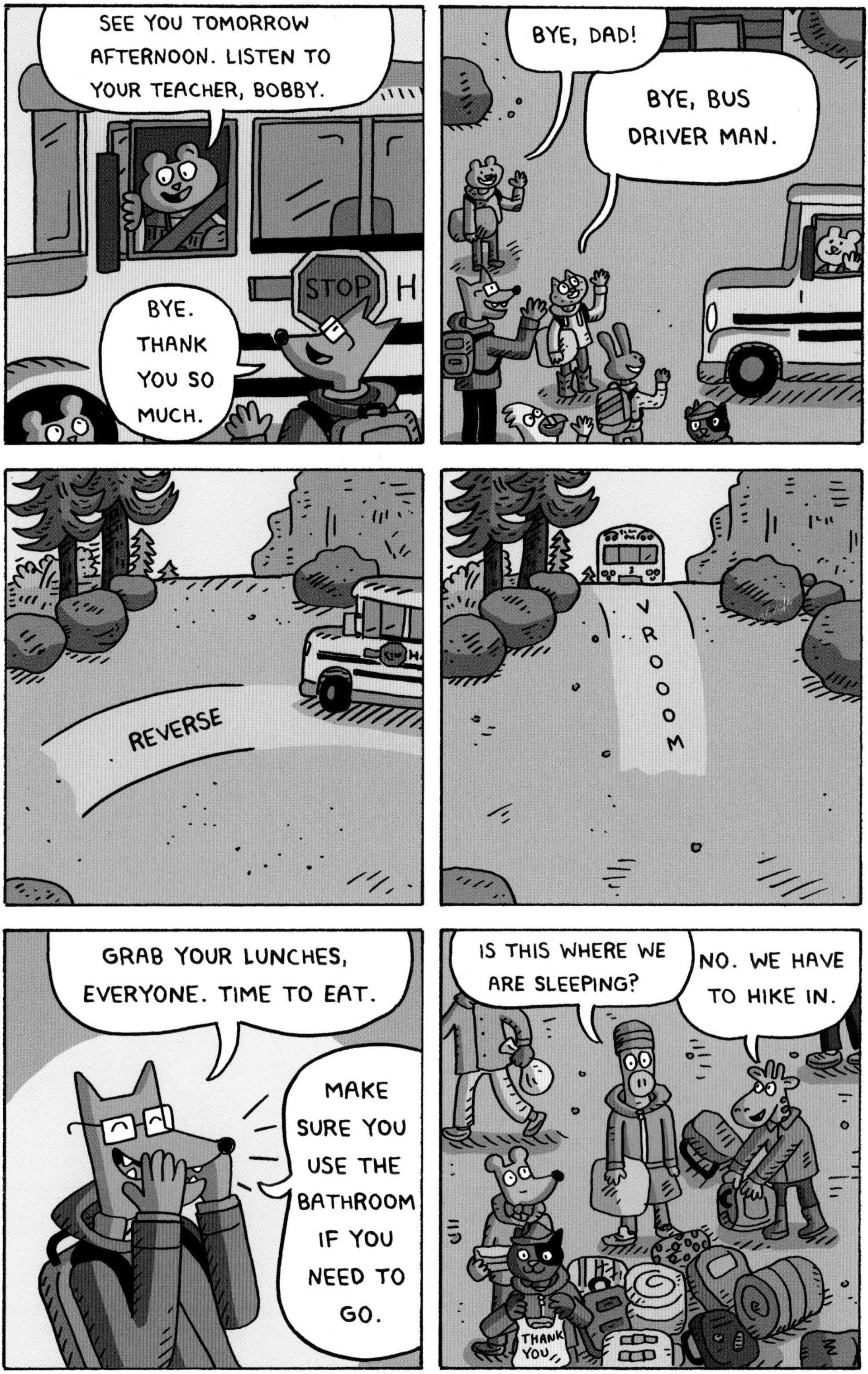
SEE YOU TOMORROW AFTERNOON. LISTEN TO YOUR TEACHER, BOBBY.
BYE. THANK YOU SO MUCH.
STOP
BYE, DAD!
BYE, BUS DRIVER MAN.
REVERSE
VROOOOM
GRAB YOUR LUNCHES, EVERYONE. TIME TO EAT.
MAKE SURE YOU USE THE BATHROOM IF YOU NEED TO GO.
IS THIS WHERE WE ARE SLEEPING?
NO. WE HAVE TO HIKE IN.
THANK YOU

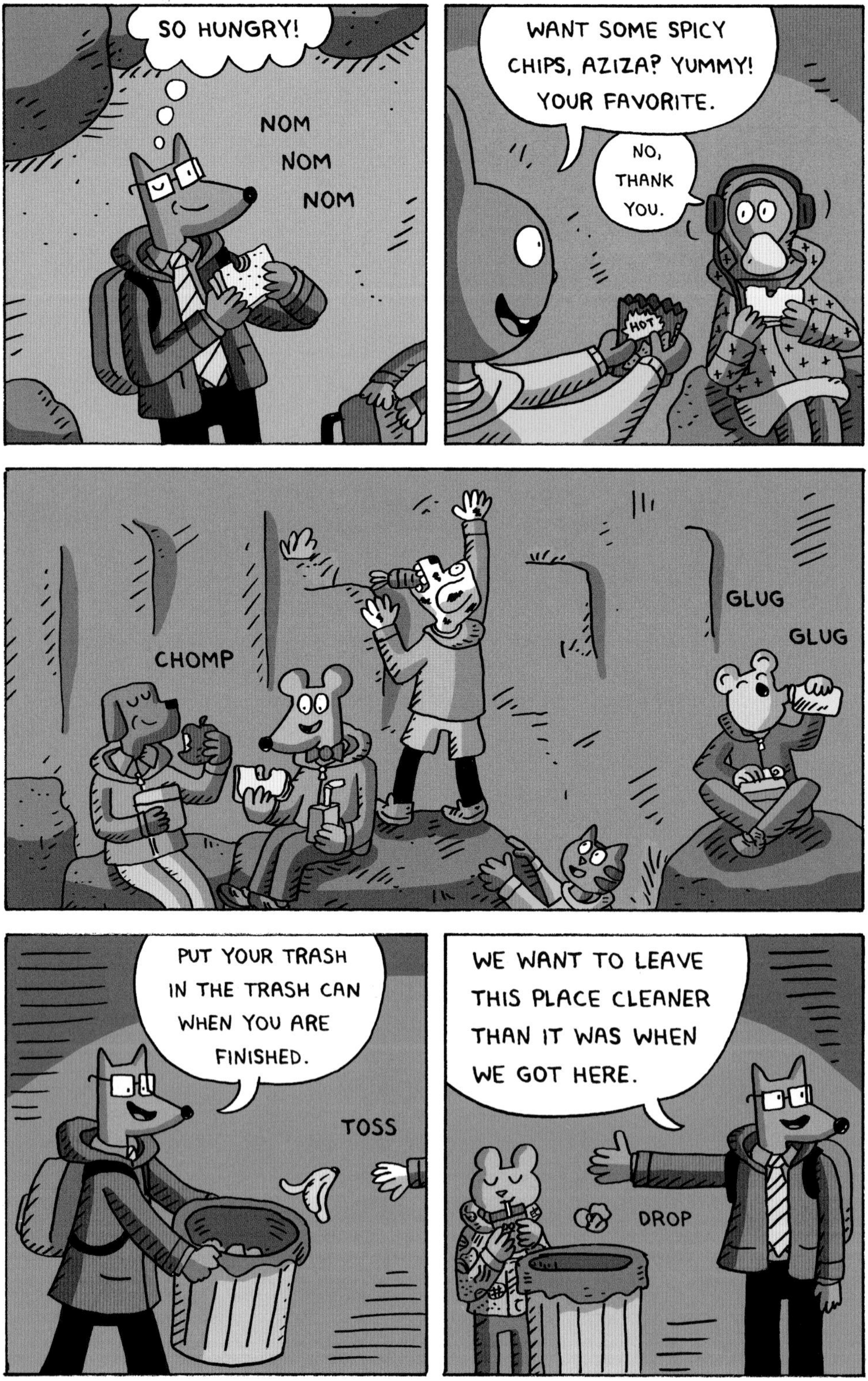
SO HUNGRY!
NOM
NOM
NOM
WANT SOME SPICY CHIPS, AZIZA? YUMMY! YOUR FAVORITE.
HOT
NO, THANK YOU.
CHOMP
GLUG
GLUG
PUT YOUR TRASH IN THE TRASH CAN WHEN YOU ARE FINISHED.
TOSS
WE WANT TO LEAVE THIS PLACE CLEANER THAN IT WAS WHEN WE GOT HERE.
DROP

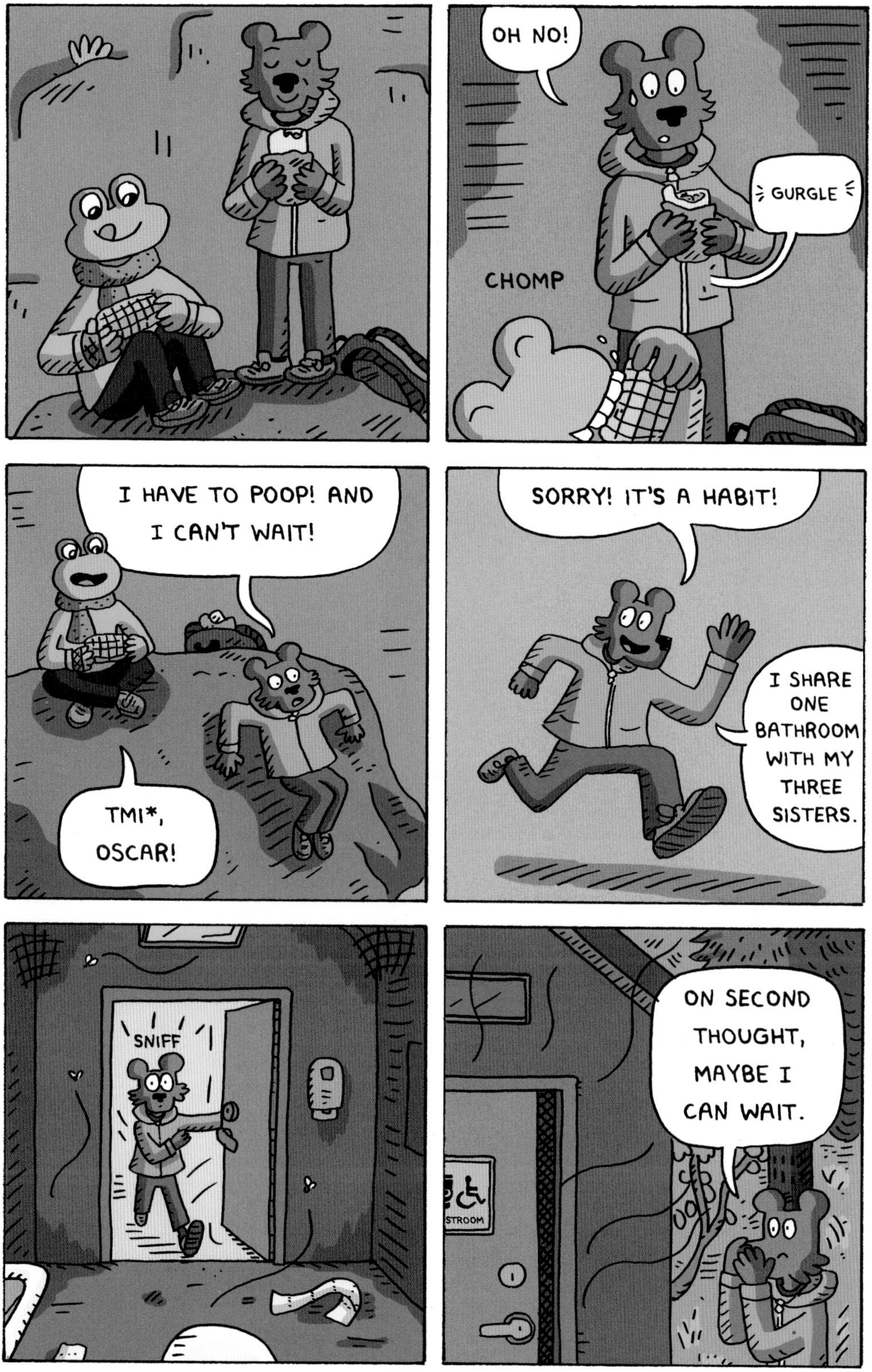
OH NO!
CHOMP
GURGLE
I HAVE TO POOP! AND I CAN'T WAIT!
TMI*, OSCAR!
SORRY! IT'S A HABIT!
I SHARE ONE BATHROOM WITH MY THREE SISTERS.
SNIFF
ON SECOND THOUGHT, MAYBE I CAN WAIT.

* TOO MUCH INFORMATION

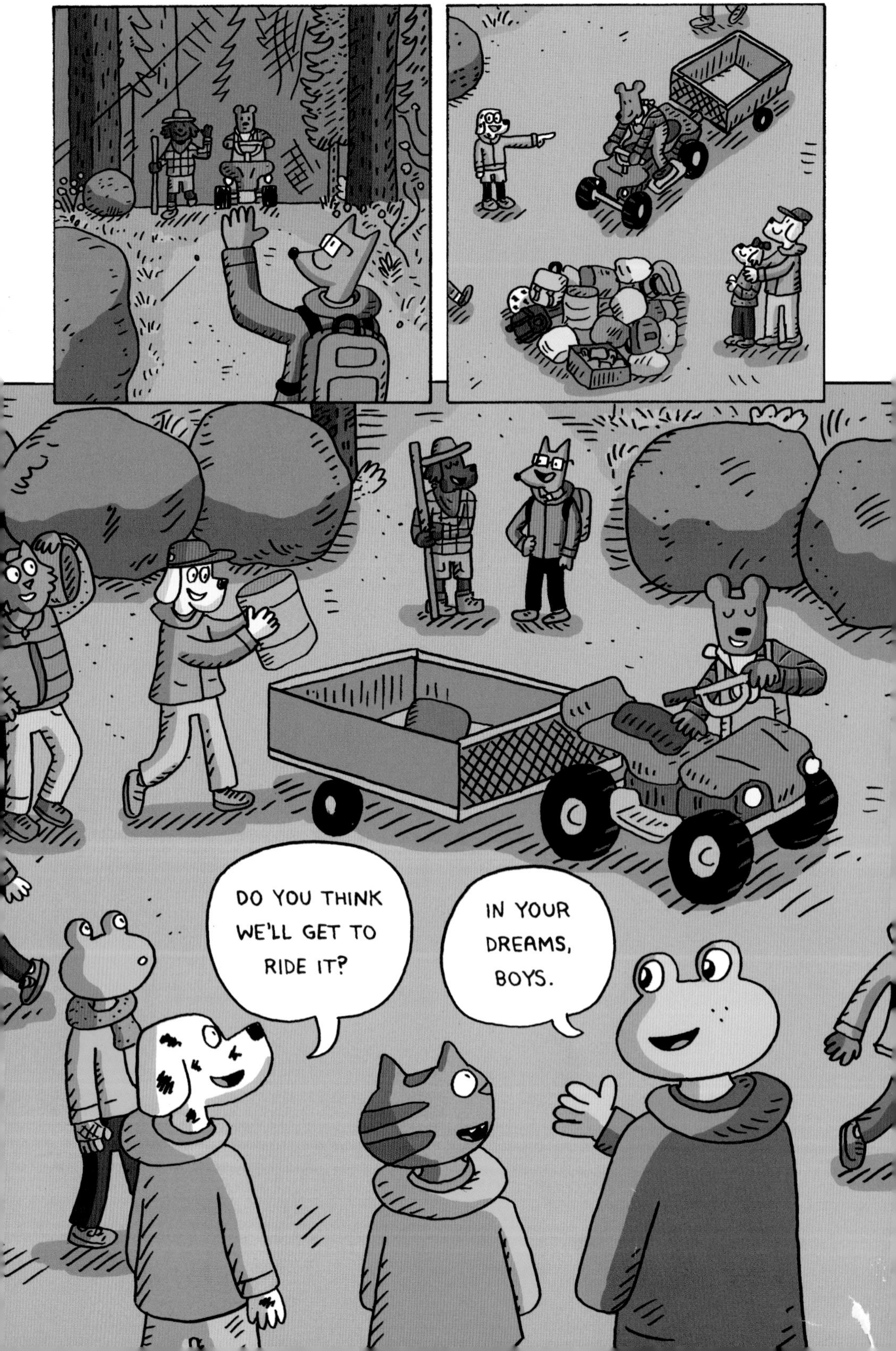
DO YOU THINK WE'LL GET TO RIDE IT?
IN YOUR DREAMS, BOYS.

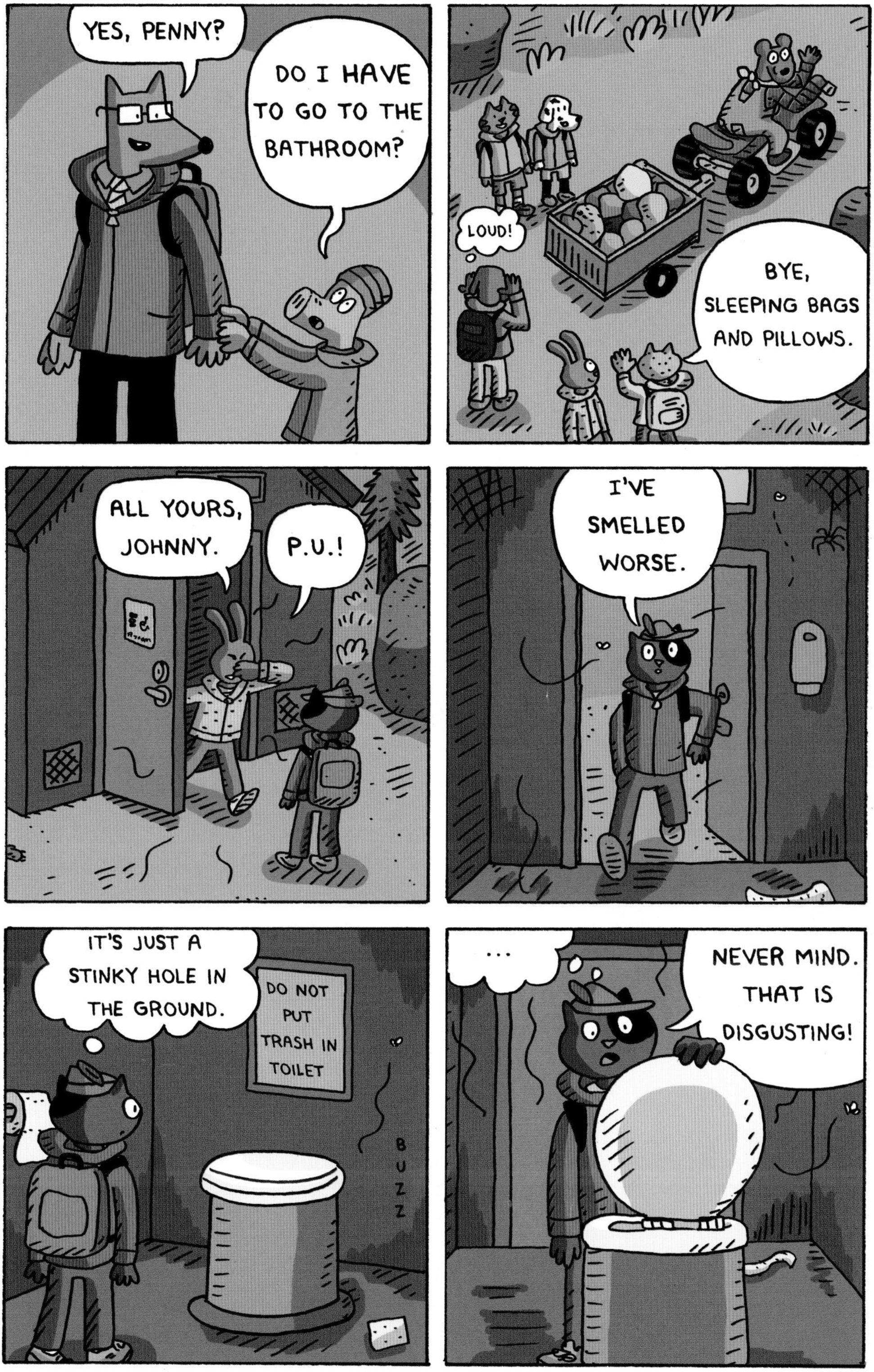
YES, PENNY?
DO I HAVE TO GO TO THE BATHROOM?
LOUD!
BYE, SLEEPING BAGS AND PILLOWS.
ALL YOURS, JOHNNY.
P.U.!
I'VE SMELLED WORSE.
IT'S JUST A STINKY HOLE IN THE GROUND.
DO NOT PUT TRASH IN TOILET
BUZZ
...
NEVER MIND. THAT IS DISGUSTING!

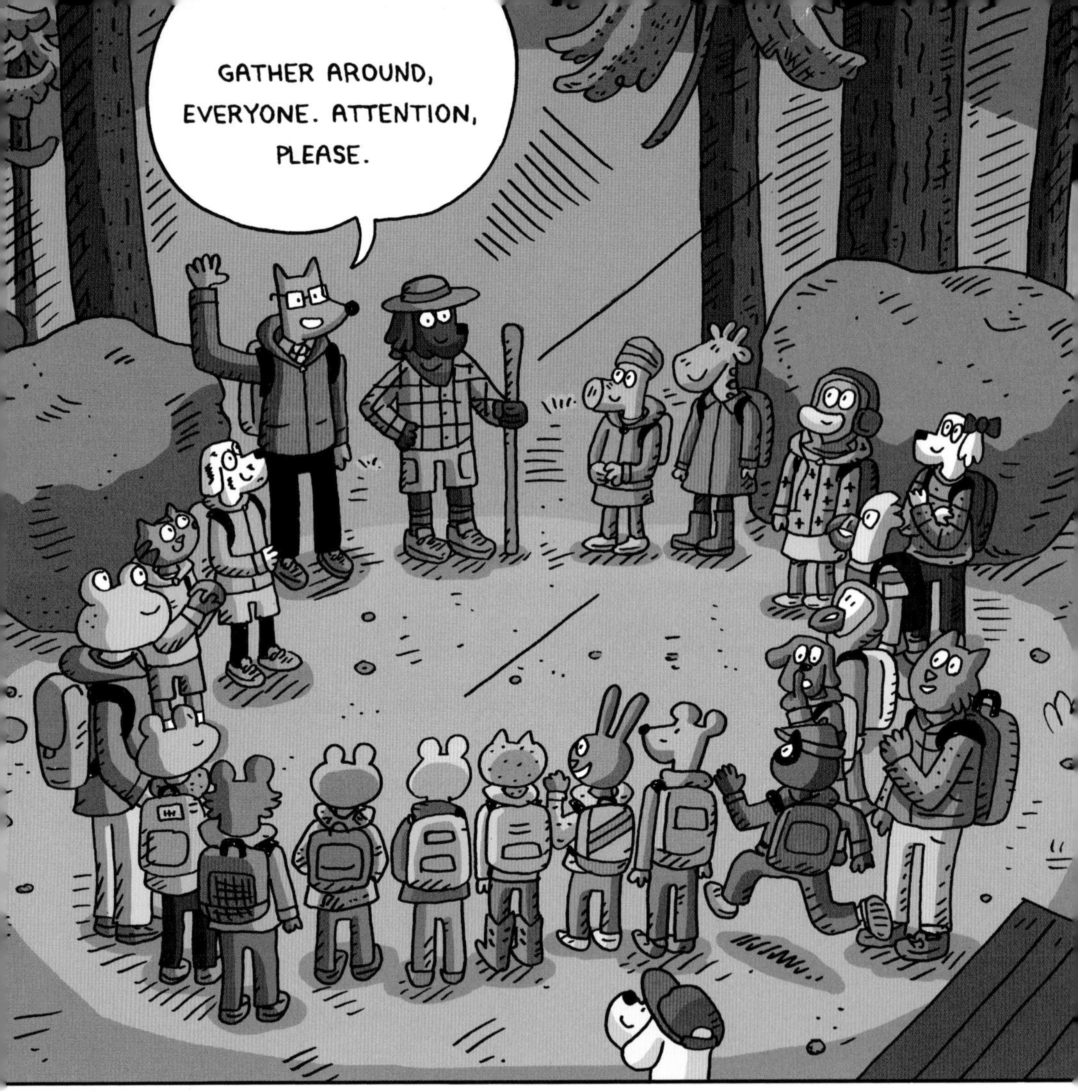
GATHER AROUND, EVERYONE. ATTENTION, PLEASE.

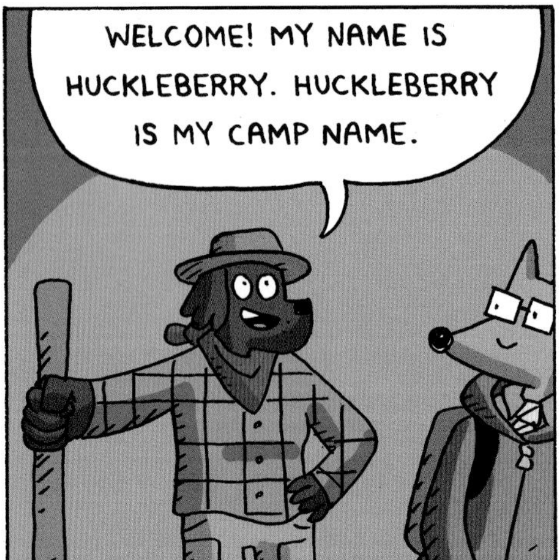
WELCOME! MY NAME IS HUCKLEBERRY. HUCKLEBERRY IS MY CAMP NAME.

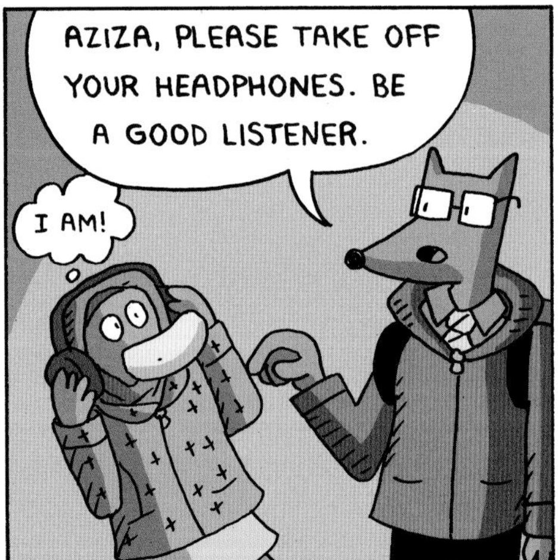
AZIZA, PLEASE TAKE OFF YOUR HEADPHONES. BE A GOOD LISTENER.
I AM!

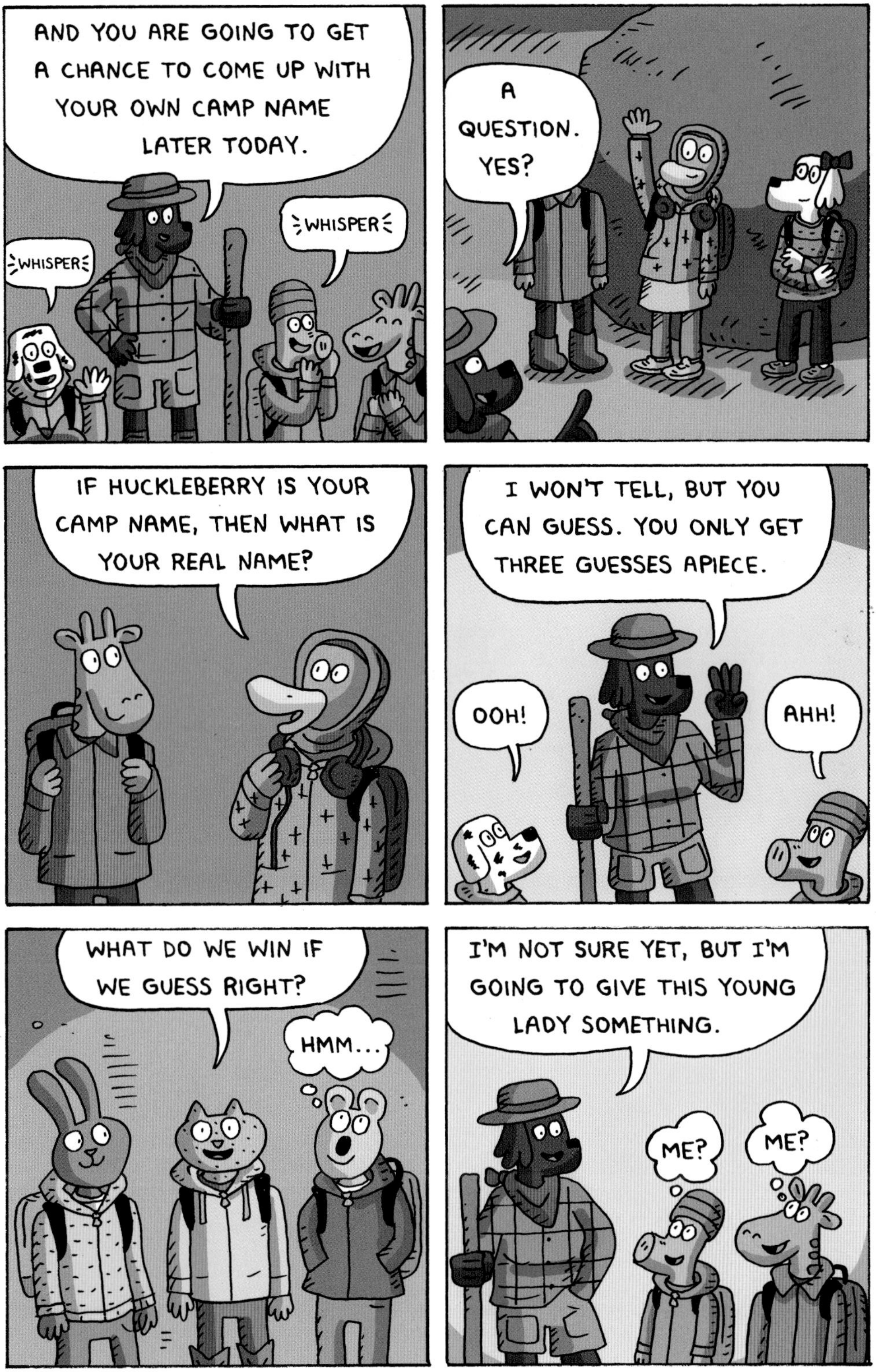
AND YOU ARE GOING TO GET A CHANCE TO COME UP WITH YOUR OWN CAMP NAME LATER TODAY.
WHISPER
WHISPER
A QUESTION. YES?
IF HUCKLEBERRY IS YOUR CAMP NAME, THEN WHAT IS YOUR REAL NAME?
I WON'T TELL, BUT YOU CAN GUESS. YOU ONLY GET THREE GUESSES APIECE.
OOH!
AHH!
WHAT DO WE WIN IF WE GUESS RIGHT?
HMM...
I'M NOT SURE YET, BUT I'M GOING TO GIVE THIS YOUNG LADY SOMETHING.
ME?
ME?

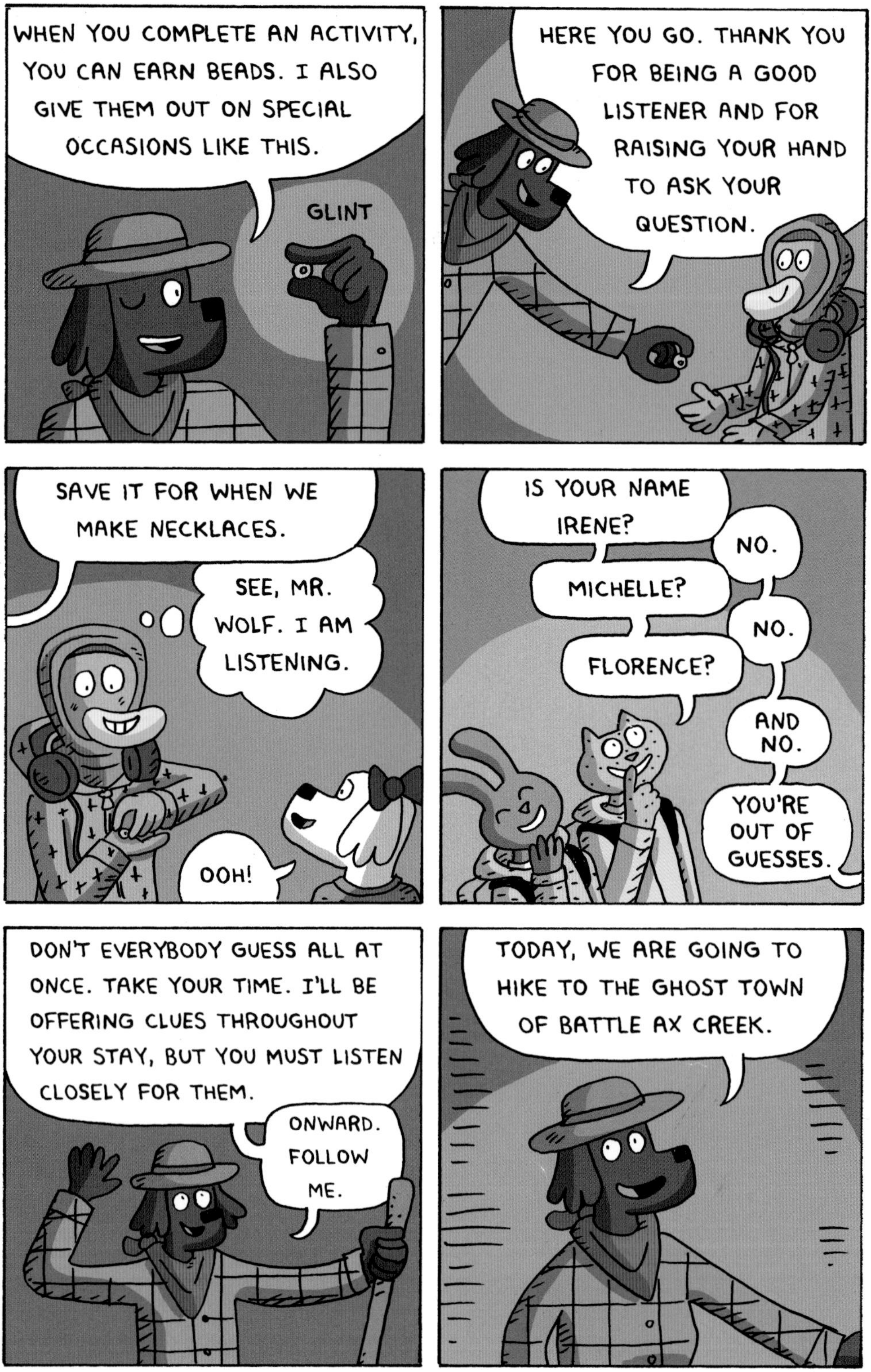
WHEN YOU COMPLETE AN ACTIVITY, YOU CAN EARN BEADS. I ALSO GIVE THEM OUT ON SPECIAL OCCASIONS LIKE THIS.
GLINT
HERE YOU GO. THANK YOU FOR BEING A GOOD LISTENER AND FOR RAISING YOUR HAND TO ASK YOUR QUESTION.
SAVE IT FOR WHEN WE MAKE NECKLACES.
SEE, MR. WOLF. I AM LISTENING.
OOH!
IS YOUR NAME IRENE?
NO.
MICHELLE?
NO.
FLORENCE?
AND NO.
YOU'RE OUT OF GUESSES.
DON'T EVERYBODY GUESS ALL AT ONCE. TAKE YOUR TIME. I'LL BE OFFERING CLUES THROUGHOUT YOUR STAY, BUT YOU MUST LISTEN CLOSELY FOR THEM.
ONWARD. FOLLOW ME.
TODAY, WE ARE GOING TO HIKE TO THE GHOST TOWN OF BATTLE AX CREEK.

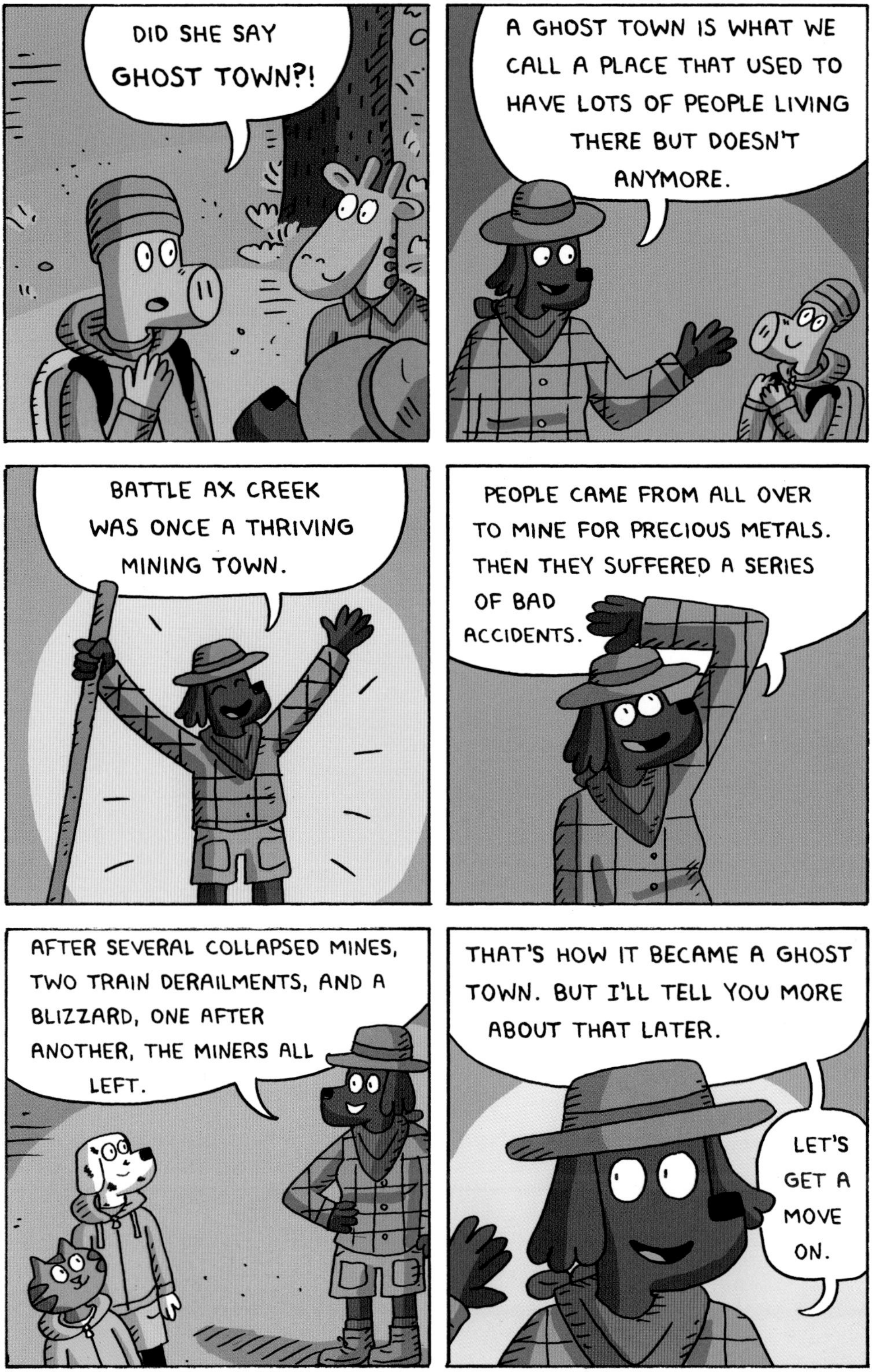
DID SHE SAY GHOST TOWN?!
A GHOST TOWN IS WHAT WE CALL A PLACE THAT USED TO HAVE LOTS OF PEOPLE LIVING THERE BUT DOESN'T ANYMORE.
BATTLE AX CREEK WAS ONCE A THRIVING MINING TOWN.
PEOPLE CAME FROM ALL OVER TO MINE FOR PRECIOUS METALS. THEN THEY SUFFERED A SERIES OF BAD ACCIDENTS.
AFTER SEVERAL COLLAPSED MINES, TWO TRAIN DERAILMENTS, AND A BLIZZARD, ONE AFTER ANOTHER, THE MINERS ALL LEFT.
THAT'S HOW IT BECAME A GHOST TOWN. BUT I'LL TELL YOU MORE ABOUT THAT LATER.
LET'S GET A MOVE ON.

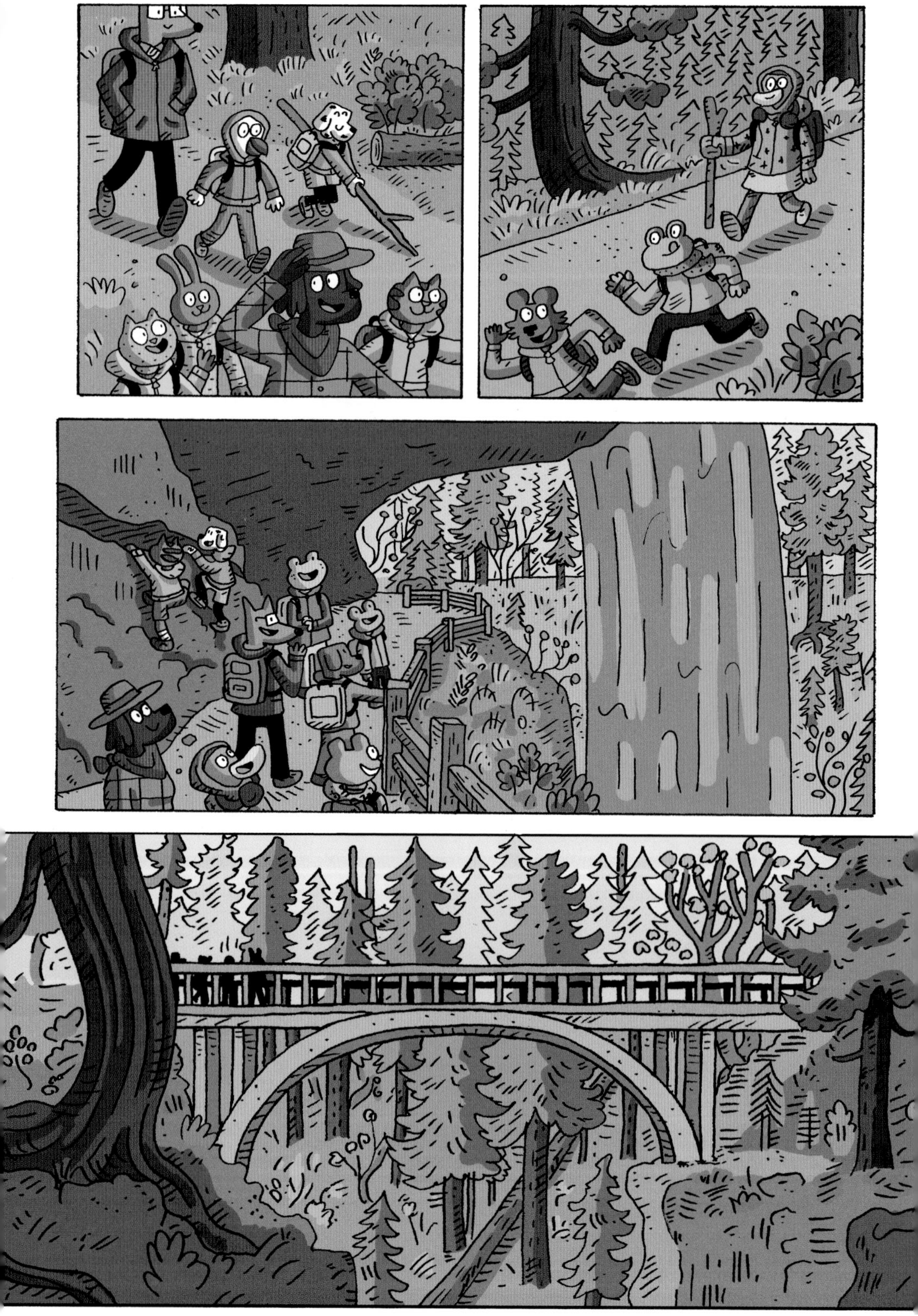

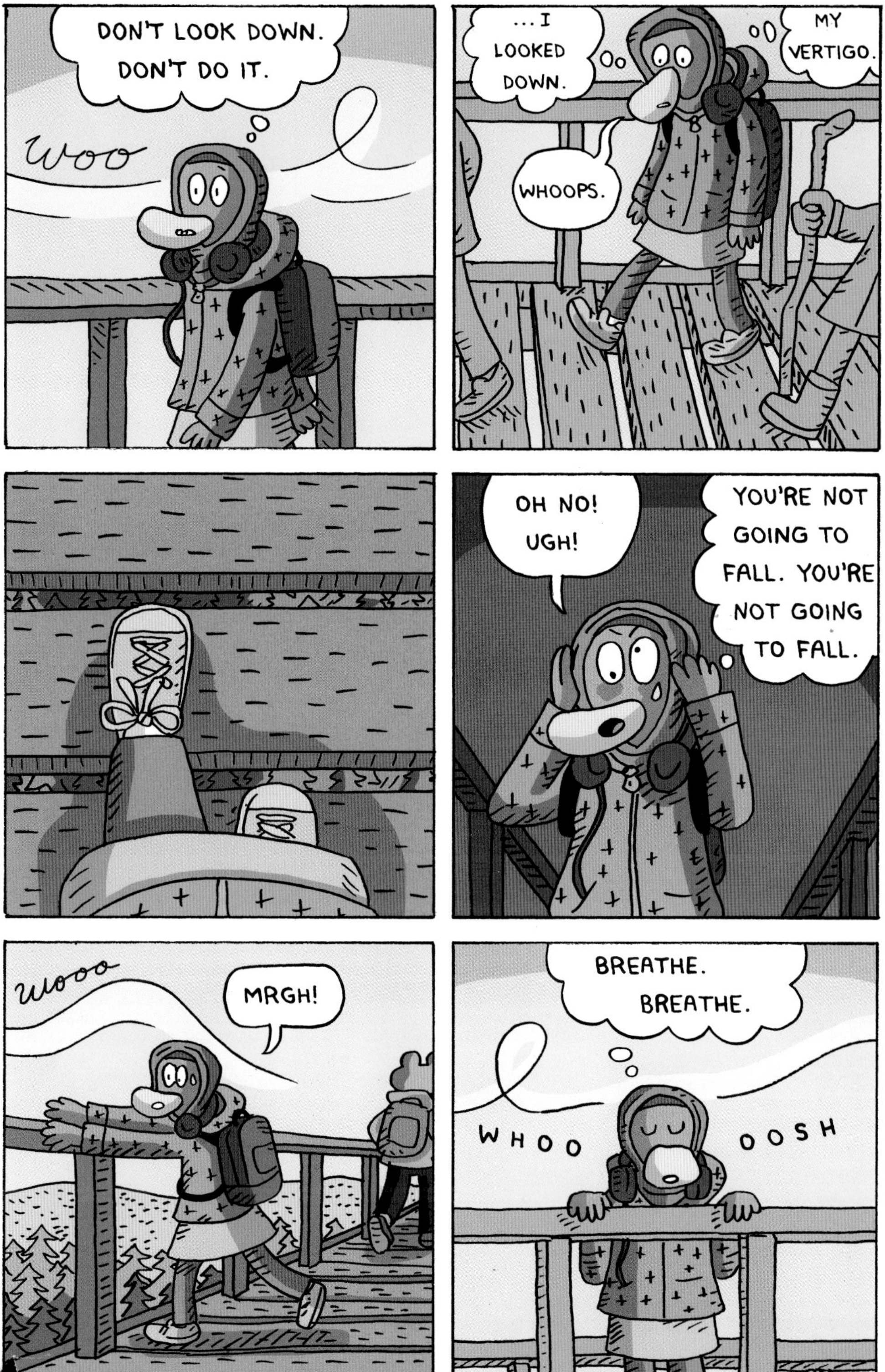
DON'T LOOK DOWN. DON'T DO IT.
WOO
...I LOOKED DOWN.
MY VERTIGO.
WHOOPS.
OH NO! UGH!
YOU'RE NOT GOING TO FALL. YOU'RE NOT GOING TO FALL.
WOOO
MRGH!
BREATHE. BREATHE.
WHOO OOSH

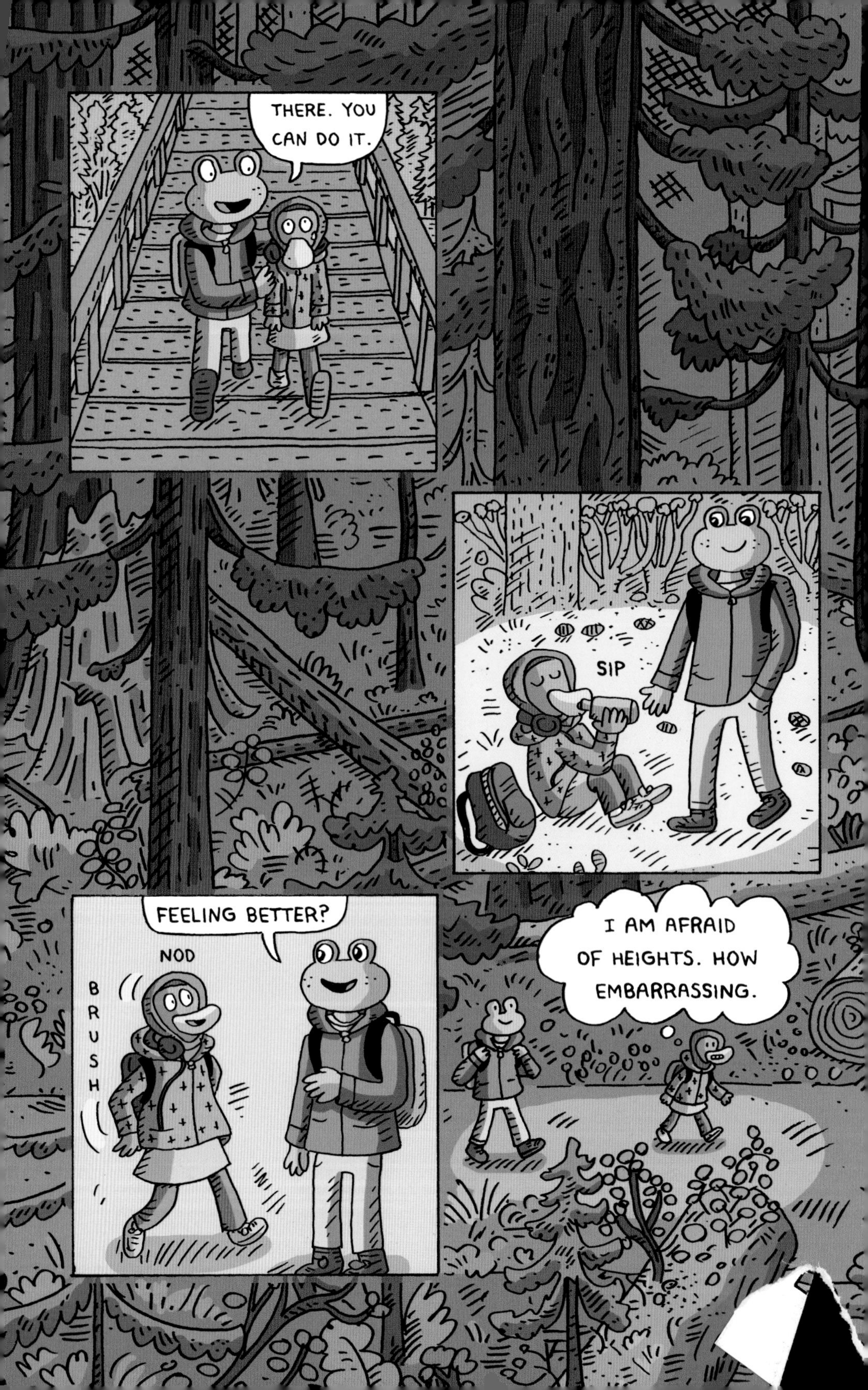
THERE. YOU CAN DO IT.
SIP
FEELING BETTER?
NOD
BRUSH
I AM AFRAID OF HEIGHTS. HOW EMBARRASSING.

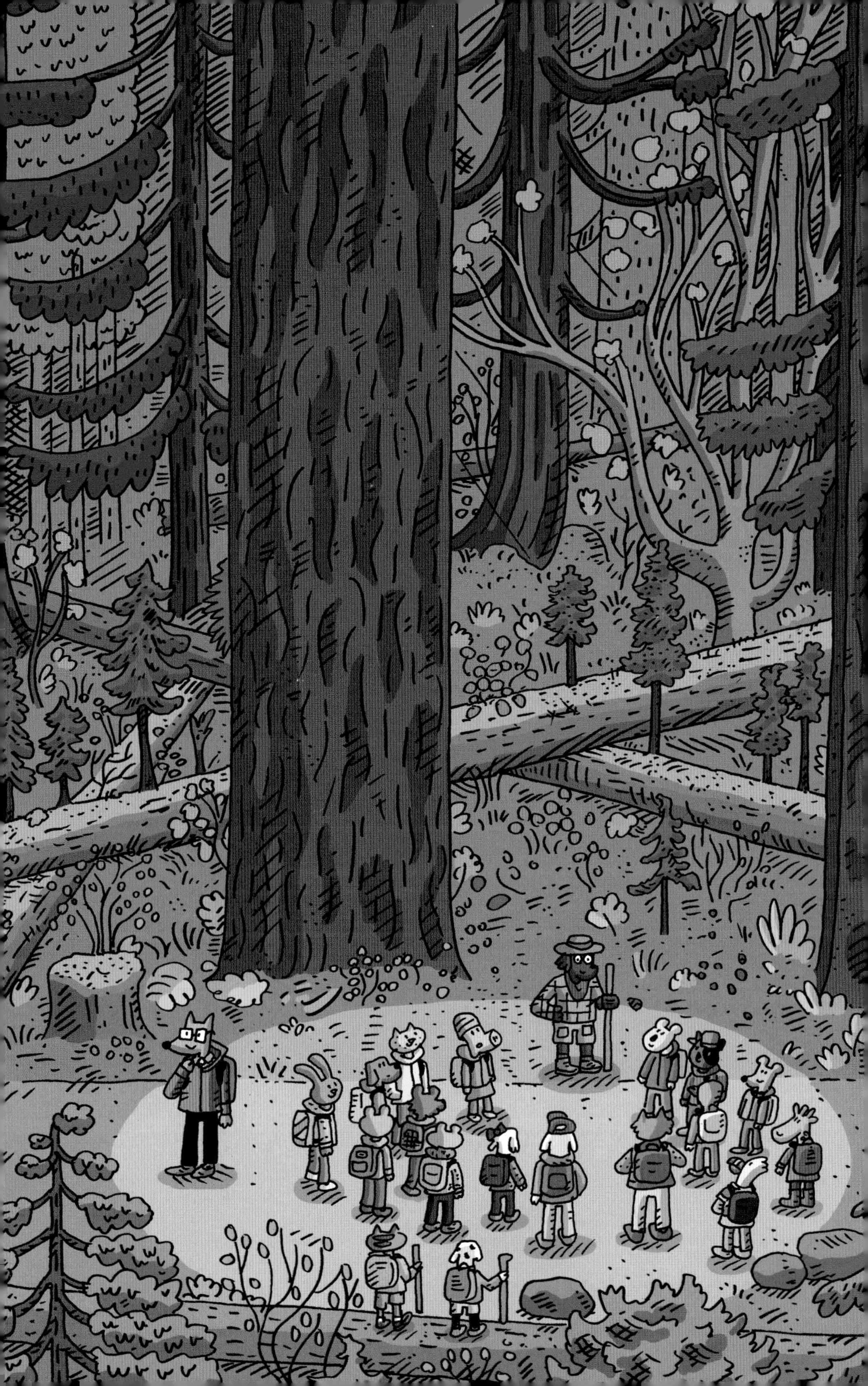

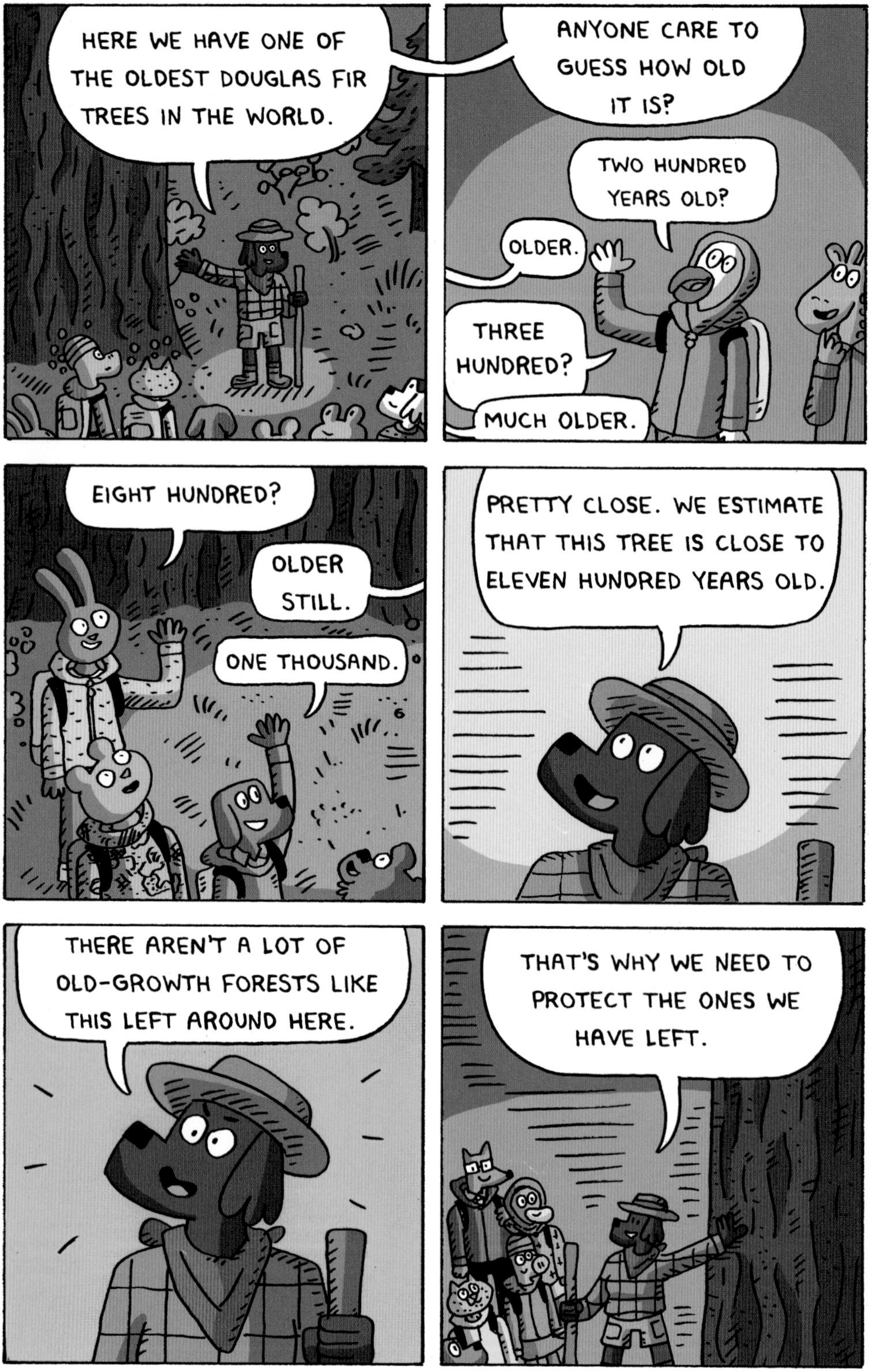
HERE WE HAVE ONE OF THE OLDEST DOUGLAS FIR TREES IN THE WORLD.
ANYONE CARE TO GUESS HOW OLD IT IS?
TWO HUNDRED YEARS OLD?
OLDER.
THREE HUNDRED?
MUCH OLDER.
EIGHT HUNDRED?
OLDER STILL.
ONE THOUSAND.
PRETTY CLOSE. WE ESTIMATE THAT THIS TREE IS CLOSE TO ELEVEN HUNDRED YEARS OLD.
THERE AREN'T A LOT OF OLD-GROWTH FORESTS LIKE THIS LEFT AROUND HERE.
THAT'S WHY WE NEED TO PROTECT THE ONES WE HAVE LEFT.

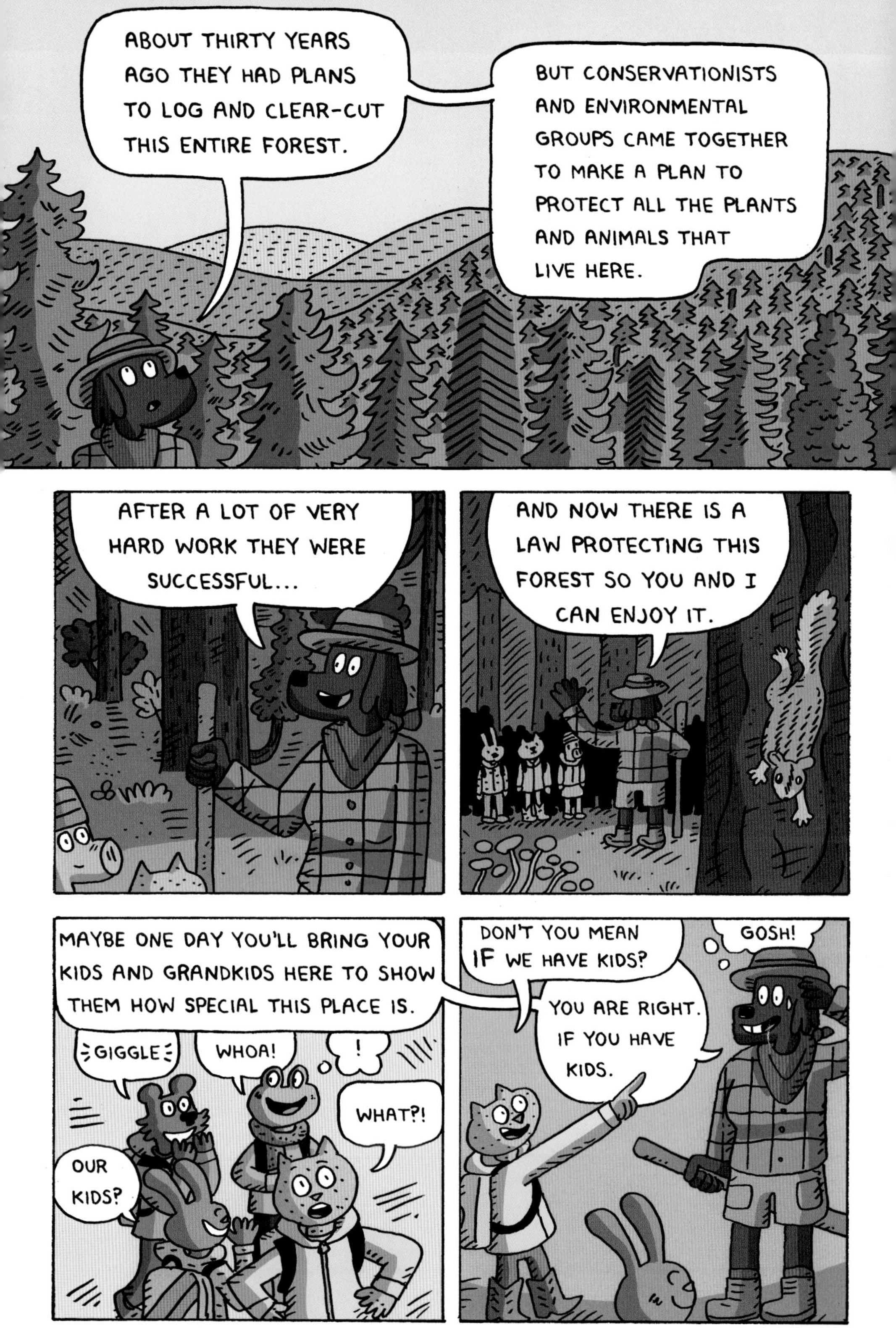

ABOUT THIRTY YEARS AGO THEY HAD PLANS TO LOG AND CLEAR-CUT THIS ENTIRE FOREST.
BUT CONSERVATIONISTS AND ENVIRONMENTAL GROUPS CAME TOGETHER TO MAKE A PLAN TO PROTECT ALL THE PLANTS AND ANIMALS THAT LIVE HERE.
AFTER A LOT OF VERY HARD WORK THEY WERE SUCCESSFUL...
AND NOW THERE IS A LAW PROTECTING THIS FOREST SO YOU AND I CAN ENJOY IT.
MAYBE ONE DAY YOU'LL BRING YOUR KIDS AND GRANDKIDS HERE TO SHOW THEM HOW SPECIAL THIS PLACE IS.
GIGGLE
WHOA!
!
WHAT?!
OUR KIDS?
DON'T YOU MEAN IF WE HAVE KIDS?
GOSH!
YOU ARE RIGHT. IF YOU HAVE KIDS.

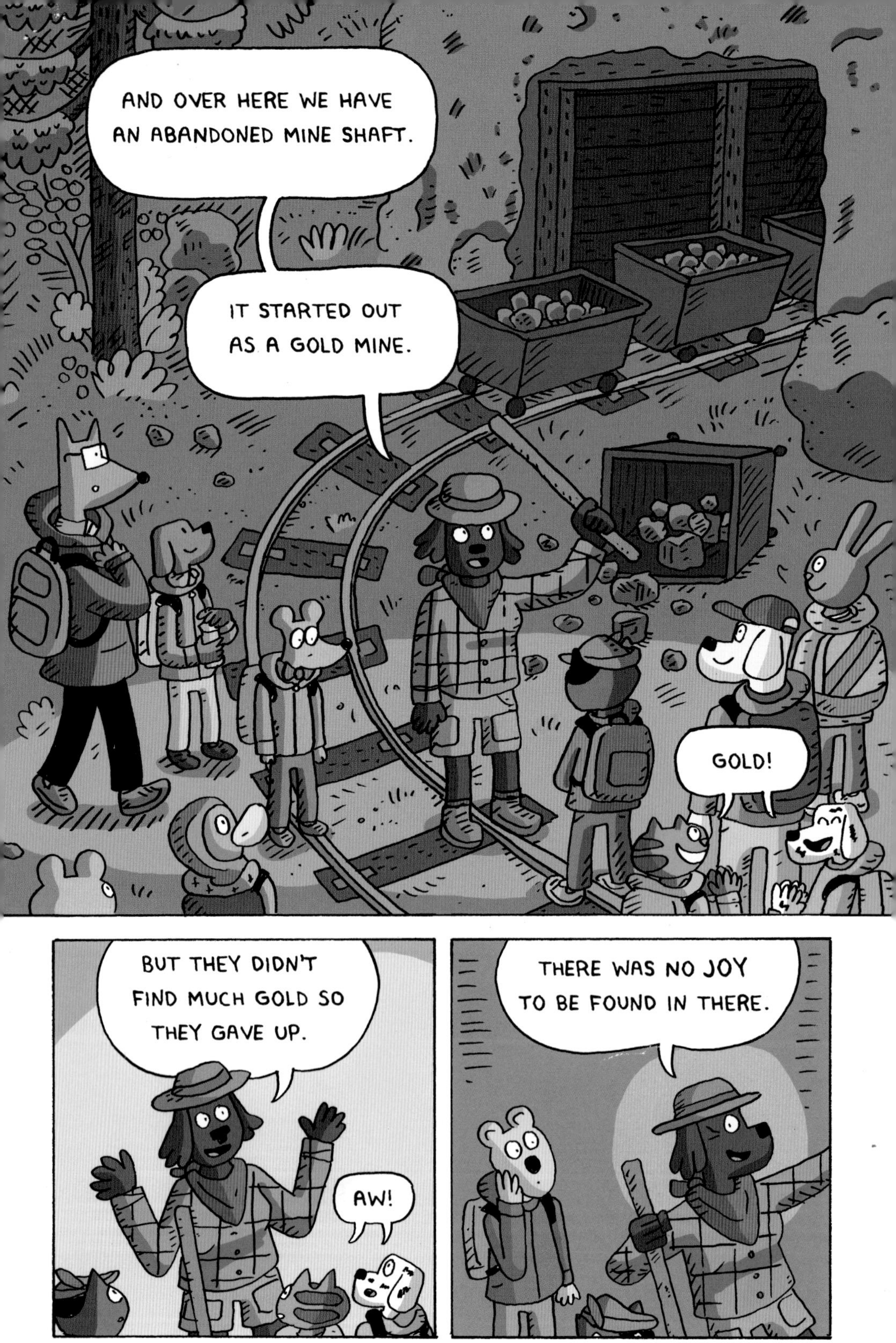
AND OVER HERE WE HAVE AN ABANDONED MINE SHAFT.
IT STARTED OUT AS A GOLD MINE.
GOLD!
BUT THEY DIDN'T FIND MUCH GOLD SO THEY GAVE UP.
AW!
THERE WAS NO JOY TO BE FOUND IN THERE.

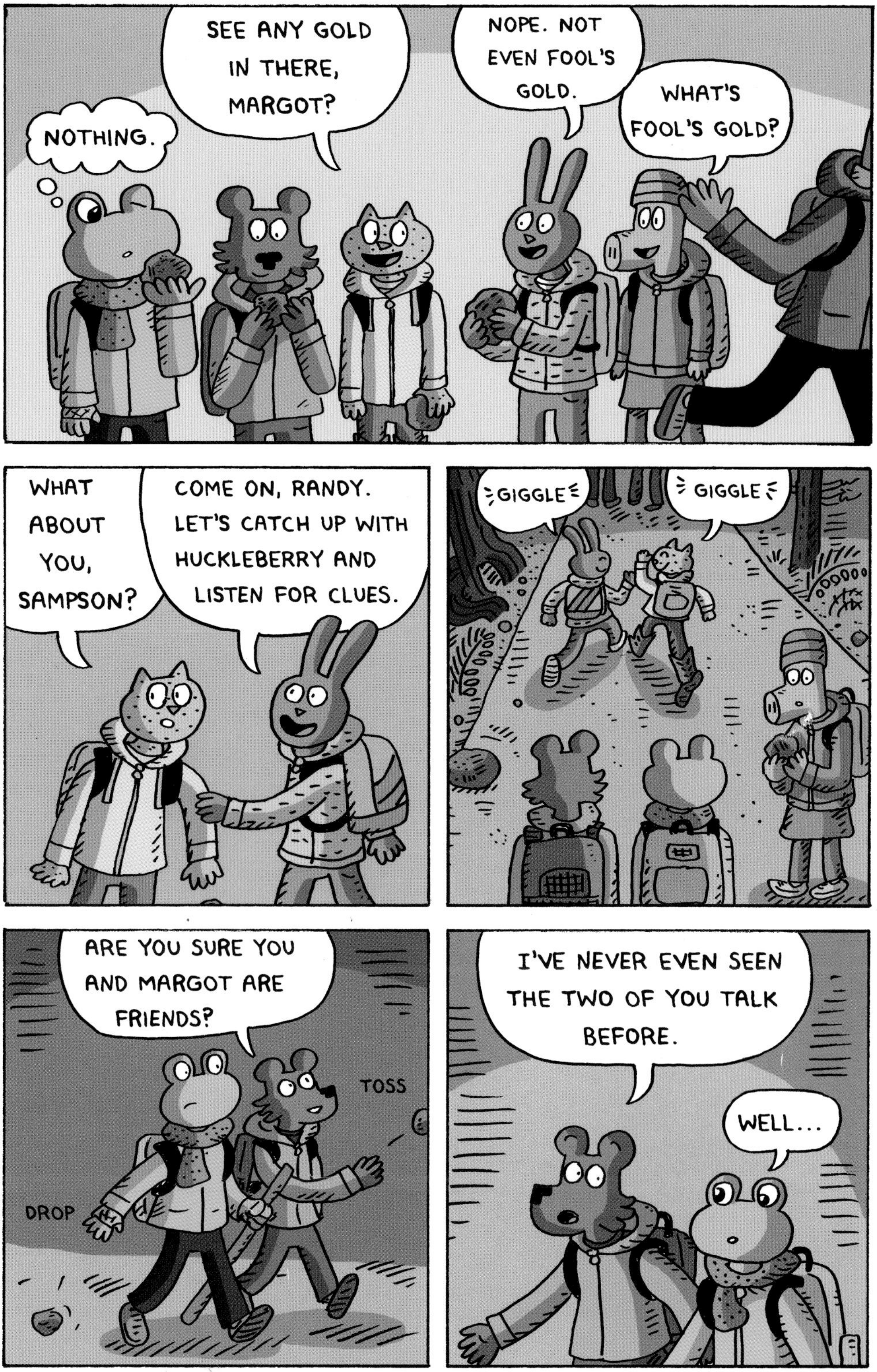
SEE ANY GOLD IN THERE, MARGOT?
NOTHING.
NOPE. NOT EVEN FOOL'S GOLD.
WHAT'S FOOL'S GOLD?
WHAT ABOUT YOU, SAMPSON?
COME ON, RANDY. LET'S CATCH UP WITH HUCKLEBERRY AND LISTEN FOR CLUES.
GIGGLE
GIGGLE
ARE YOU SURE YOU AND MARGOT ARE FRIENDS?
TOSS
DROP
I'VE NEVER EVEN SEEN THE TWO OF YOU TALK BEFORE.
WELL...

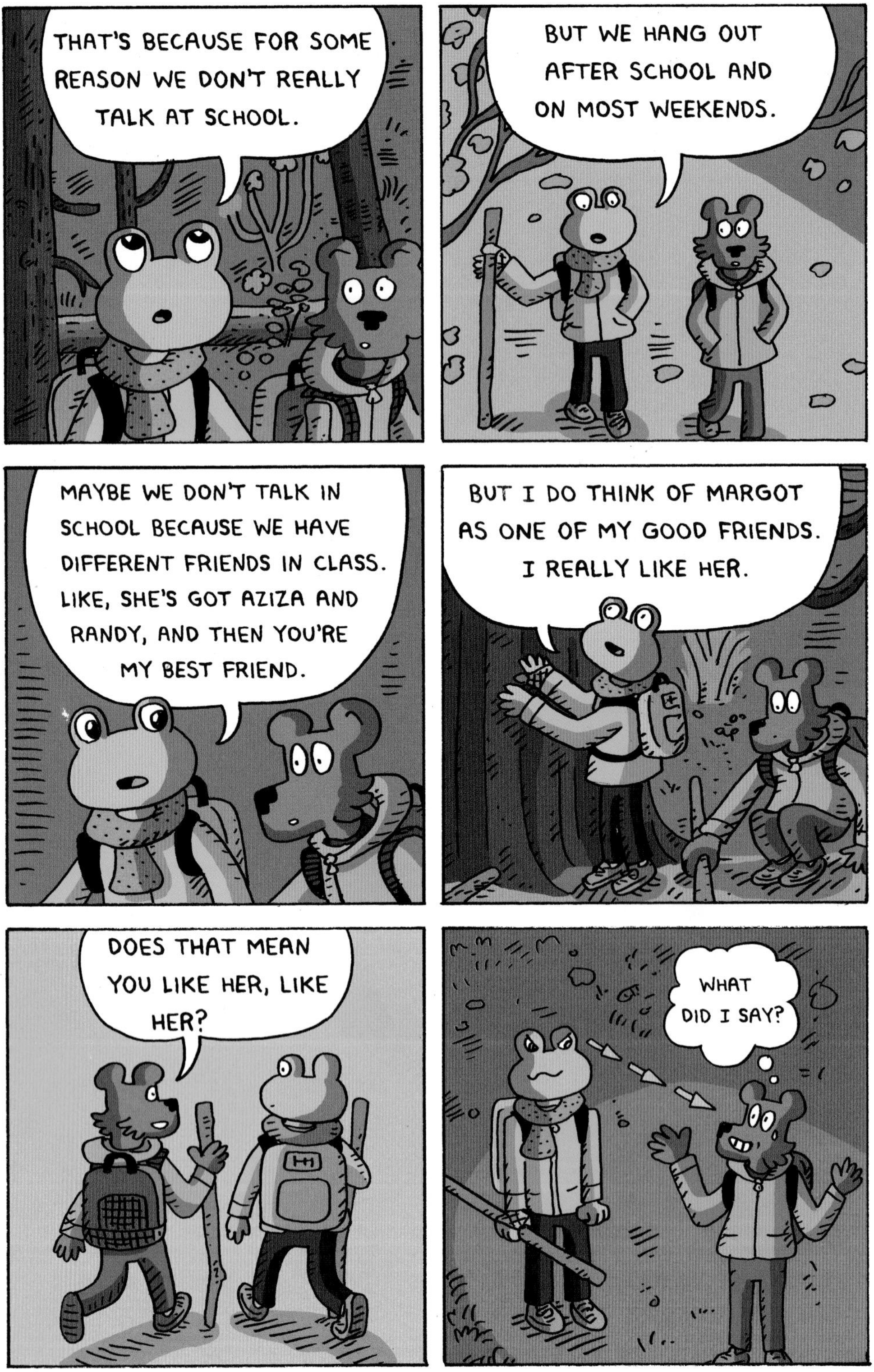
THAT'S BECAUSE FOR SOME REASON WE DON'T REALLY TALK AT SCHOOL.
BUT WE HANG OUT AFTER SCHOOL AND ON MOST WEEKENDS.
MAYBE WE DON'T TALK IN SCHOOL BECAUSE WE HAVE DIFFERENT FRIENDS IN CLASS. LIKE, SHE'S GOT AZIZA AND RANDY, AND THEN YOU'RE MY BEST FRIEND.
BUT I DO THINK OF MARGOT AS ONE OF MY GOOD FRIENDS. I REALLY LIKE HER.
DOES THAT MEAN YOU LIKE HER, LIKE HER?
WHAT DID I SAY?

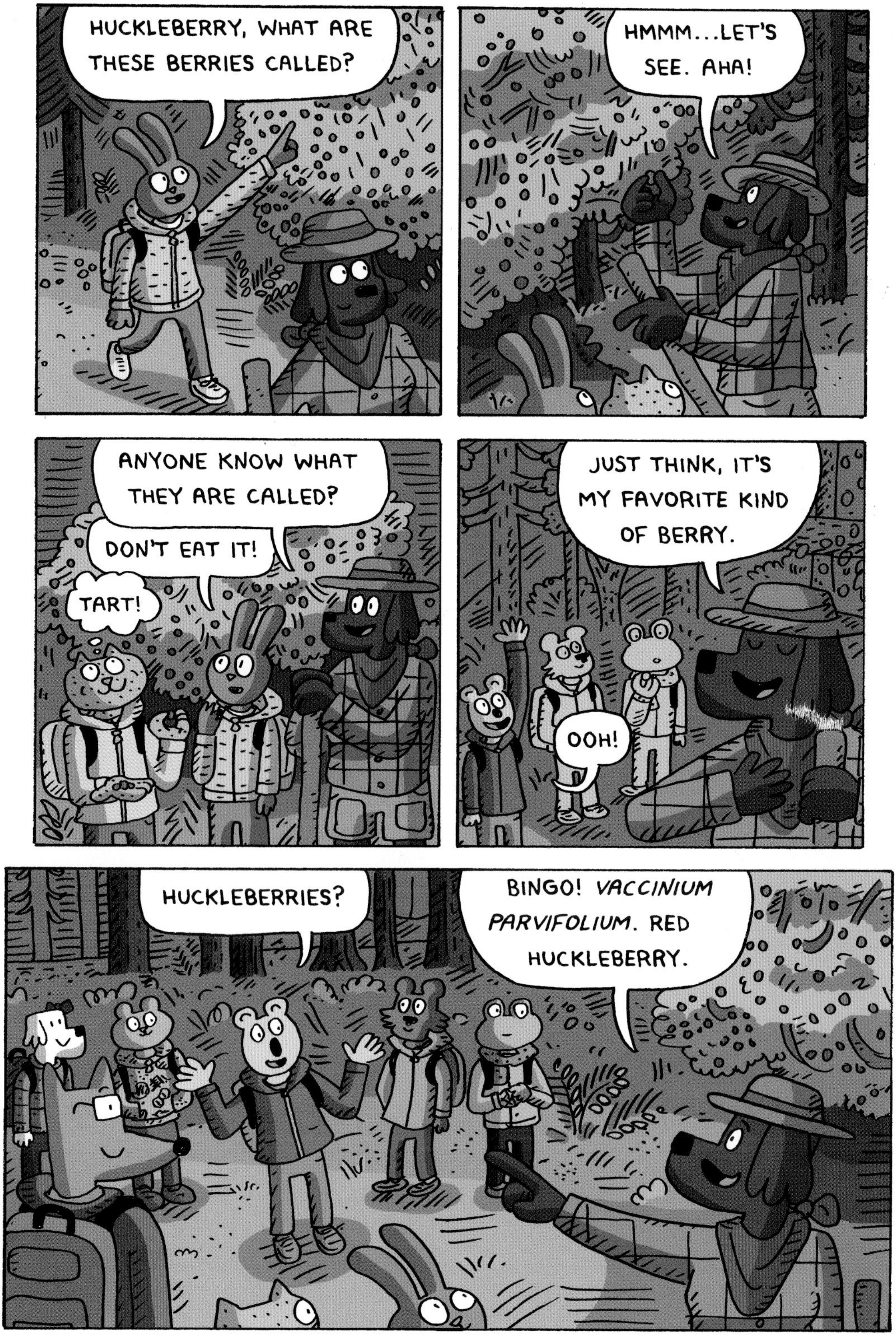
HUCKLEBERRY, WHAT ARE THESE BERRIES CALLED?
HMMM...LET'S SEE. AHA!
ANYONE KNOW WHAT THEY ARE CALLED?
DON'T EAT IT!
TART!
JUST THINK, IT'S MY FAVORITE KIND OF BERRY.
OOH!
HUCKLEBERRIES?
BINGO! *VACCINIUM PARVIFOLIUM*. RED HUCKLEBERRY.

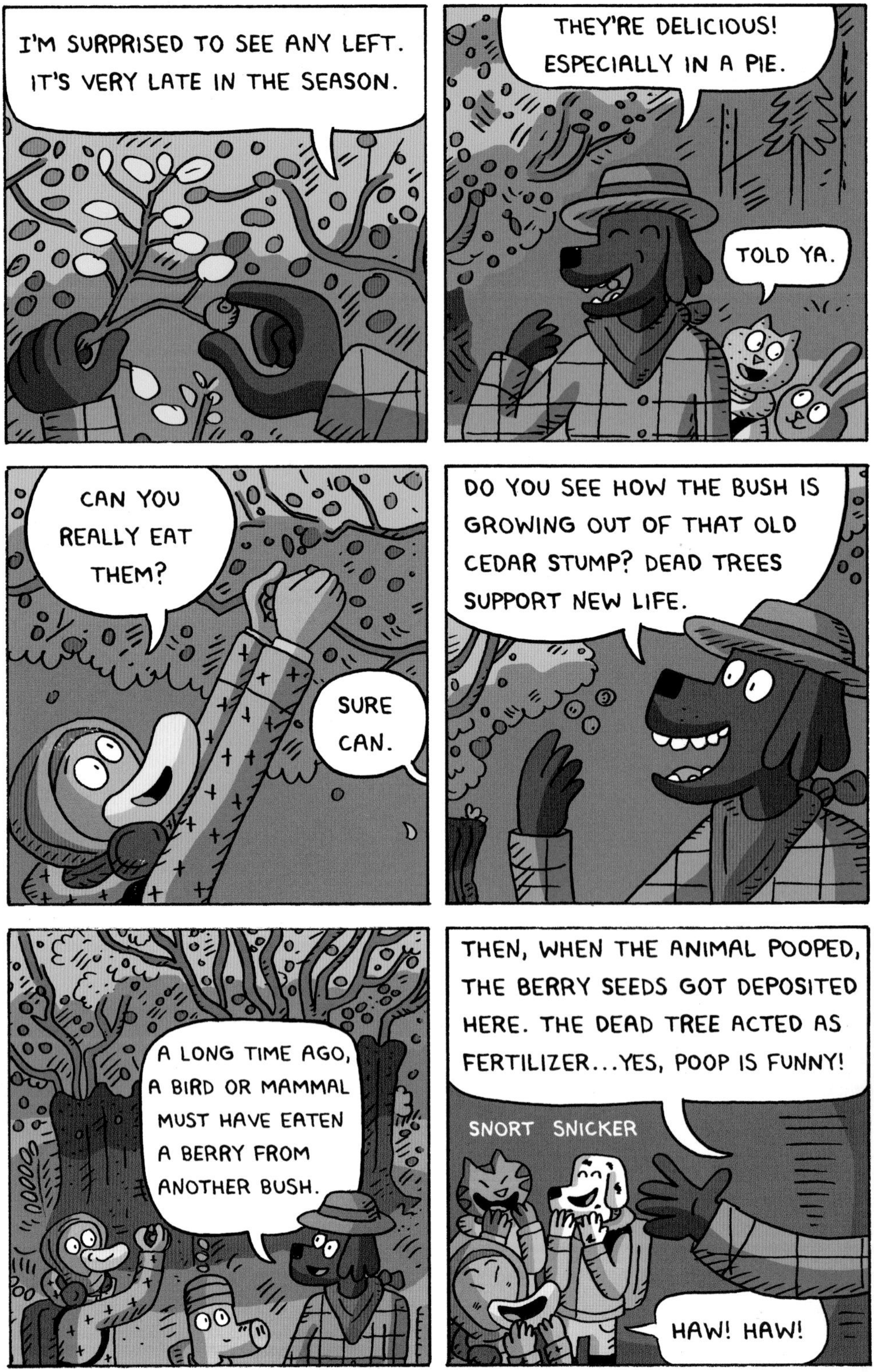
I'M SURPRISED TO SEE ANY LEFT. IT'S VERY LATE IN THE SEASON.
THEY'RE DELICIOUS! ESPECIALLY IN A PIE.
TOLD YA.
CAN YOU REALLY EAT THEM?
SURE CAN.
DO YOU SEE HOW THE BUSH IS GROWING OUT OF THAT OLD CEDAR STUMP? DEAD TREES SUPPORT NEW LIFE.
A LONG TIME AGO, A BIRD OR MAMMAL MUST HAVE EATEN A BERRY FROM ANOTHER BUSH.
THEN, WHEN THE ANIMAL POOPED, THE BERRY SEEDS GOT DEPOSITED HERE. THE DEAD TREE ACTED AS FERTILIZER...YES, POOP IS FUNNY!
SNORT
SNICKER
HAW! HAW!

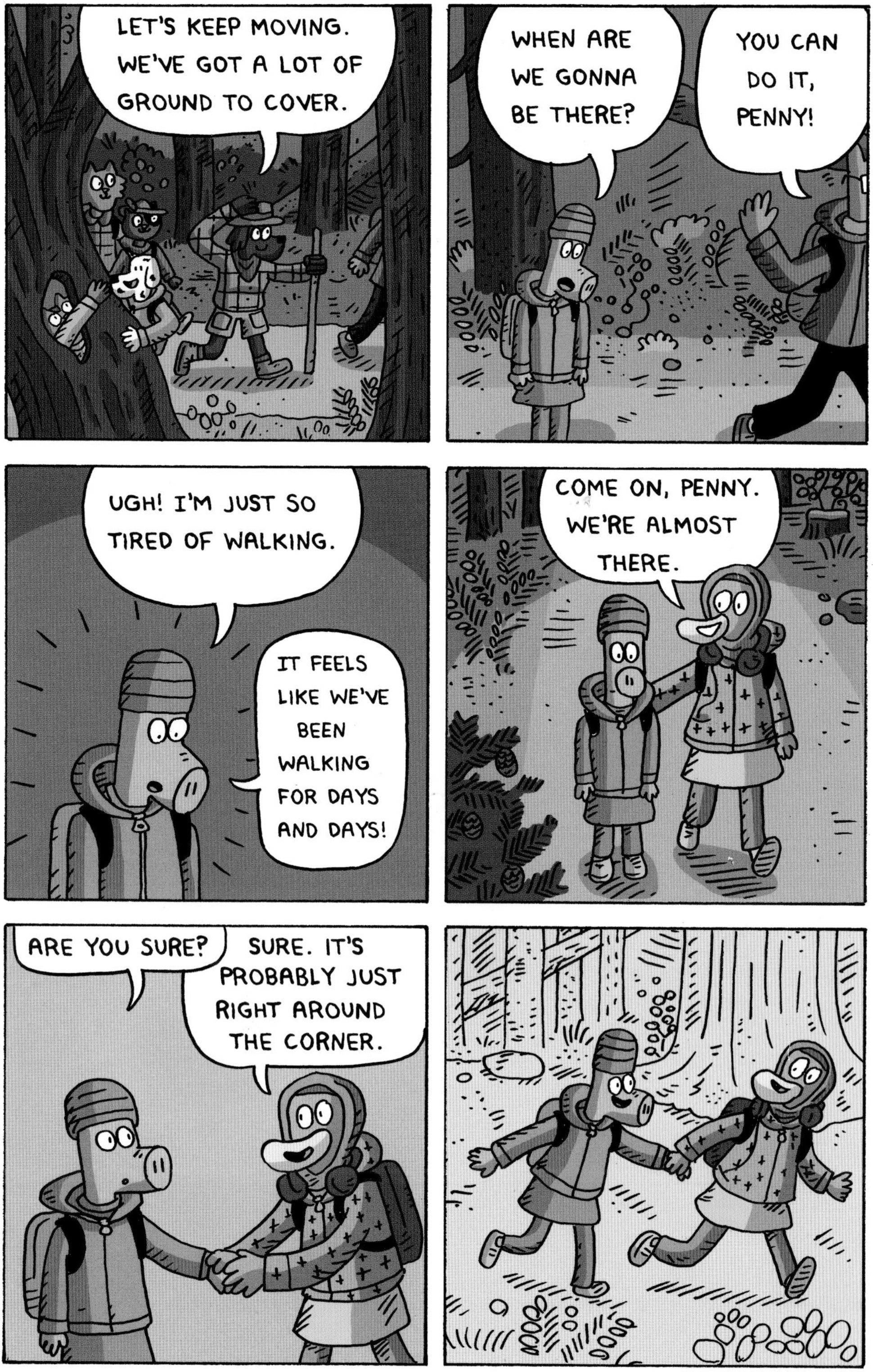
LET'S KEEP MOVING. WE'VE GOT A LOT OF GROUND TO COVER.
WHEN ARE WE GONNA BE THERE?
YOU CAN DO IT, PENNY!
UGH! I'M JUST SO TIRED OF WALKING.
IT FEELS LIKE WE'VE BEEN WALKING FOR DAYS AND DAYS!
COME ON, PENNY. WE'RE ALMOST THERE.
ARE YOU SURE?
SURE. IT'S PROBABLY JUST RIGHT AROUND THE CORNER.

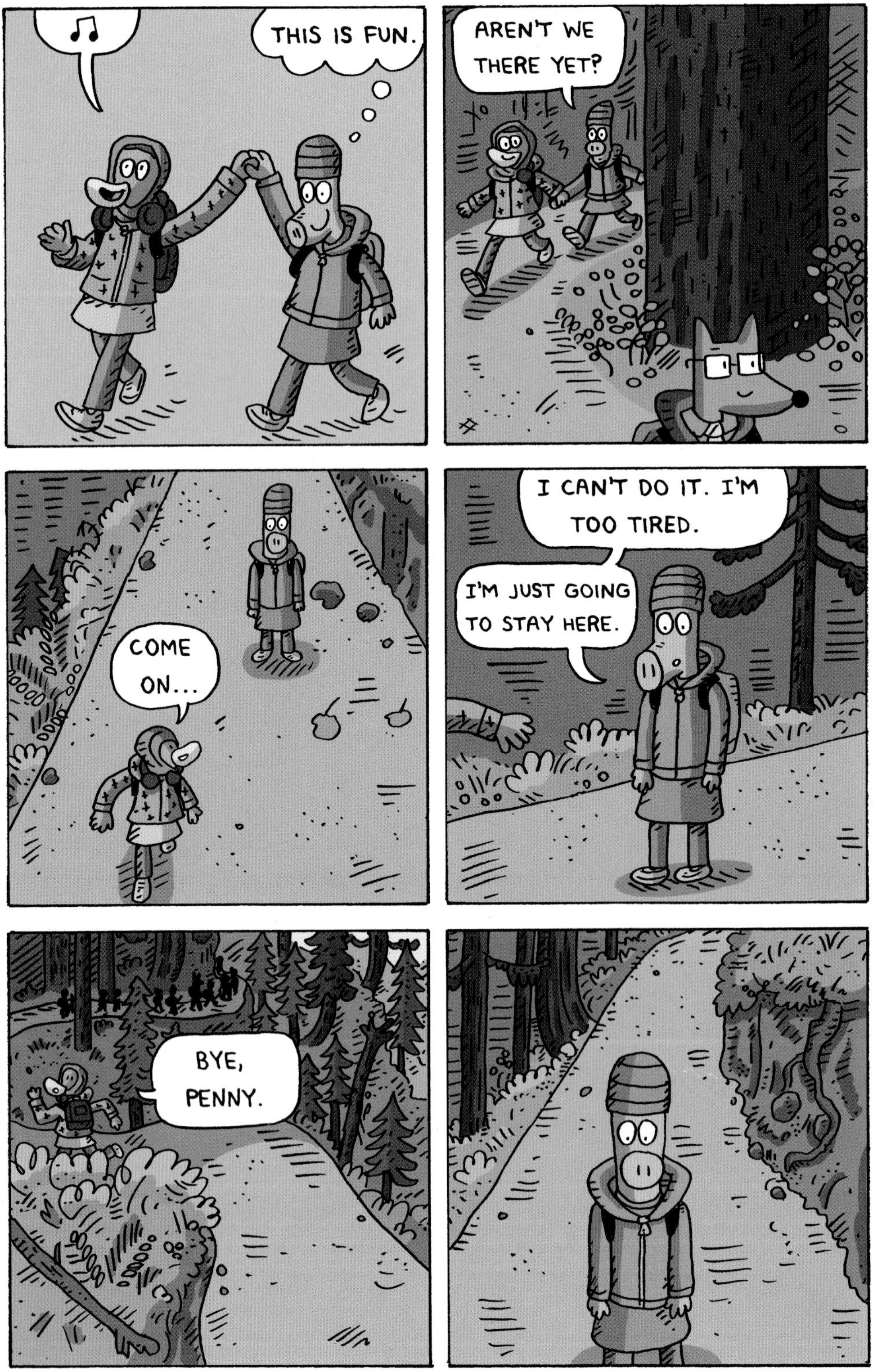
♫
THIS IS FUN.
AREN'T WE THERE YET?
COME ON...
I CAN'T DO IT. I'M TOO TIRED.
I'M JUST GOING TO STAY HERE.
BYE, PENNY.

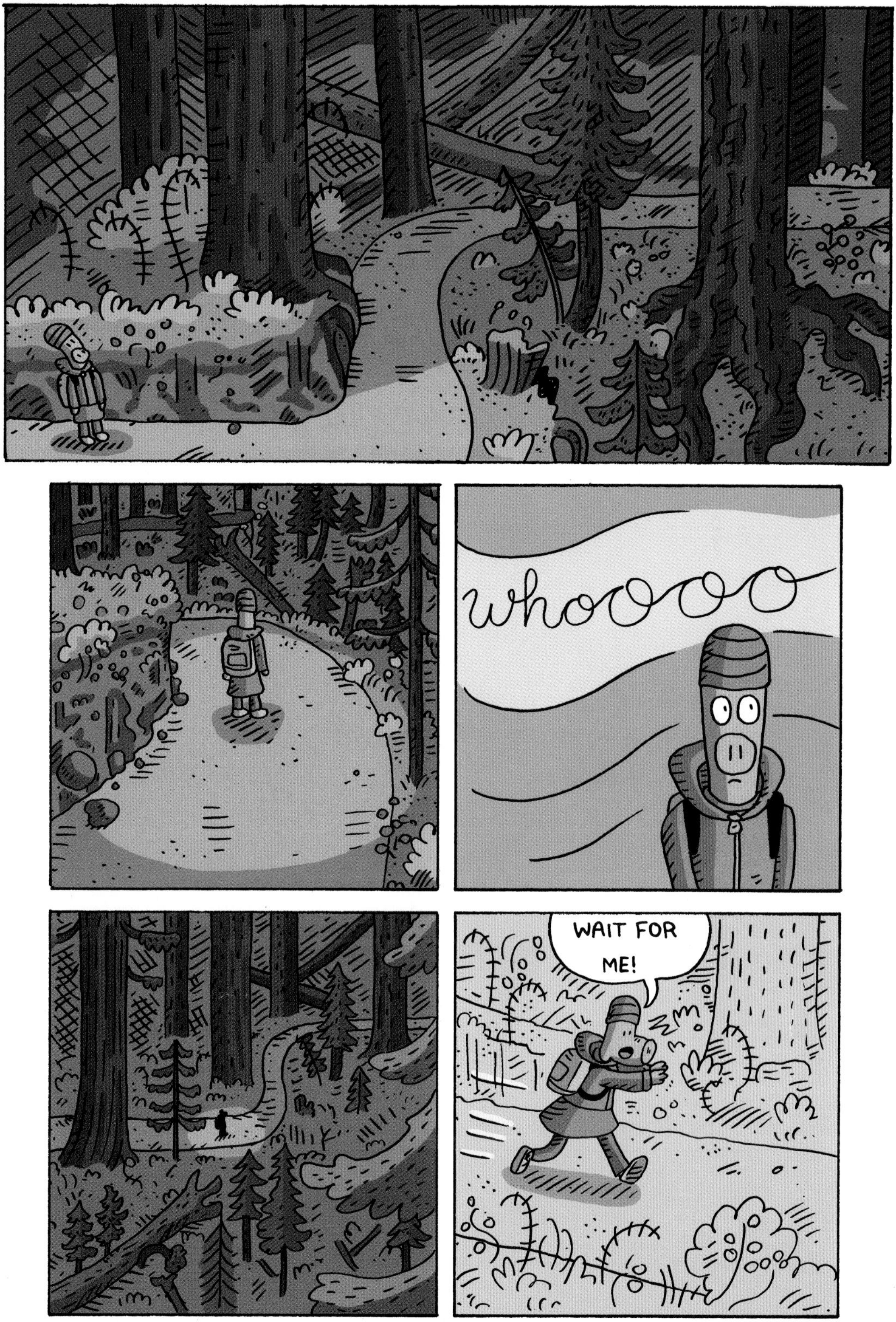
whoOOOO
WAIT FOR ME!

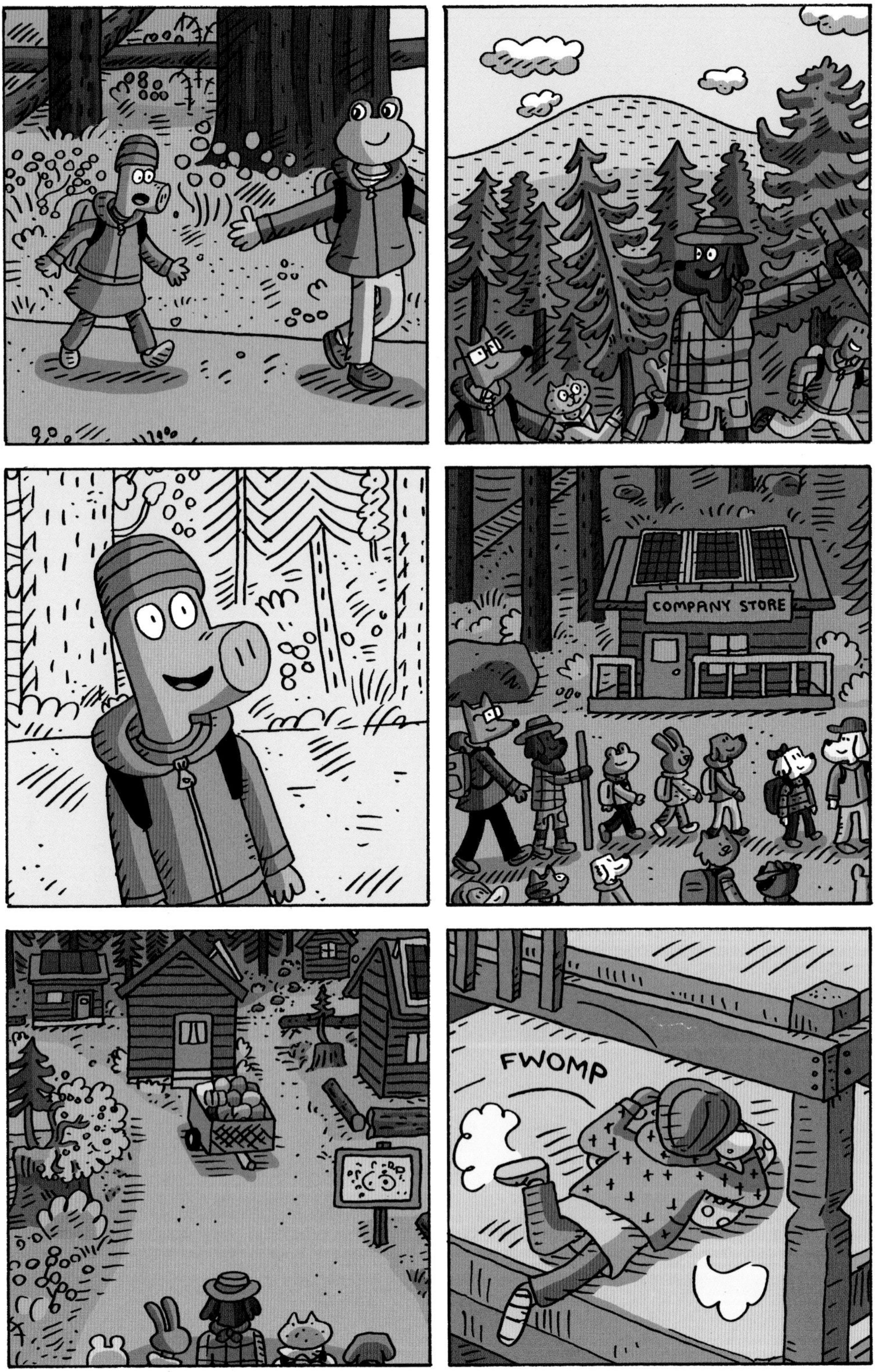
COMPANY STORE
FWOMP

CHAPTER THREE
New Friends

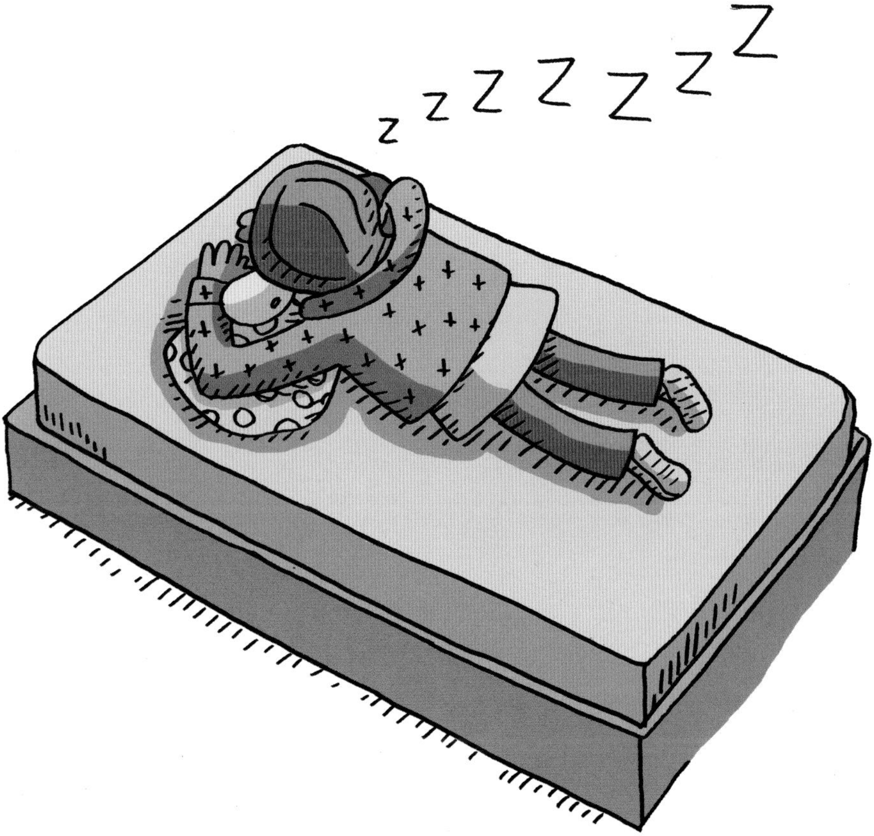

z z Z Z Z Z Z

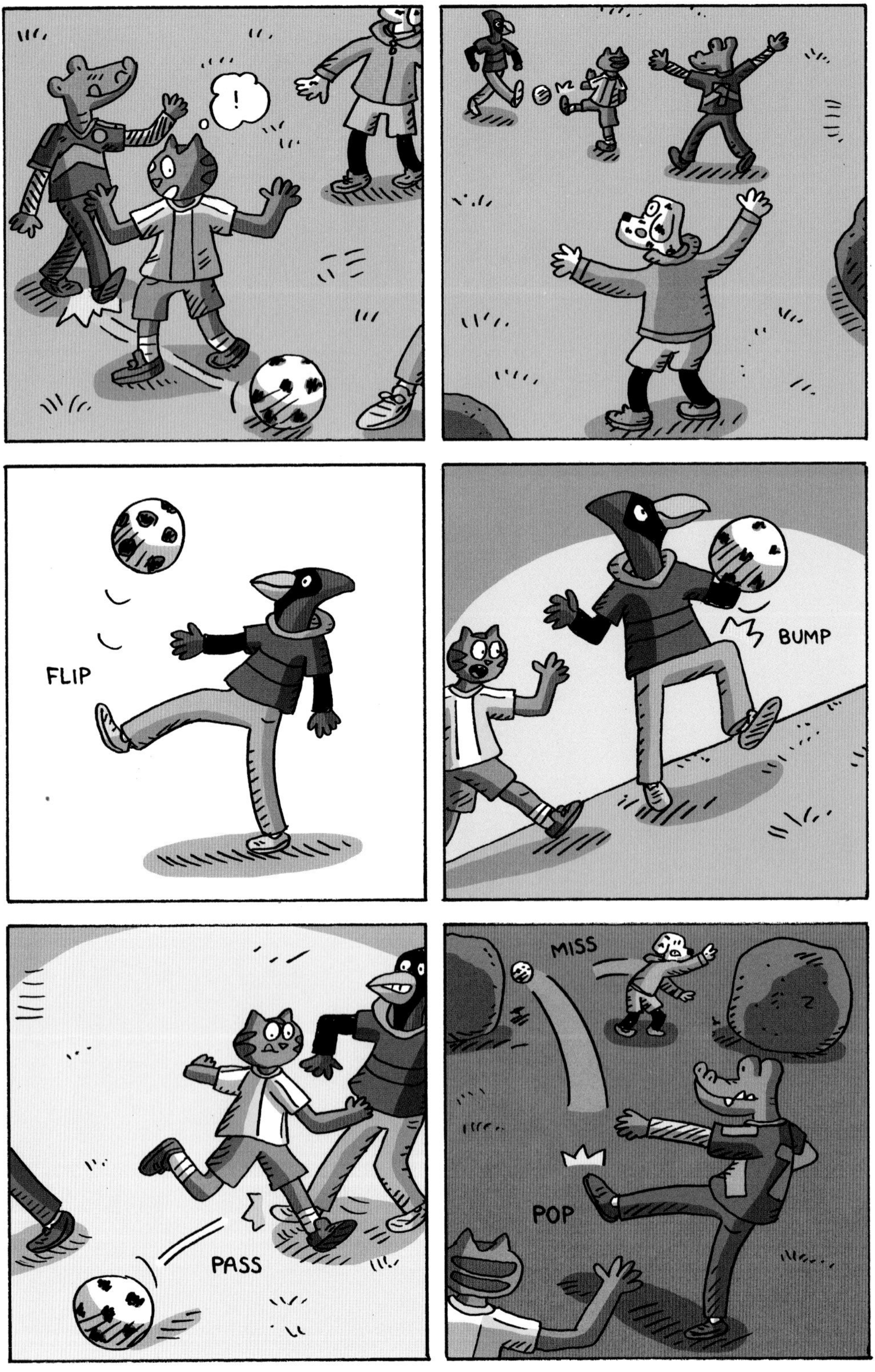
!
FLIP
BUMP
PASS
MISS
POP

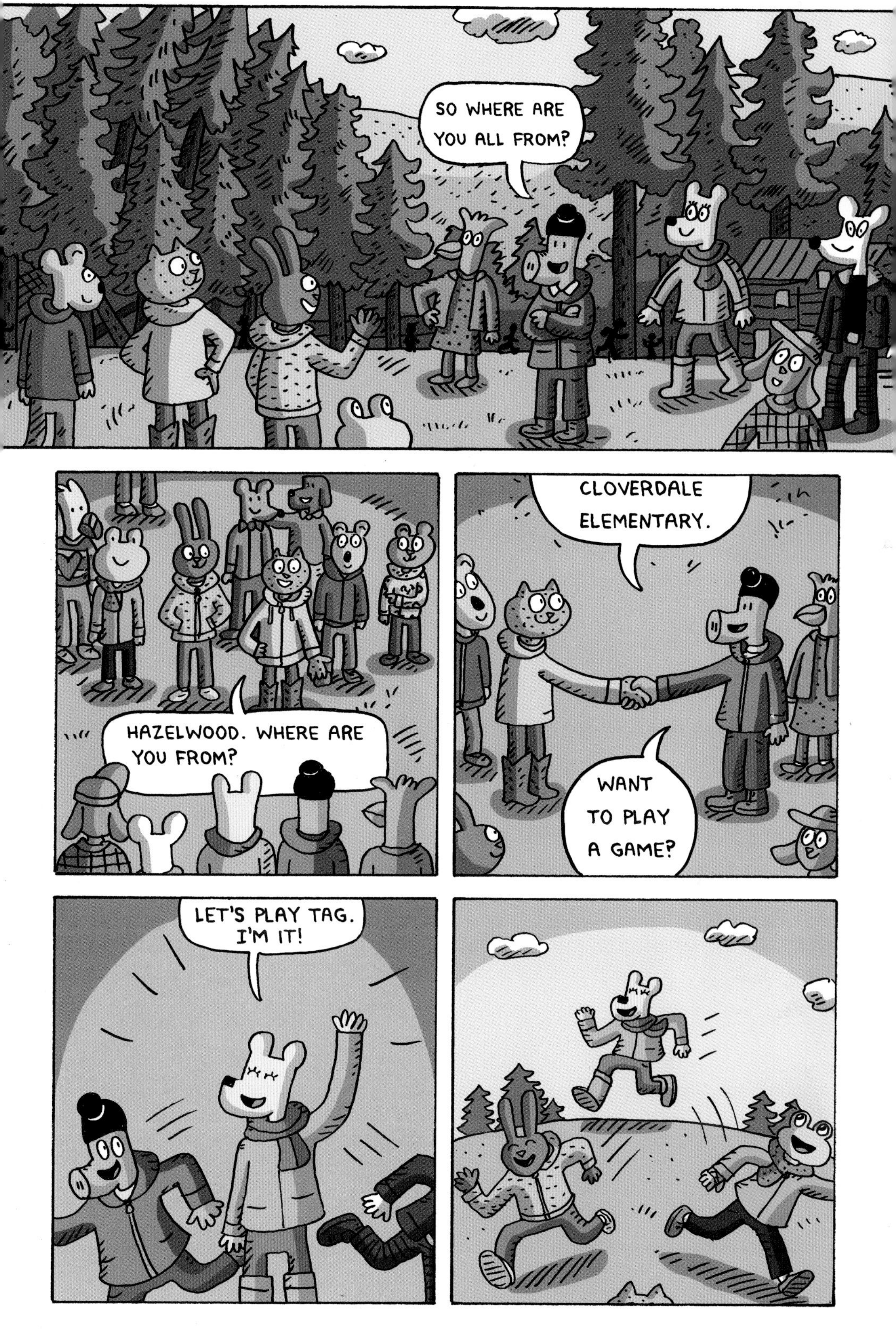
SO WHERE ARE YOU ALL FROM?
HAZELWOOD. WHERE ARE YOU FROM?
CLOVERDALE ELEMENTARY.
WANT TO PLAY A GAME?
LET'S PLAY TAG. I'M IT!

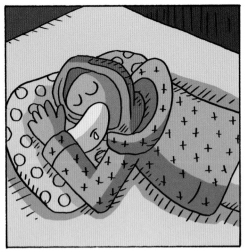

SSSSL...HUH?!

WHOA!

WHAT DAY IS IT? WHERE AM I? WHAT AM I DOING HERE?

I MUST HAVE PASSED OUT.

HOW ARE YOU FEELING, AZIZA? DID YOU GET SOME SLEEP? YOU MUST HAVE BEEN EXHAUSTED.

...

GO ON AND FIND YOUR FRIENDS. EVERYONE IS PLAYING IN THE MEADOW.

OKAY. THANK YOU, GENEVIEVE.

CALL ME GI-GI.

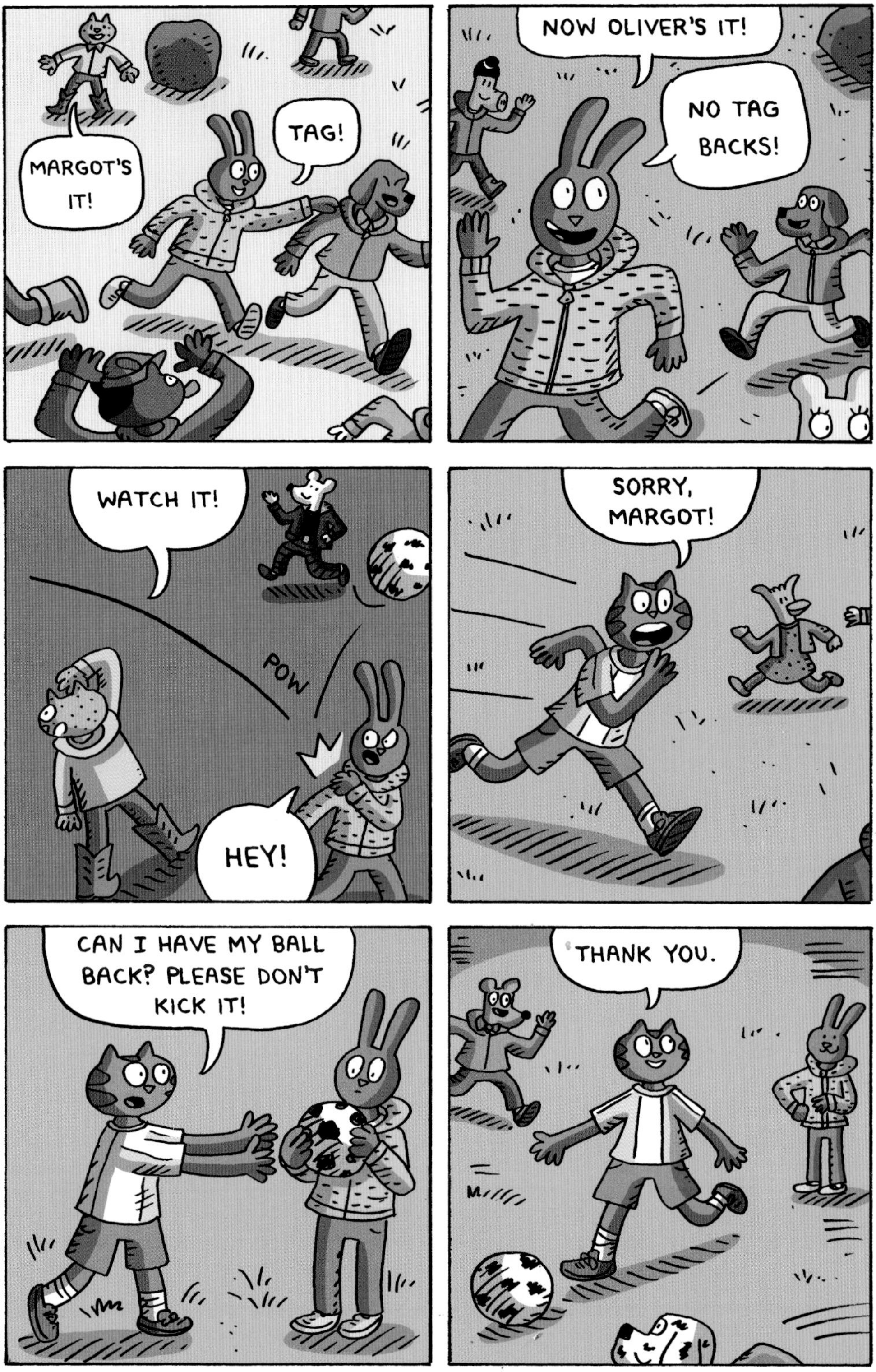
MARGOT'S IT!
TAG!
NOW OLIVER'S IT!
NO TAG BACKS!
WATCH IT!
POW
HEY!
SORRY, MARGOT!
CAN I HAVE MY BALL BACK? PLEASE DON'T KICK IT!
THANK YOU.

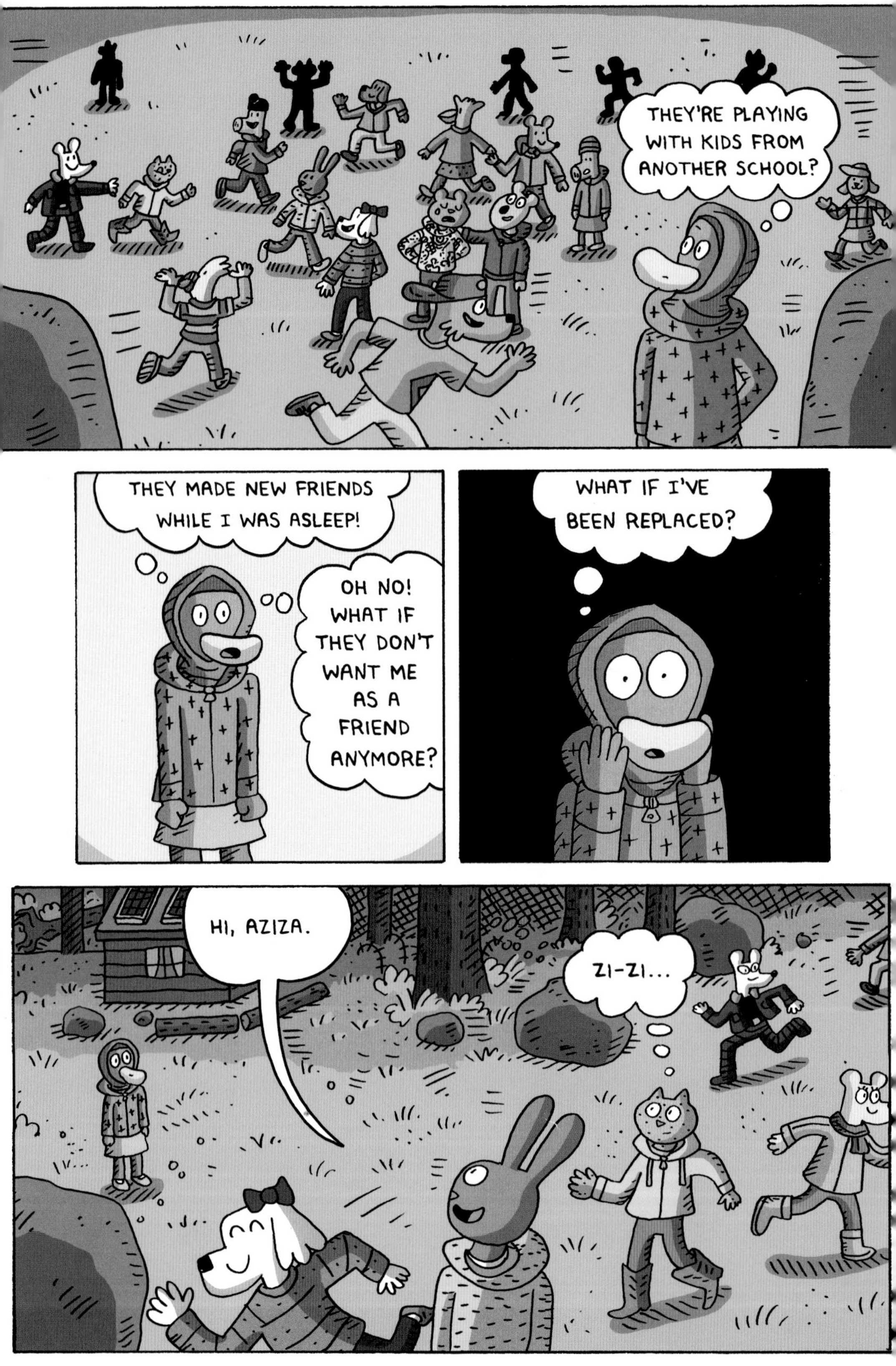
THEY'RE PLAYING WITH KIDS FROM ANOTHER SCHOOL?
THEY MADE NEW FRIENDS WHILE I WAS ASLEEP!
OH NO! WHAT IF THEY DON'T WANT ME AS A FRIEND ANYMORE?
WHAT IF I'VE BEEN REPLACED?
HI, AZIZA.
ZI-ZI...

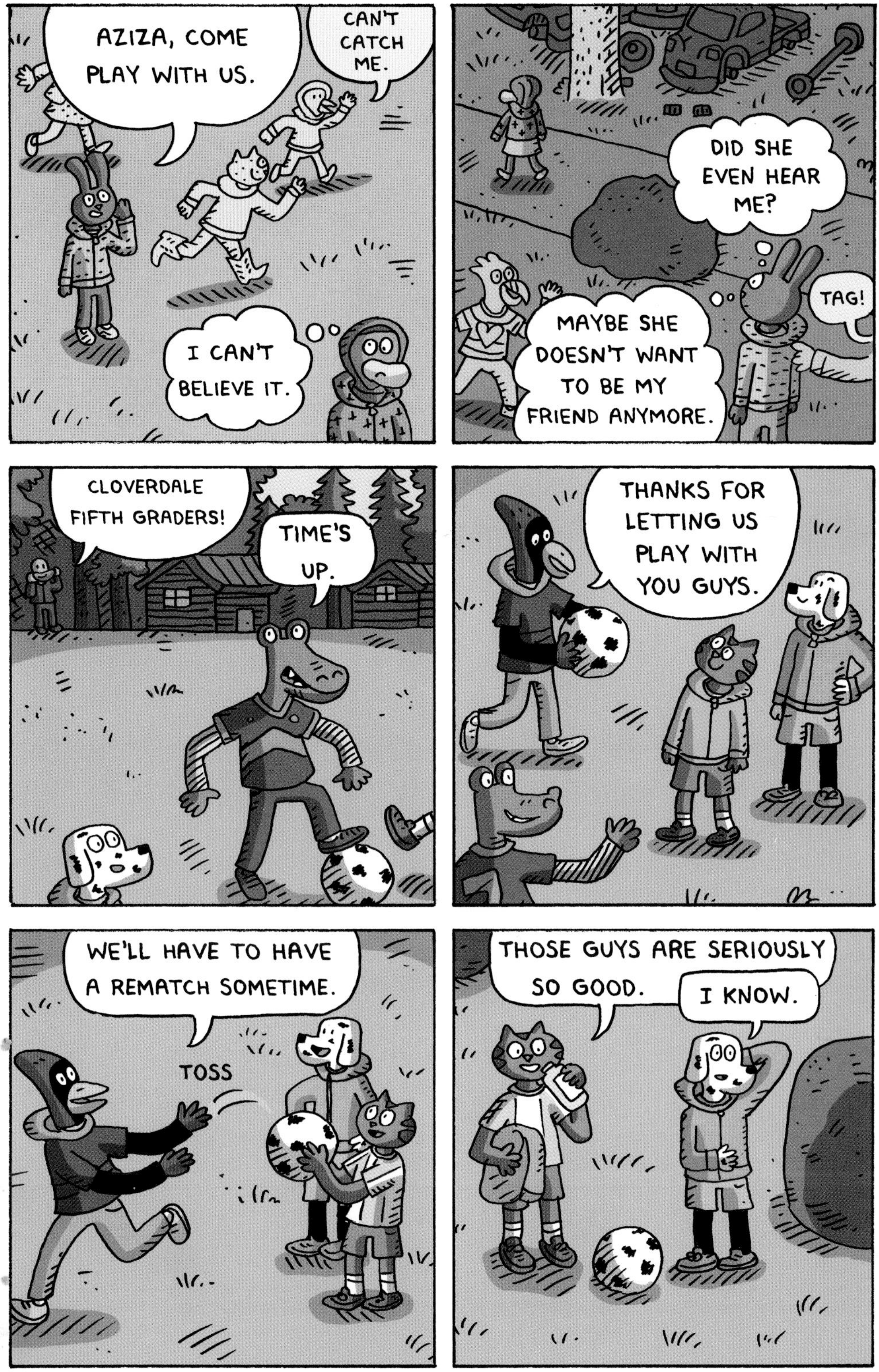
AZIZA, COME PLAY WITH US.
CAN'T CATCH ME.
I CAN'T BELIEVE IT.
DID SHE EVEN HEAR ME?
MAYBE SHE DOESN'T WANT TO BE MY FRIEND ANYMORE.
TAG!
CLOVERDALE FIFTH GRADERS!
TIME'S UP.
THANKS FOR LETTING US PLAY WITH YOU GUYS.
WE'LL HAVE TO HAVE A REMATCH SOMETIME.
TOSS
THOSE GUYS ARE SERIOUSLY SO GOOD.
I KNOW.

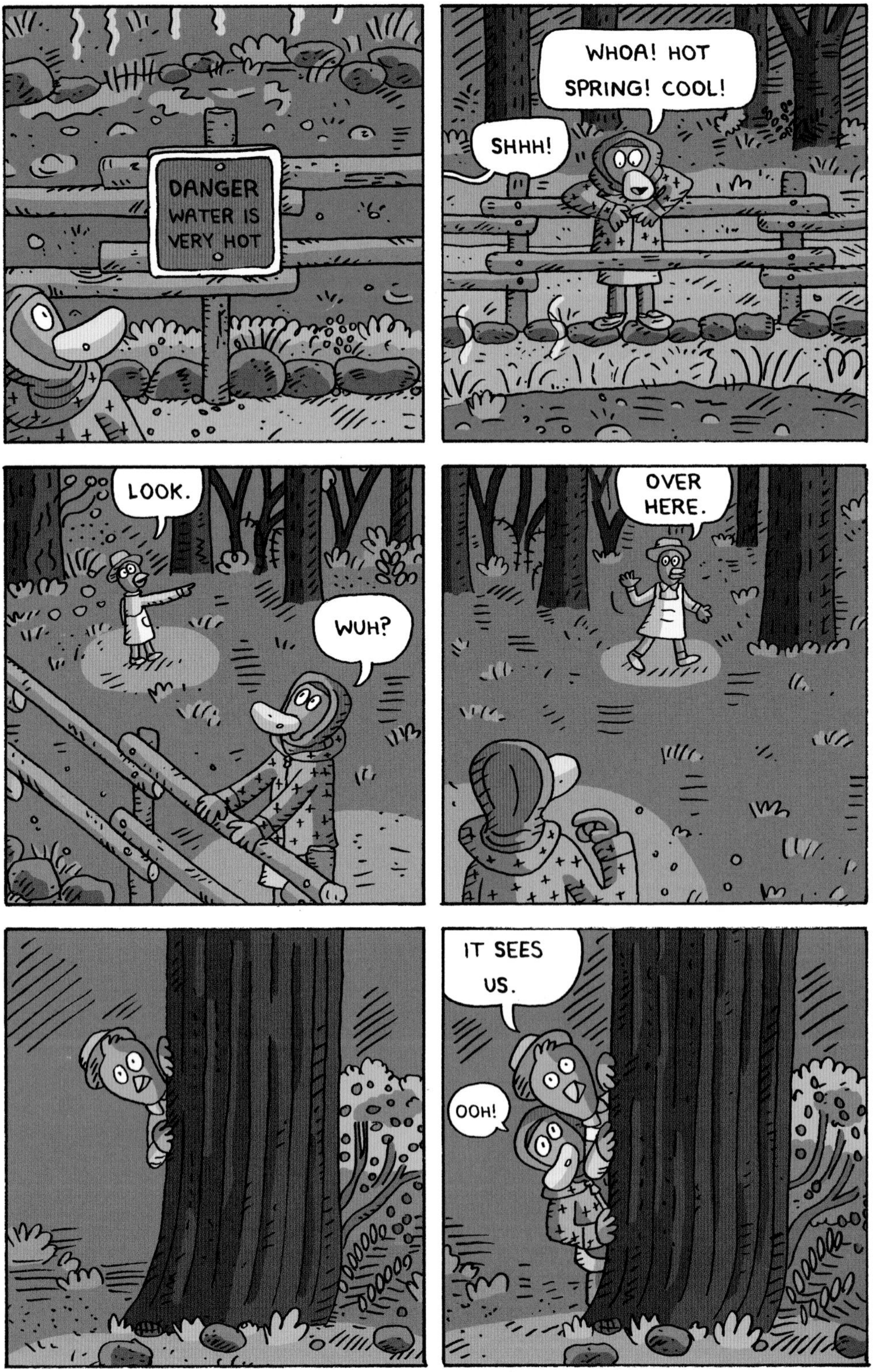
DANGER WATER IS VERY HOT
WHOA! HOT SPRING! COOL!
SHHH!
LOOK.
WUH?
OVER HERE.
IT SEES US.
OOH!

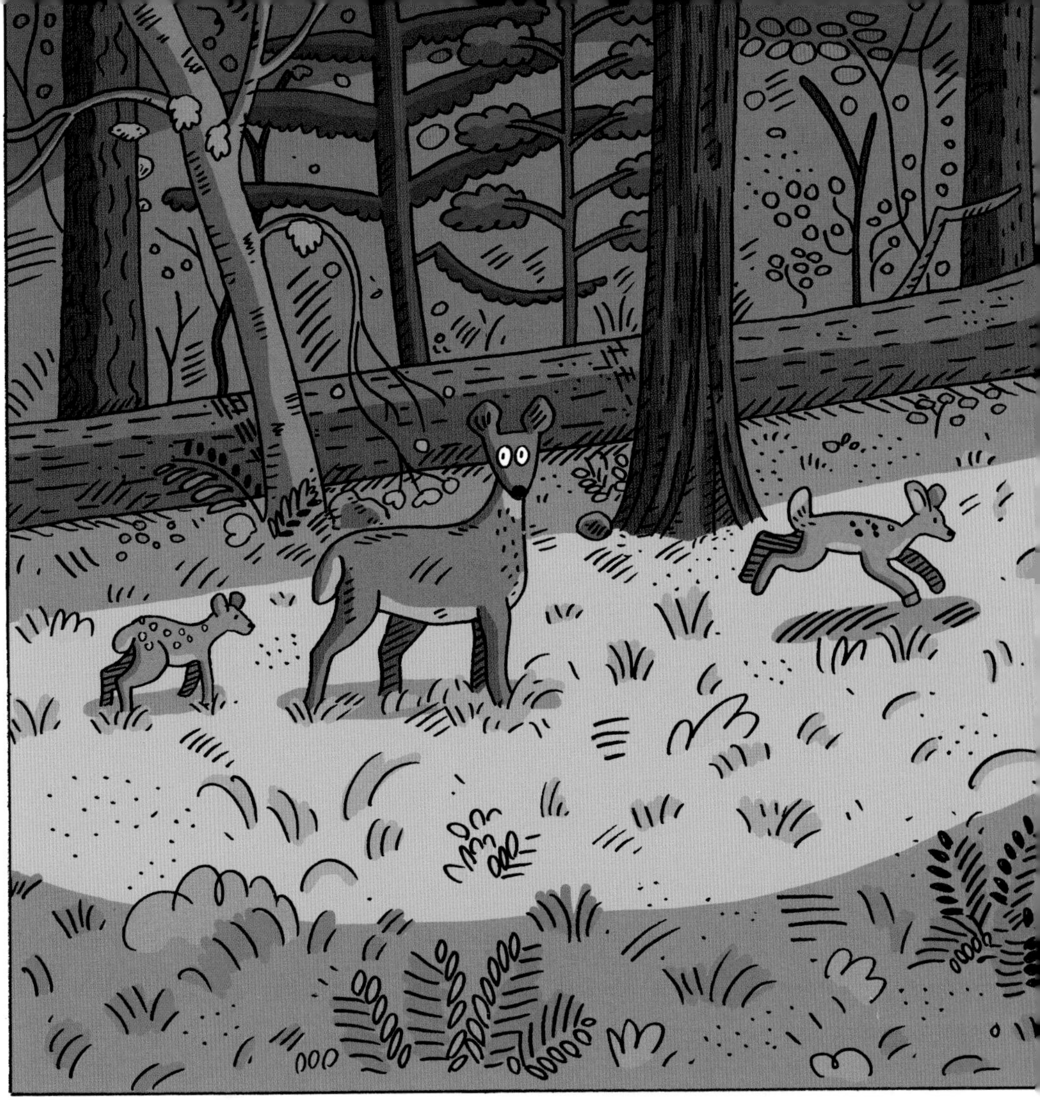

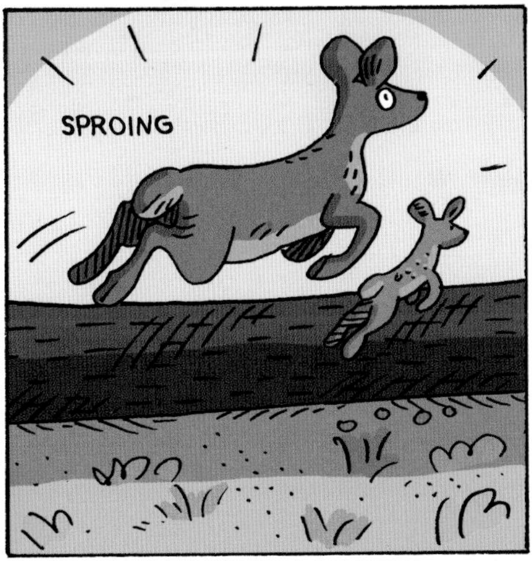
SPROING

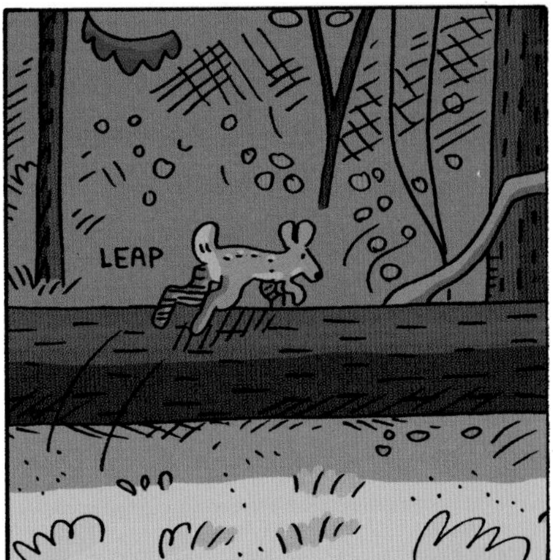
LEAP

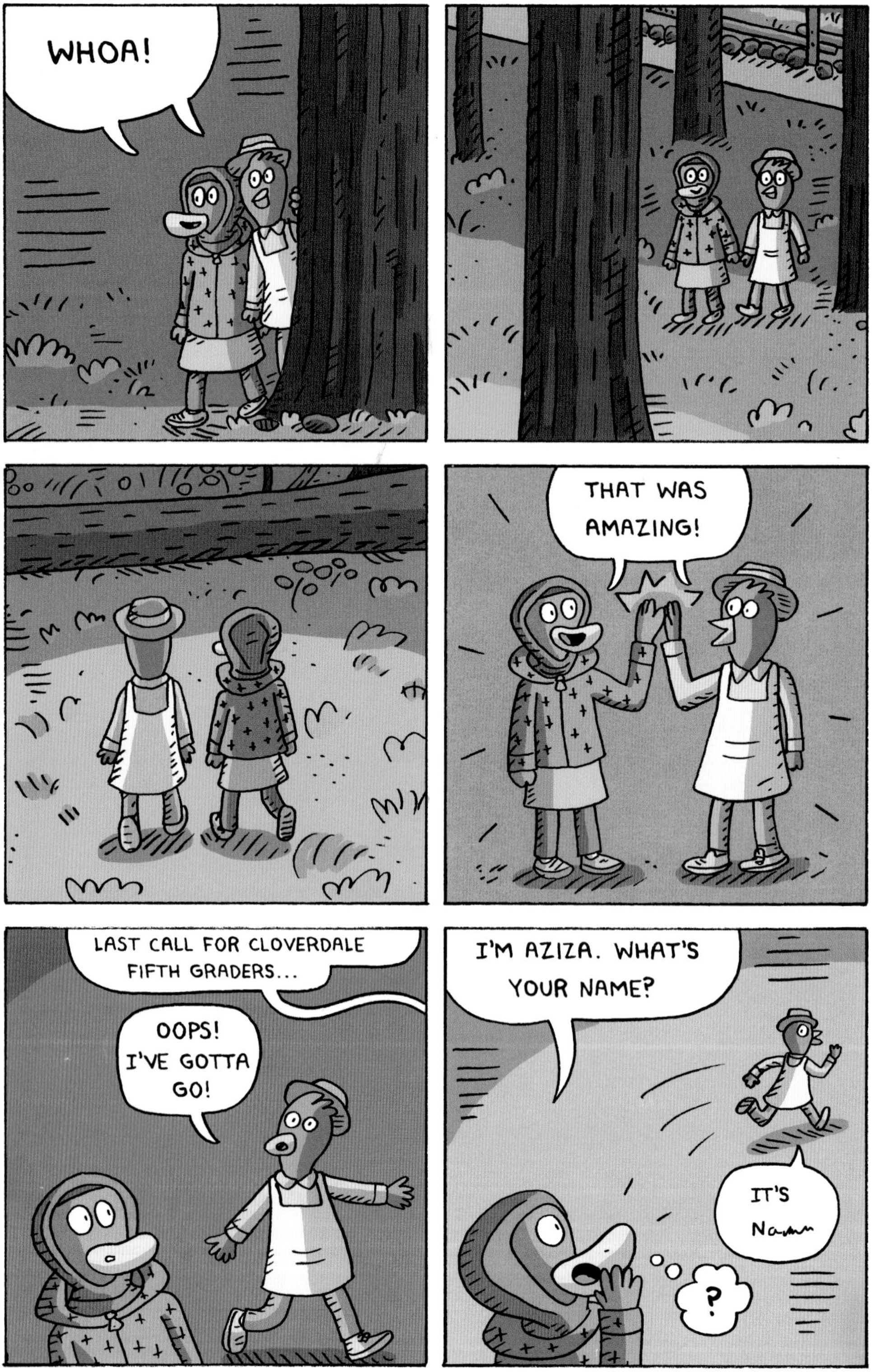
WHOA!
THAT WAS AMAZING!
LAST CALL FOR CLOVERDALE FIFTH GRADERS...
OOPS! I'VE GOTTA GO!
I'M AZIZA. WHAT'S YOUR NAME?
IT'S
?

CHAPTER FOUR
Camp Names

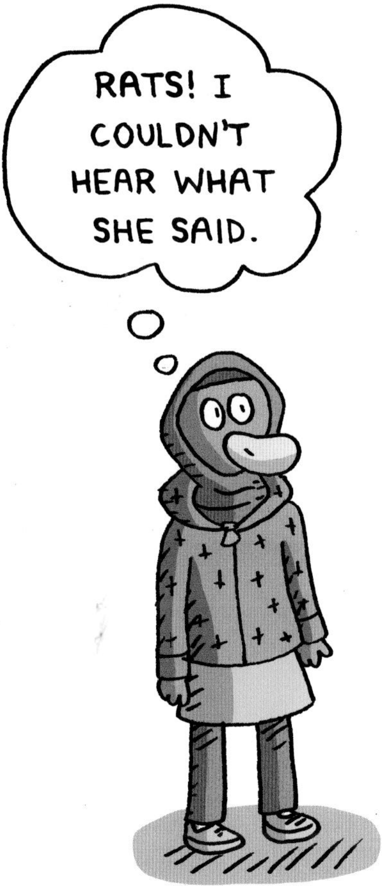
RATS! I COULDN'T HEAR WHAT SHE SAID.

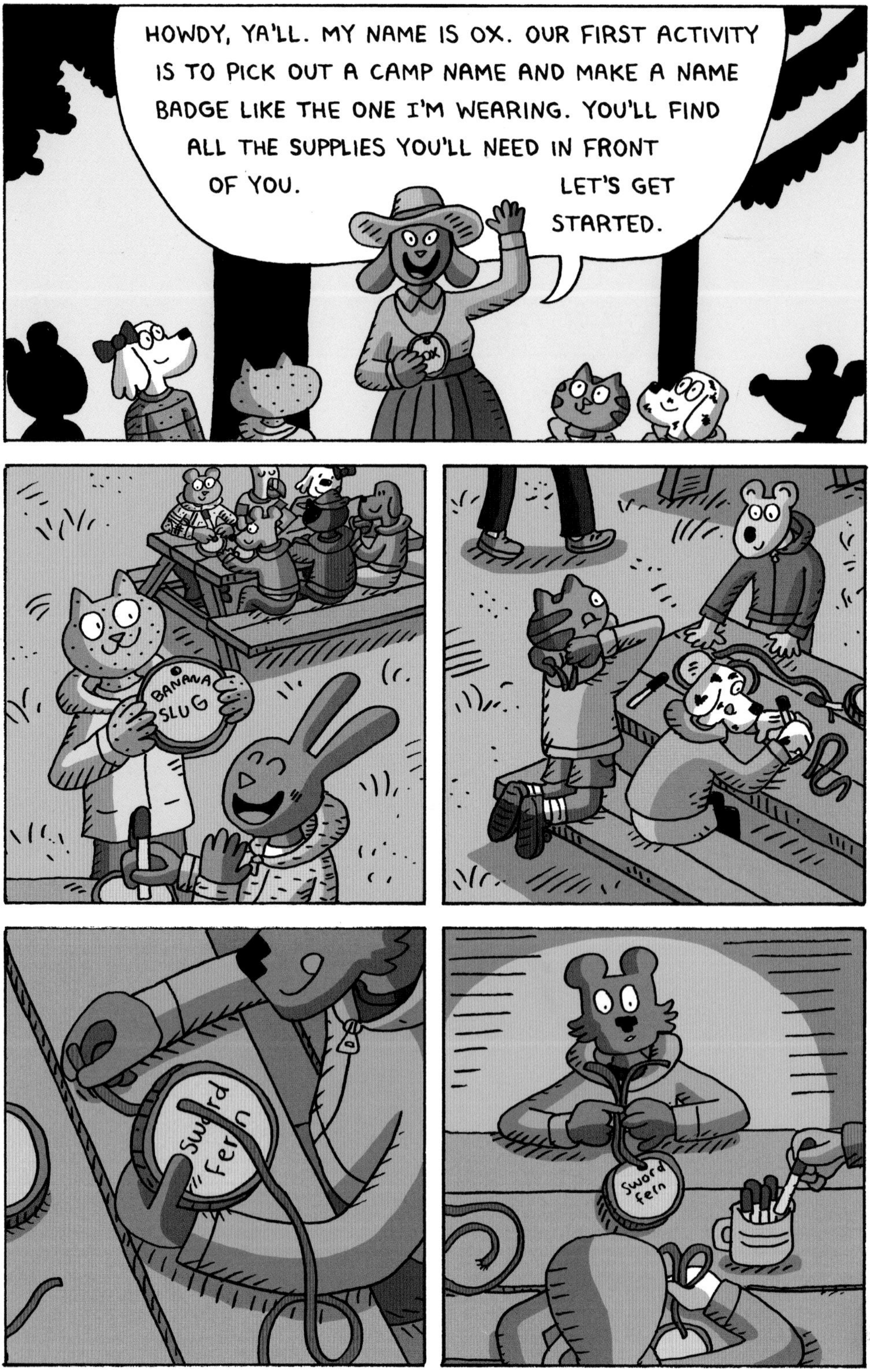
HOWDY, YA'LL. MY NAME IS OX. OUR FIRST ACTIVITY IS TO PICK OUT A CAMP NAME AND MAKE A NAME BADGE LIKE THE ONE I'M WEARING. YOU'LL FIND ALL THE SUPPLIES YOU'LL NEED IN FRONT OF YOU.
LET'S GET STARTED.
OX
BANANA SLUG
Sword Fern
Sword Fern

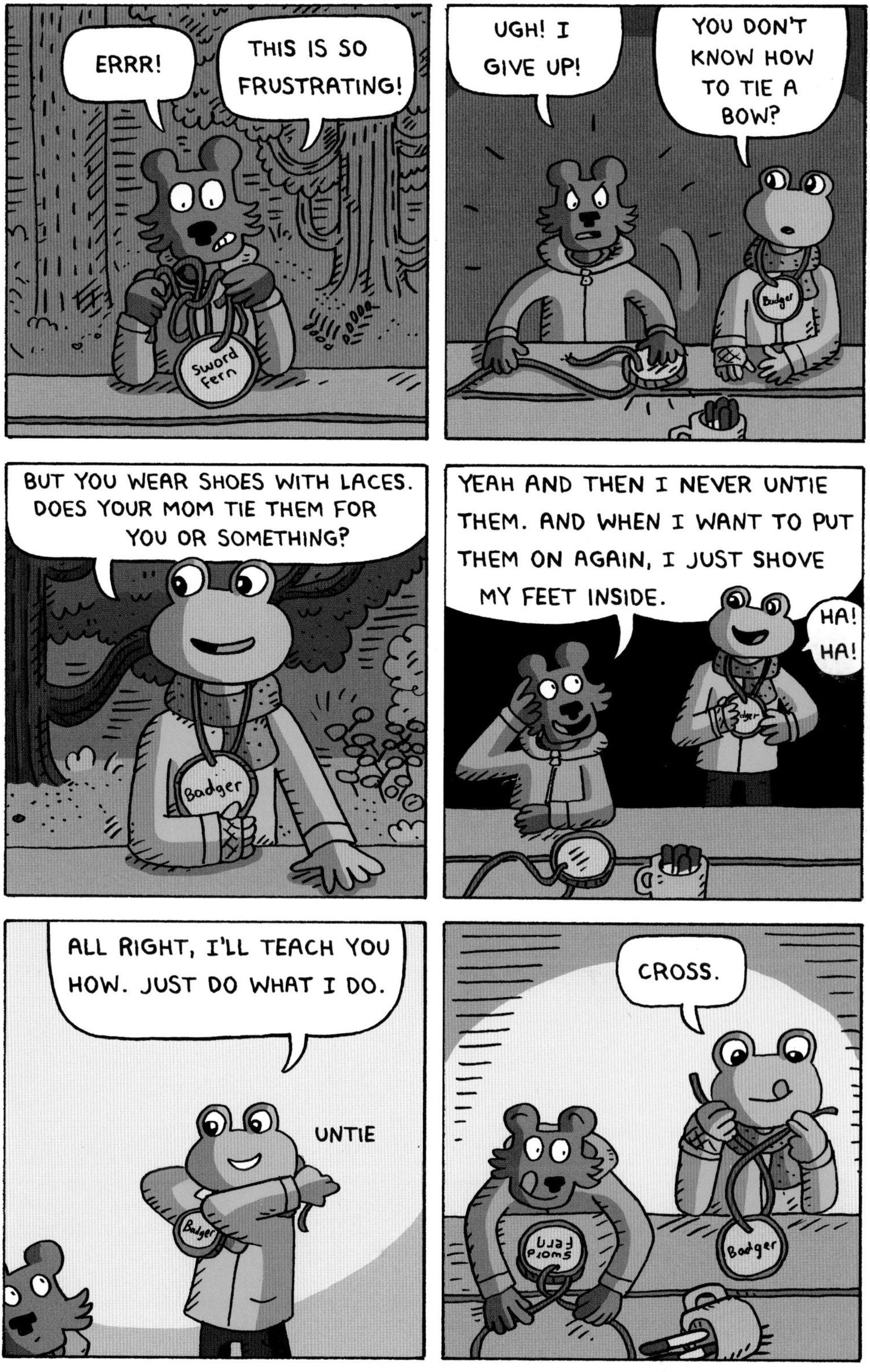
ERRR!
THIS IS SO FRUSTRATING!
Sword Fern
UGH! I GIVE UP!
YOU DON'T KNOW HOW TO TIE A BOW?
Badger
BUT YOU WEAR SHOES WITH LACES. DOES YOUR MOM TIE THEM FOR YOU OR SOMETHING?
Badger
YEAH AND THEN I NEVER UNTIE THEM. AND WHEN I WANT TO PUT THEM ON AGAIN, I JUST SHOVE MY FEET INSIDE.
HA! HA!
ALL RIGHT, I'LL TEACH YOU HOW. JUST DO WHAT I DO.
UNTIE
Badger
CROSS.
Badger

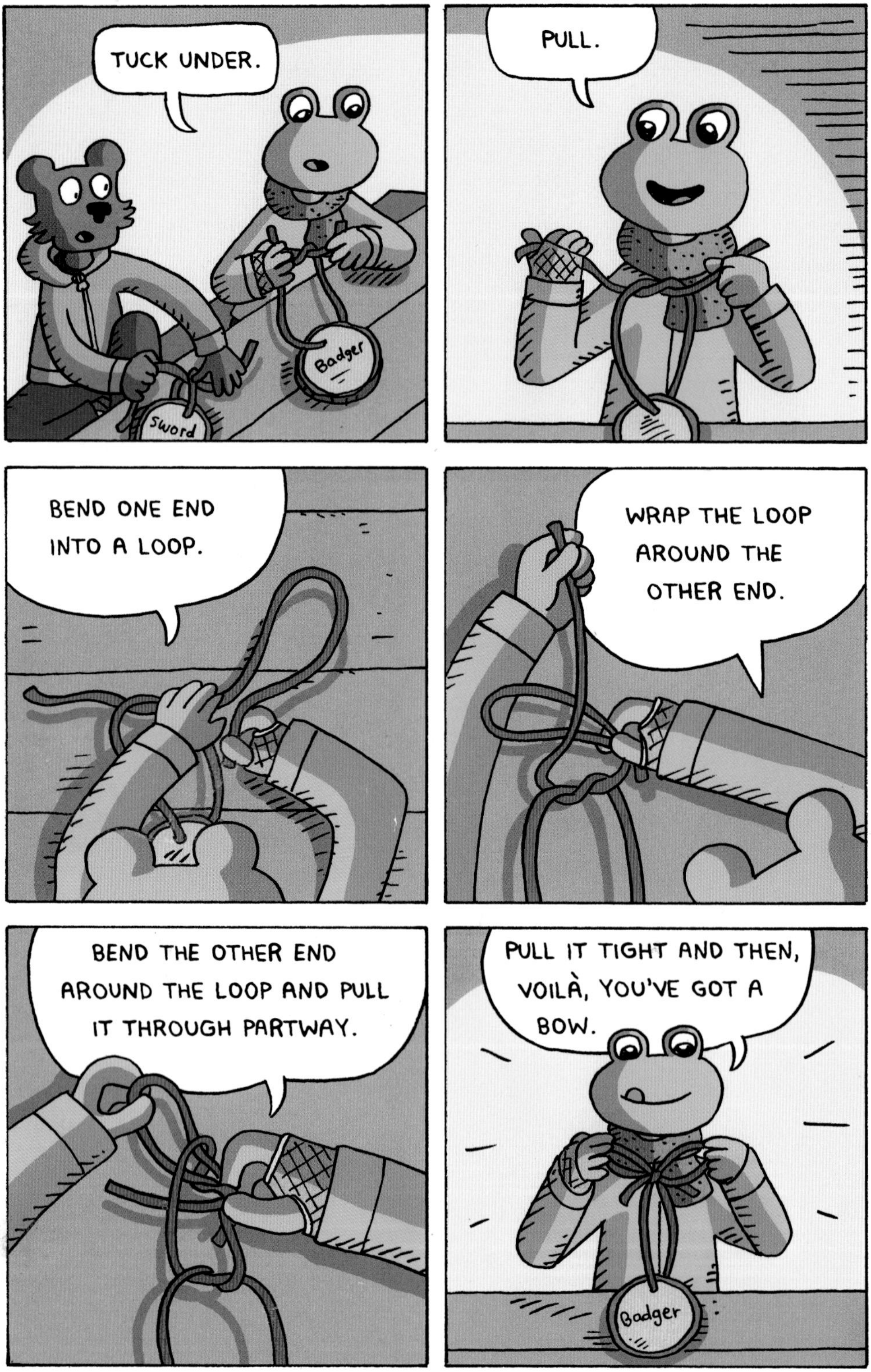
TUCK UNDER.
Badger
Sword
PULL.
BEND ONE END INTO A LOOP.
WRAP THE LOOP AROUND THE OTHER END.
BEND THE OTHER END AROUND THE LOOP AND PULL IT THROUGH PARTWAY.
PULL IT TIGHT AND THEN, VOILÀ, YOU'VE GOT A BOW.
Badger

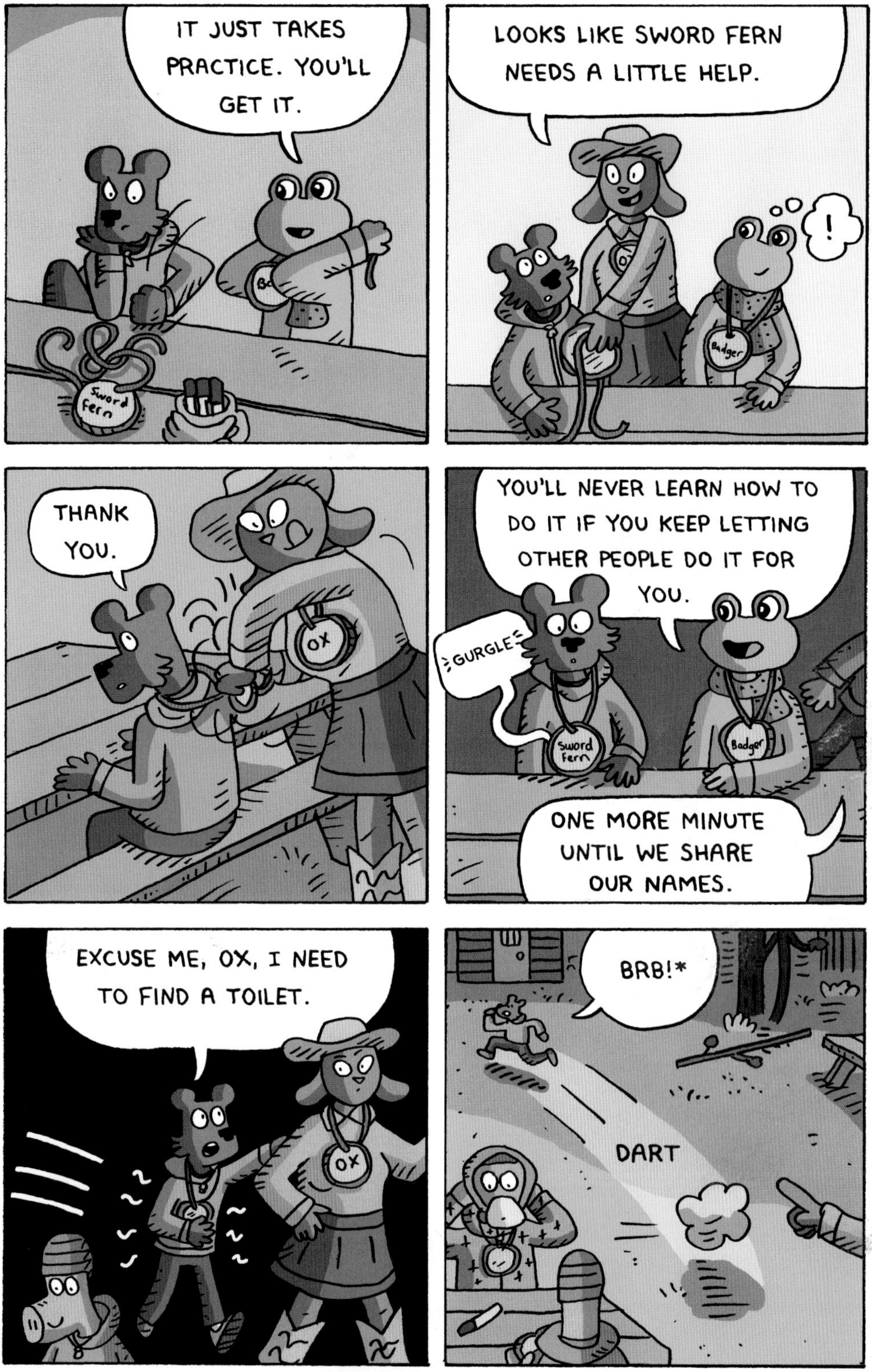
IT JUST TAKES PRACTICE. YOU'LL GET IT.
Sword Fern
LOOKS LIKE SWORD FERN NEEDS A LITTLE HELP.
!
Badger
THANK YOU.
OX
YOU'LL NEVER LEARN HOW TO DO IT IF YOU KEEP LETTING OTHER PEOPLE DO IT FOR YOU.
GURGLE
Sword Fern
Badger
ONE MORE MINUTE UNTIL WE SHARE OUR NAMES.
EXCUSE ME, OX, I NEED TO FIND A TOILET.
OX
BRB!*
DART

*BE RIGHT BACK

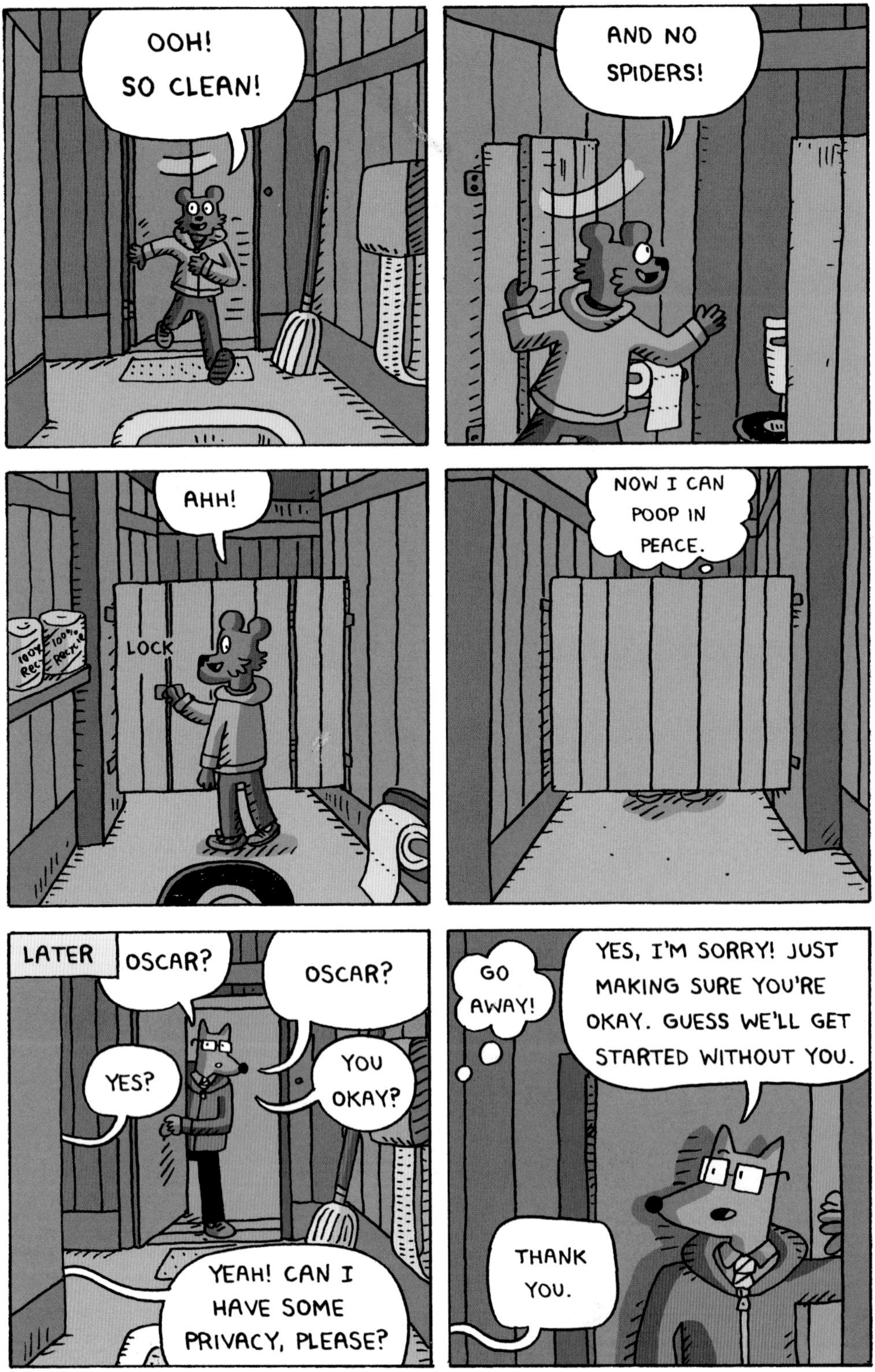
OOH!
SO CLEAN!
AND NO SPIDERS!
AHH!
LOCK
100% RECYCLE
100% REC
NOW I CAN POOP IN PEACE.
LATER
OSCAR?
OSCAR?
YES?
YOU OKAY?
YEAH! CAN I HAVE SOME PRIVACY, PLEASE?
GO AWAY!
YES, I'M SORRY! JUST MAKING SURE YOU'RE OKAY. GUESS WE'LL GET STARTED WITHOUT YOU.
THANK YOU.

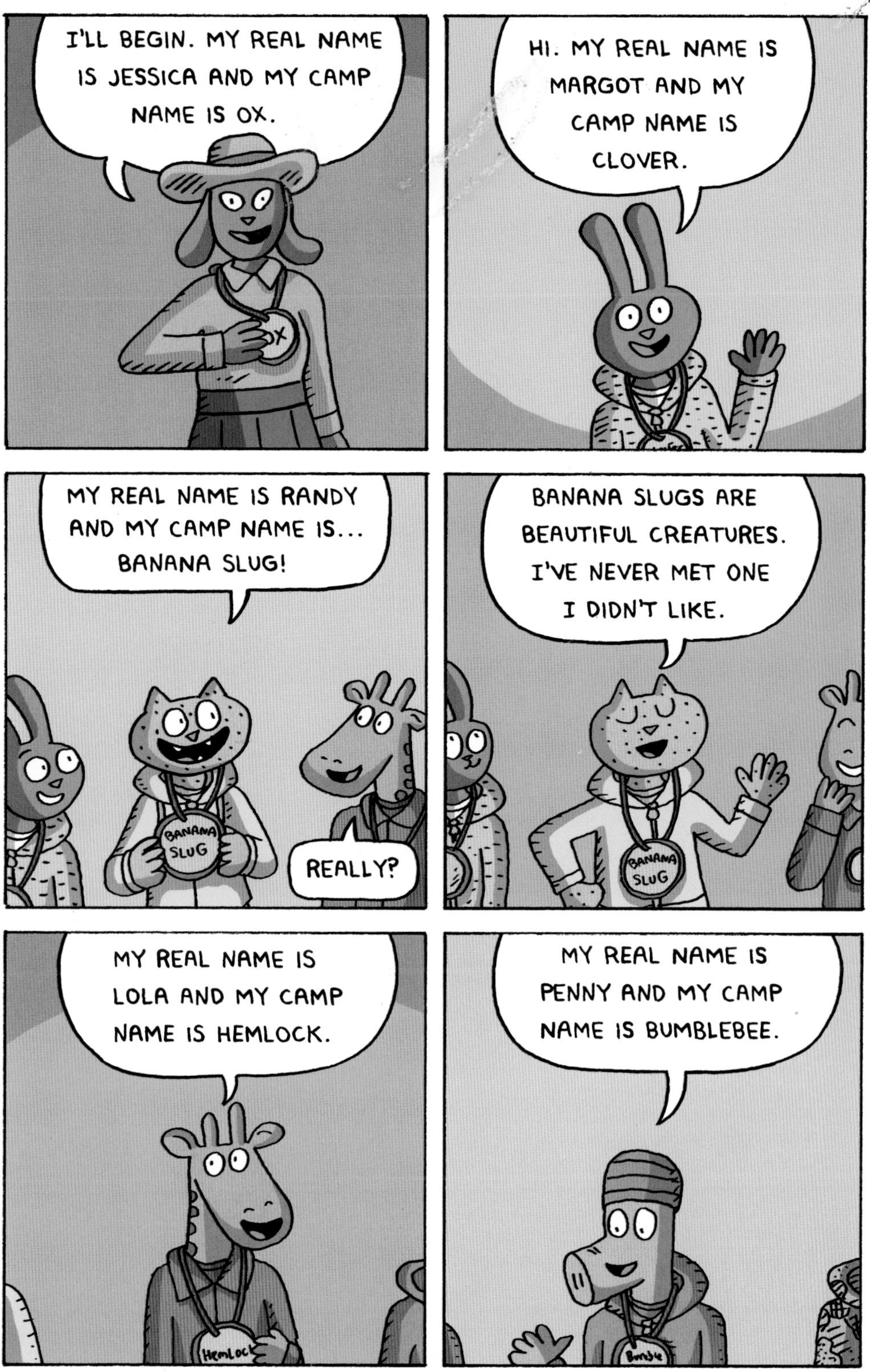
I'LL BEGIN. MY REAL NAME IS JESSICA AND MY CAMP NAME IS OX.
HI. MY REAL NAME IS MARGOT AND MY CAMP NAME IS CLOVER.
MY REAL NAME IS RANDY AND MY CAMP NAME IS... BANANA SLUG!
BANANA SLUG
REALLY?
BANANA SLUGS ARE BEAUTIFUL CREATURES. I'VE NEVER MET ONE I DIDN'T LIKE.
BANANA SLUG
MY REAL NAME IS LOLA AND MY CAMP NAME IS HEMLOCK.
Hemlock
MY REAL NAME IS PENNY AND MY CAMP NAME IS BUMBLEBEE.

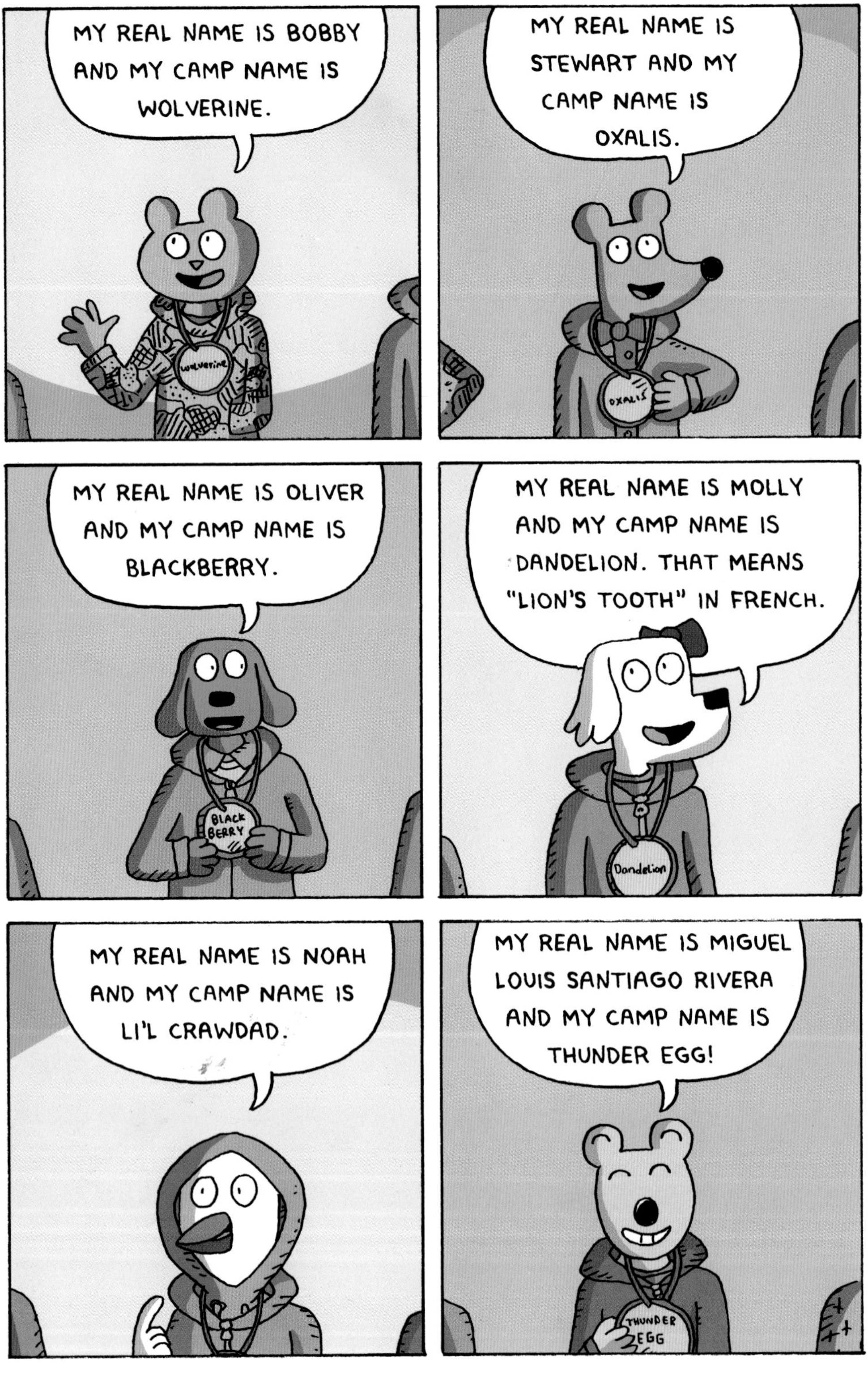
MY REAL NAME IS BOBBY AND MY CAMP NAME IS WOLVERINE.
Wolverine
MY REAL NAME IS STEWART AND MY CAMP NAME IS OXALIS.
OXALIS
MY REAL NAME IS OLIVER AND MY CAMP NAME IS BLACKBERRY.
BLACK BERRY
MY REAL NAME IS MOLLY AND MY CAMP NAME IS DANDELION. THAT MEANS "LION'S TOOTH" IN FRENCH.
Dandelion
MY REAL NAME IS NOAH AND MY CAMP NAME IS LI'L CRAWDAD.
MY REAL NAME IS MIGUEL LOUIS SANTIAGO RIVERA AND MY CAMP NAME IS THUNDER EGG!
THUNDER EGG

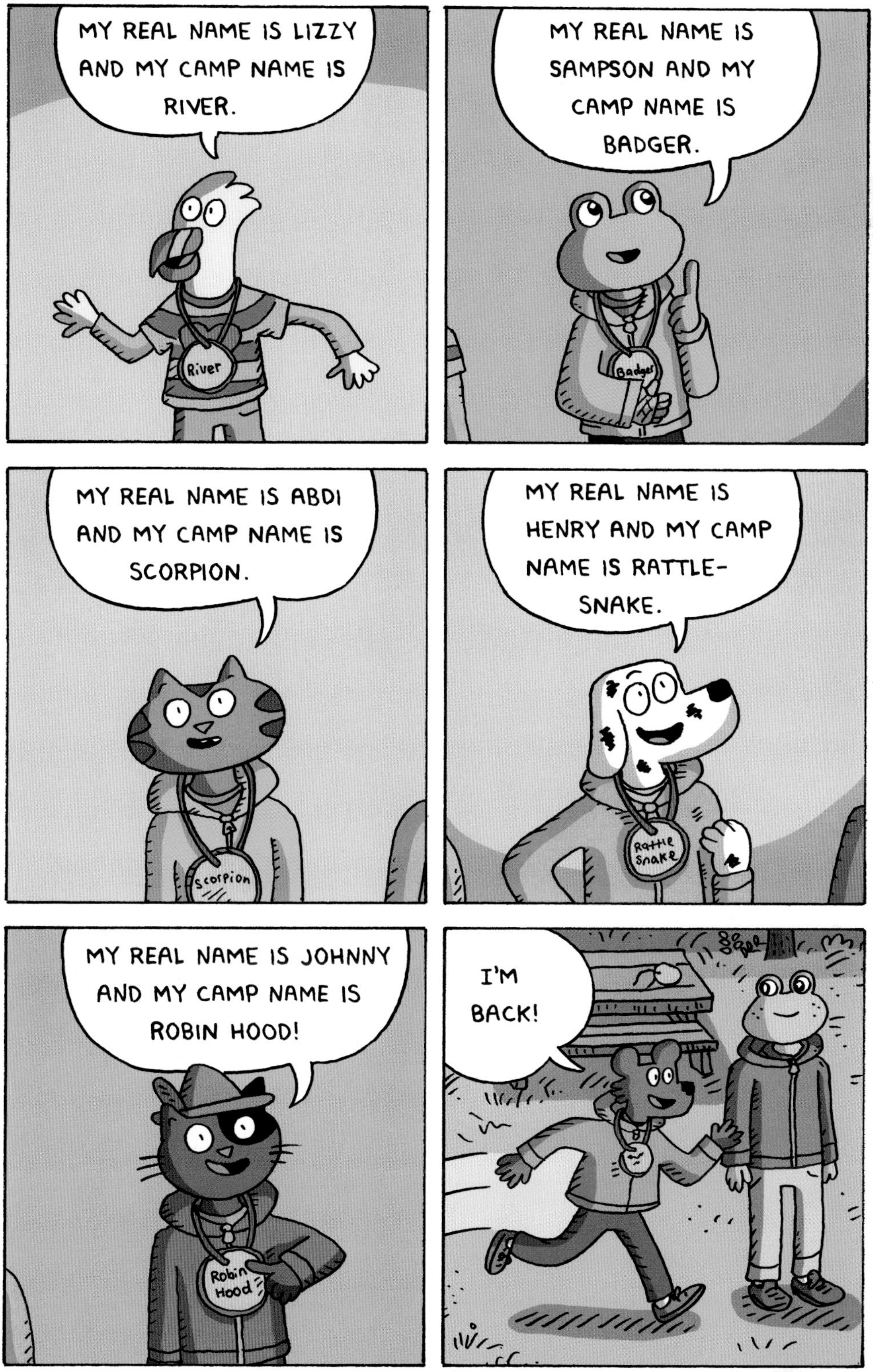
MY REAL NAME IS LIZZY AND MY CAMP NAME IS RIVER.
River
MY REAL NAME IS SAMPSON AND MY CAMP NAME IS BADGER.
Badger
MY REAL NAME IS ABDI AND MY CAMP NAME IS SCORPION.
Scorpion
MY REAL NAME IS HENRY AND MY CAMP NAME IS RATTLE-SNAKE.
Rattle snake
MY REAL NAME IS JOHNNY AND MY CAMP NAME IS ROBIN HOOD!
Robin Hood
I'M BACK!

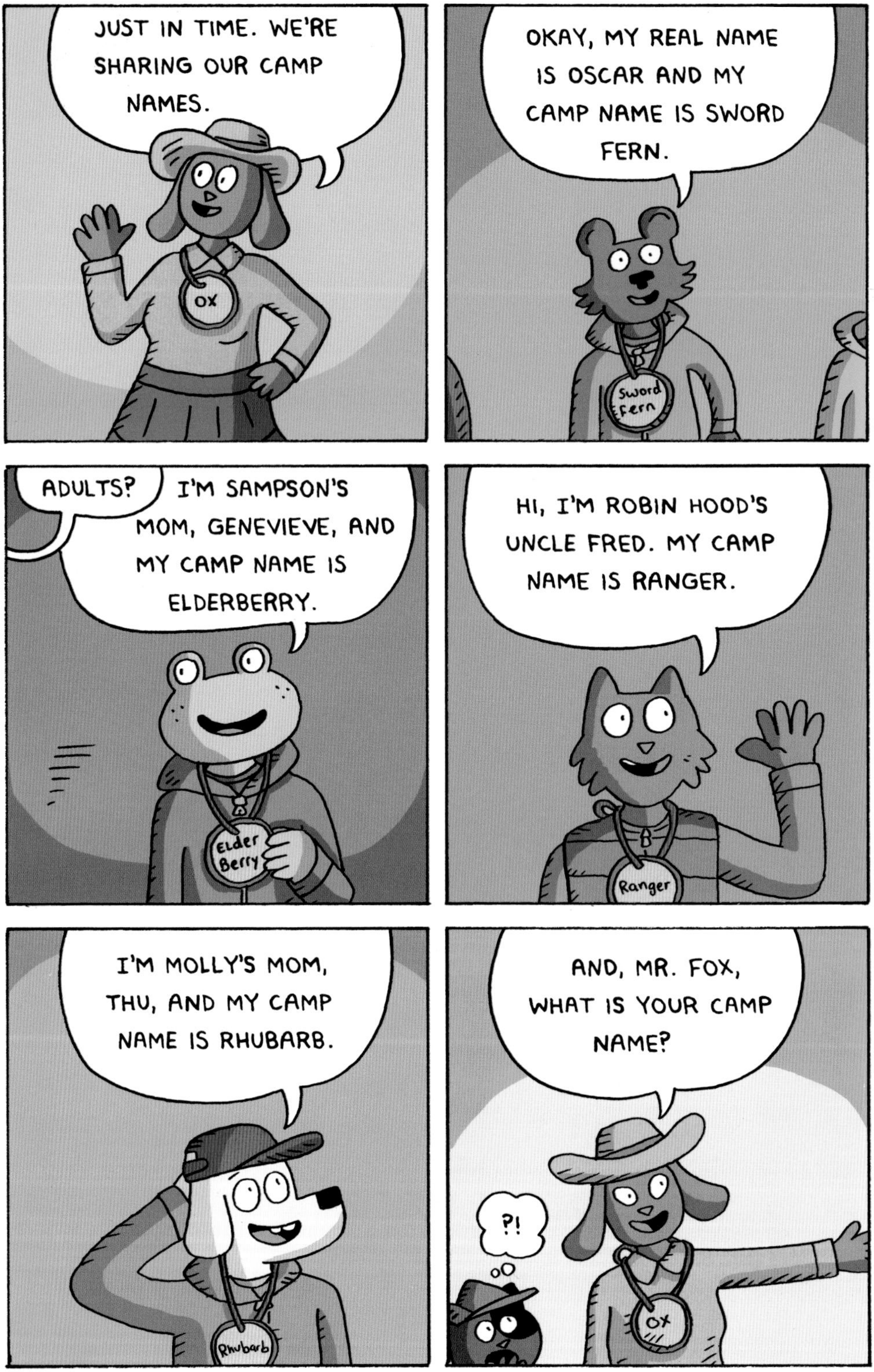
JUST IN TIME. WE'RE SHARING OUR CAMP NAMES.
OX
OKAY, MY REAL NAME IS OSCAR AND MY CAMP NAME IS SWORD FERN.
Sword Fern
ADULTS?
I'M SAMPSON'S MOM, GENEVIEVE, AND MY CAMP NAME IS ELDERBERRY.
Elder Berry
HI, I'M ROBIN HOOD'S UNCLE FRED. MY CAMP NAME IS RANGER.
Ranger
I'M MOLLY'S MOM, THU, AND MY CAMP NAME IS RHUBARB.
Rhubarb
AND, MR. FOX, WHAT IS YOUR CAMP NAME?
?!
OX

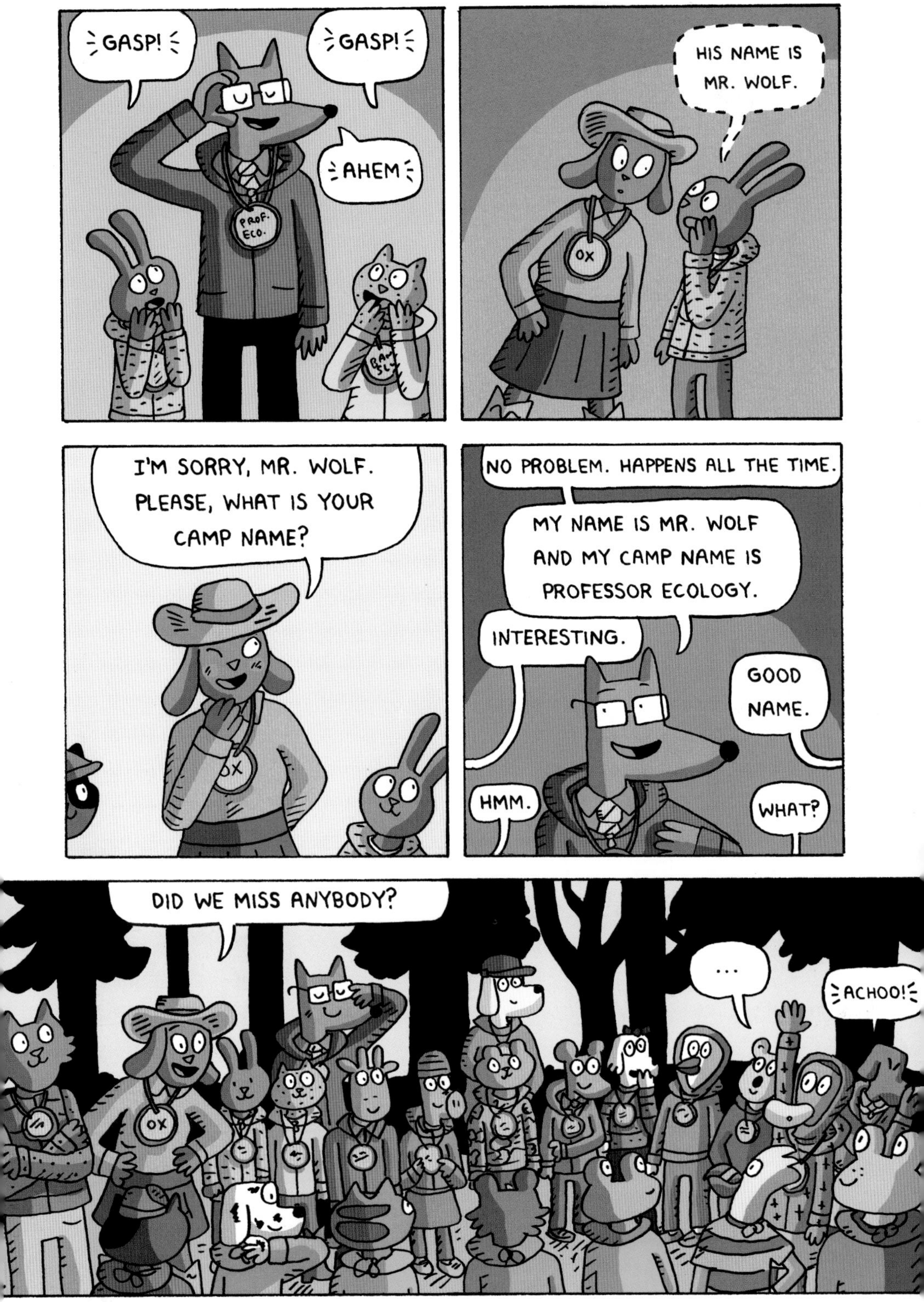
GASP!
GASP!
AHEM
PROF. ECO.
HIS NAME IS MR. WOLF.
OX
I'M SORRY, MR. WOLF. PLEASE, WHAT IS YOUR CAMP NAME?
OX
NO PROBLEM. HAPPENS ALL THE TIME.
MY NAME IS MR. WOLF AND MY CAMP NAME IS PROFESSOR ECOLOGY.
INTERESTING.
GOOD NAME.
HMM.
WHAT?
DID WE MISS ANYBODY?
...
ACHOO!
OX

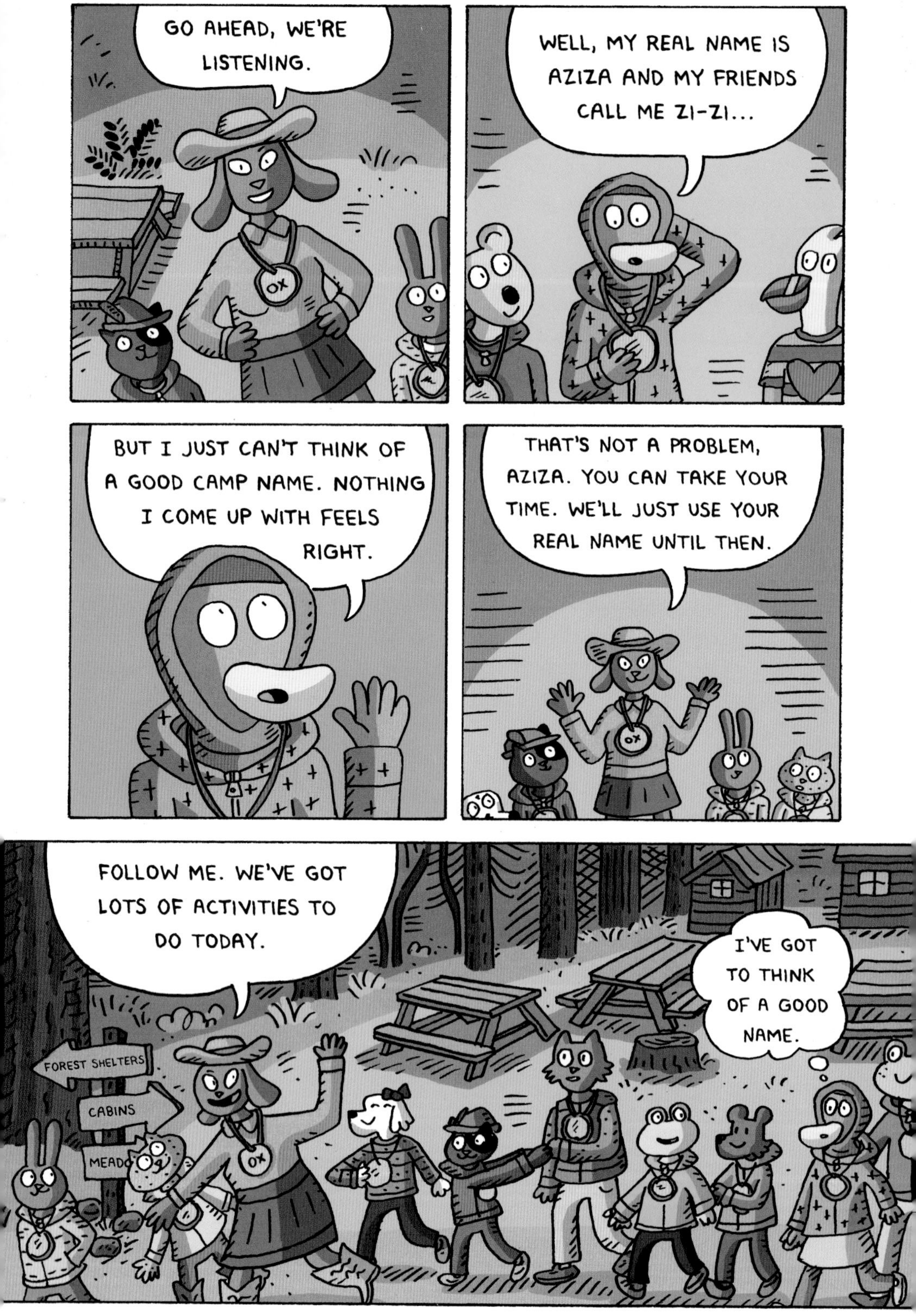
GO AHEAD, WE'RE LISTENING.
WELL, MY REAL NAME IS AZIZA AND MY FRIENDS CALL ME ZI-ZI...
BUT I JUST CAN'T THINK OF A GOOD CAMP NAME. NOTHING I COME UP WITH FEELS RIGHT.
THAT'S NOT A PROBLEM, AZIZA. YOU CAN TAKE YOUR TIME. WE'LL JUST USE YOUR REAL NAME UNTIL THEN.
OX
FOLLOW ME. WE'VE GOT LOTS OF ACTIVITIES TO DO TODAY.
FOREST SHELTERS
CABINS
I'VE GOT TO THINK OF A GOOD NAME.

FIRST ACTIVITY: A VISIT TO THE POWER HOUSE

HERE IS WHERE WE GET MOST OF OUR ELECTRICITY.

THE FORCE OF THE FALLING WATER TURNS THE BLADES OF THE TURBINES.

SHHHHH

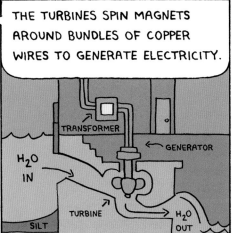

THE TURBINES SPIN MAGNETS AROUND BUNDLES OF COPPER WIRES TO GENERATE ELECTRICITY.

TRANSFORMER

GENERATOR

H_2O IN

TURBINE

SILT

H_2O OUT

YOU HAVE SOLAR POWER, TOO, RIGHT?

GOOD OBSERVATION, AZIZA. THANKS FOR POINTING THAT OUT.

THESE ROOFTOP SOLAR PANELS ARE BUSY GENERATING ENERGY, EVEN ON CLOUDY DAYS.

STAFF

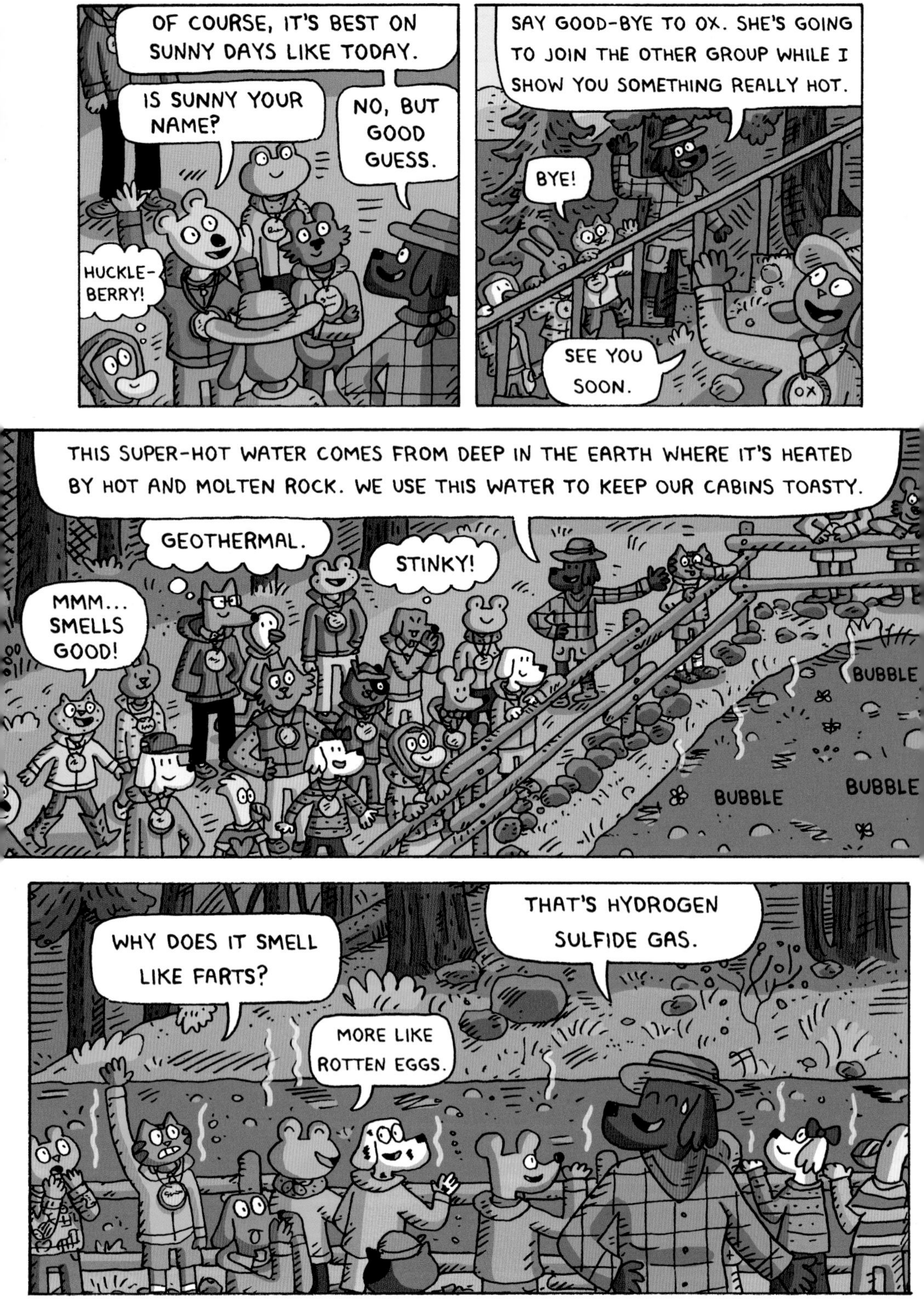
OF COURSE, IT'S BEST ON SUNNY DAYS LIKE TODAY.
IS SUNNY YOUR NAME?
NO, BUT GOOD GUESS.
HUCKLE-BERRY!
SAY GOOD-BYE TO OX. SHE'S GOING TO JOIN THE OTHER GROUP WHILE I SHOW YOU SOMETHING REALLY HOT.
BYE!
SEE YOU SOON.
OX
THIS SUPER-HOT WATER COMES FROM DEEP IN THE EARTH WHERE IT'S HEATED BY HOT AND MOLTEN ROCK. WE USE THIS WATER TO KEEP OUR CABINS TOASTY.
GEOTHERMAL.
STINKY!
MMM... SMELLS GOOD!
BUBBLE
BUBBLE
BUBBLE
WHY DOES IT SMELL LIKE FARTS?
THAT'S HYDROGEN SULFIDE GAS.
MORE LIKE ROTTEN EGGS.

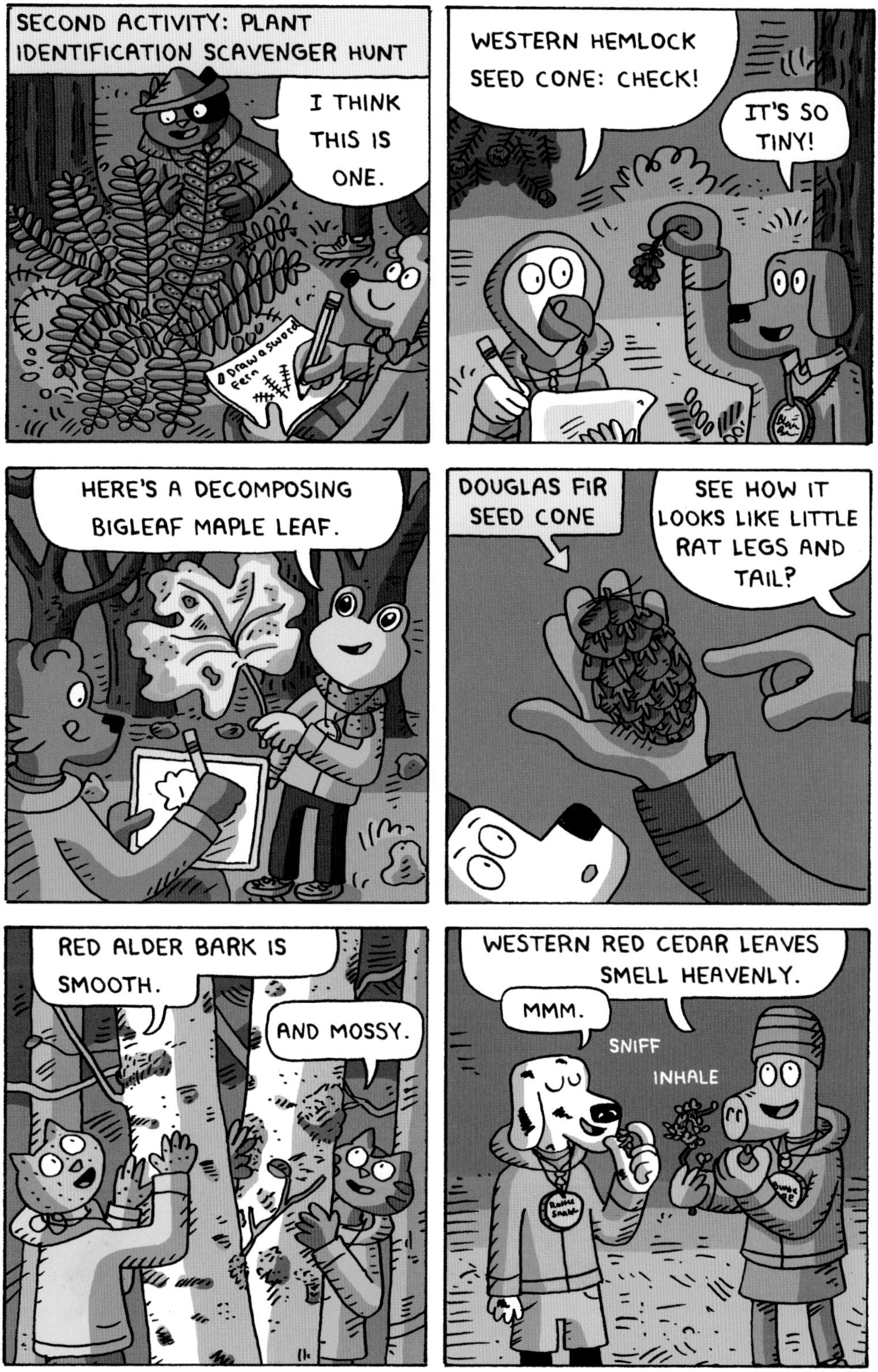
SECOND ACTIVITY: PLANT IDENTIFICATION SCAVENGER HUNT
I THINK THIS IS ONE.
Draw a sword fern
WESTERN HEMLOCK SEED CONE: CHECK!
IT'S SO TINY!
HERE'S A DECOMPOSING BIGLEAF MAPLE LEAF.
DOUGLAS FIR SEED CONE
SEE HOW IT LOOKS LIKE LITTLE RAT LEGS AND TAIL?
RED ALDER BARK IS SMOOTH.
AND MOSSY.
WESTERN RED CEDAR LEAVES SMELL HEAVENLY.
MMM.
SNIFF
INHALE

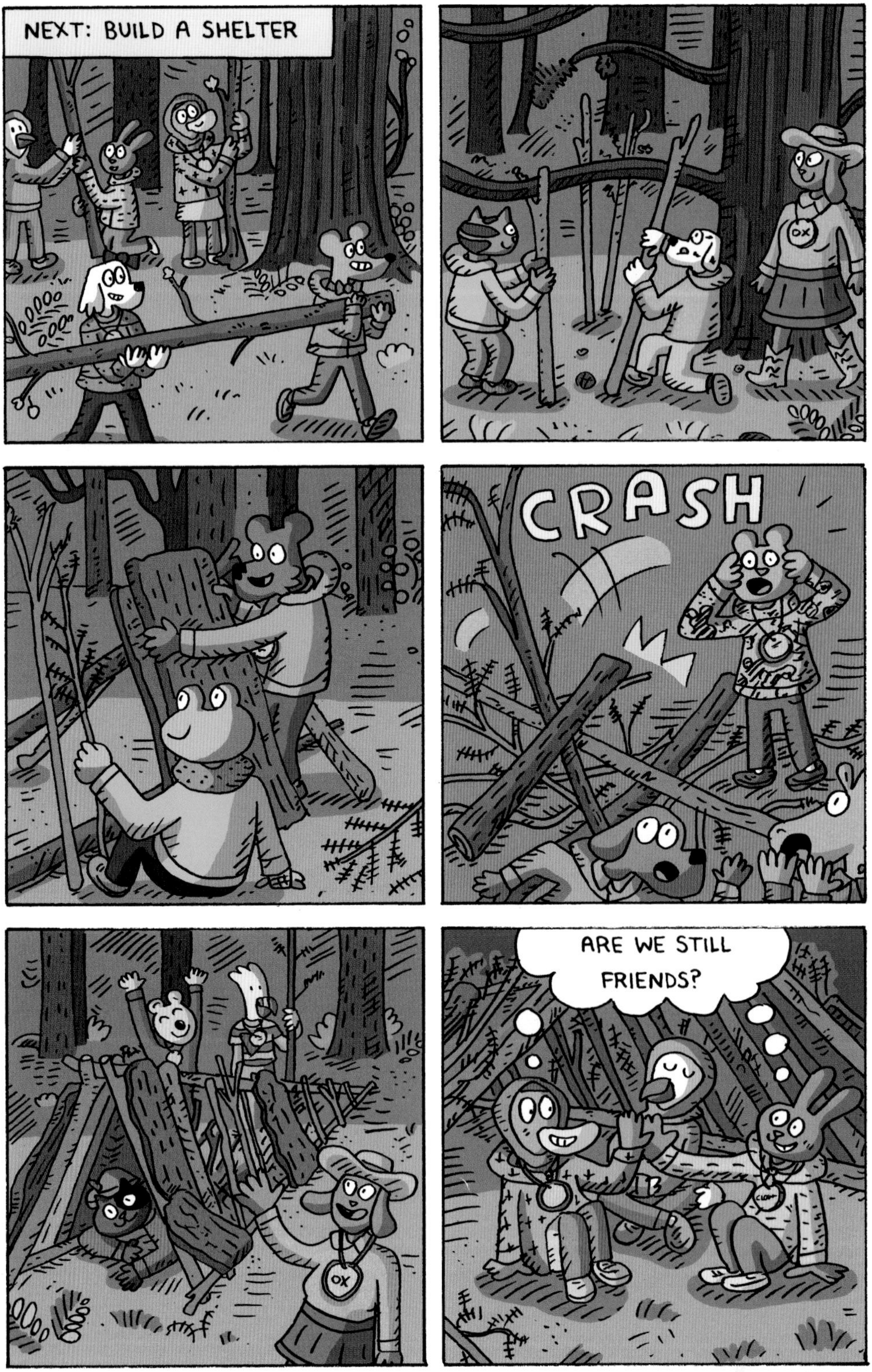
NEXT: BUILD A SHELTER
CRASH
ARE WE STILL FRIENDS?

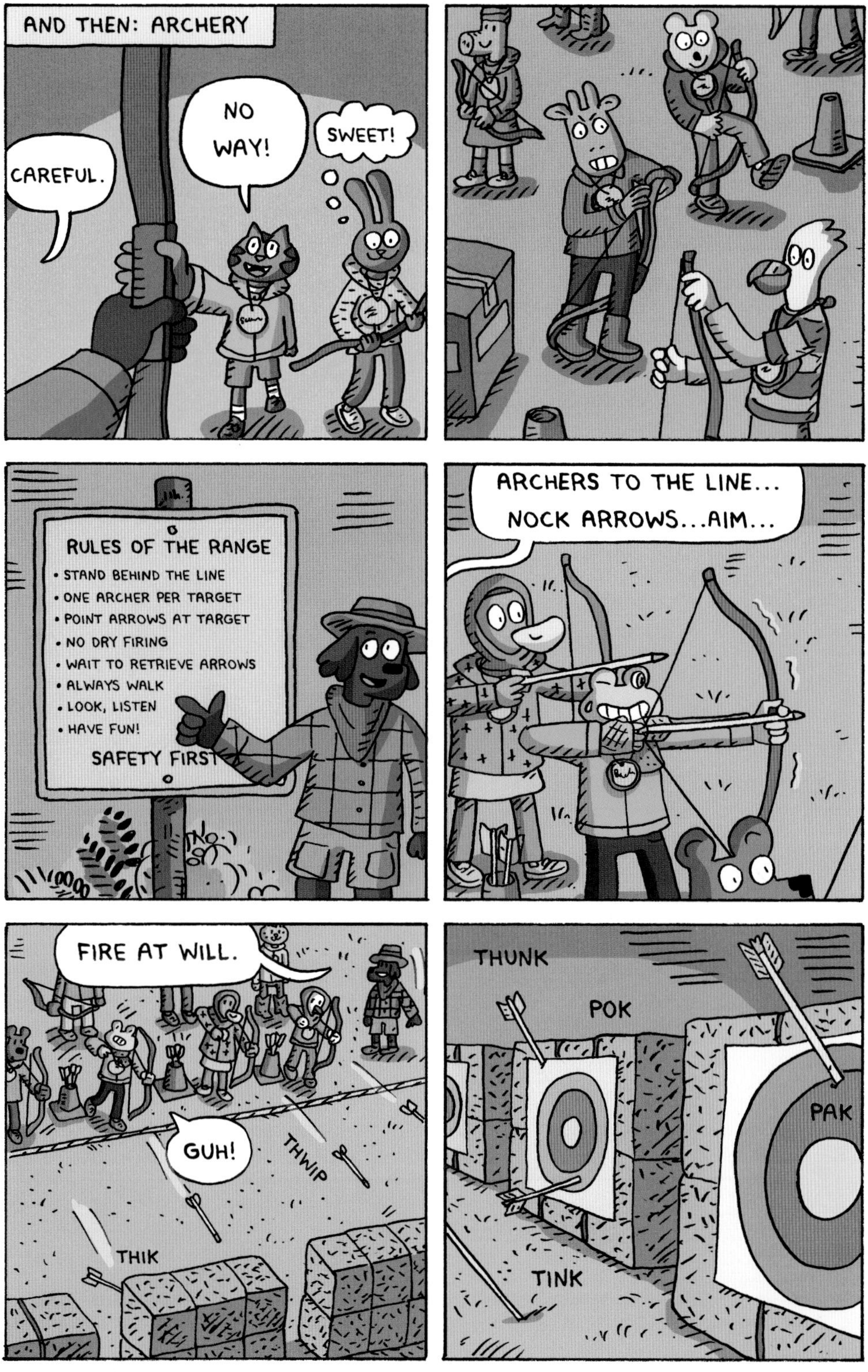
AND THEN: ARCHERY
CAREFUL.
NO WAY!
SWEET!
RULES OF THE RANGE
• STAND BEHIND THE LINE
• ONE ARCHER PER TARGET
• POINT ARROWS AT TARGET
• NO DRY FIRING
• WAIT TO RETRIEVE ARROWS
• ALWAYS WALK
• LOOK, LISTEN
• HAVE FUN!
SAFETY FIRST
ARCHERS TO THE LINE... NOCK ARROWS...AIM...
FIRE AT WILL.
GUH!
THWIP
THIK
THUNK
POK
PAK
TINK

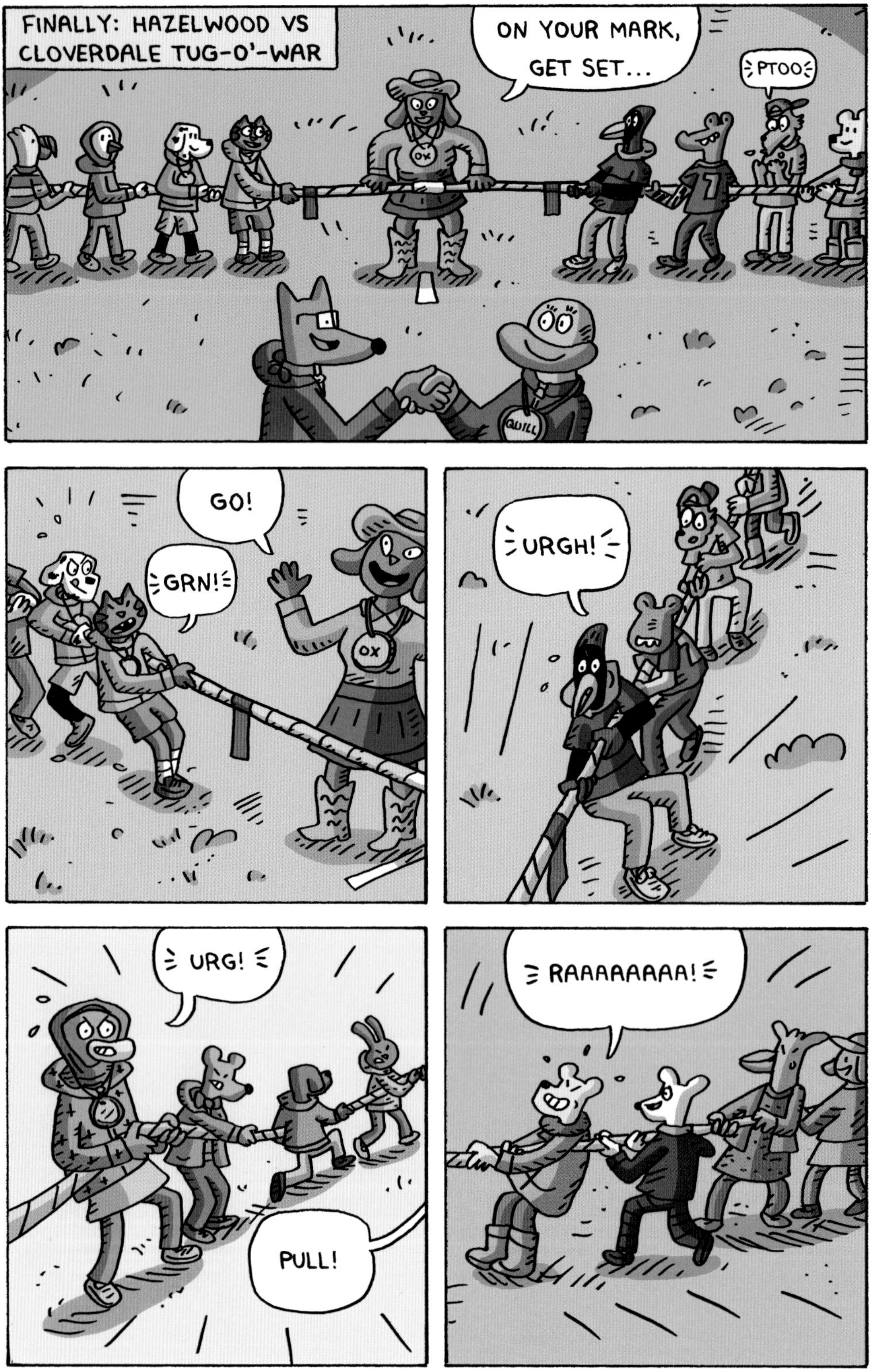
FINALLY: HAZELWOOD VS CLOVERDALE TUG-O'-WAR
ON YOUR MARK, GET SET...
PTOO
QUILL
GO!
GRN!
OX
URGH!
URG!
PULL!
RAAAAAAAA!

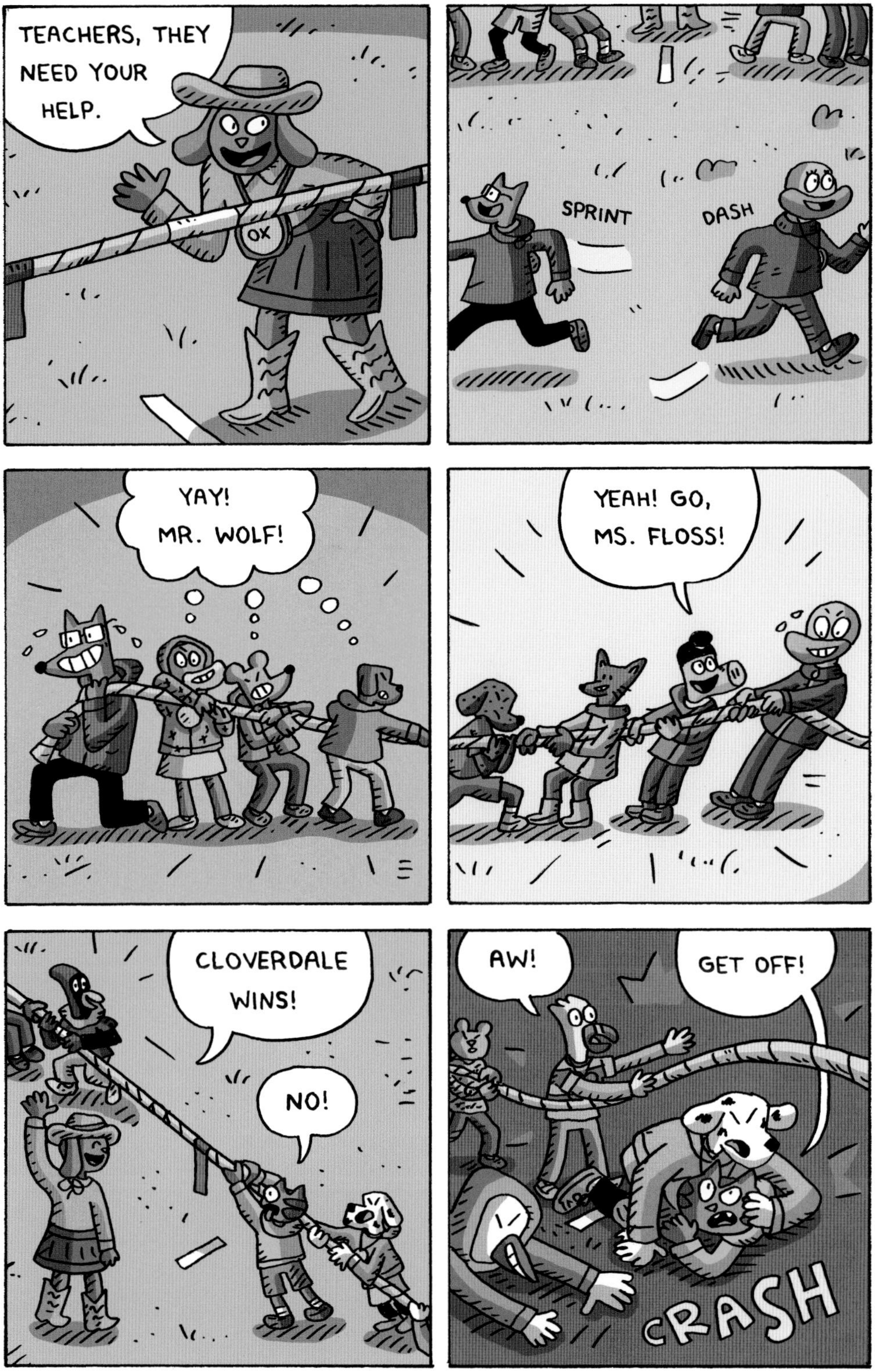
TEACHERS, THEY NEED YOUR HELP.
OX
SPRINT
DASH
YAY! MR. WOLF!
YEAH! GO, MS. FLOSS!
CLOVERDALE WINS!
NO!
AW!
GET OFF!
CRASH

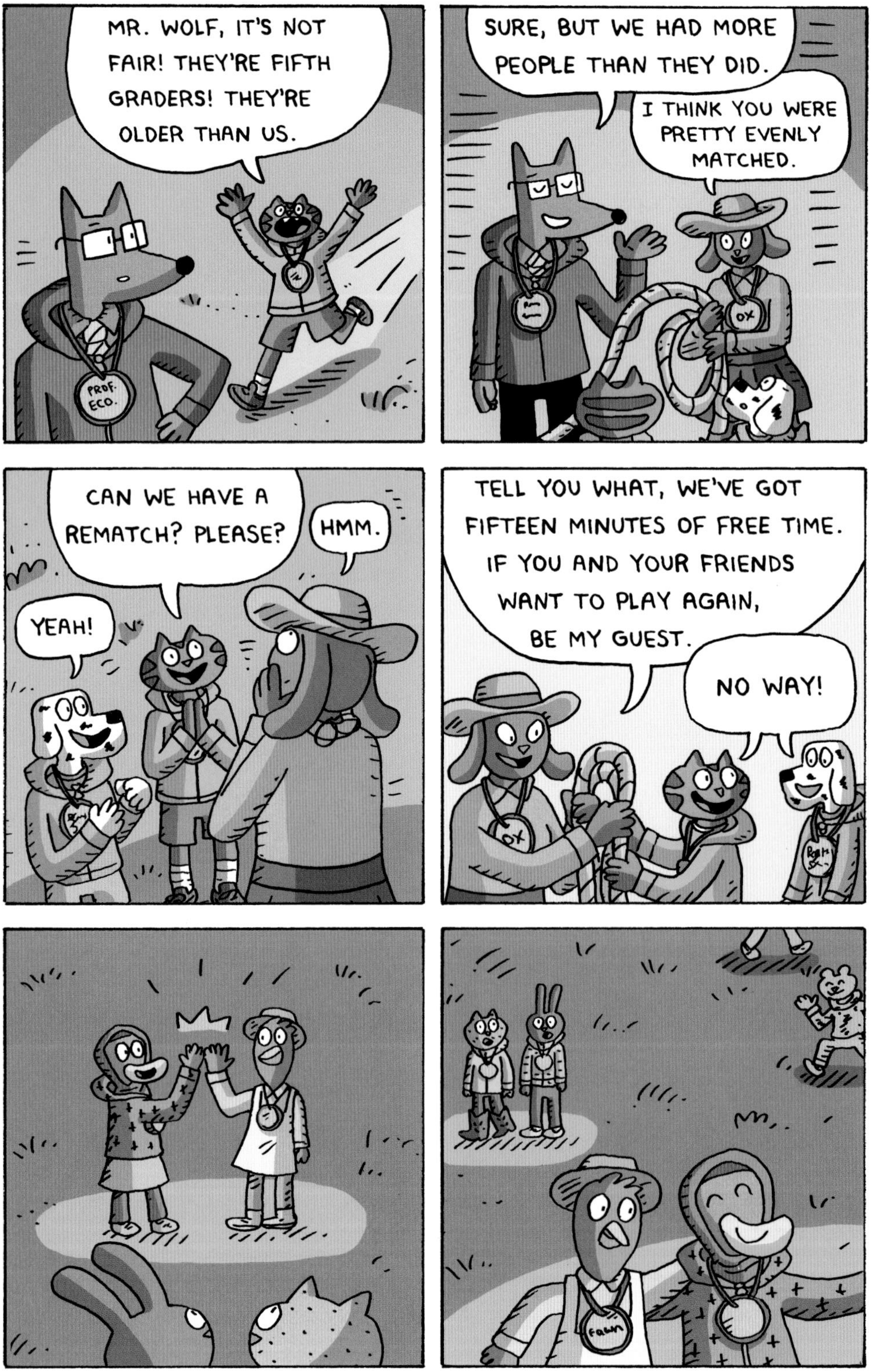
MR. WOLF, IT'S NOT FAIR! THEY'RE FIFTH GRADERS! THEY'RE OLDER THAN US.
PROF. ECO.
SURE, BUT WE HAD MORE PEOPLE THAN THEY DID.
I THINK YOU WERE PRETTY EVENLY MATCHED.
OX
CAN WE HAVE A REMATCH? PLEASE?
HMM.
YEAH!
TELL YOU WHAT, WE'VE GOT FIFTEEN MINUTES OF FREE TIME. IF YOU AND YOUR FRIENDS WANT TO PLAY AGAIN, BE MY GUEST.
NO WAY!
OX

CHAPTER FIVE
Out of Bounds

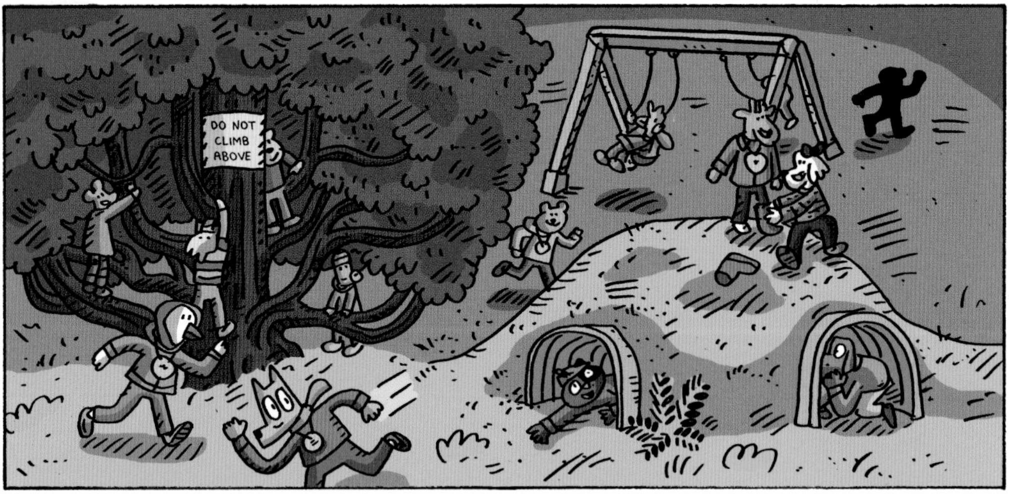
DO NOT CLIMB ABOVE

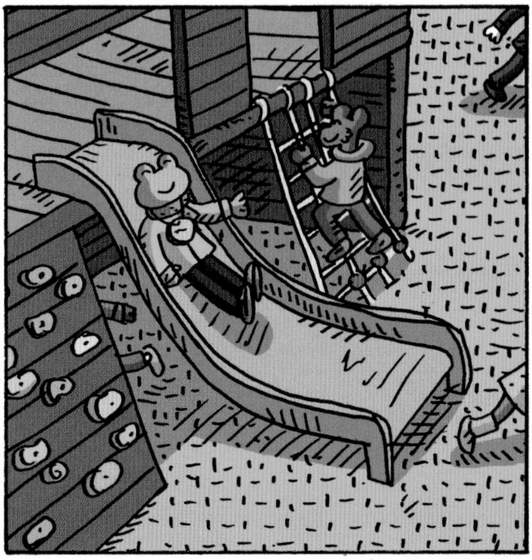

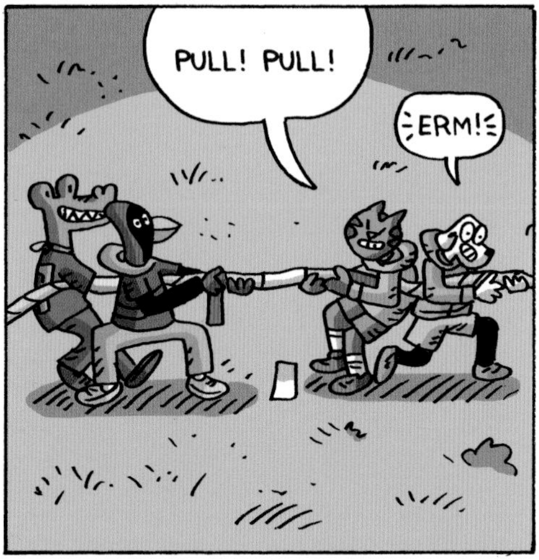
PULL! PULL!
ERM!

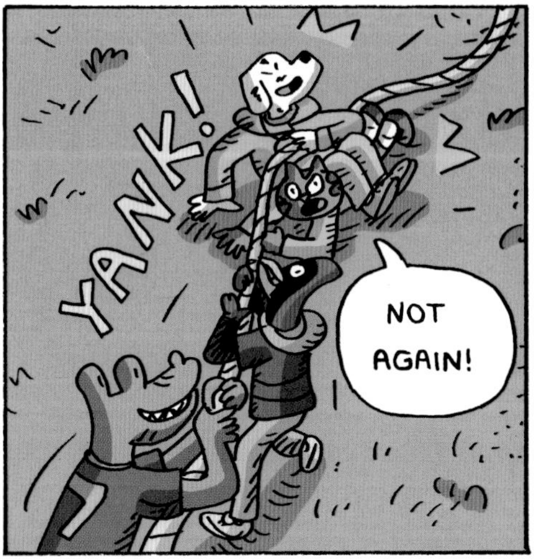
YANK!
NOT AGAIN!

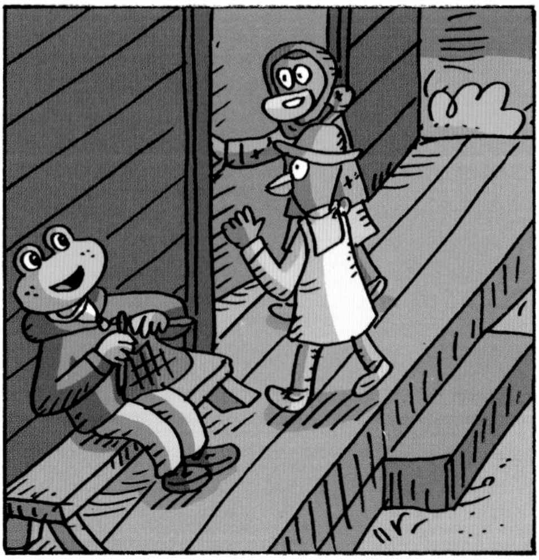

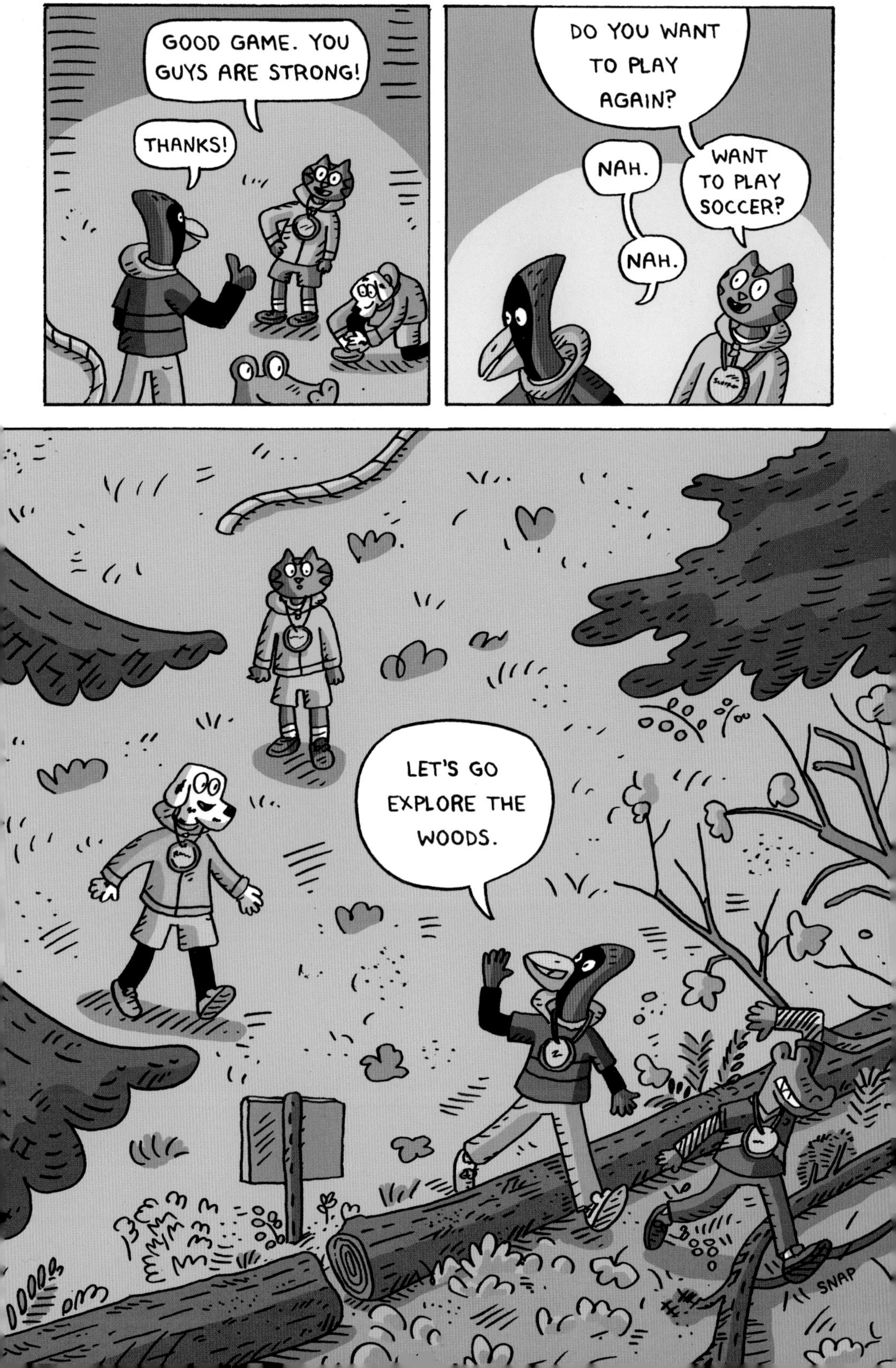
GOOD GAME. YOU GUYS ARE STRONG!
THANKS!
DO YOU WANT TO PLAY AGAIN?
NAH.
NAH.
WANT TO PLAY SOCCER?
LET'S GO EXPLORE THE WOODS.
SNAP

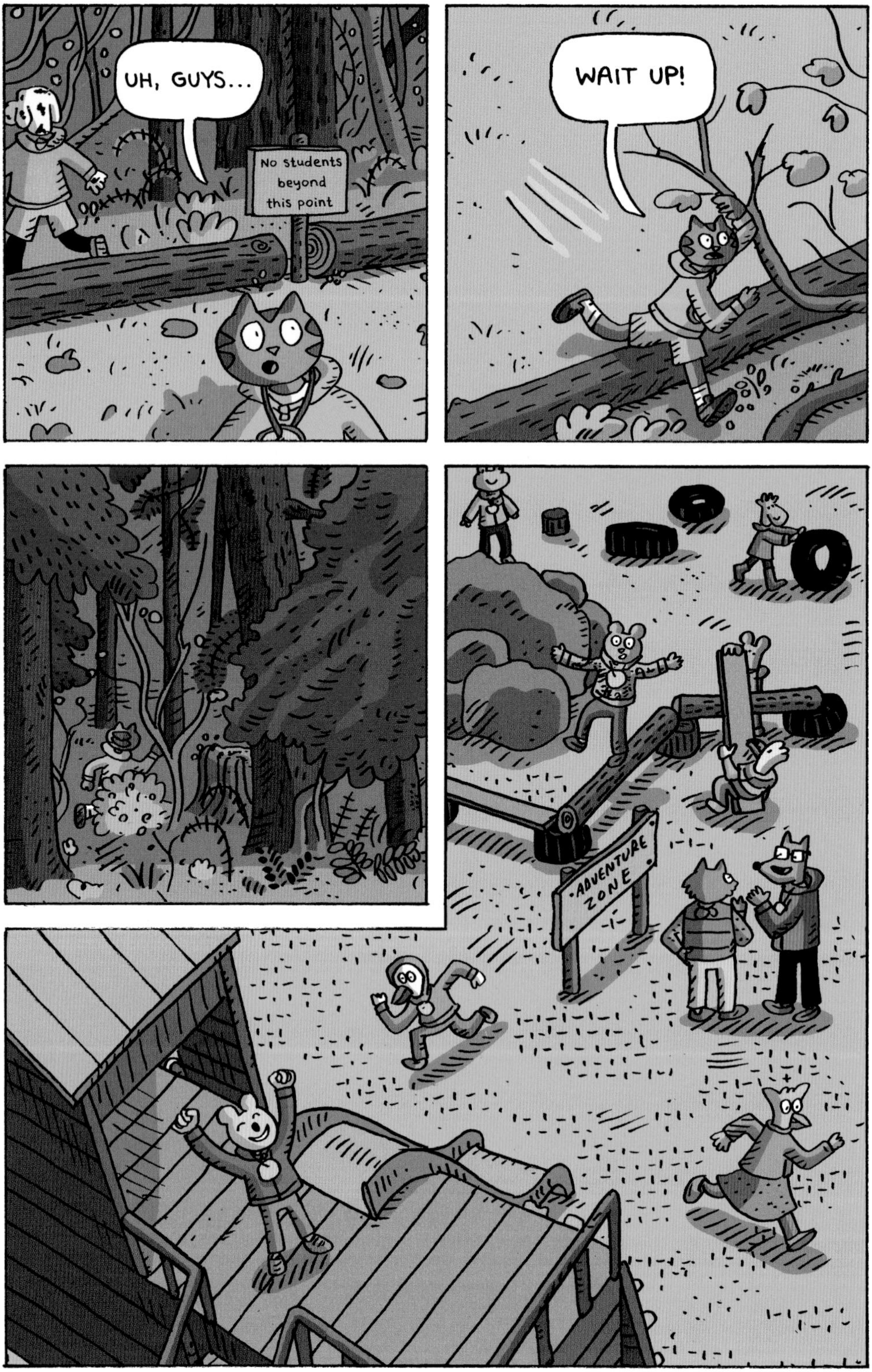
UH, GUYS...
No students beyond this point
WAIT UP!
ADVENTURE ZONE

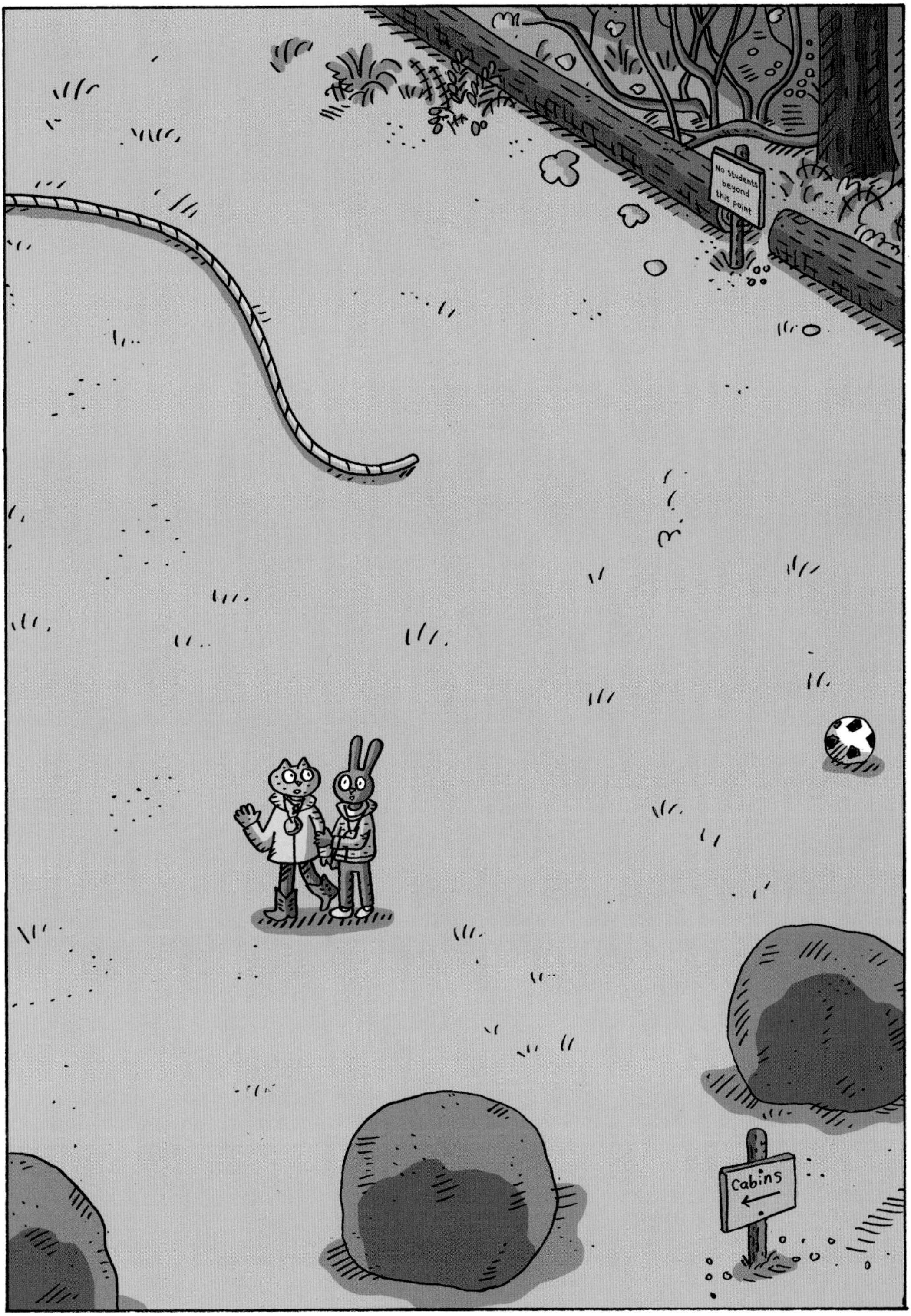
No students beyond this point
Cabins

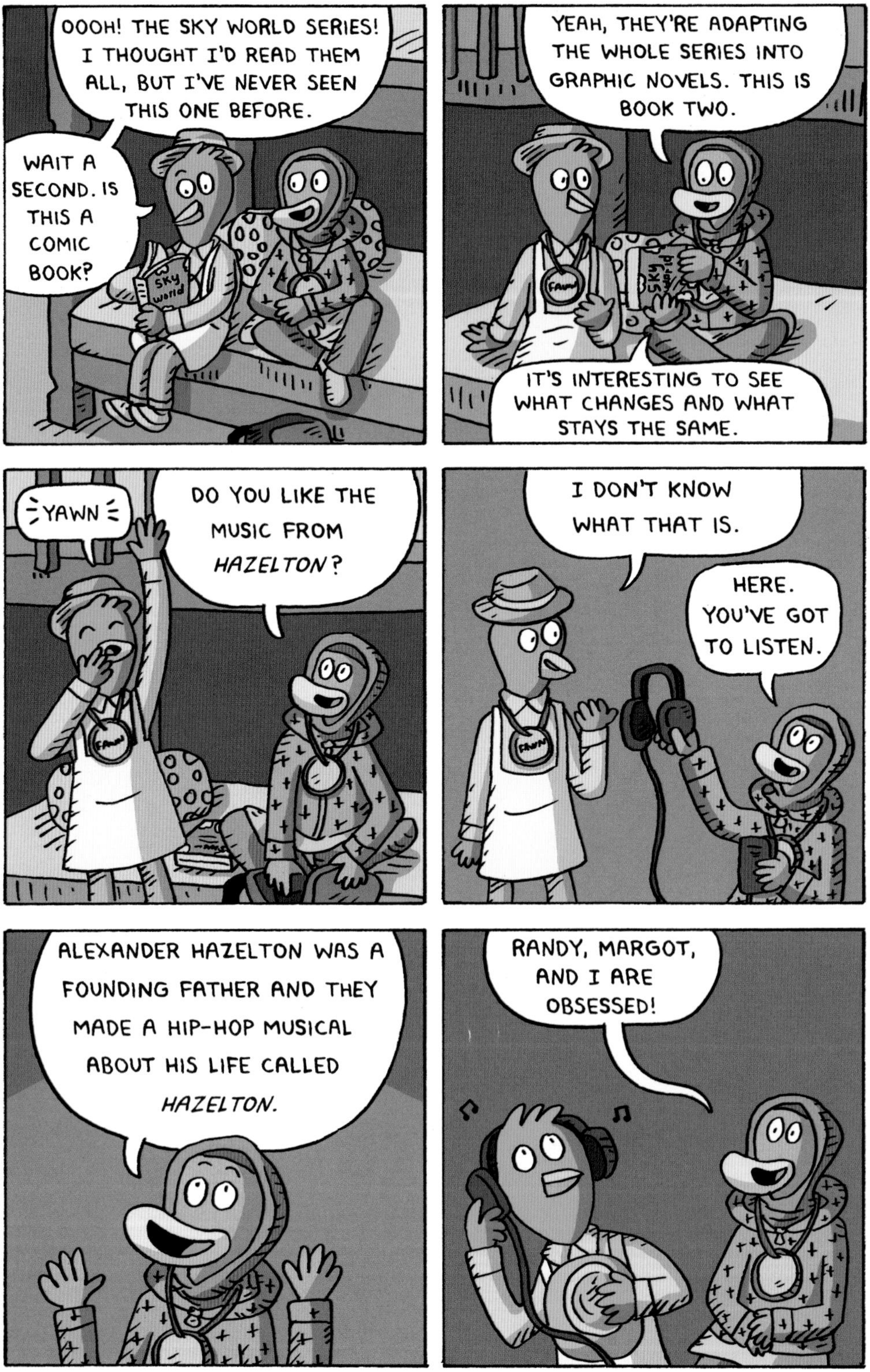
OOOH! THE SKY WORLD SERIES! I THOUGHT I'D READ THEM ALL, BUT I'VE NEVER SEEN THIS ONE BEFORE.
WAIT A SECOND. IS THIS A COMIC BOOK?
SKY WORLD
YEAH, THEY'RE ADAPTING THE WHOLE SERIES INTO GRAPHIC NOVELS. THIS IS BOOK TWO.
IT'S INTERESTING TO SEE WHAT CHANGES AND WHAT STAYS THE SAME.
YAWN
DO YOU LIKE THE MUSIC FROM *HAZELTON*?
I DON'T KNOW WHAT THAT IS.
HERE. YOU'VE GOT TO LISTEN.
ALEXANDER HAZELTON WAS A FOUNDING FATHER AND THEY MADE A HIP-HOP MUSICAL ABOUT HIS LIFE CALLED *HAZELTON*.
RANDY, MARGOT, AND I ARE OBSESSED!

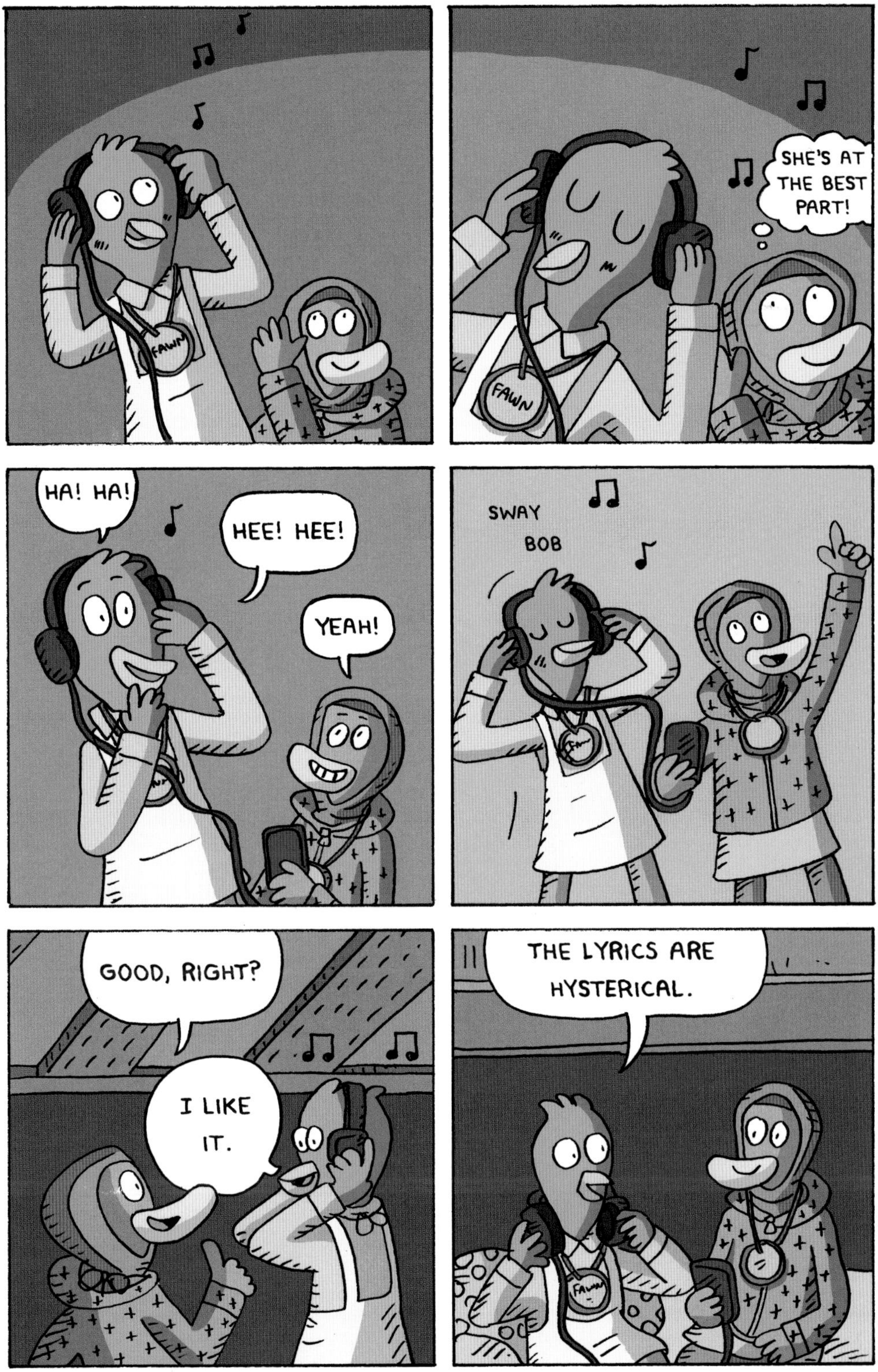
SHE'S AT THE BEST PART!
HA! HA!
HEE! HEE!
YEAH!
SWAY
BOB
GOOD, RIGHT?
I LIKE IT.
THE LYRICS ARE HYSTERICAL.

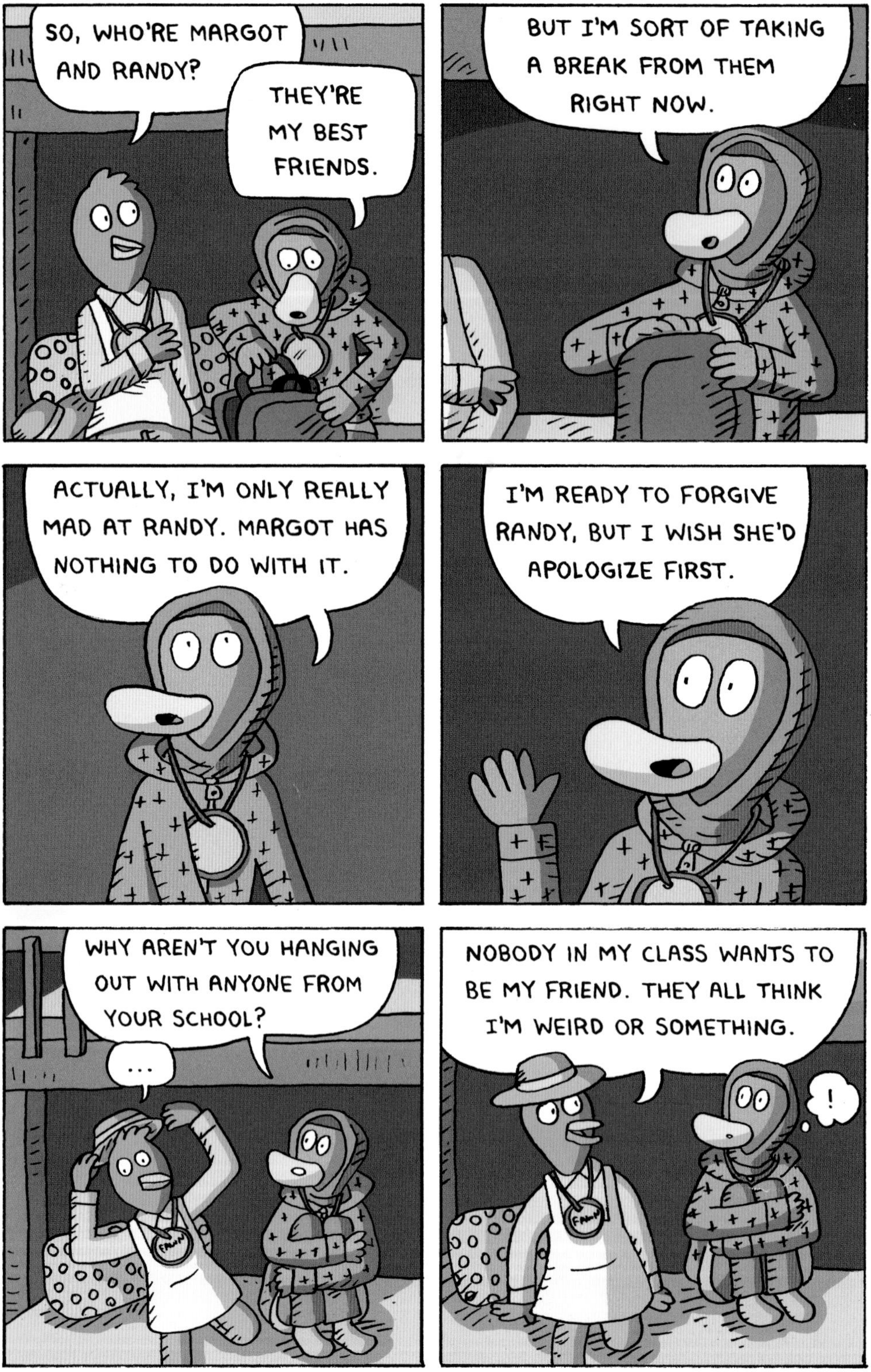
SO, WHO'RE MARGOT AND RANDY?
THEY'RE MY BEST FRIENDS.
BUT I'M SORT OF TAKING A BREAK FROM THEM RIGHT NOW.
ACTUALLY, I'M ONLY REALLY MAD AT RANDY. MARGOT HAS NOTHING TO DO WITH IT.
I'M READY TO FORGIVE RANDY, BUT I WISH SHE'D APOLOGIZE FIRST.
WHY AREN'T YOU HANGING OUT WITH ANYONE FROM YOUR SCHOOL?
...
NOBODY IN MY CLASS WANTS TO BE MY FRIEND. THEY ALL THINK I'M WEIRD OR SOMETHING.
!

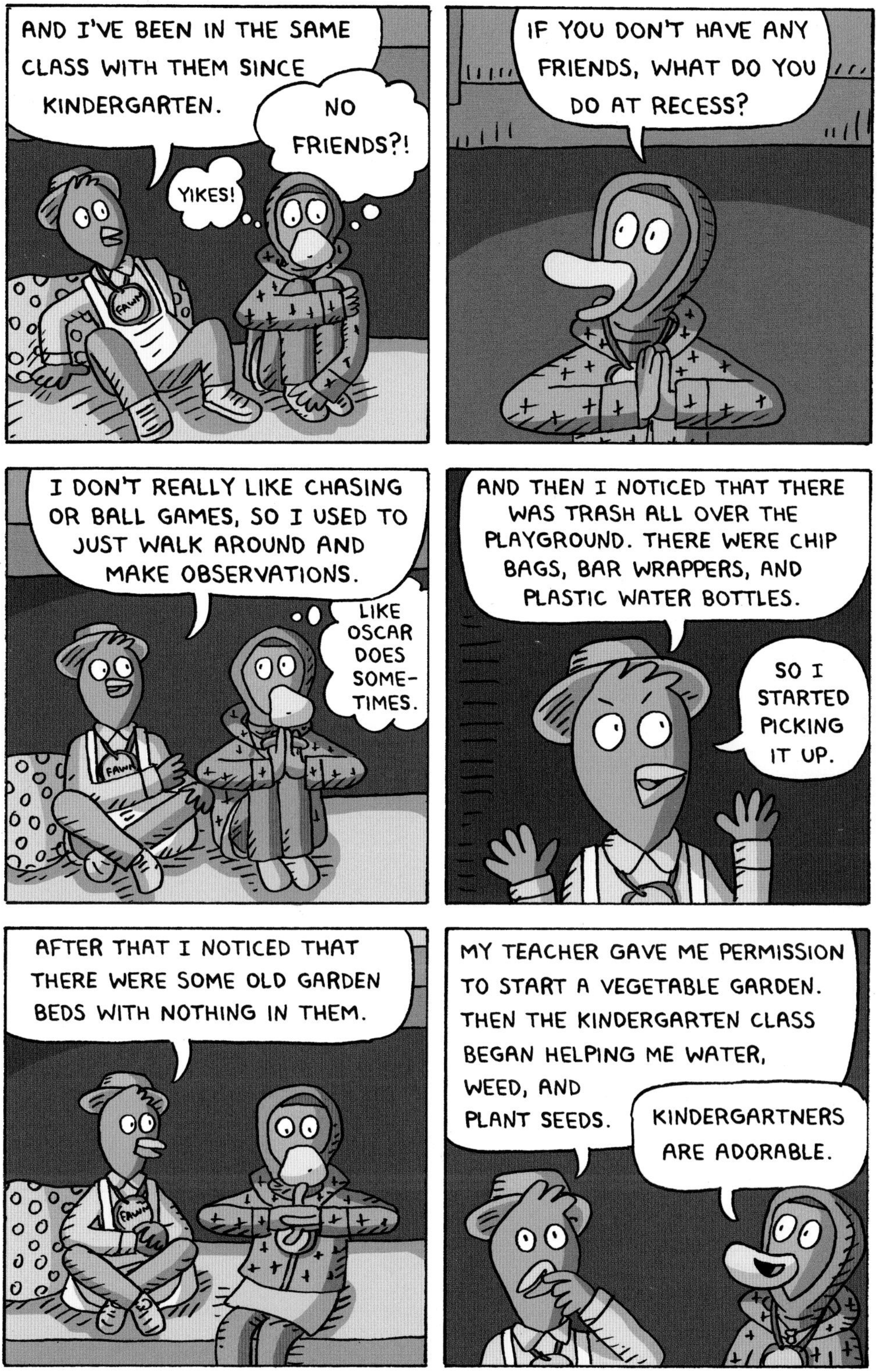

AND I'VE BEEN IN THE SAME CLASS WITH THEM SINCE KINDERGARTEN.
YIKES!
NO FRIENDS?!
IF YOU DON'T HAVE ANY FRIENDS, WHAT DO YOU DO AT RECESS?
I DON'T REALLY LIKE CHASING OR BALL GAMES, SO I USED TO JUST WALK AROUND AND MAKE OBSERVATIONS.
LIKE OSCAR DOES SOME-TIMES.
AND THEN I NOTICED THAT THERE WAS TRASH ALL OVER THE PLAYGROUND. THERE WERE CHIP BAGS, BAR WRAPPERS, AND PLASTIC WATER BOTTLES.
SO I STARTED PICKING IT UP.
AFTER THAT I NOTICED THAT THERE WERE SOME OLD GARDEN BEDS WITH NOTHING IN THEM.
MY TEACHER GAVE ME PERMISSION TO START A VEGETABLE GARDEN. THEN THE KINDERGARTEN CLASS BEGAN HELPING ME WATER, WEED, AND PLANT SEEDS.
KINDERGARTNERS ARE ADORABLE.

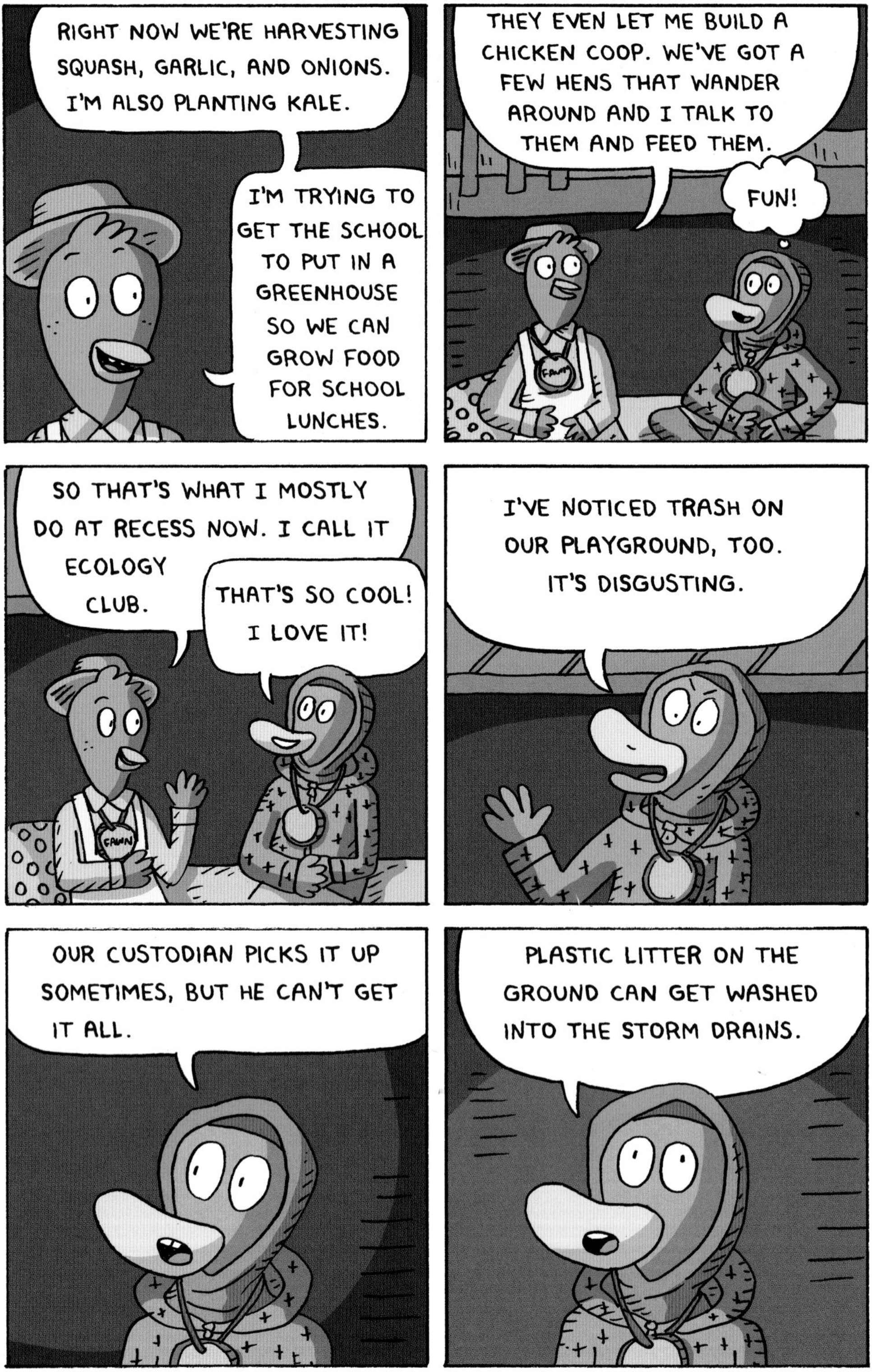
RIGHT NOW WE'RE HARVESTING SQUASH, GARLIC, AND ONIONS. I'M ALSO PLANTING KALE.
I'M TRYING TO GET THE SCHOOL TO PUT IN A GREENHOUSE SO WE CAN GROW FOOD FOR SCHOOL LUNCHES.
THEY EVEN LET ME BUILD A CHICKEN COOP. WE'VE GOT A FEW HENS THAT WANDER AROUND AND I TALK TO THEM AND FEED THEM.
FUN!
SO THAT'S WHAT I MOSTLY DO AT RECESS NOW. I CALL IT ECOLOGY CLUB.
THAT'S SO COOL! I LOVE IT!
I'VE NOTICED TRASH ON OUR PLAYGROUND, TOO. IT'S DISGUSTING.
OUR CUSTODIAN PICKS IT UP SOMETIMES, BUT HE CAN'T GET IT ALL.
PLASTIC LITTER ON THE GROUND CAN GET WASHED INTO THE STORM DRAINS.

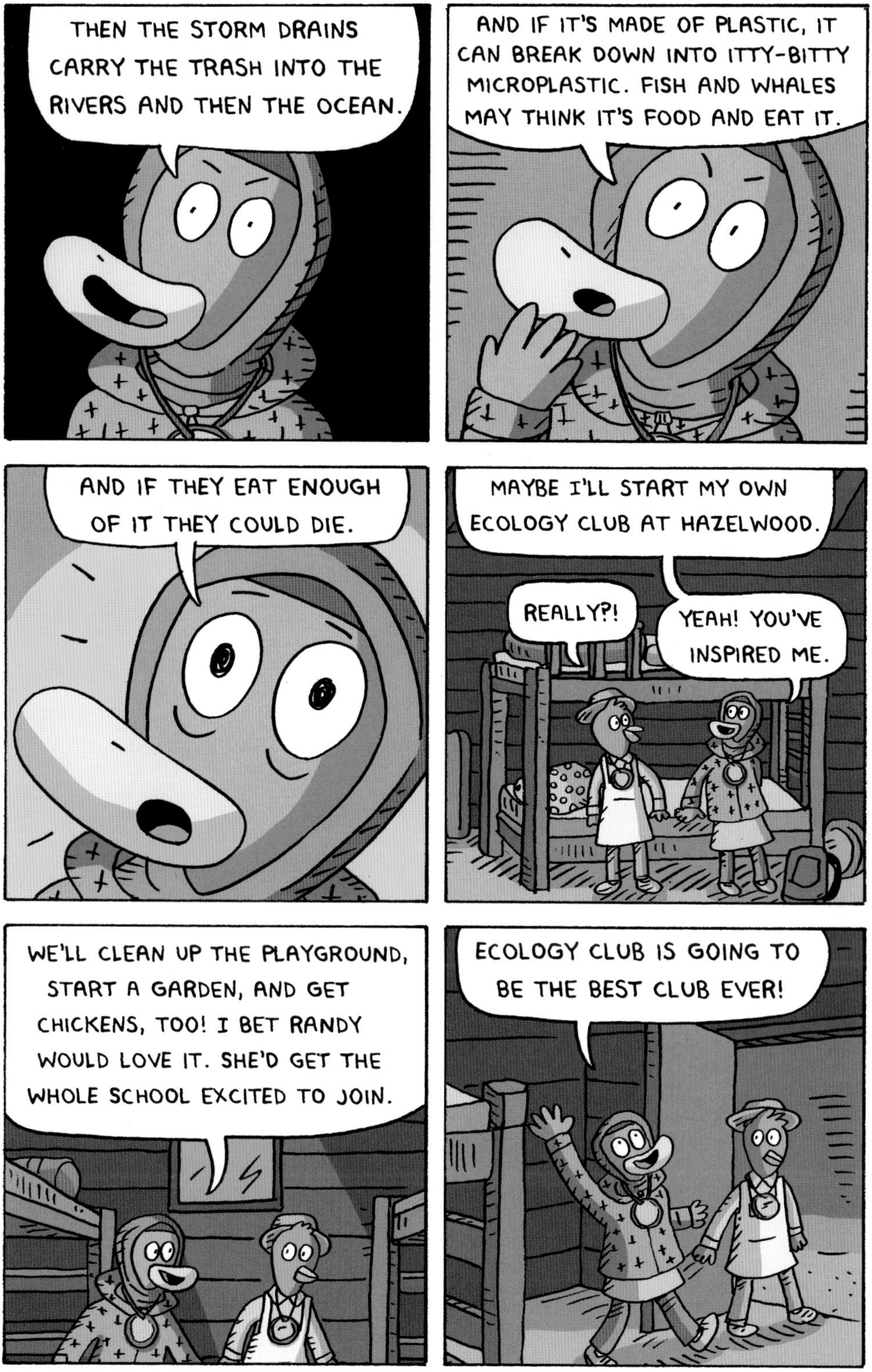
THEN THE STORM DRAINS CARRY THE TRASH INTO THE RIVERS AND THEN THE OCEAN.
AND IF IT'S MADE OF PLASTIC, IT CAN BREAK DOWN INTO ITTY-BITTY MICROPLASTIC. FISH AND WHALES MAY THINK IT'S FOOD AND EAT IT.
AND IF THEY EAT ENOUGH OF IT THEY COULD DIE.
MAYBE I'LL START MY OWN ECOLOGY CLUB AT HAZELWOOD.
REALLY?!
YEAH! YOU'VE INSPIRED ME.
WE'LL CLEAN UP THE PLAYGROUND, START A GARDEN, AND GET CHICKENS, TOO! I BET RANDY WOULD LOVE IT. SHE'D GET THE WHOLE SCHOOL EXCITED TO JOIN.
ECOLOGY CLUB IS GOING TO BE THE BEST CLUB EVER!

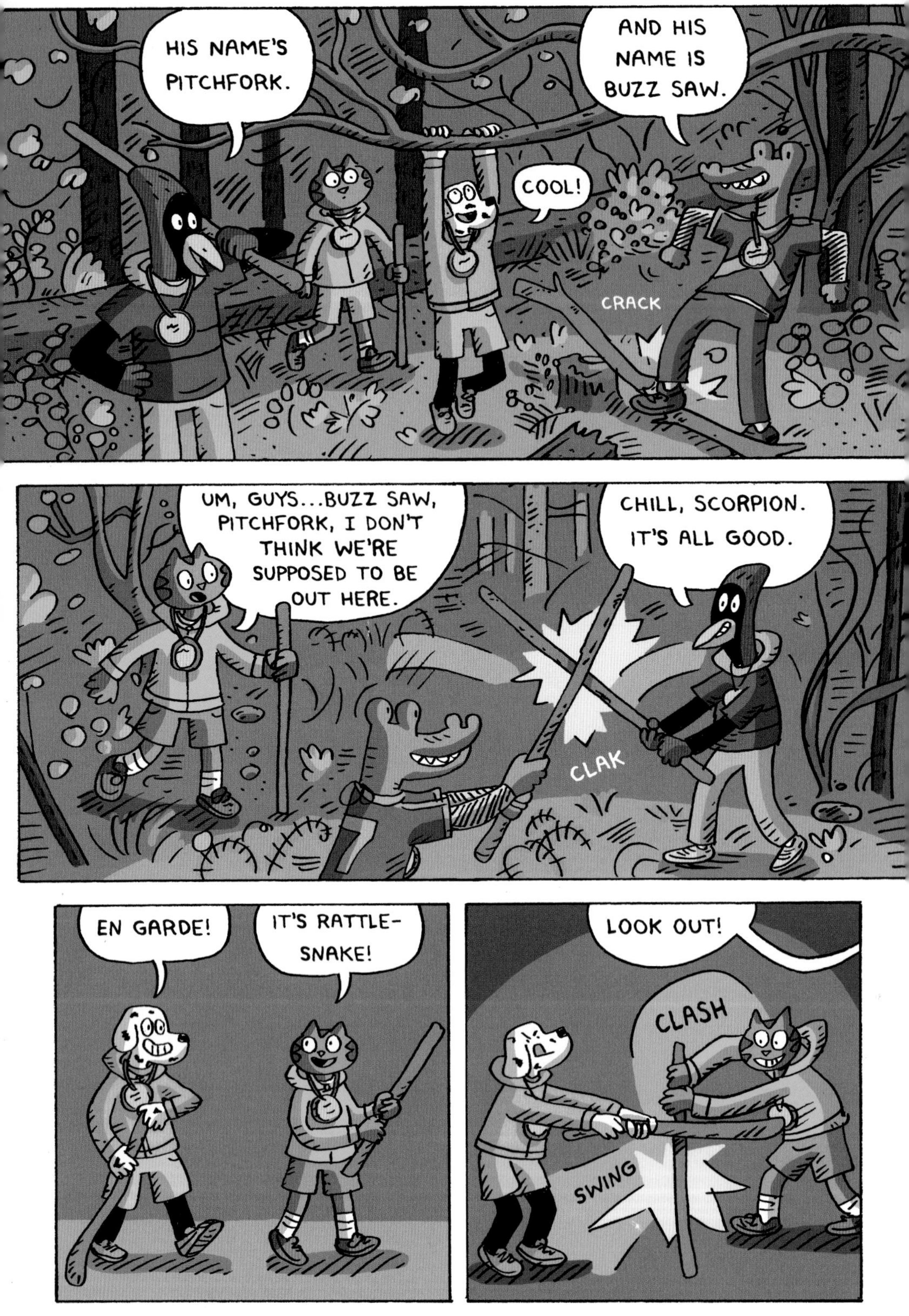
HIS NAME'S PITCHFORK.
AND HIS NAME IS BUZZ SAW.
COOL!
CRACK
UM, GUYS...BUZZ SAW, PITCHFORK, I DON'T THINK WE'RE SUPPOSED TO BE OUT HERE.
CHILL, SCORPION. IT'S ALL GOOD.
CLAK
EN GARDE!
IT'S RATTLE-SNAKE!
LOOK OUT!
CLASH
SWING

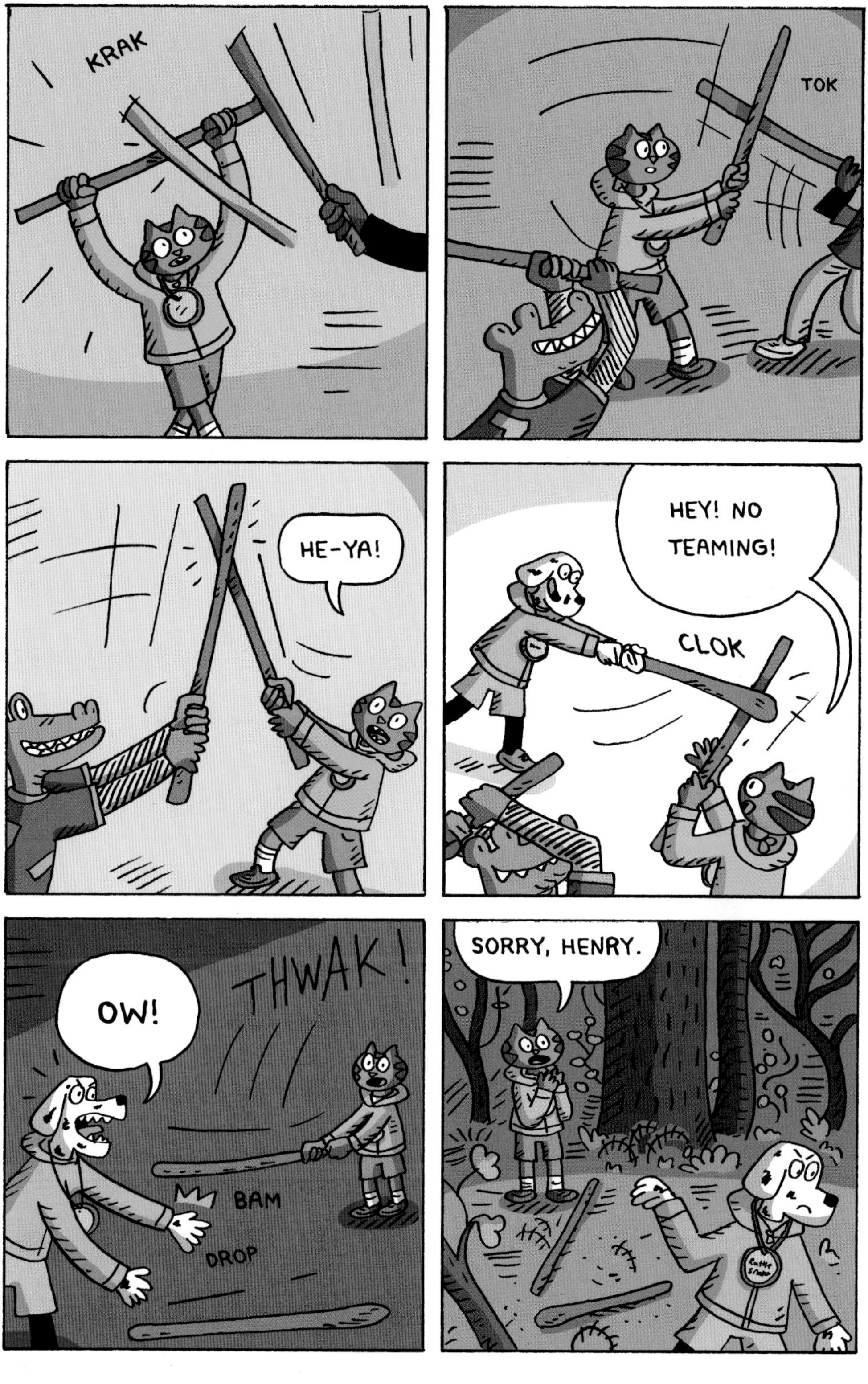
KRAK
TOK
HE-YA!
HEY! NO TEAMING!
CLOK
OW!
THWAK!
BAM
DROP
SORRY, HENRY.

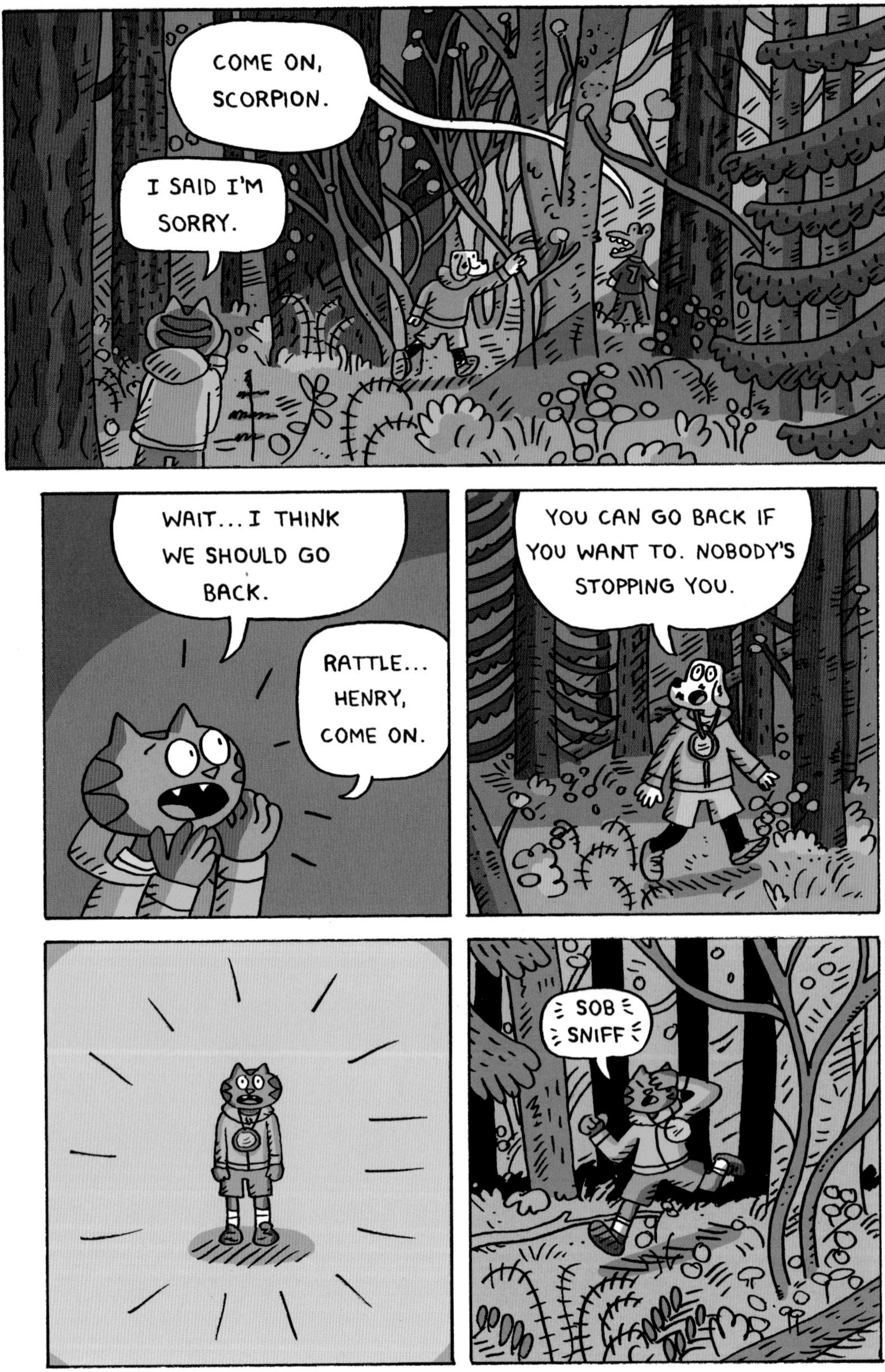
COME ON, SCORPION.
I SAID I'M SORRY.
WAIT... I THINK WE SHOULD GO BACK.
RATTLE... HENRY, COME ON.
YOU CAN GO BACK IF YOU WANT TO. NOBODY'S STOPPING YOU.
SOB SNIFF

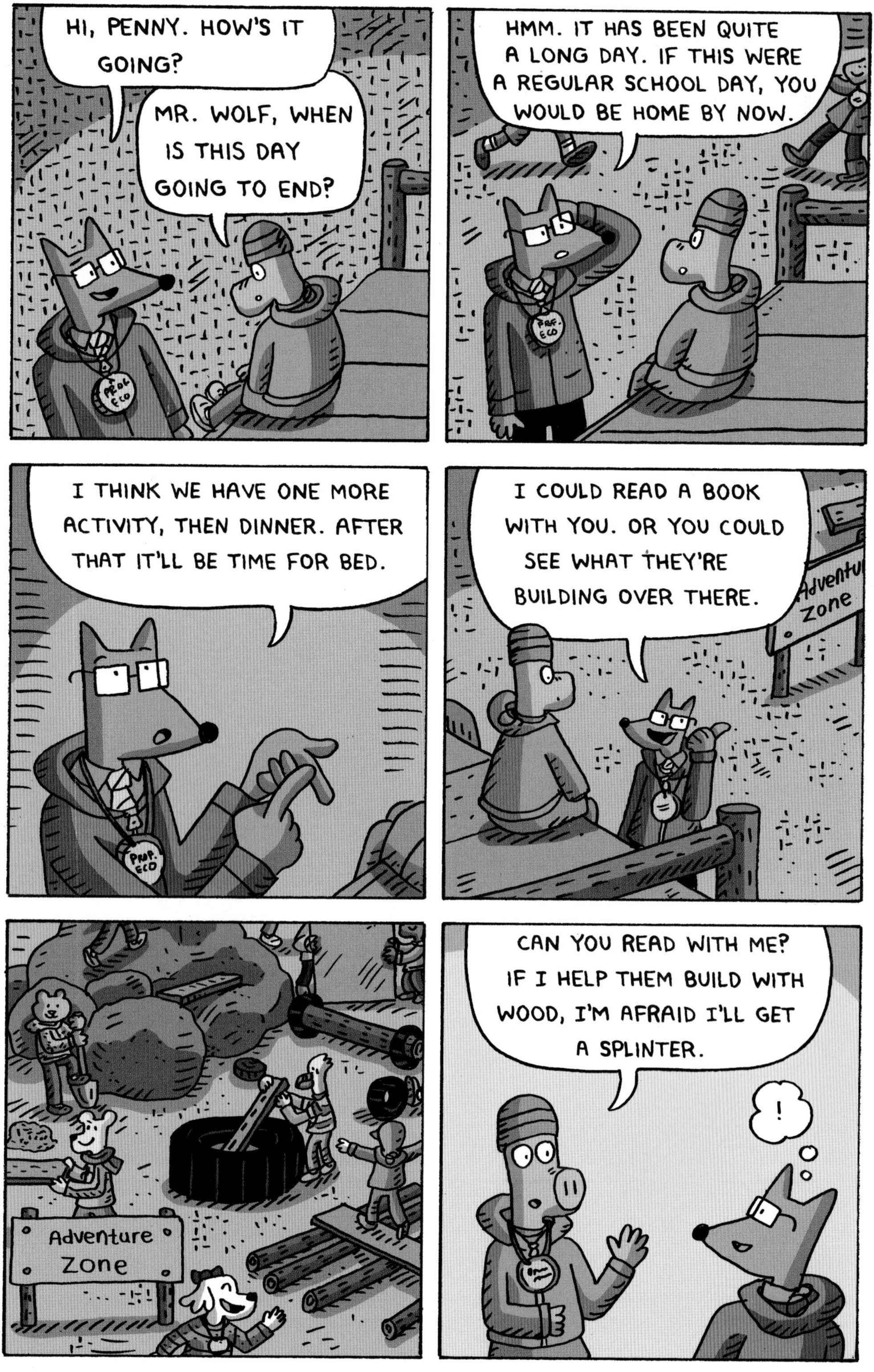
HI, PENNY. HOW'S IT GOING?
MR. WOLF, WHEN IS THIS DAY GOING TO END?
HMM. IT HAS BEEN QUITE A LONG DAY. IF THIS WERE A REGULAR SCHOOL DAY, YOU WOULD BE HOME BY NOW.
I THINK WE HAVE ONE MORE ACTIVITY, THEN DINNER. AFTER THAT IT'LL BE TIME FOR BED.
I COULD READ A BOOK WITH YOU. OR YOU COULD SEE WHAT THEY'RE BUILDING OVER THERE.
Adventure Zone
CAN YOU READ WITH ME? IF I HELP THEM BUILD WITH WOOD, I'M AFRAID I'LL GET A SPLINTER.
!

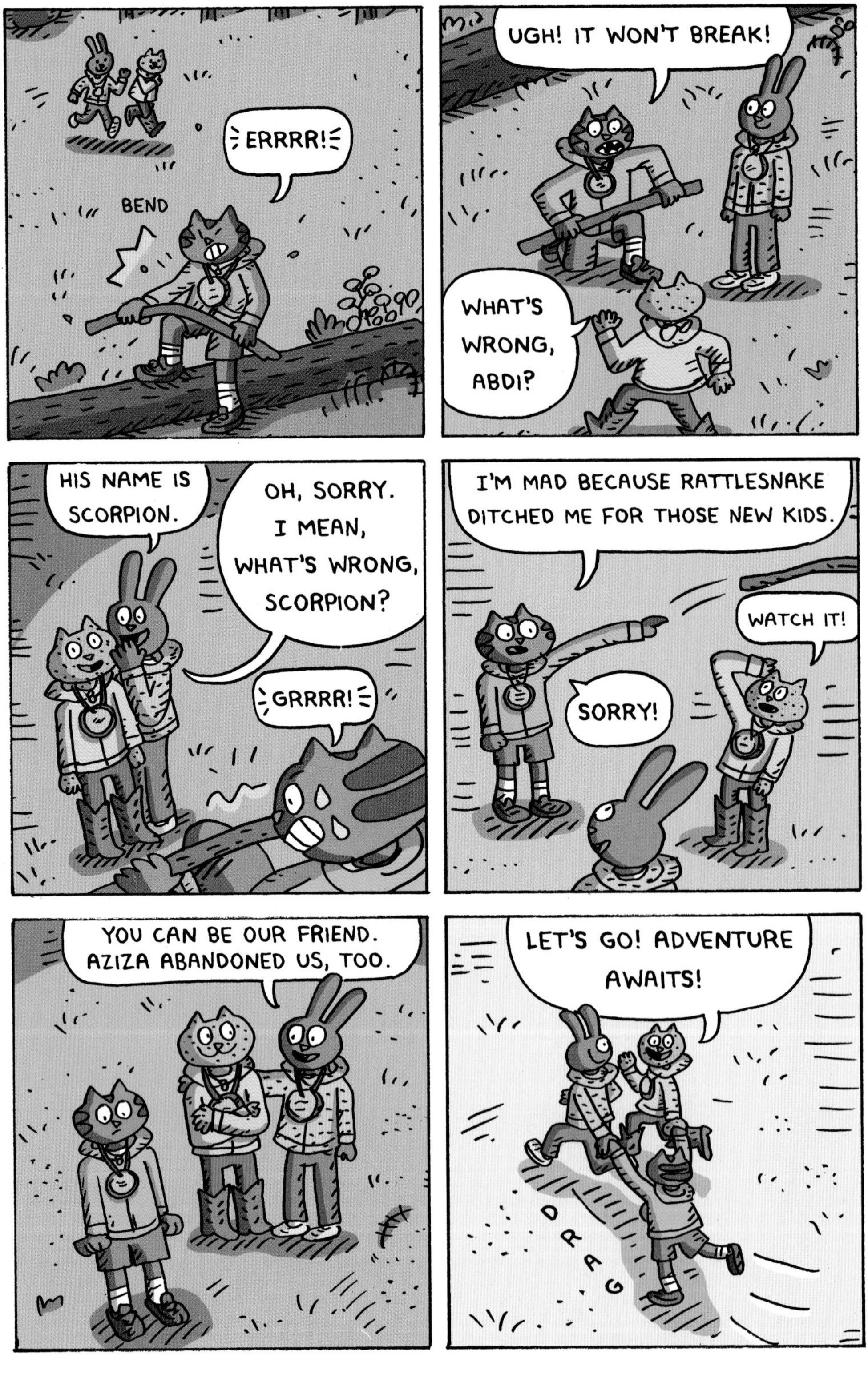
ERRRR!
BEND
UGH! IT WON'T BREAK!
WHAT'S WRONG, ABDI?
HIS NAME IS SCORPION.
OH, SORRY. I MEAN, WHAT'S WRONG, SCORPION?
GRRRR!
I'M MAD BECAUSE RATTLESNAKE DITCHED ME FOR THOSE NEW KIDS.
WATCH IT!
SORRY!
YOU CAN BE OUR FRIEND. AZIZA ABANDONED US, TOO.
LET'S GO! ADVENTURE AWAITS!
DRAG

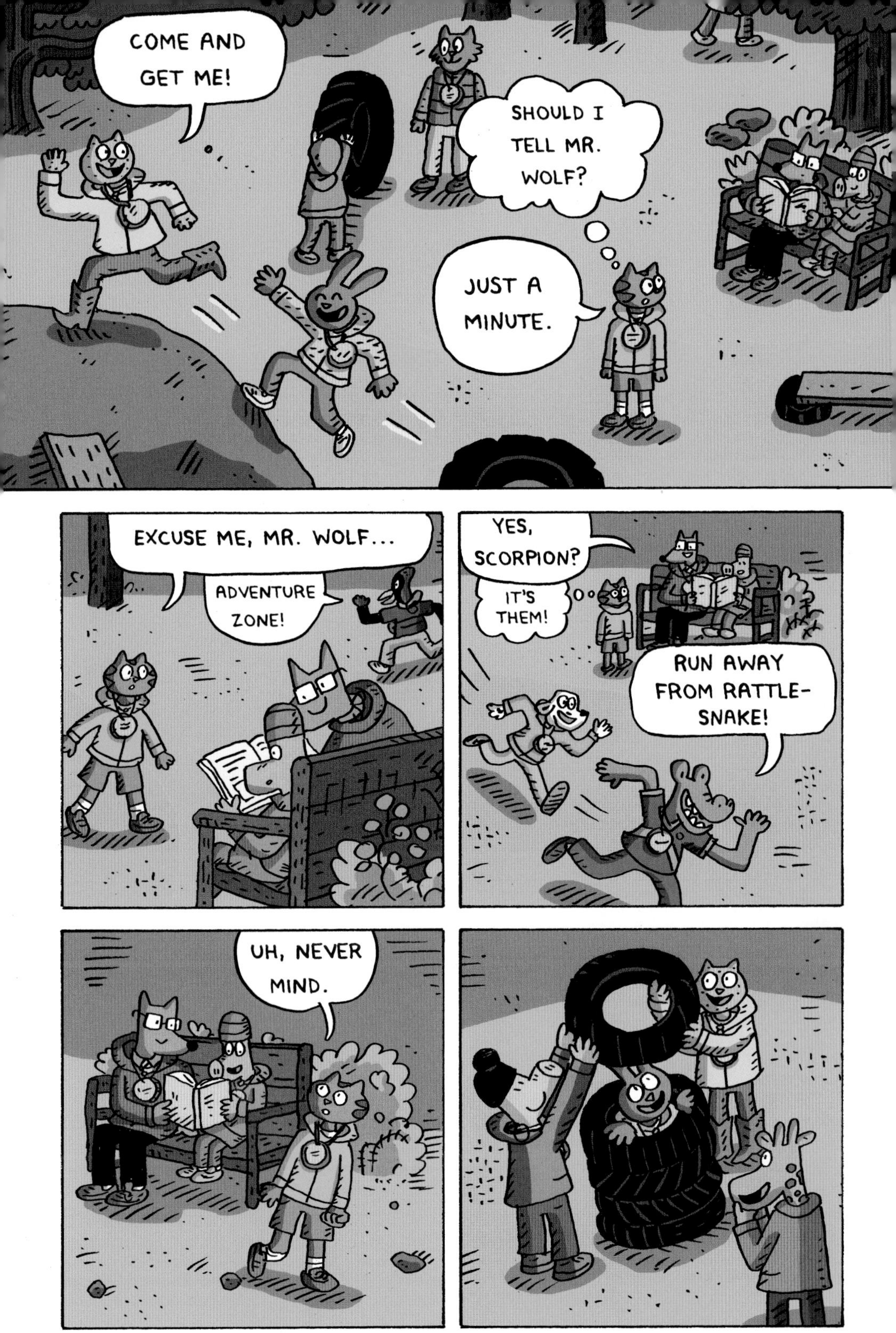
COME AND GET ME!
SHOULD I TELL MR. WOLF?
JUST A MINUTE.
EXCUSE ME, MR. WOLF...
ADVENTURE ZONE!
YES, SCORPION?
IT'S THEM!
RUN AWAY FROM RATTLE-SNAKE!
UH, NEVER MIND.

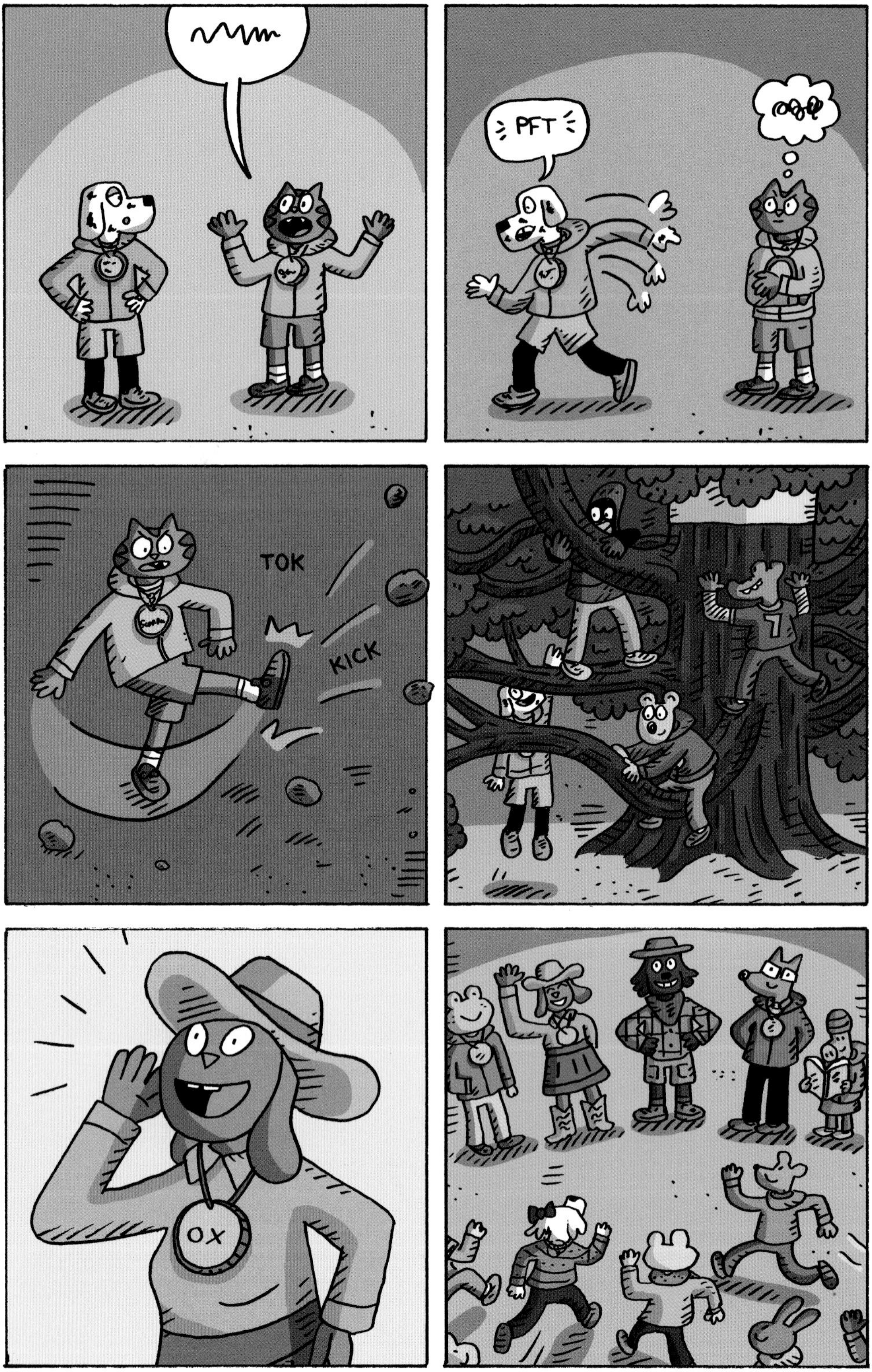
PFT
TOK
KICK
OX

CHAPTER SIX
No Dancing

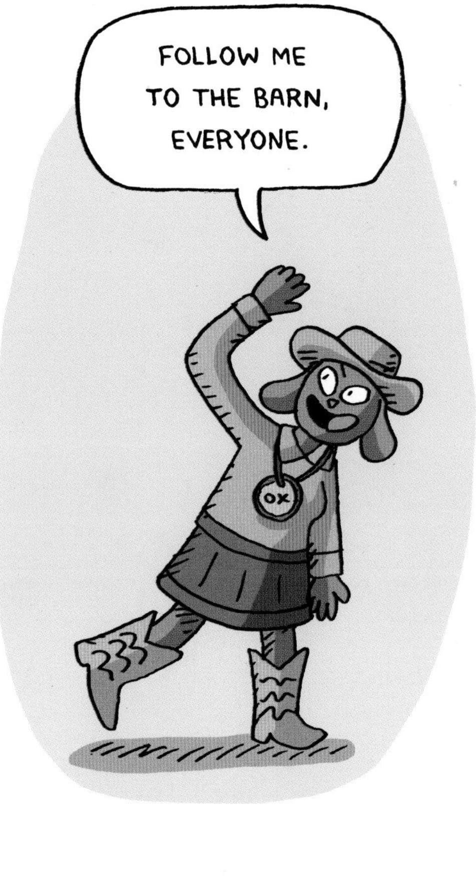
FOLLOW ME TO THE BARN, EVERYONE.

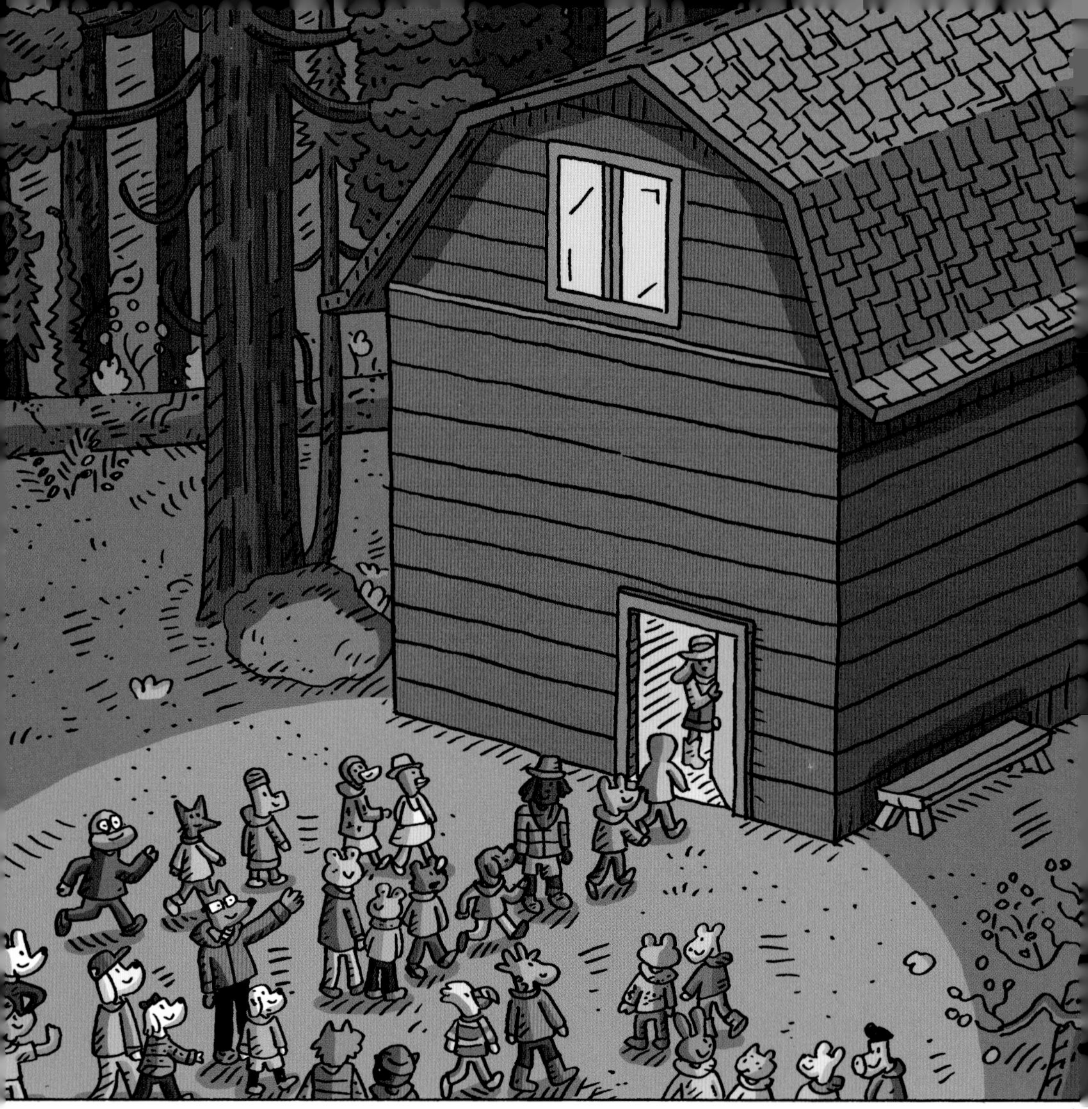

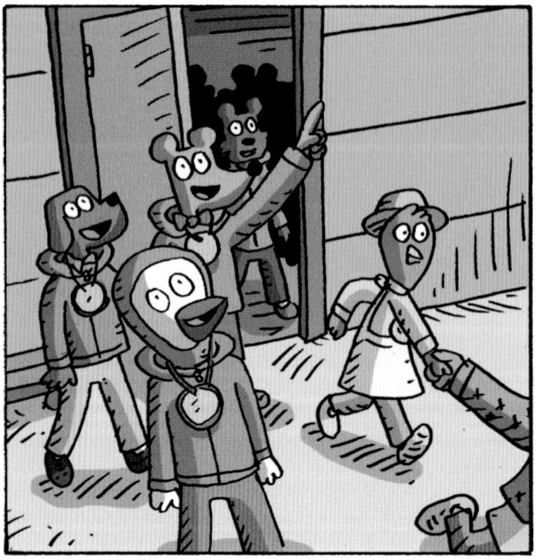

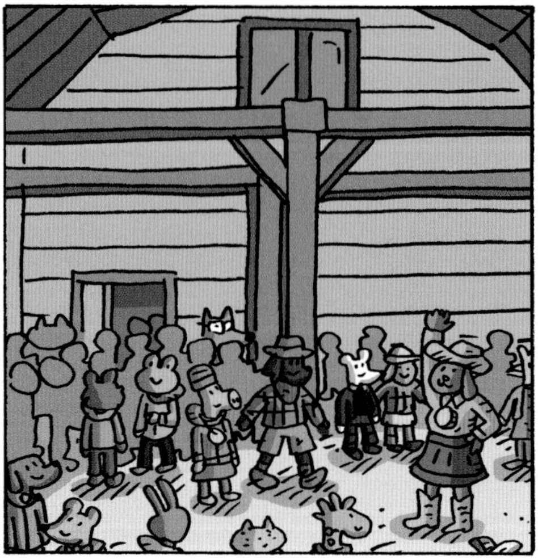

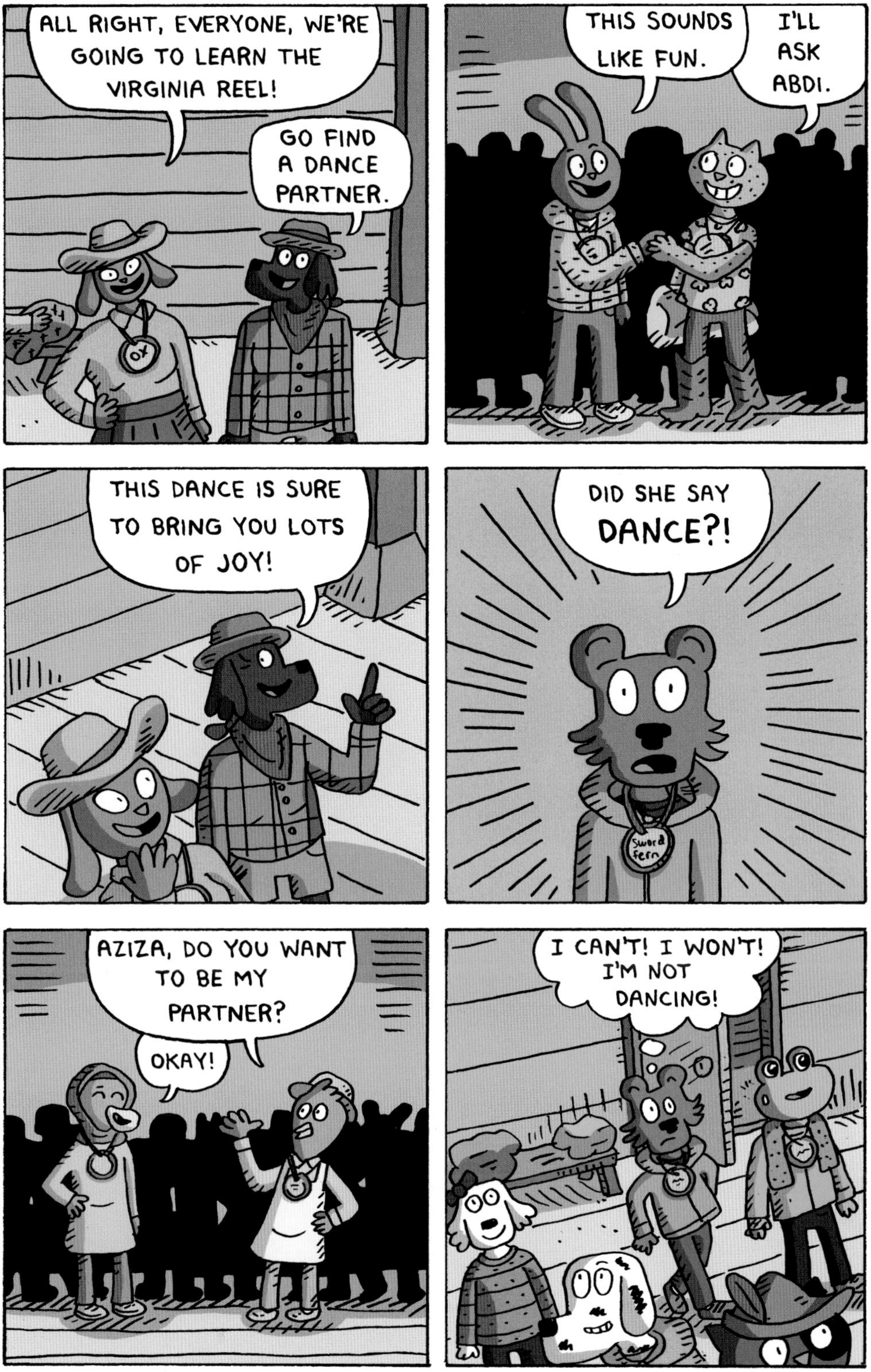
ALL RIGHT, EVERYONE, WE'RE GOING TO LEARN THE VIRGINIA REEL!
GO FIND A DANCE PARTNER.
THIS SOUNDS LIKE FUN.
I'LL ASK ABDI.
THIS DANCE IS SURE TO BRING YOU LOTS OF JOY!
DID SHE SAY DANCE?!
AZIZA, DO YOU WANT TO BE MY PARTNER?
OKAY!
I CAN'T! I WON'T! I'M NOT DANCING!

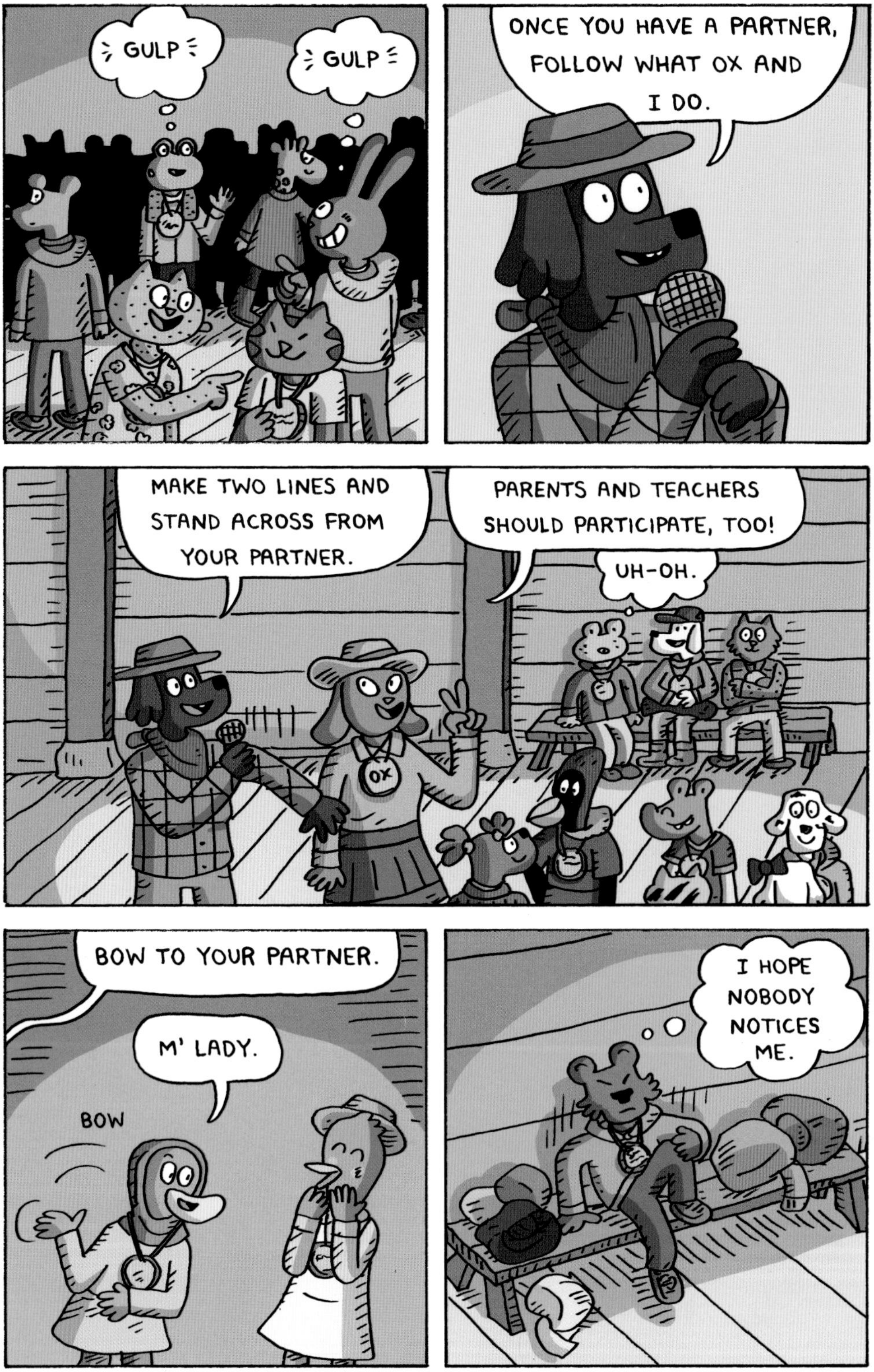
GULP
GULP
ONCE YOU HAVE A PARTNER, FOLLOW WHAT OX AND I DO.
MAKE TWO LINES AND STAND ACROSS FROM YOUR PARTNER.
PARENTS AND TEACHERS SHOULD PARTICIPATE, TOO!
UH-OH.
OX
BOW TO YOUR PARTNER.
M' LADY.
BOW
I HOPE NOBODY NOTICES ME.

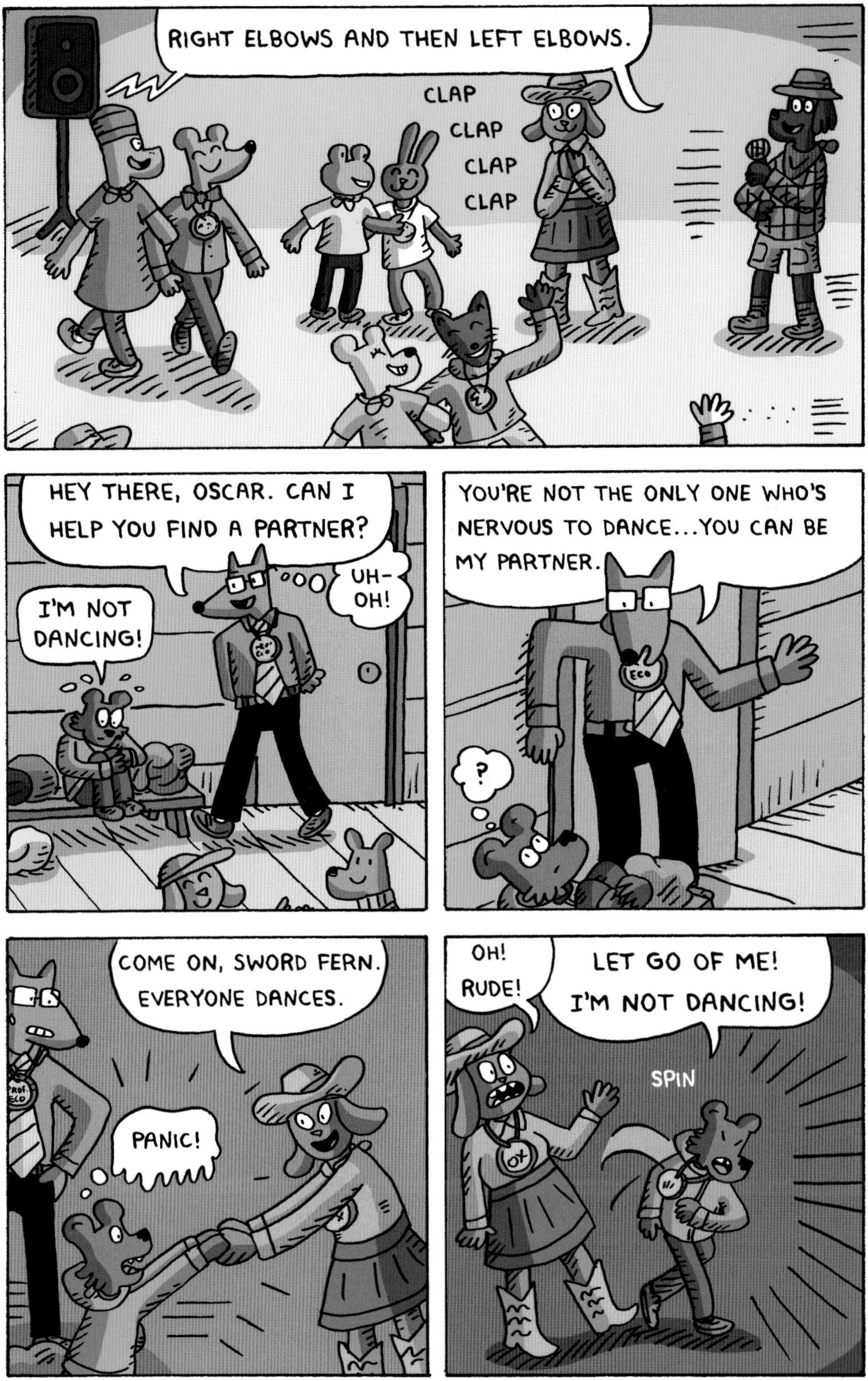
RIGHT ELBOWS AND THEN LEFT ELBOWS.
CLAP
CLAP
CLAP
CLAP
HEY THERE, OSCAR. CAN I HELP YOU FIND A PARTNER?
I'M NOT DANCING!
UH-OH!
YOU'RE NOT THE ONLY ONE WHO'S NERVOUS TO DANCE...YOU CAN BE MY PARTNER.
?
COME ON, SWORD FERN. EVERYONE DANCES.
PANIC!
OH! RUDE!
LET GO OF ME! I'M NOT DANCING!
SPIN

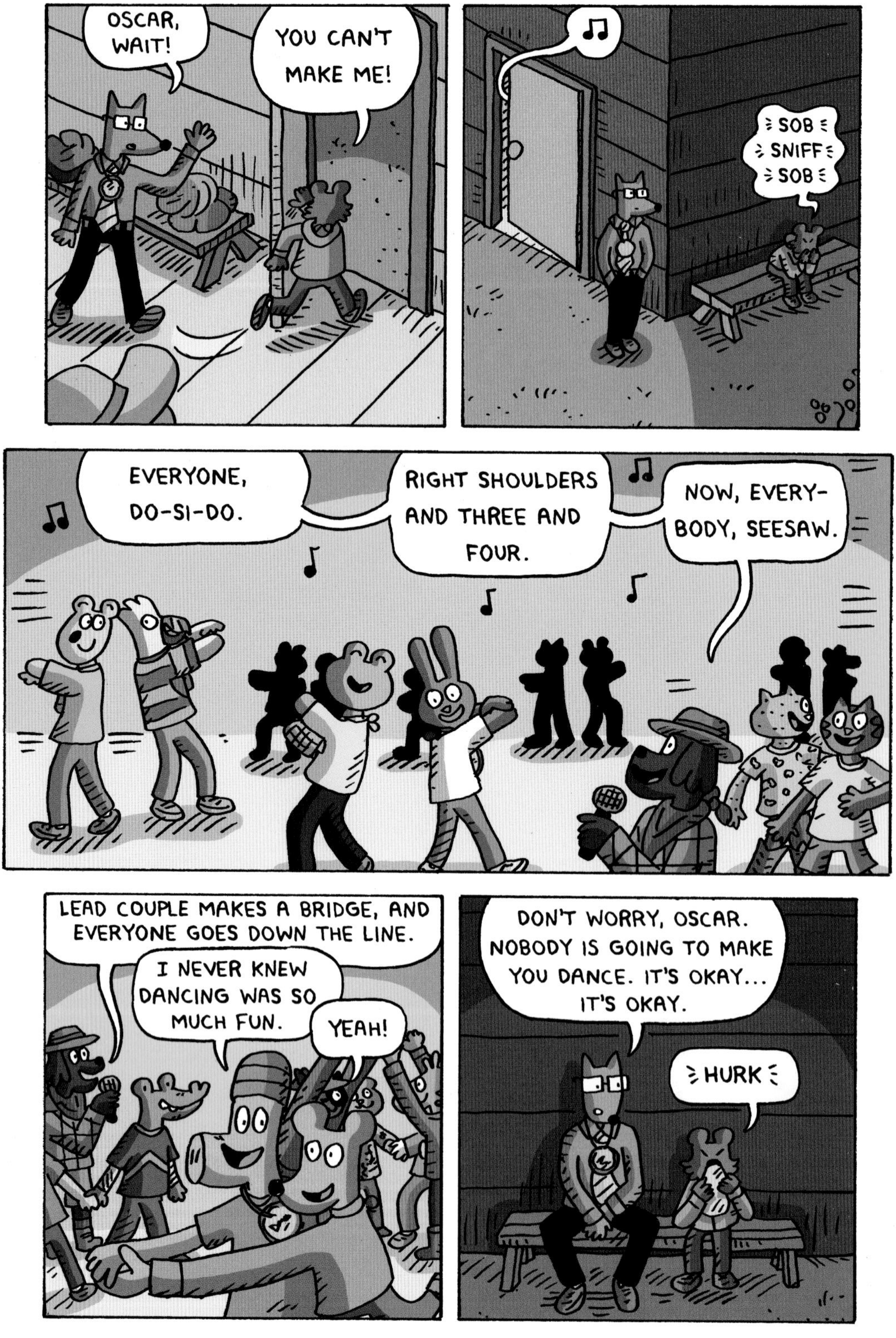
OSCAR, WAIT!
YOU CAN'T MAKE ME!
♫
SOB SNIFF SOB
EVERYONE, DO-SI-DO.
RIGHT SHOULDERS AND THREE AND FOUR.
NOW, EVERY-BODY, SEESAW.
LEAD COUPLE MAKES A BRIDGE, AND EVERYONE GOES DOWN THE LINE.
I NEVER KNEW DANCING WAS SO MUCH FUN.
YEAH!
DON'T WORRY, OSCAR. NOBODY IS GOING TO MAKE YOU DANCE. IT'S OKAY... IT'S OKAY.
HURK

CHAPTER SEVEN
The Headless Miner

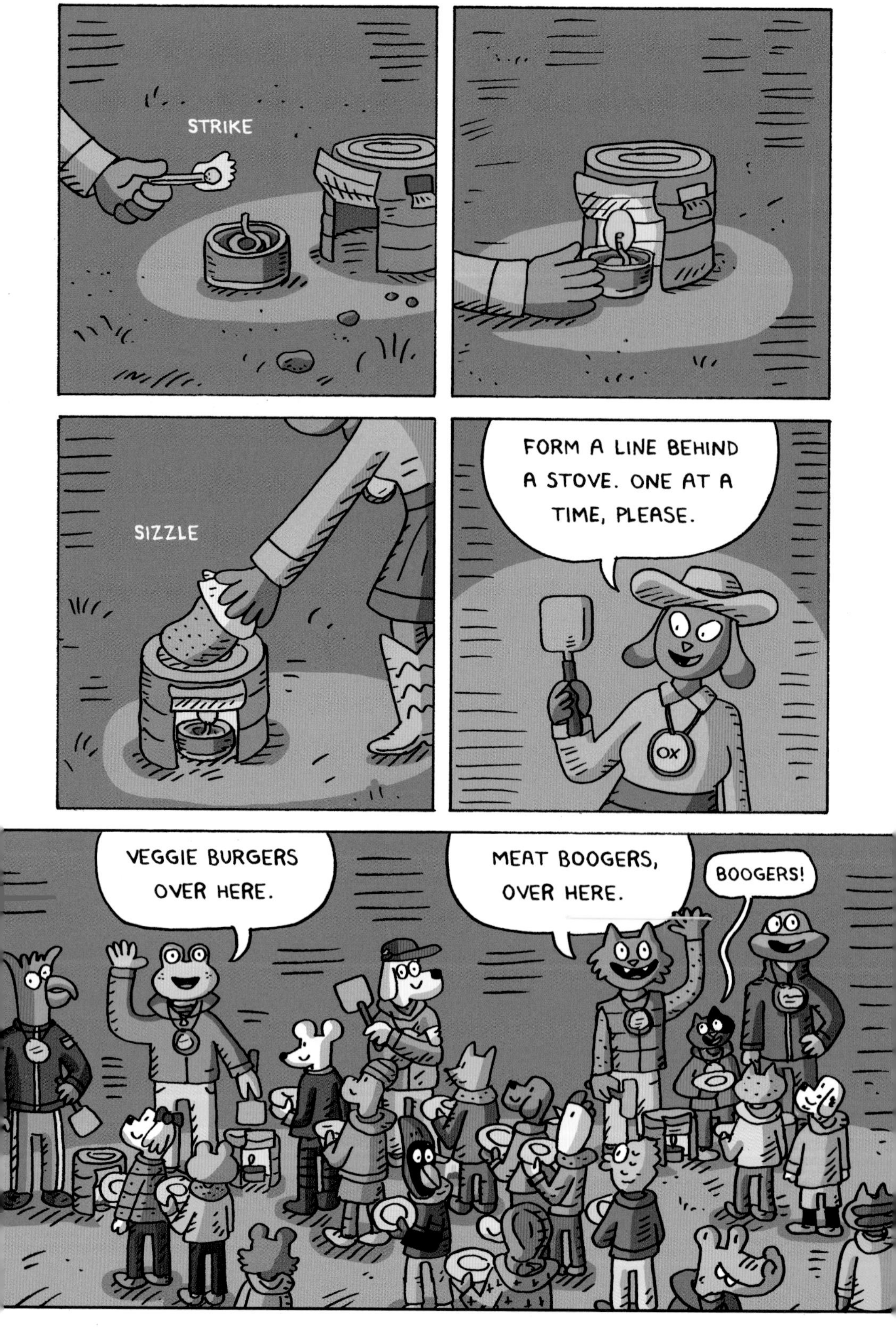
STRIKE
SIZZLE
FORM A LINE BEHIND A STOVE. ONE AT A TIME, PLEASE.
OX
VEGGIE BURGERS OVER HERE.
MEAT BOOGERS, OVER HERE.
BOOGERS!

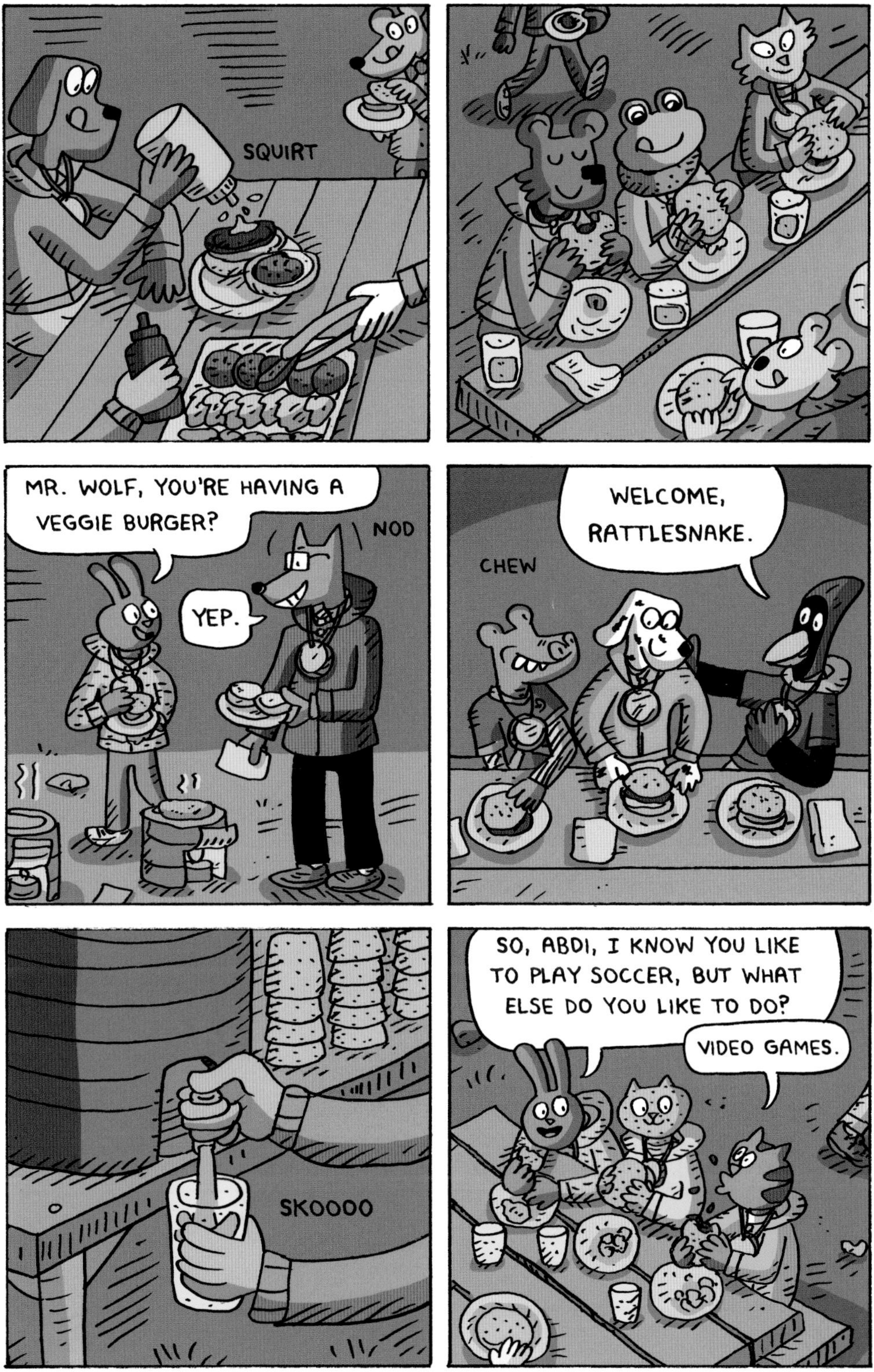
SQUIRT
MR. WOLF, YOU'RE HAVING A VEGGIE BURGER?
NOD
YEP.
CHEW
WELCOME, RATTLESNAKE.
SKOOOO
SO, ABDI, I KNOW YOU LIKE TO PLAY SOCCER, BUT WHAT ELSE DO YOU LIKE TO DO?
VIDEO GAMES.

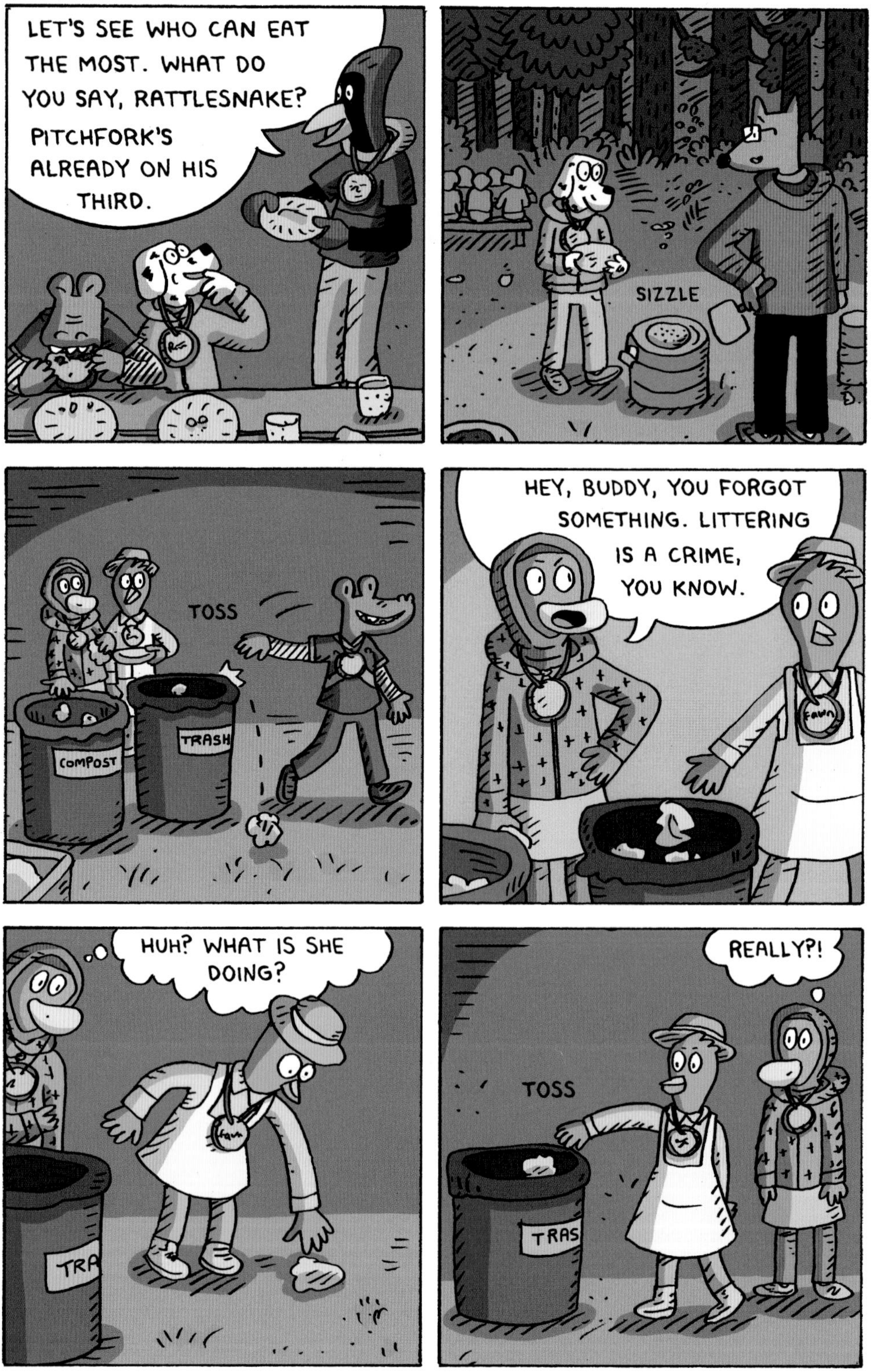
LET'S SEE WHO CAN EAT THE MOST. WHAT DO YOU SAY, RATTLESNAKE? PITCHFORK'S ALREADY ON HIS THIRD.
SIZZLE
TOSS
TRASH
COMPOST
HEY, BUDDY, YOU FORGOT SOMETHING. LITTERING IS A CRIME, YOU KNOW.
HUH? WHAT IS SHE DOING?
TRA
TOSS
TRAS
REALLY?!

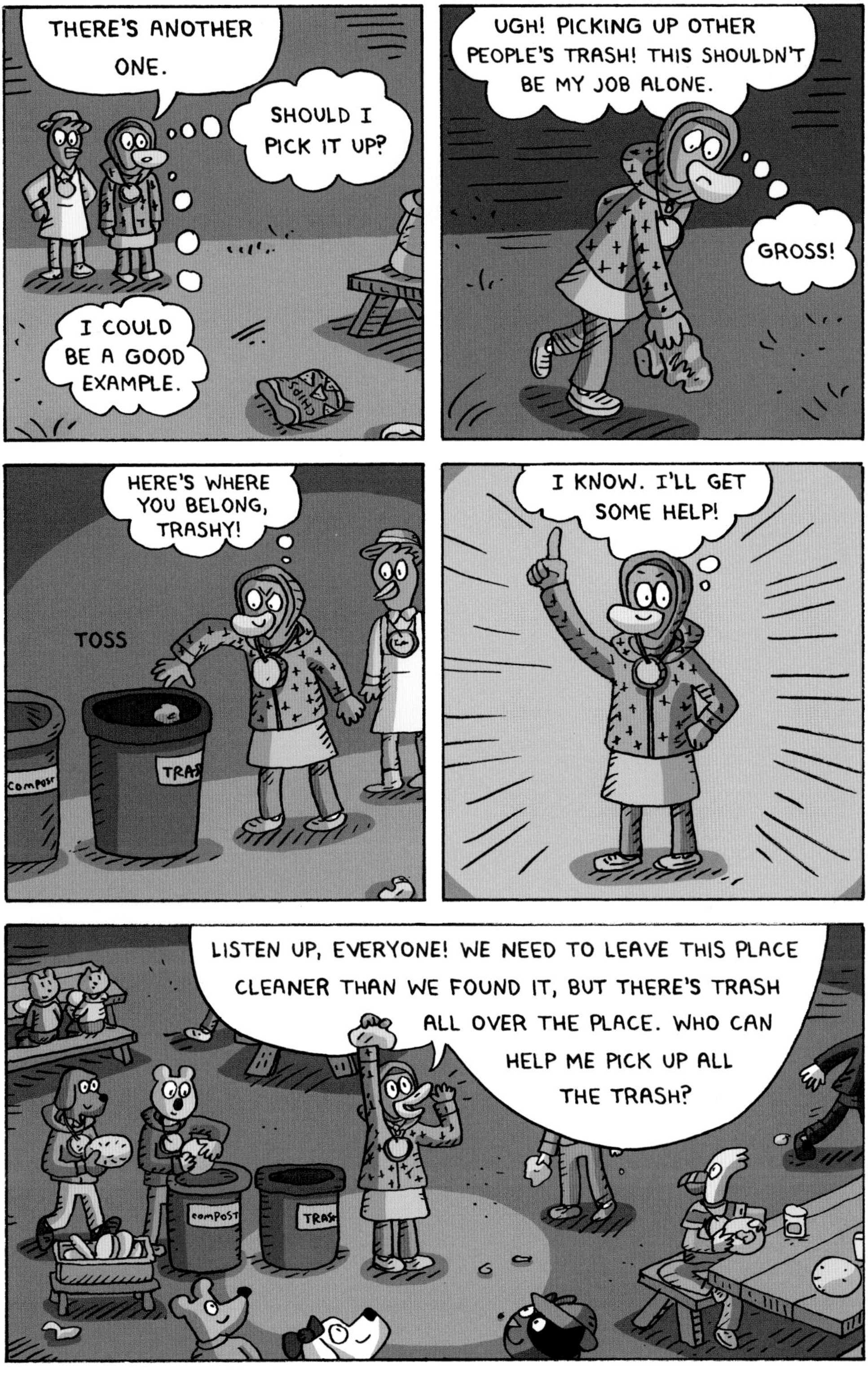
THERE'S ANOTHER ONE.
SHOULD I PICK IT UP?
I COULD BE A GOOD EXAMPLE.
CHIPS
UGH! PICKING UP OTHER PEOPLE'S TRASH! THIS SHOULDN'T BE MY JOB ALONE.
GROSS!
HERE'S WHERE YOU BELONG, TRASHY!
TOSS
COMPOST
TRASH
I KNOW. I'LL GET SOME HELP!
LISTEN UP, EVERYONE! WE NEED TO LEAVE THIS PLACE CLEANER THAN WE FOUND IT, BUT THERE'S TRASH ALL OVER THE PLACE. WHO CAN HELP ME PICK UP ALL THE TRASH?
COMPOST
TRASH

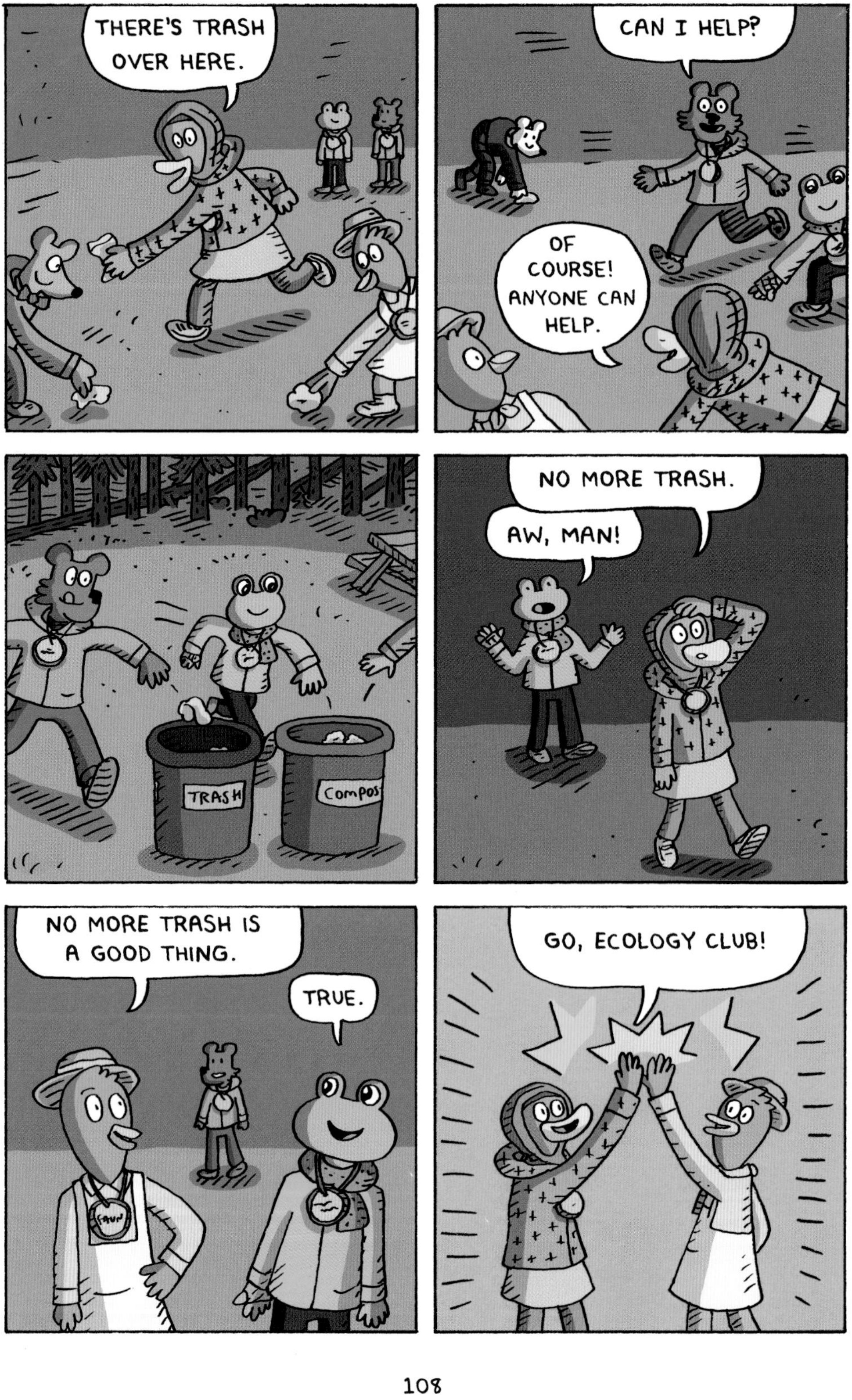
THERE'S TRASH OVER HERE.
CAN I HELP?
OF COURSE! ANYONE CAN HELP.
TRASH
Compos
NO MORE TRASH.
AW, MAN!
NO MORE TRASH IS A GOOD THING.
TRUE.
GO, ECOLOGY CLUB!

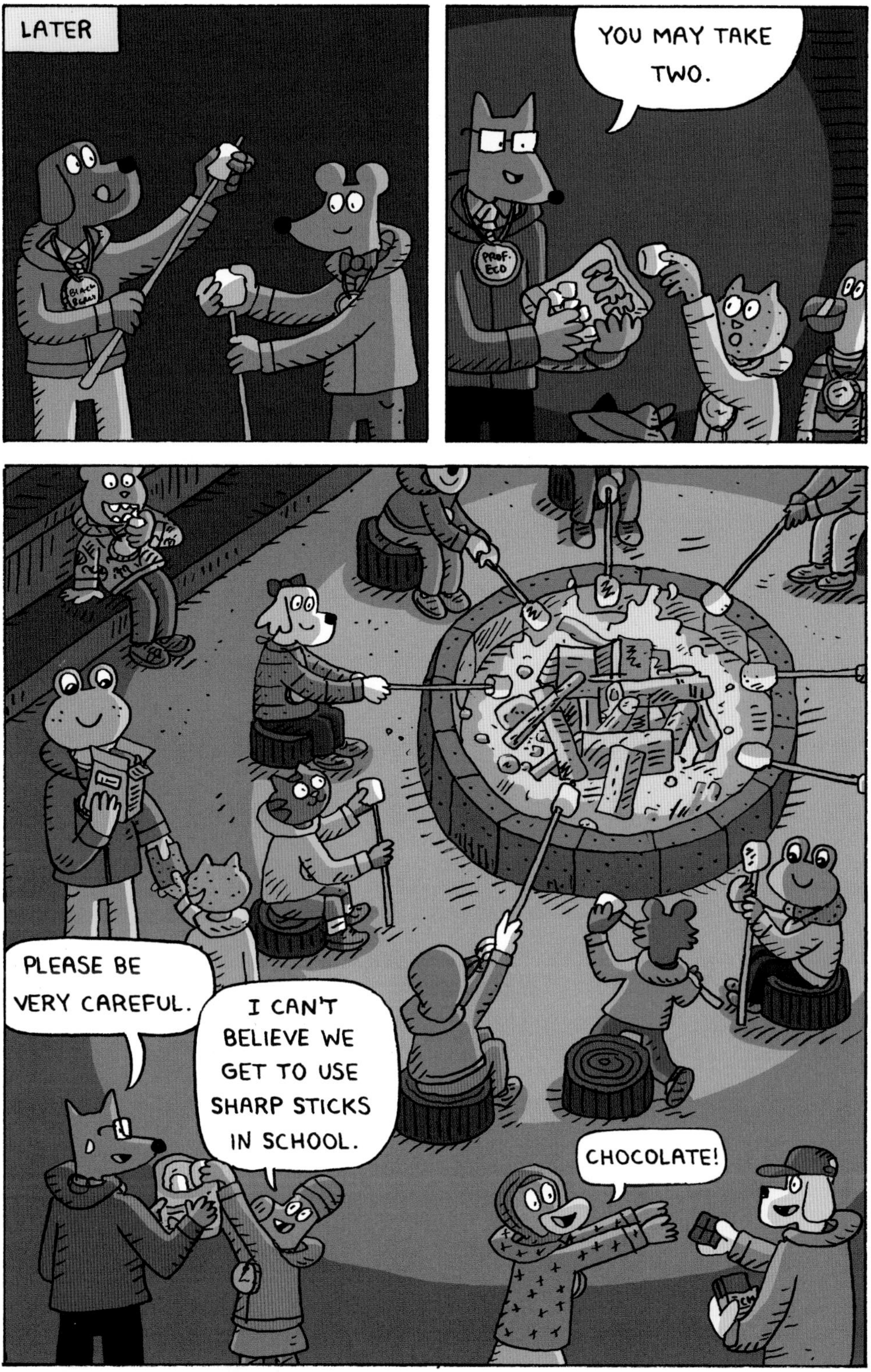
LATER
YOU MAY TAKE TWO.
PLEASE BE VERY CAREFUL.
I CAN'T BELIEVE WE GET TO USE SHARP STICKS IN SCHOOL.
CHOCOLATE!

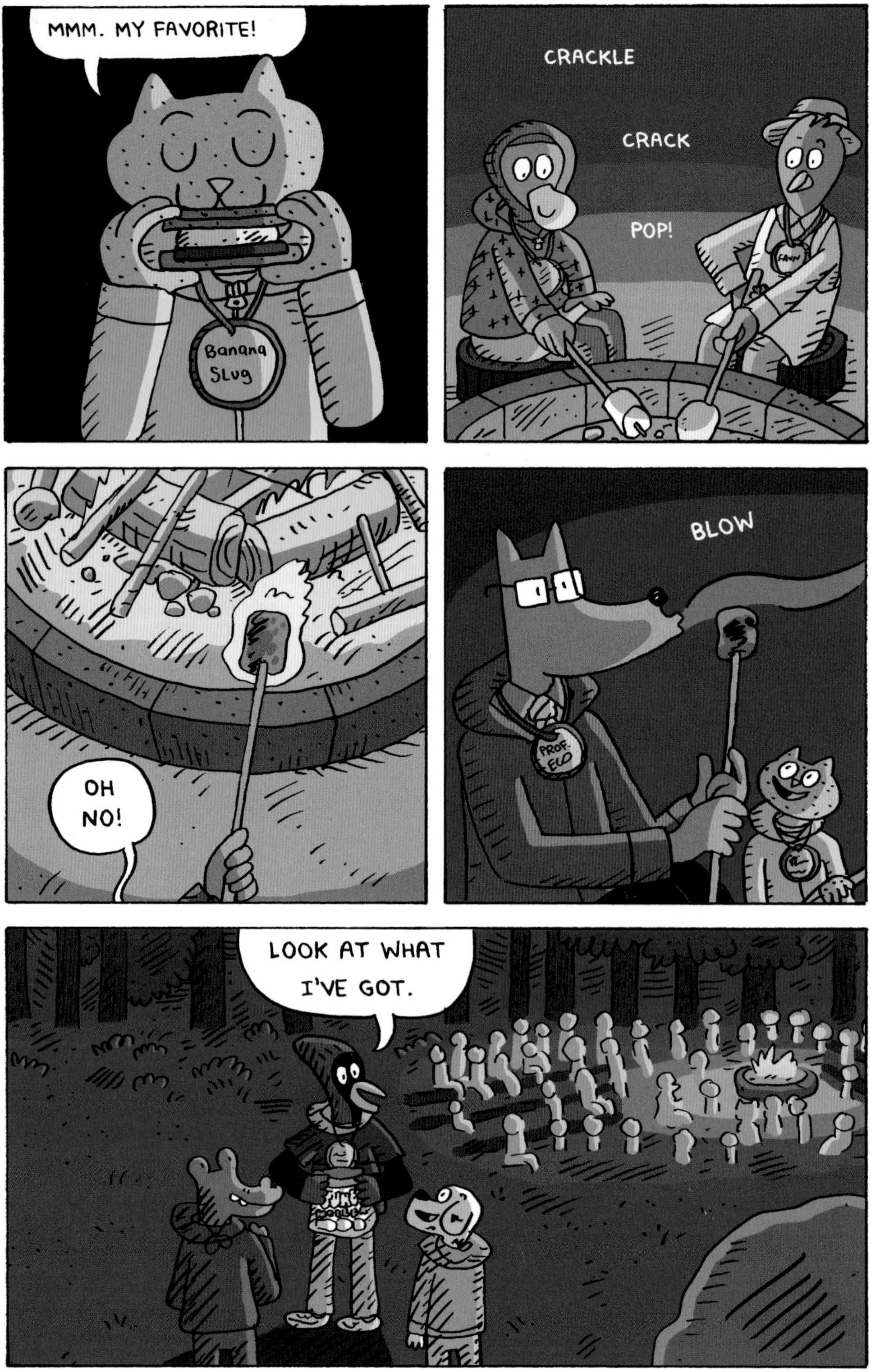
MMM. MY FAVORITE!
Banana Slug
CRACKLE
CRACK
POP!
OH NO!
BLOW
PROF. ECO
LOOK AT WHAT I'VE GOT.

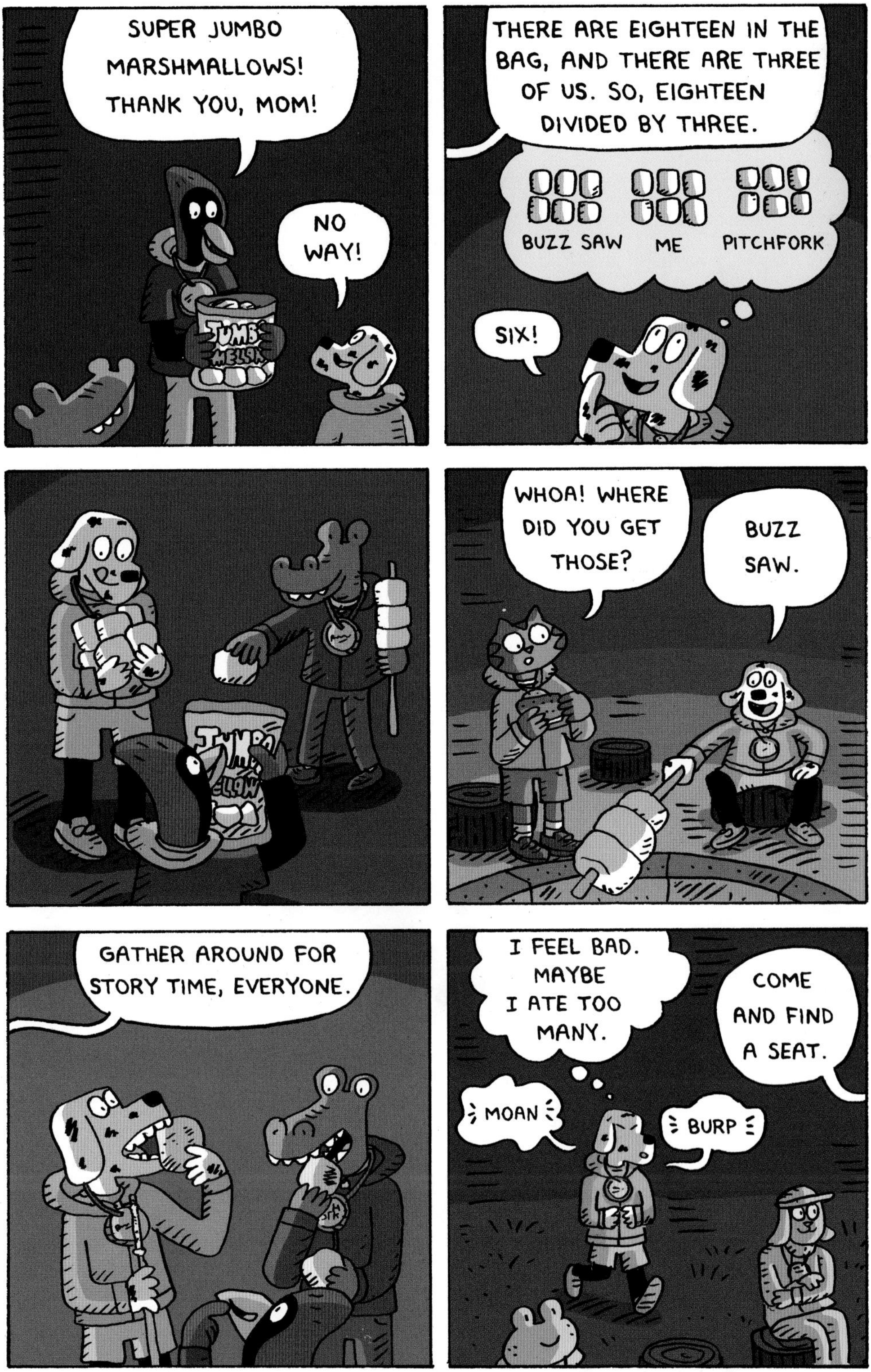
SUPER JUMBO MARSHMALLOWS! THANK YOU, MOM!
NO WAY!
THERE ARE EIGHTEEN IN THE BAG, AND THERE ARE THREE OF US. SO, EIGHTEEN DIVIDED BY THREE.
BUZZ SAW
ME
PITCHFORK
SIX!
WHOA! WHERE DID YOU GET THOSE?
BUZZ SAW.
GATHER AROUND FOR STORY TIME, EVERYONE.
I FEEL BAD. MAYBE I ATE TOO MANY.
COME AND FIND A SEAT.
MOAN
BURP

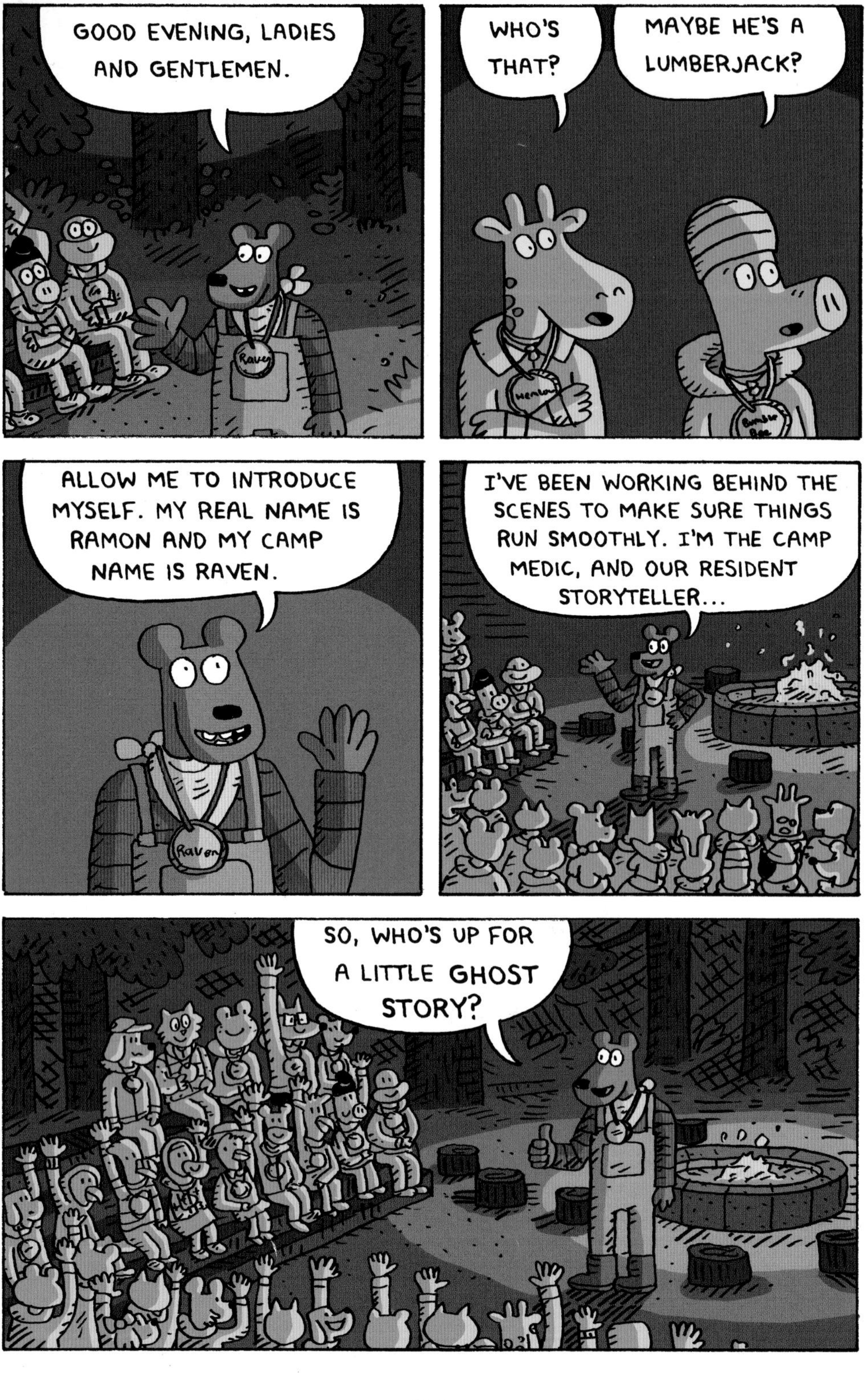
GOOD EVENING, LADIES AND GENTLEMEN.
WHO'S THAT?
MAYBE HE'S A LUMBERJACK?
ALLOW ME TO INTRODUCE MYSELF. MY REAL NAME IS RAMON AND MY CAMP NAME IS RAVEN.
I'VE BEEN WORKING BEHIND THE SCENES TO MAKE SURE THINGS RUN SMOOTHLY. I'M THE CAMP MEDIC, AND OUR RESIDENT STORYTELLER...
SO, WHO'S UP FOR A LITTLE GHOST STORY?

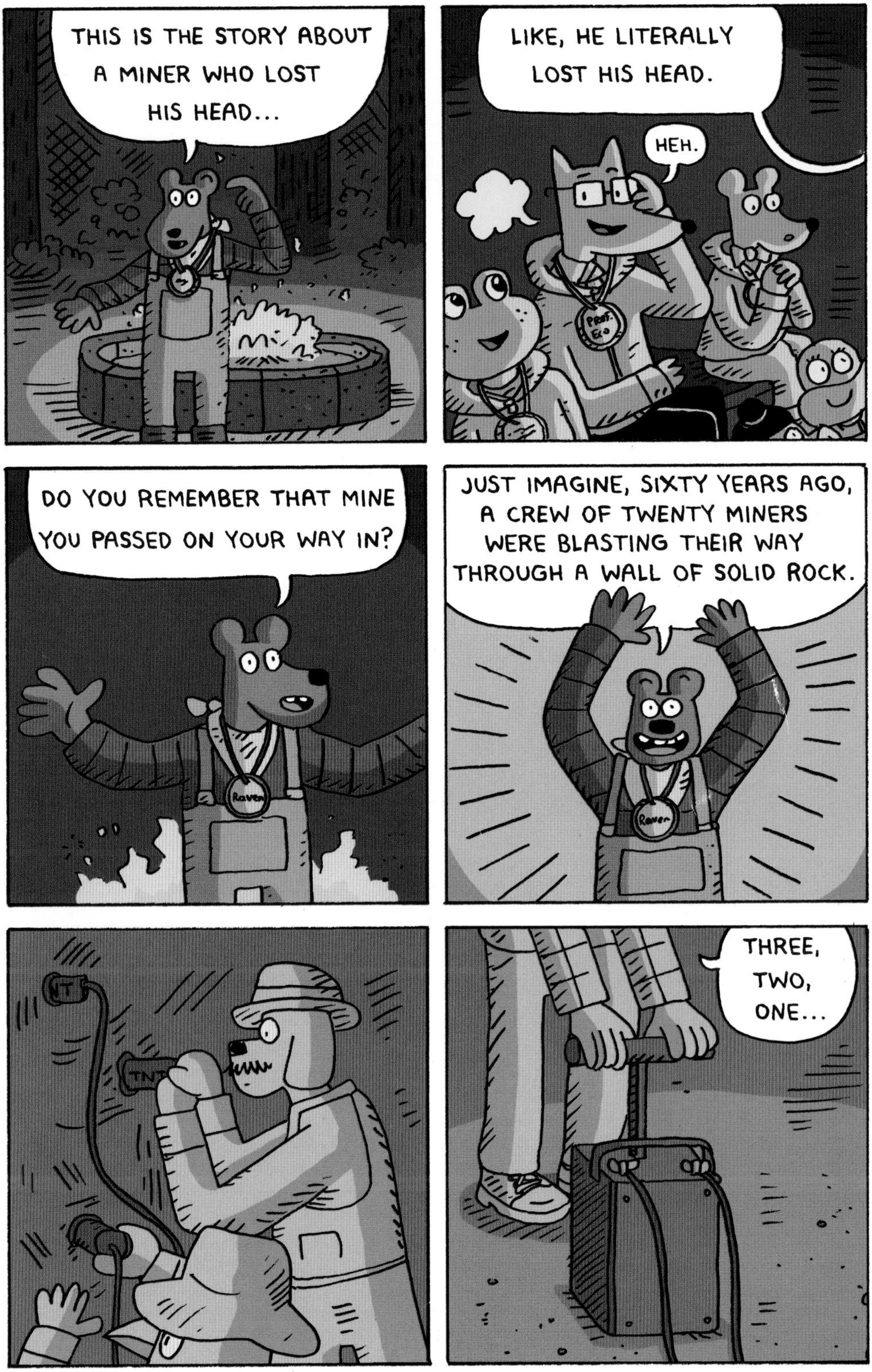
THIS IS THE STORY ABOUT A MINER WHO LOST HIS HEAD...
LIKE, HE LITERALLY LOST HIS HEAD.
HEH.
DO YOU REMEMBER THAT MINE YOU PASSED ON YOUR WAY IN?
JUST IMAGINE, SIXTY YEARS AGO, A CREW OF TWENTY MINERS WERE BLASTING THEIR WAY THROUGH A WALL OF SOLID ROCK.
TNT
THREE, TWO, ONE...

BLAM!

SOMETIMES THEY'D GET LUCKY AND FIND GOLD...

BUT THIS ONE TIME, THEY WERE NOT SO LUCKY...THERE WAS A CAVE-IN. TWENTY MINERS WENT IN AND ONLY NINETEEN CAME OUT.

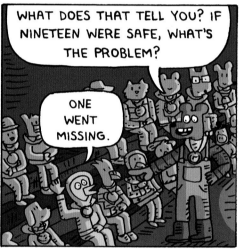

WHAT DOES THAT TELL YOU? IF NINETEEN WERE SAFE, WHAT'S THE PROBLEM?

ONE WENT MISSING.

EXACTLY. WHEN THE SMOKE AND DUST SETTLED, THE MINERS WENT BACK INSIDE TO SEARCH FOR THEIR MISSING FRIEND.

Raven

AFTER DIGGING THROUGH THE DEBRIS, THEY UNCOVERED HIS FEET AND LEGS. THEY PULLED AND PULLED TO FREE THEIR FRIEND...

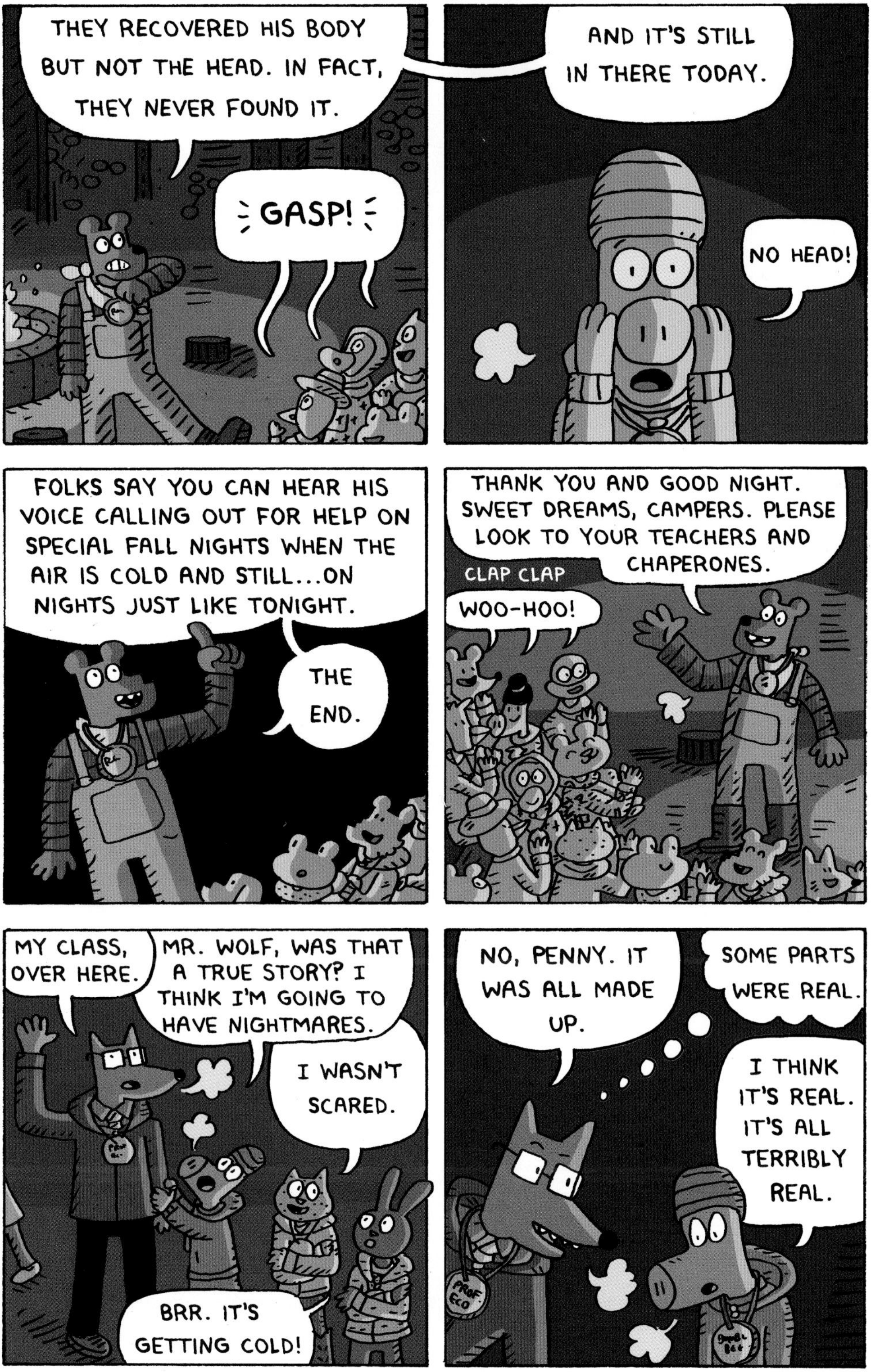
THEY RECOVERED HIS BODY BUT NOT THE HEAD. IN FACT, THEY NEVER FOUND IT.
AND IT'S STILL IN THERE TODAY.
GASP!
NO HEAD!
FOLKS SAY YOU CAN HEAR HIS VOICE CALLING OUT FOR HELP ON SPECIAL FALL NIGHTS WHEN THE AIR IS COLD AND STILL...ON NIGHTS JUST LIKE TONIGHT.
THE END.
THANK YOU AND GOOD NIGHT. SWEET DREAMS, CAMPERS. PLEASE LOOK TO YOUR TEACHERS AND CHAPERONES.
CLAP CLAP
WOO-HOO!
MY CLASS, OVER HERE.
MR. WOLF, WAS THAT A TRUE STORY? I THINK I'M GOING TO HAVE NIGHTMARES.
I WASN'T SCARED.
BRR. IT'S GETTING COLD!
NO, PENNY. IT WAS ALL MADE UP.
SOME PARTS WERE REAL.
I THINK IT'S REAL. IT'S ALL TERRIBLY REAL.

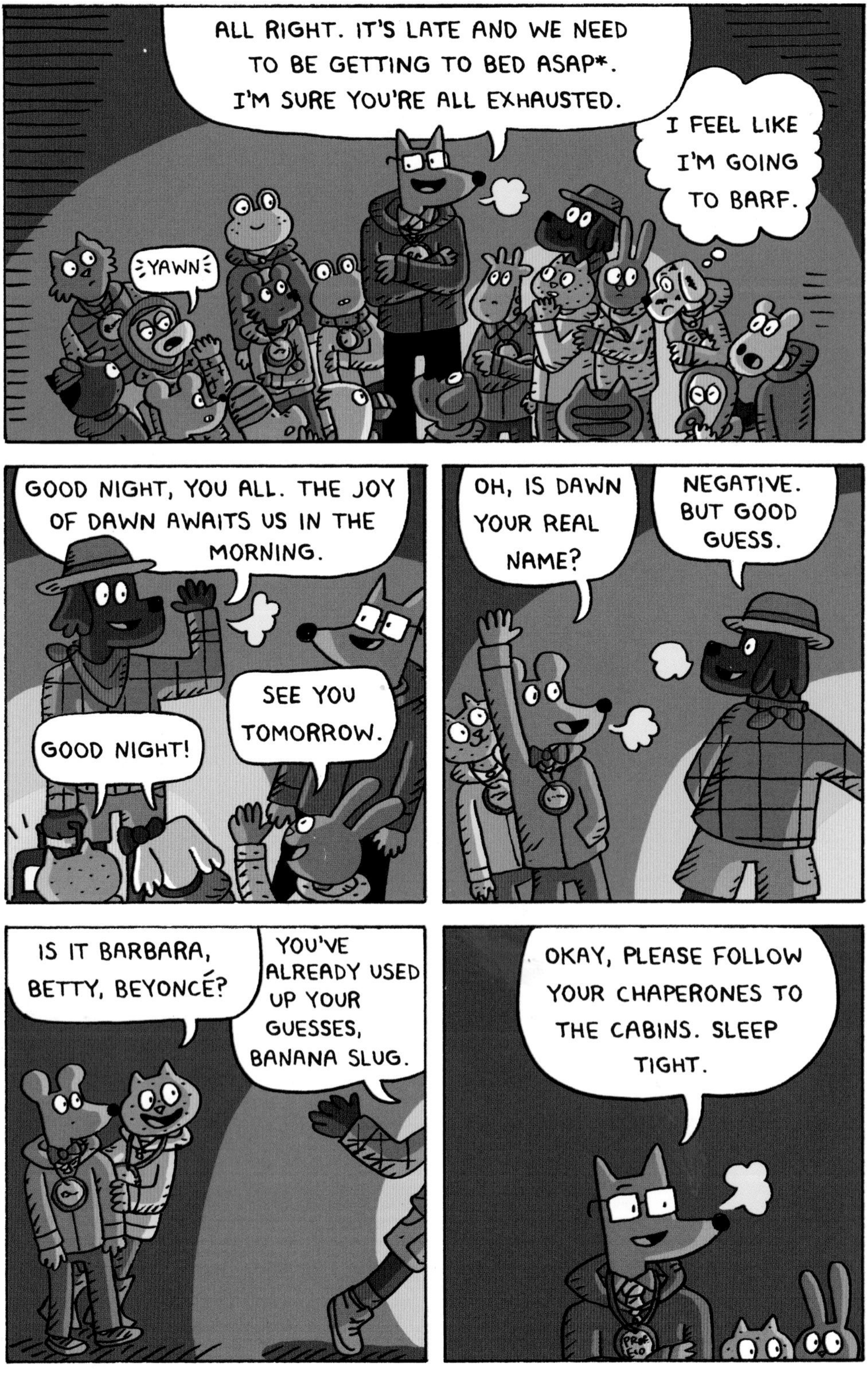
ALL RIGHT. IT'S LATE AND WE NEED TO BE GETTING TO BED ASAP*. I'M SURE YOU'RE ALL EXHAUSTED.
YAWN
I FEEL LIKE I'M GOING TO BARF.
GOOD NIGHT, YOU ALL. THE JOY OF DAWN AWAITS US IN THE MORNING.
GOOD NIGHT!
SEE YOU TOMORROW.
OH, IS DAWN YOUR REAL NAME?
NEGATIVE. BUT GOOD GUESS.
IS IT BARBARA, BETTY, BEYONCÉ?
YOU'VE ALREADY USED UP YOUR GUESSES, BANANA SLUG.
OKAY, PLEASE FOLLOW YOUR CHAPERONES TO THE CABINS. SLEEP TIGHT.

*AS SOON AS POSSIBLE

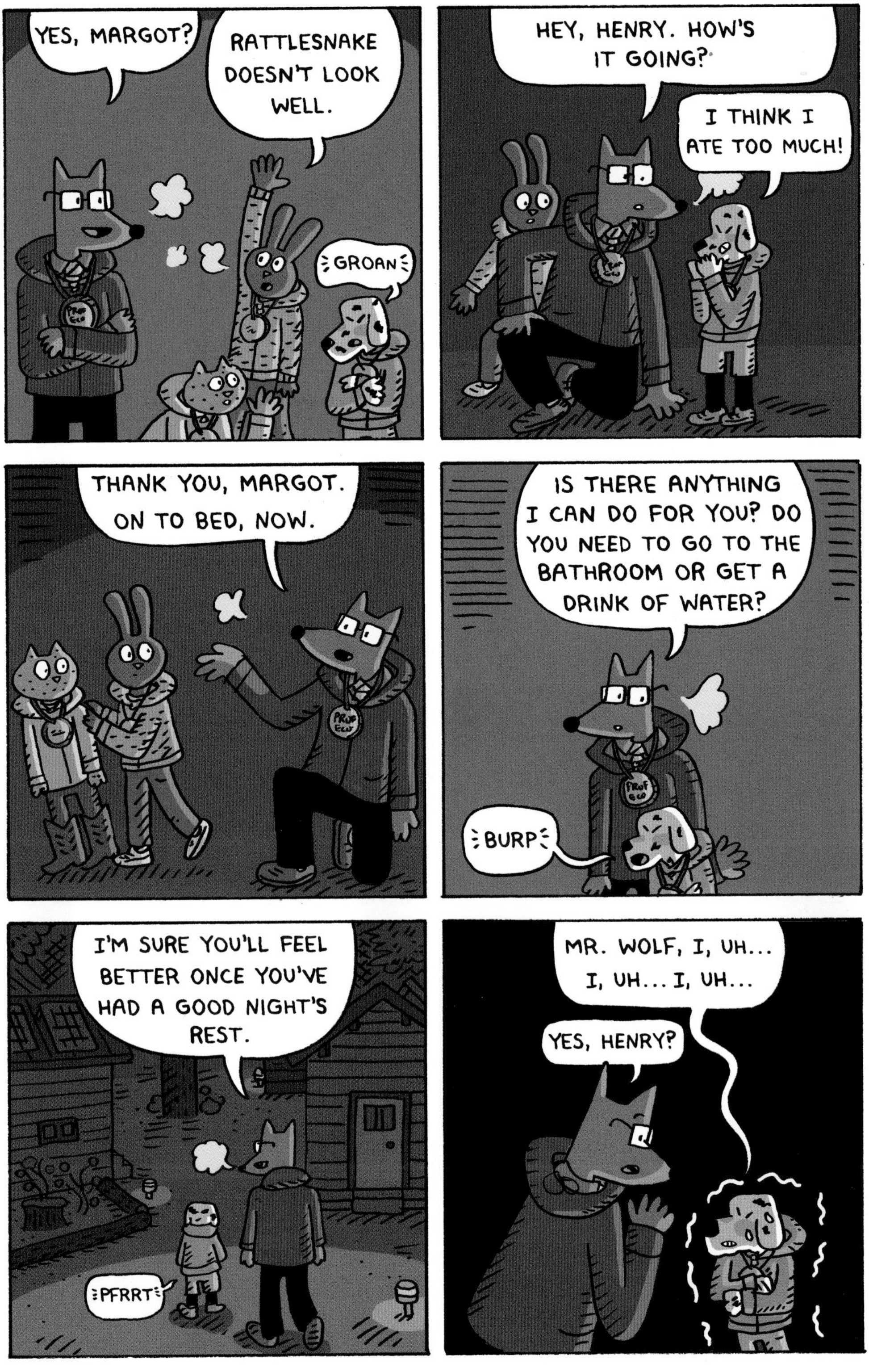
YES, MARGOT?
RATTLESNAKE DOESN'T LOOK WELL.
GROAN
HEY, HENRY. HOW'S IT GOING?
I THINK I ATE TOO MUCH!
THANK YOU, MARGOT. ON TO BED, NOW.
IS THERE ANYTHING I CAN DO FOR YOU? DO YOU NEED TO GO TO THE BATHROOM OR GET A DRINK OF WATER?
BURP
I'M SURE YOU'LL FEEL BETTER ONCE YOU'VE HAD A GOOD NIGHT'S REST.
PFRRT
MR. WOLF, I, UH... I, UH... I, UH...
YES, HENRY?

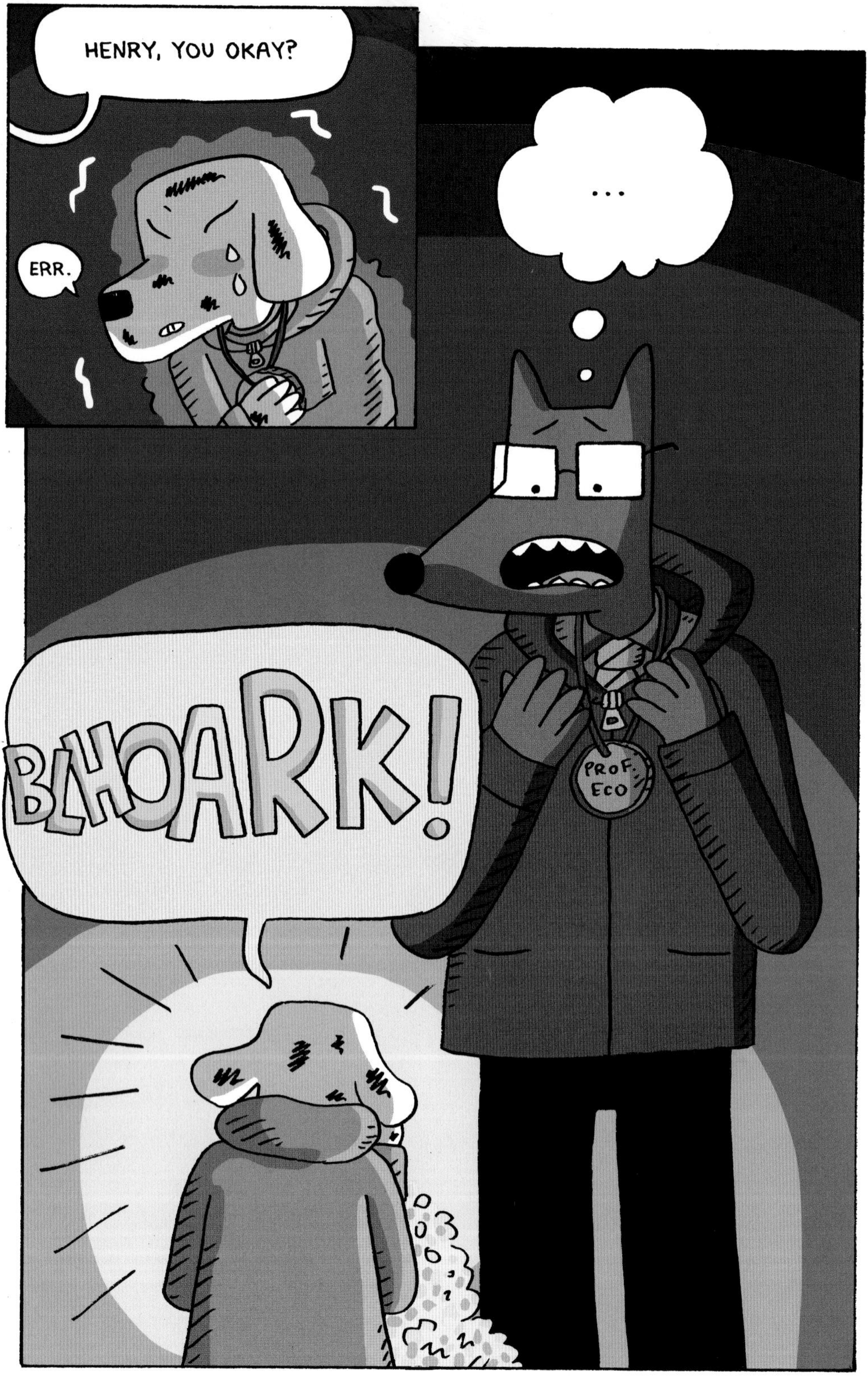
HENRY, YOU OKAY?
ERR.
...
BLHOARK!
PROF. ECO

CHAPTER EIGHT

Surprise

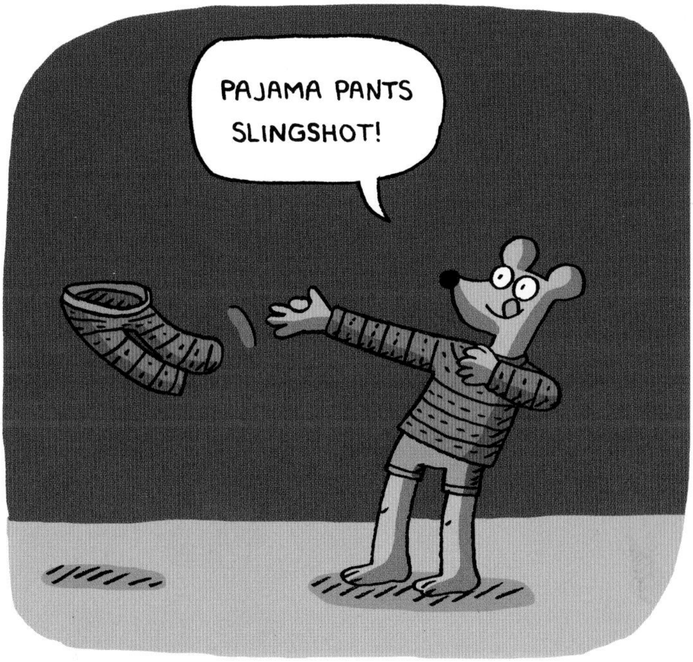
PAJAMA PANTS SLINGSHOT!

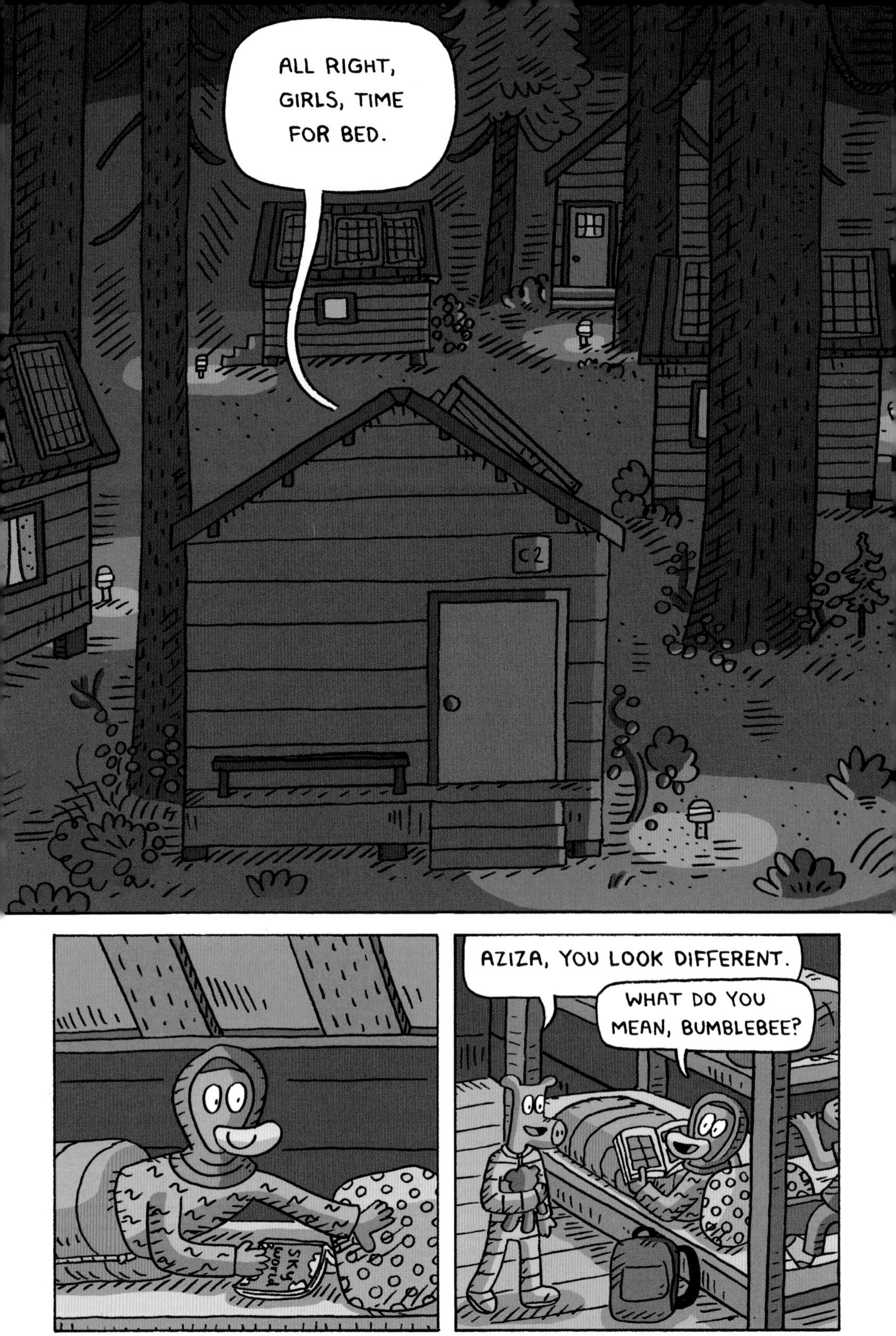
ALL RIGHT, GIRLS, TIME FOR BED.
C2
SKY WORLD
AZIZA, YOU LOOK DIFFERENT.
WHAT DO YOU MEAN, BUMBLEBEE?

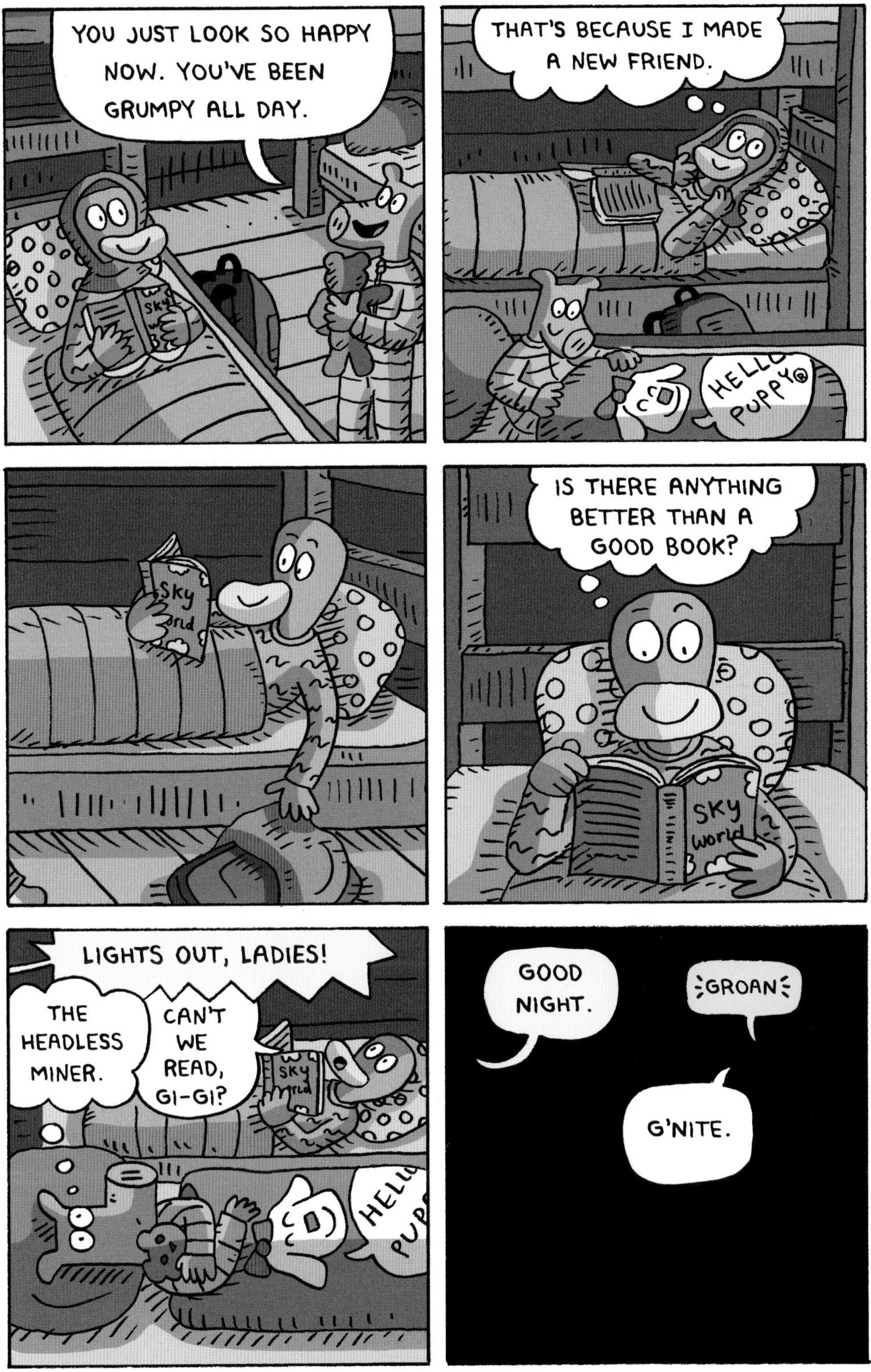
YOU JUST LOOK SO HAPPY NOW. YOU'VE BEEN GRUMPY ALL DAY.
THAT'S BECAUSE I MADE A NEW FRIEND.
HELLO PUPPY®
IS THERE ANYTHING BETTER THAN A GOOD BOOK?
SKY World
LIGHTS OUT, LADIES!
THE HEADLESS MINER.
CAN'T WE READ, GI-GI?
GOOD NIGHT.
GROAN
G'NITE.

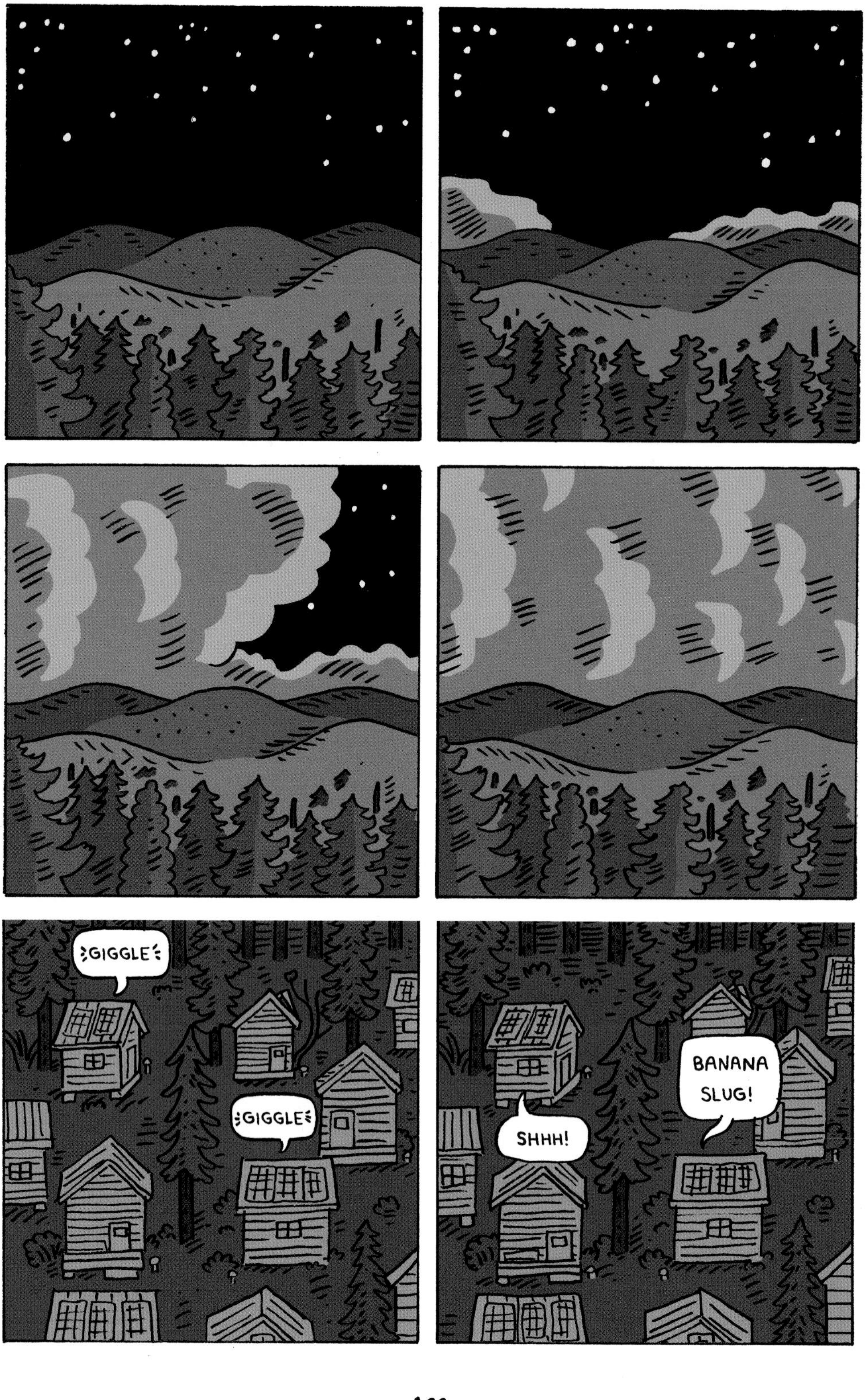
GIGGLE
GIGGLE
BANANA SLUG!
SHHH!

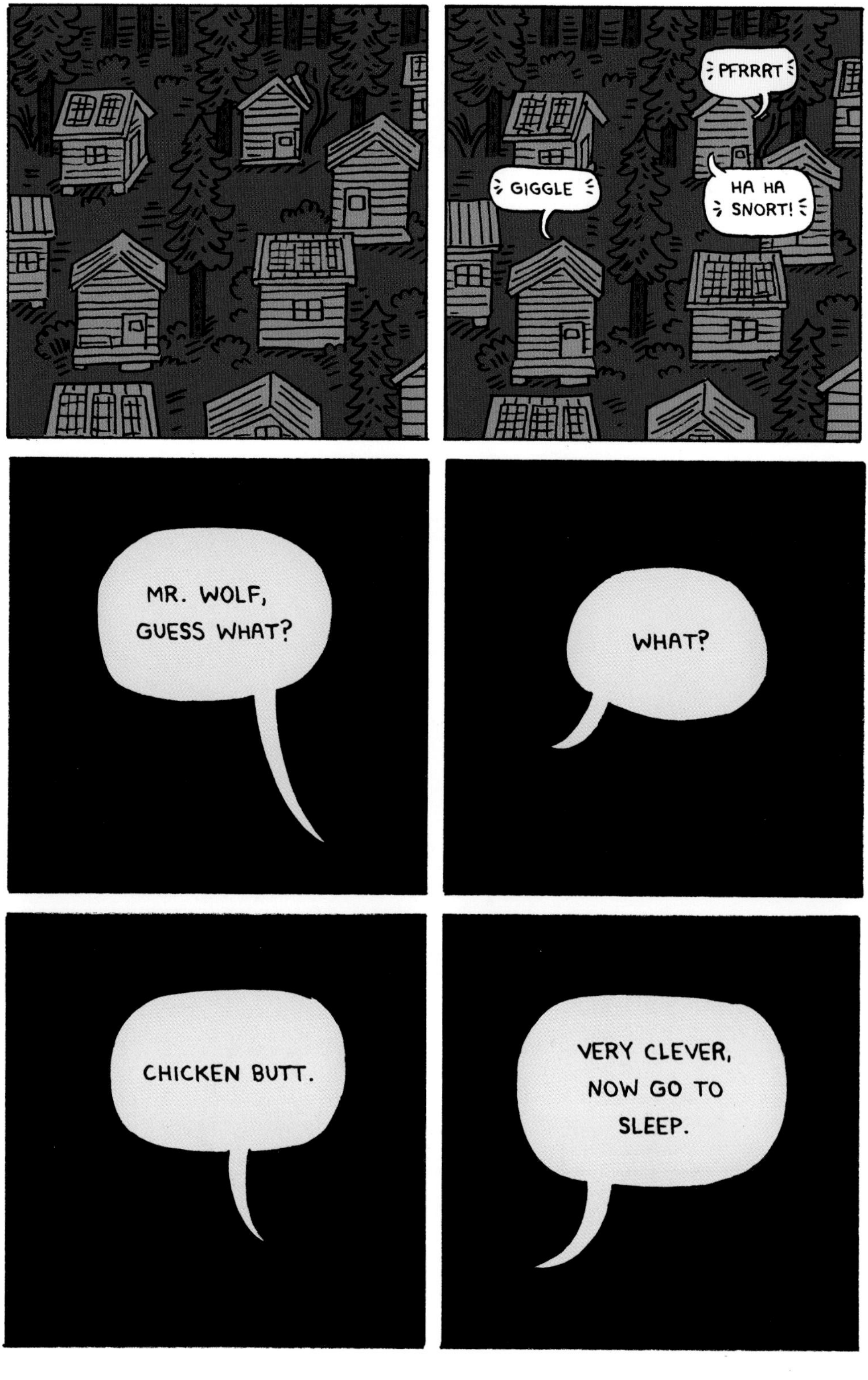
PFRRRT
GIGGLE
HA HA SNORT!
MR. WOLF, GUESS WHAT?
WHAT?
CHICKEN BUTT.
VERY CLEVER, NOW GO TO SLEEP.

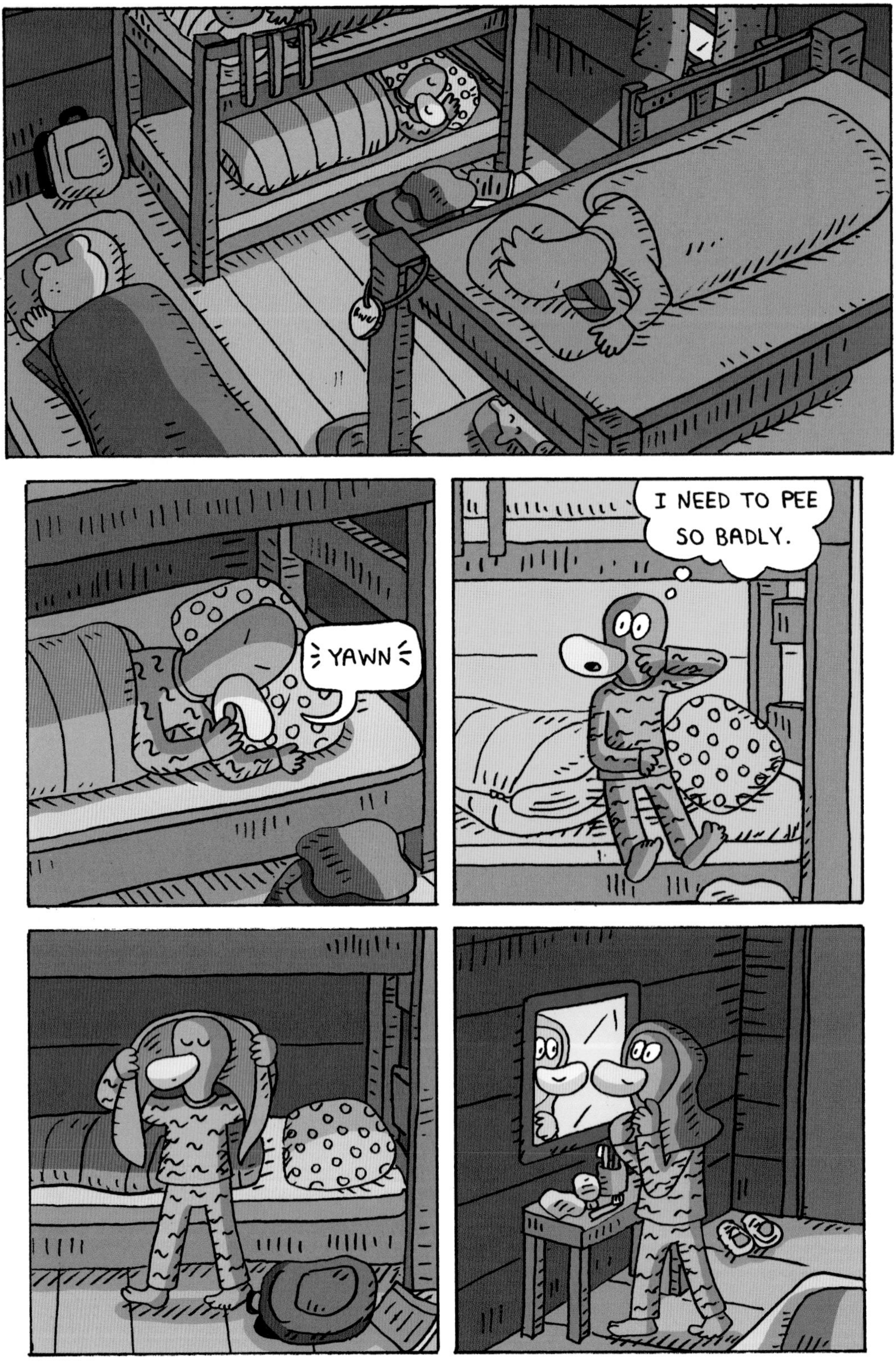
YAWN
I NEED TO PEE SO BADLY.

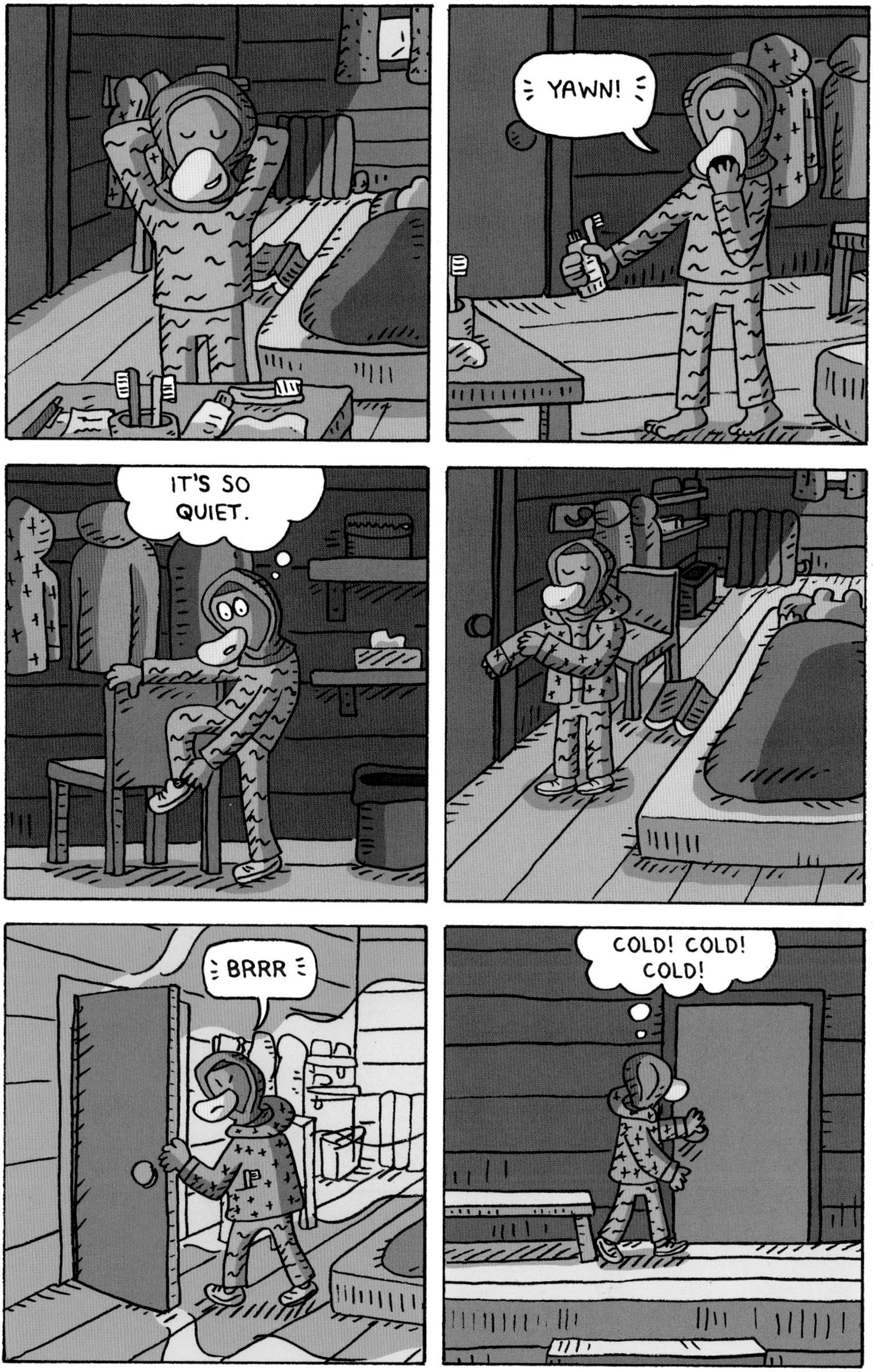
YAWN!
IT'S SO QUIET.
BRRR
COLD! COLD! COLD!

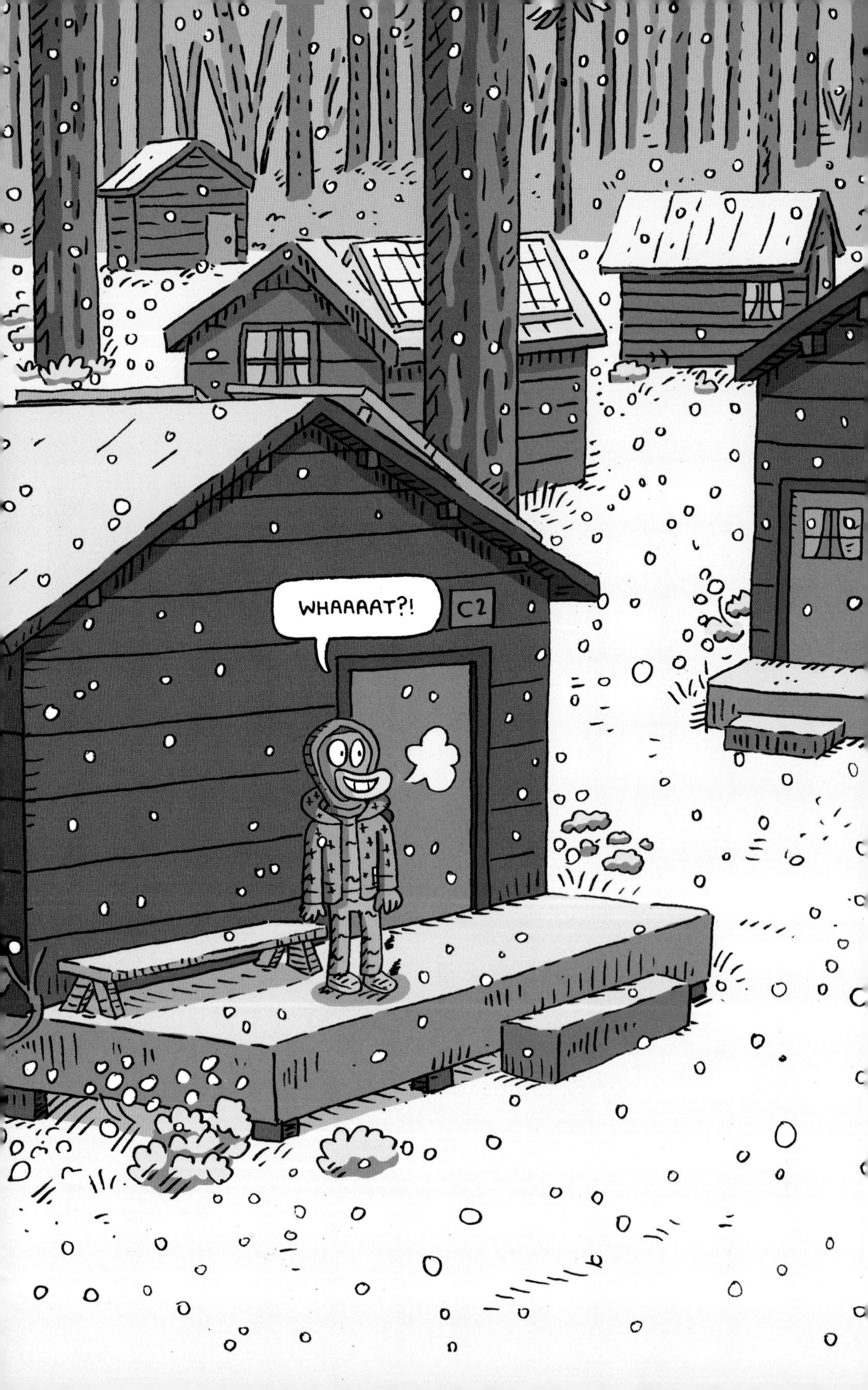
WHAAAAT?!
C2

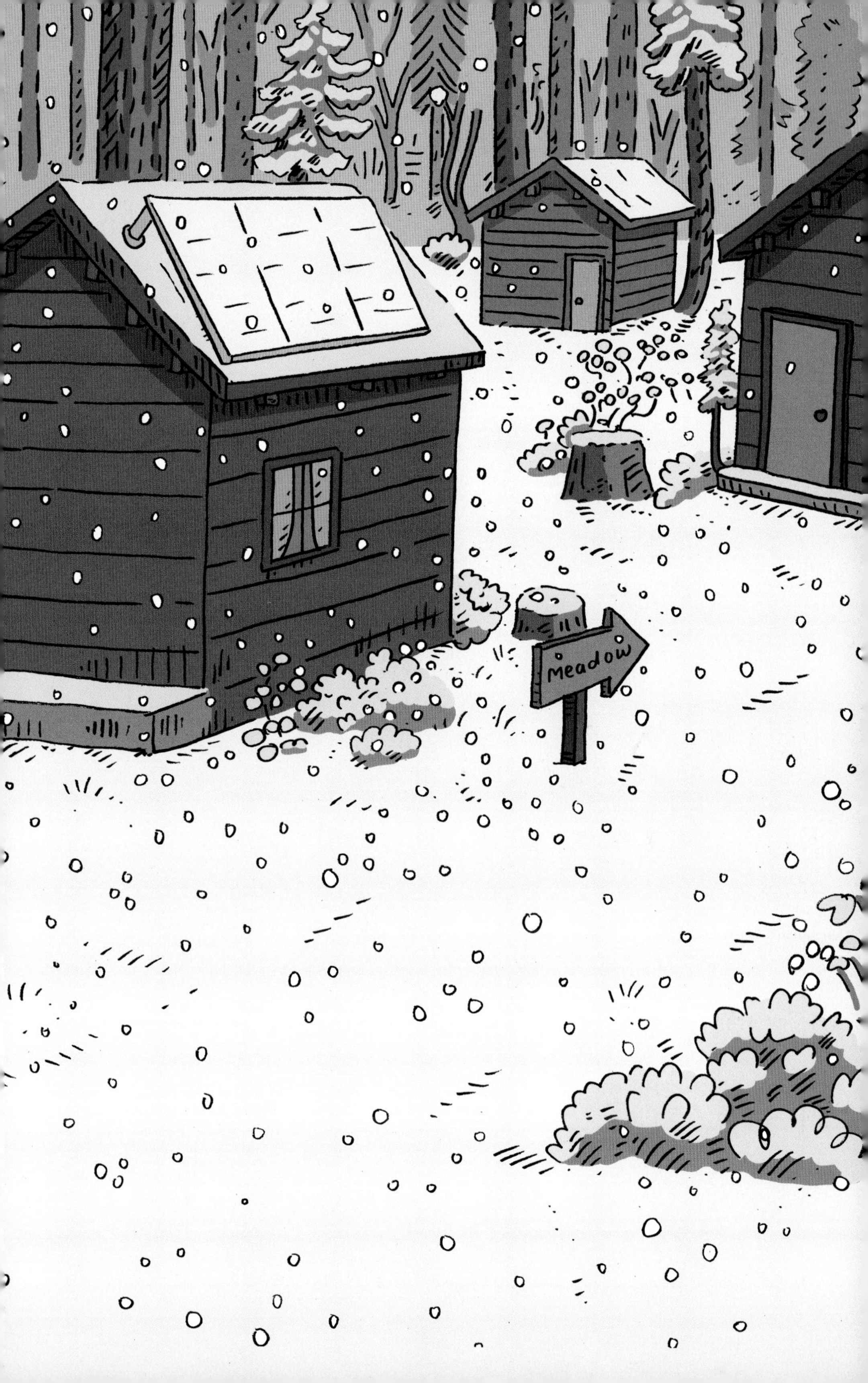
Meadow

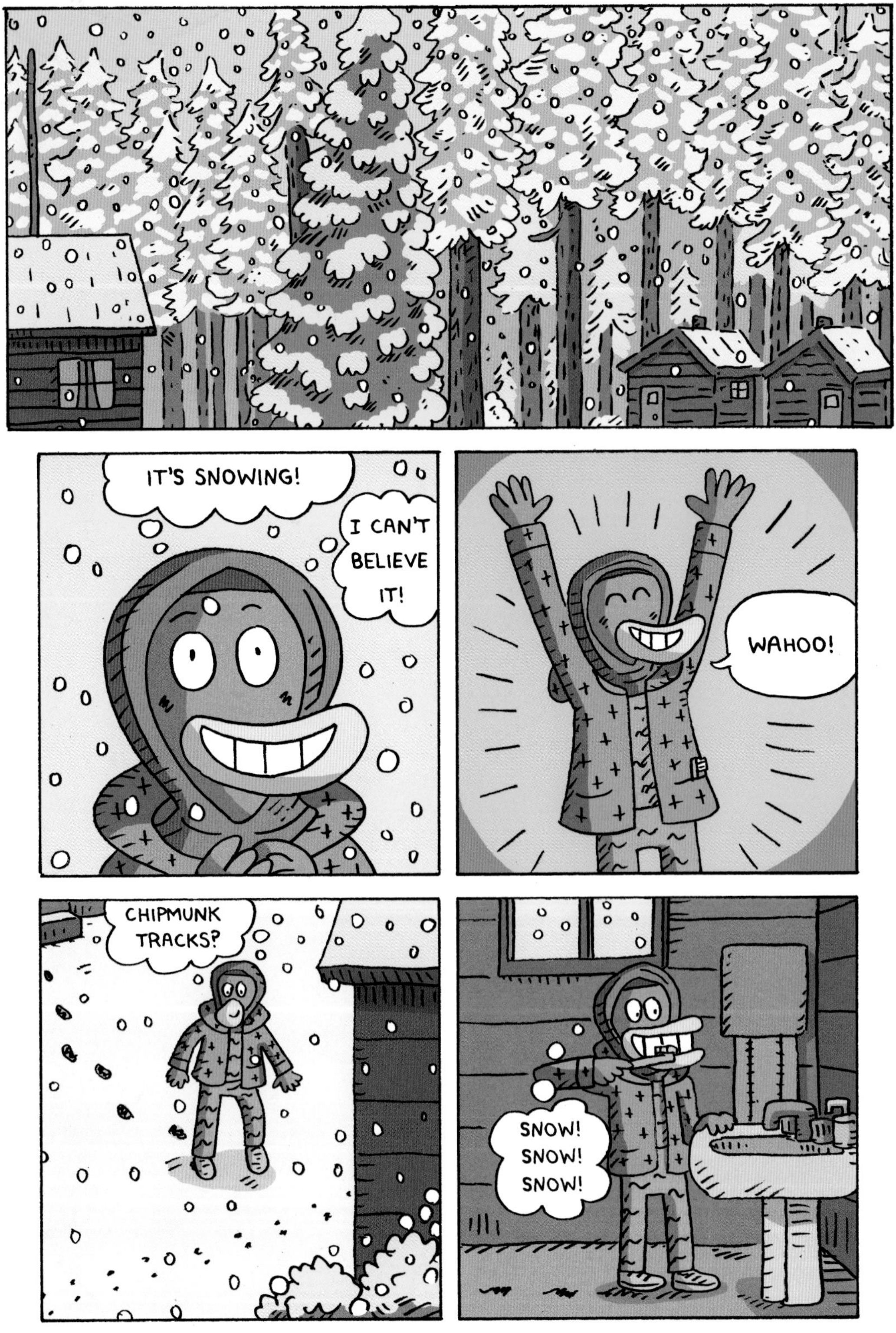
IT'S SNOWING!
I CAN'T BELIEVE IT!
WAHOO!
CHIPMUNK TRACKS?
SNOW! SNOW! SNOW!

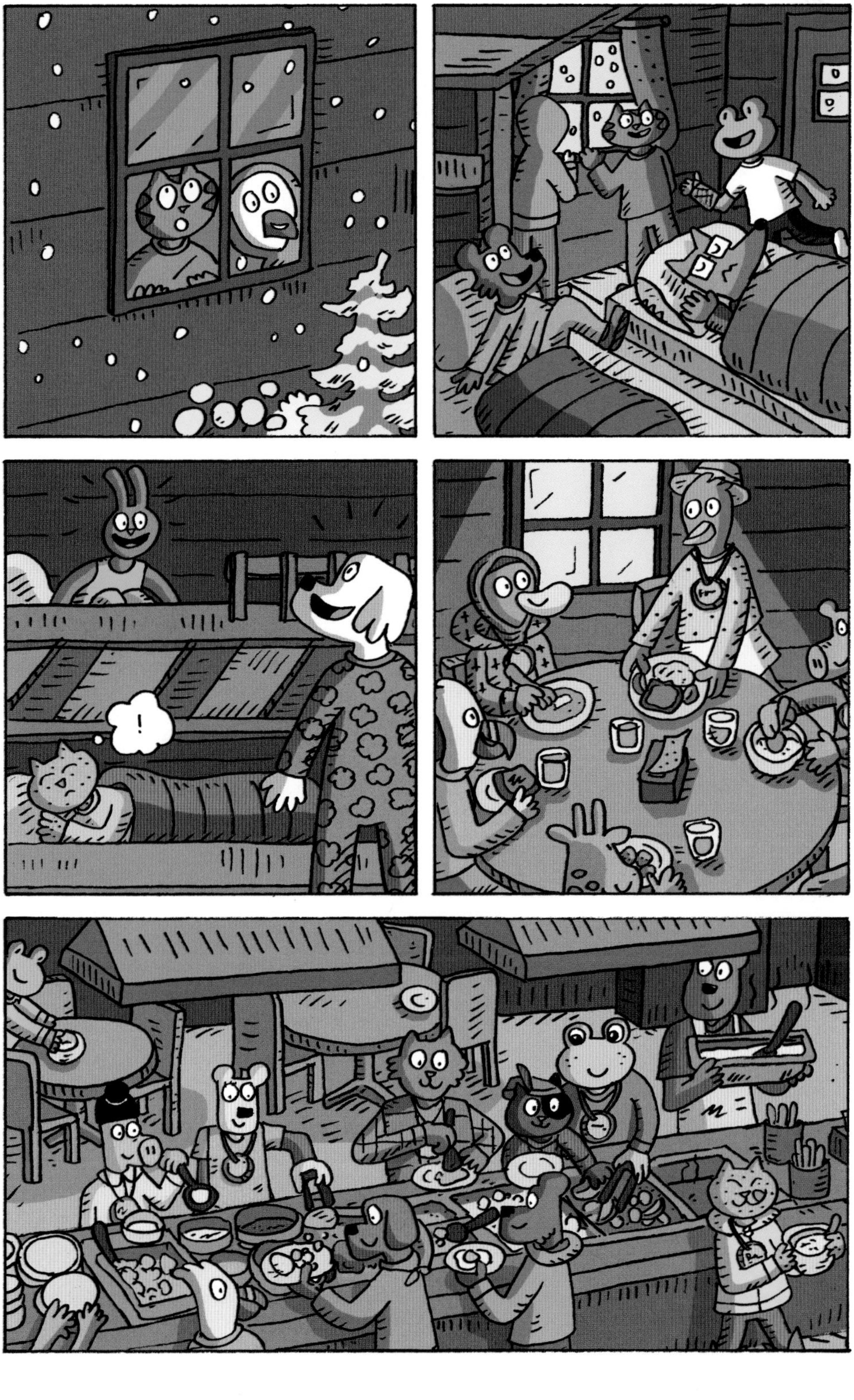
!

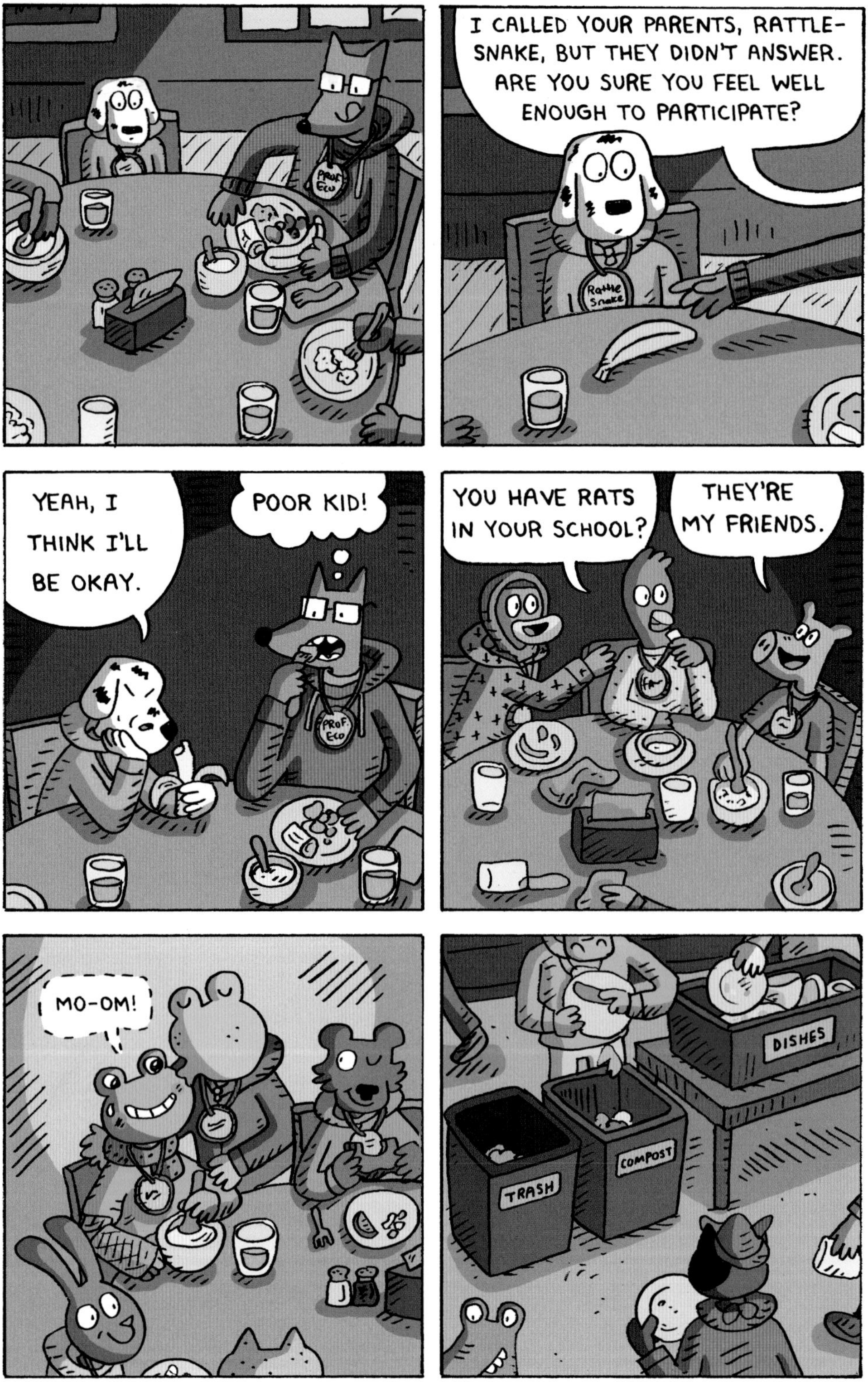
I CALLED YOUR PARENTS, RATTLESNAKE, BUT THEY DIDN'T ANSWER. ARE YOU SURE YOU FEEL WELL ENOUGH TO PARTICIPATE?
YEAH, I THINK I'LL BE OKAY.
POOR KID!
YOU HAVE RATS IN YOUR SCHOOL?
THEY'RE MY FRIENDS.
MO-OM!
DISHES
COMPOST
TRASH

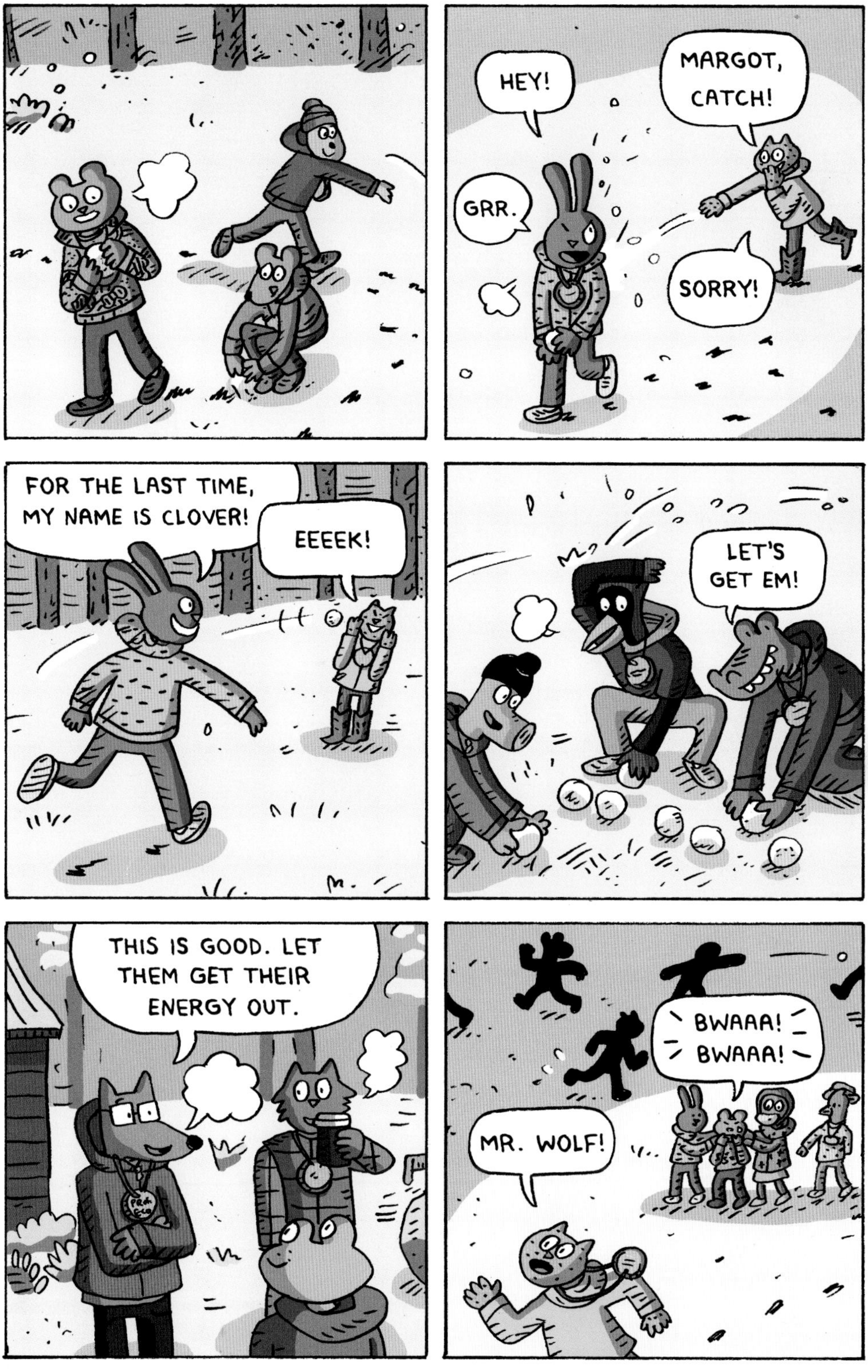
HEY!
MARGOT, CATCH!
GRR.
SORRY!
FOR THE LAST TIME, MY NAME IS CLOVER!
EEEEK!
LET'S GET EM!
THIS IS GOOD. LET THEM GET THEIR ENERGY OUT.
BWAAA! BWAAA!
MR. WOLF!

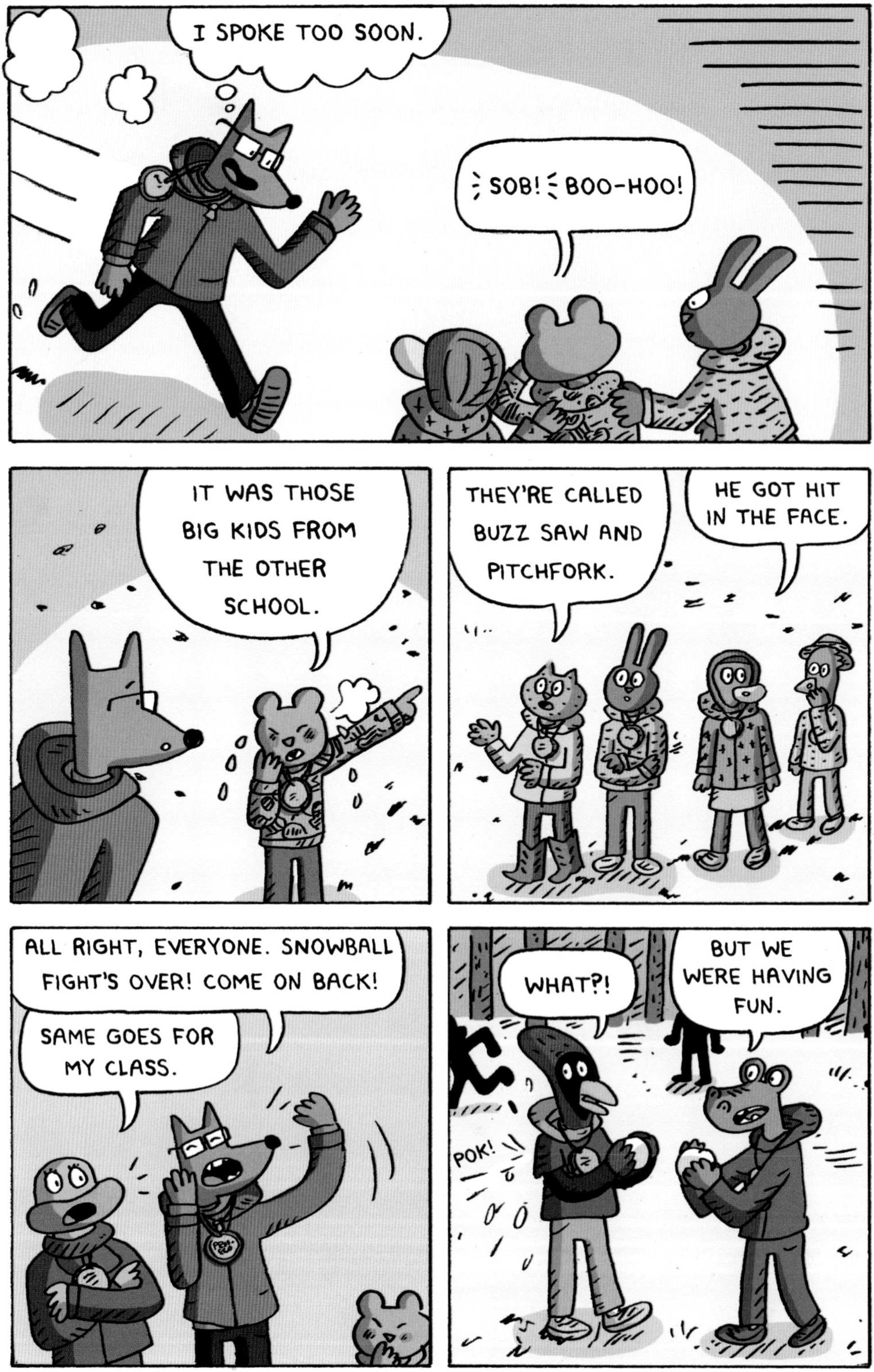
I SPOKE TOO SOON.
SOB! BOO-HOO!
IT WAS THOSE BIG KIDS FROM THE OTHER SCHOOL.
THEY'RE CALLED BUZZ SAW AND PITCHFORK.
HE GOT HIT IN THE FACE.
ALL RIGHT, EVERYONE. SNOWBALL FIGHT'S OVER! COME ON BACK!
SAME GOES FOR MY CLASS.
WHAT?!
BUT WE WERE HAVING FUN.
POK!

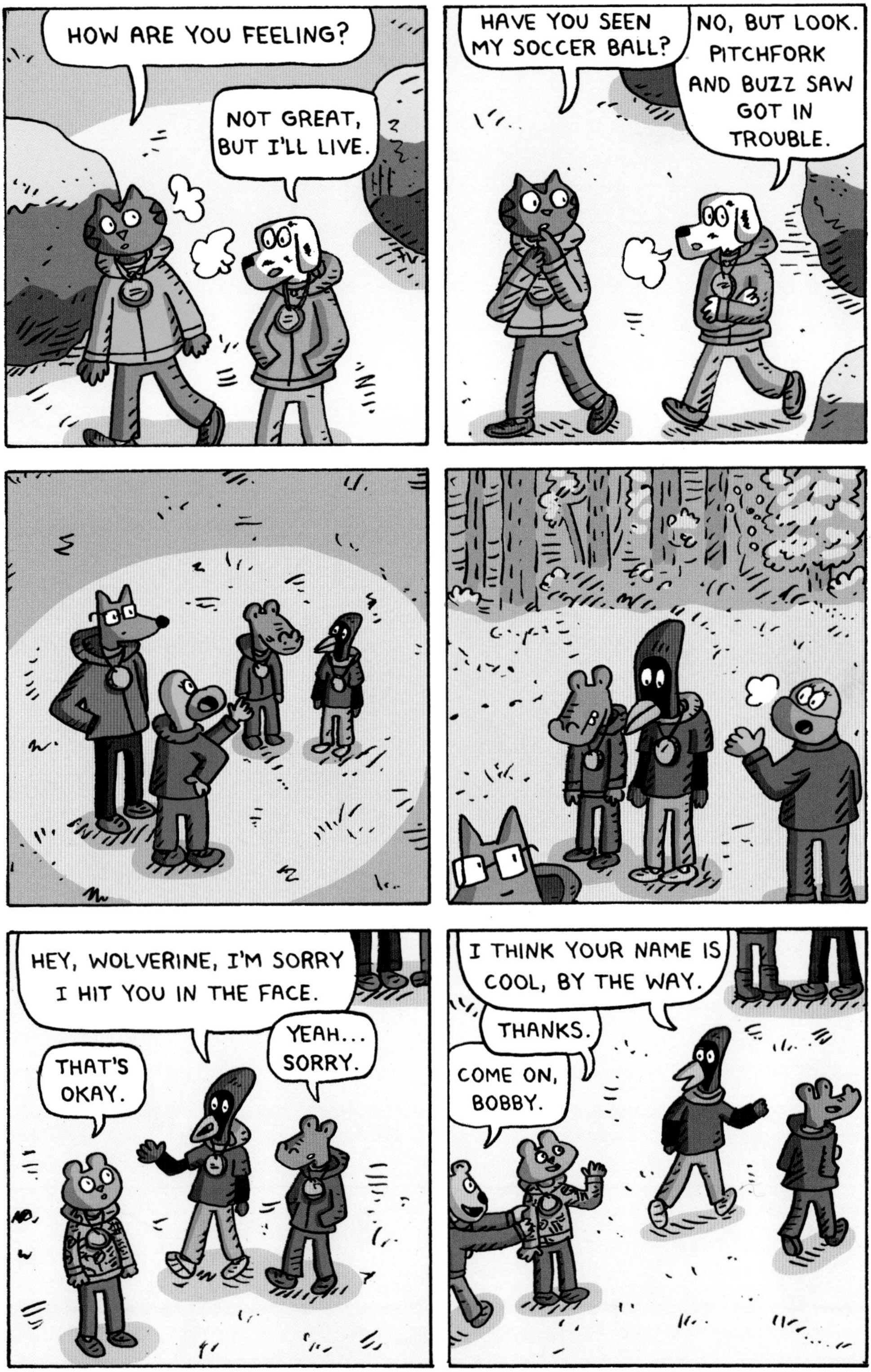
HOW ARE YOU FEELING?
NOT GREAT, BUT I'LL LIVE.
HAVE YOU SEEN MY SOCCER BALL?
NO, BUT LOOK. PITCHFORK AND BUZZ SAW GOT IN TROUBLE.
HEY, WOLVERINE, I'M SORRY I HIT YOU IN THE FACE.
THAT'S OKAY.
YEAH... SORRY.
I THINK YOUR NAME IS COOL, BY THE WAY.
THANKS.
COME ON, BOBBY.

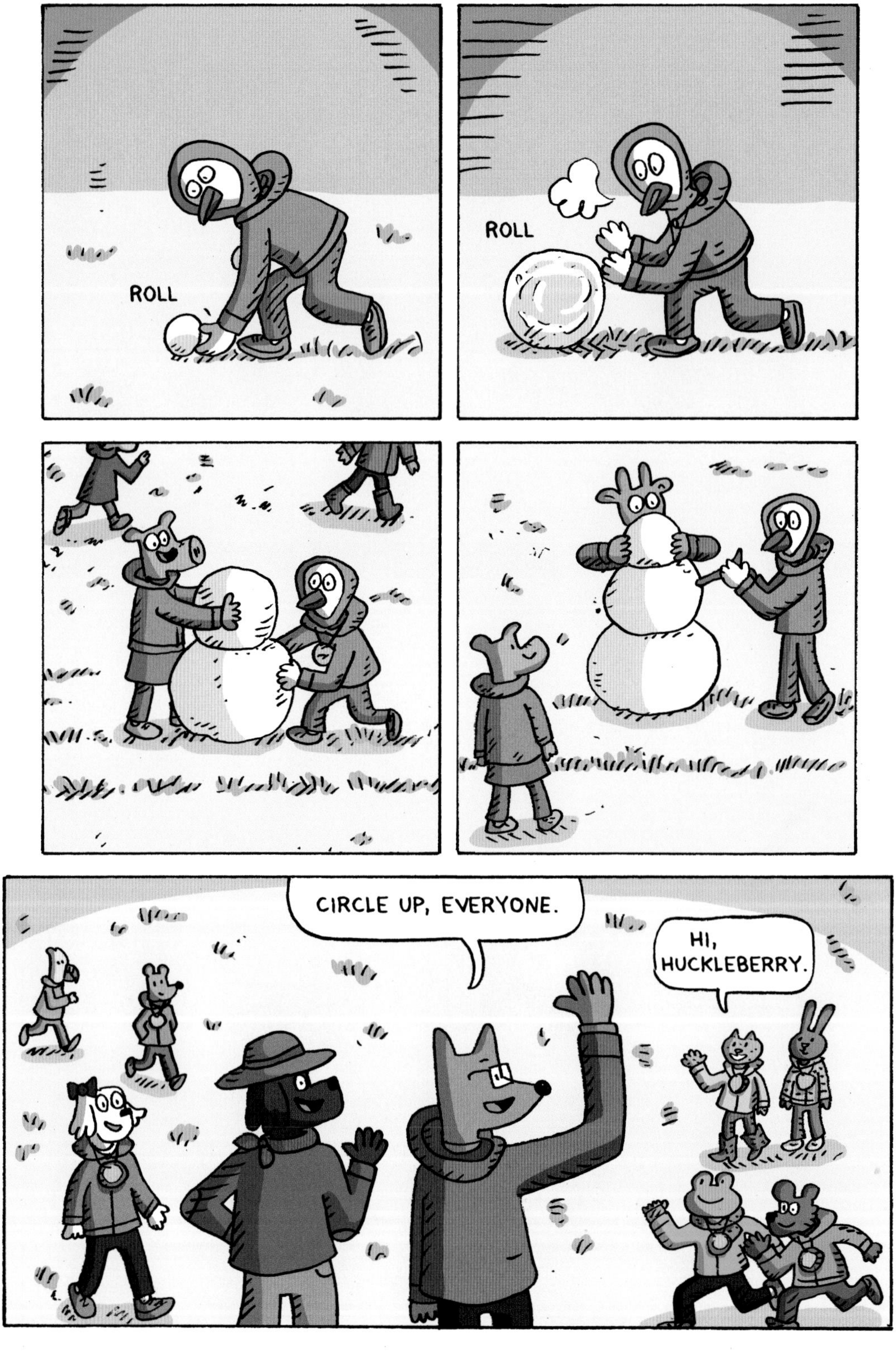
ROLL
ROLL
CIRCLE UP, EVERYONE.
HI, HUCKLEBERRY.

CHAPTER NINE
A Rare Sight

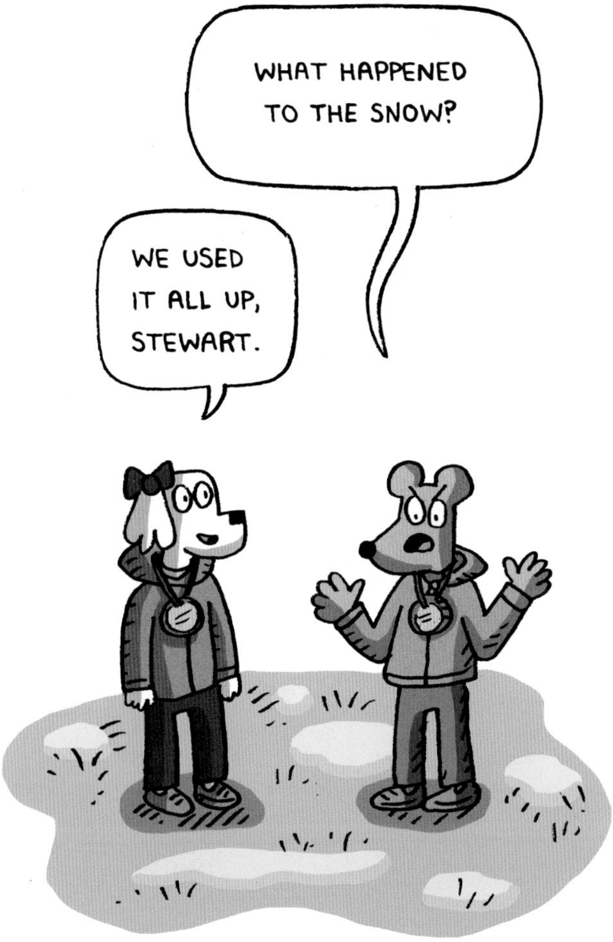
WHAT HAPPENED TO THE SNOW?
WE USED IT ALL UP, STEWART.

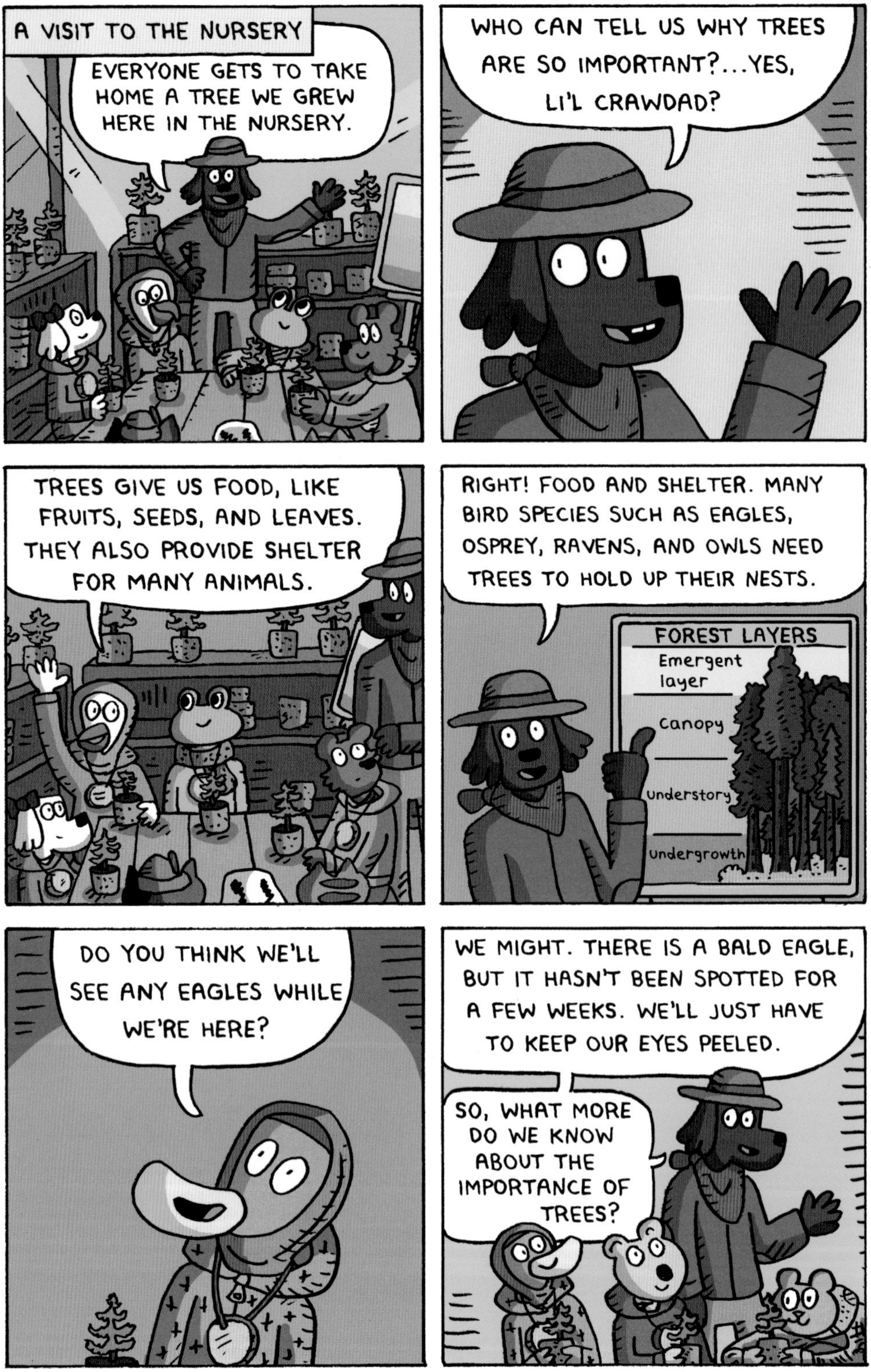
A VISIT TO THE NURSERY
EVERYONE GETS TO TAKE HOME A TREE WE GREW HERE IN THE NURSERY.
WHO CAN TELL US WHY TREES ARE SO IMPORTANT?...YES, LI'L CRAWDAD?
TREES GIVE US FOOD, LIKE FRUITS, SEEDS, AND LEAVES. THEY ALSO PROVIDE SHELTER FOR MANY ANIMALS.
RIGHT! FOOD AND SHELTER. MANY BIRD SPECIES SUCH AS EAGLES, OSPREY, RAVENS, AND OWLS NEED TREES TO HOLD UP THEIR NESTS.
FOREST LAYERS
Emergent layer
Canopy
understory
undergrowth
DO YOU THINK WE'LL SEE ANY EAGLES WHILE WE'RE HERE?
WE MIGHT. THERE IS A BALD EAGLE, BUT IT HASN'T BEEN SPOTTED FOR A FEW WEEKS. WE'LL JUST HAVE TO KEEP OUR EYES PEELED.
SO, WHAT MORE DO WE KNOW ABOUT THE IMPORTANCE OF TREES?

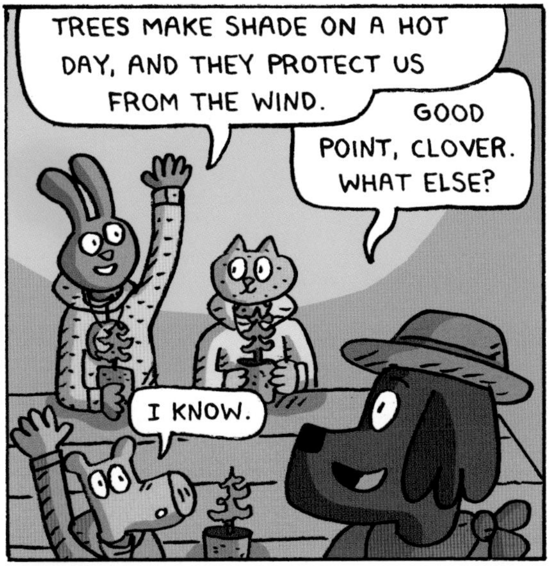
TREES MAKE SHADE ON A HOT DAY, AND THEY PROTECT US FROM THE WIND.
GOOD POINT, CLOVER. WHAT ELSE?
I KNOW.

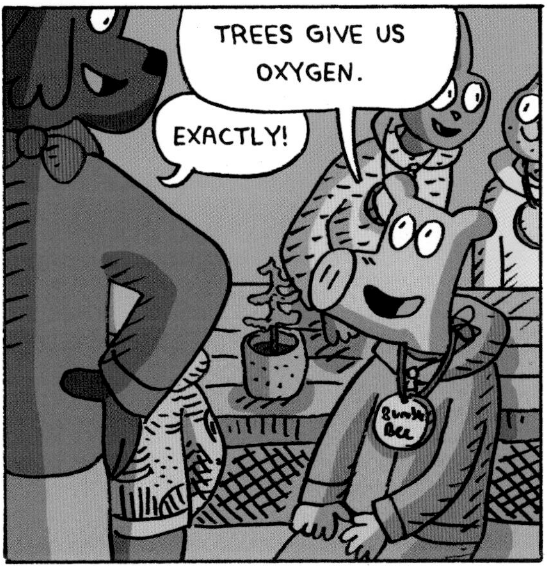
TREES GIVE US OXYGEN.
EXACTLY!

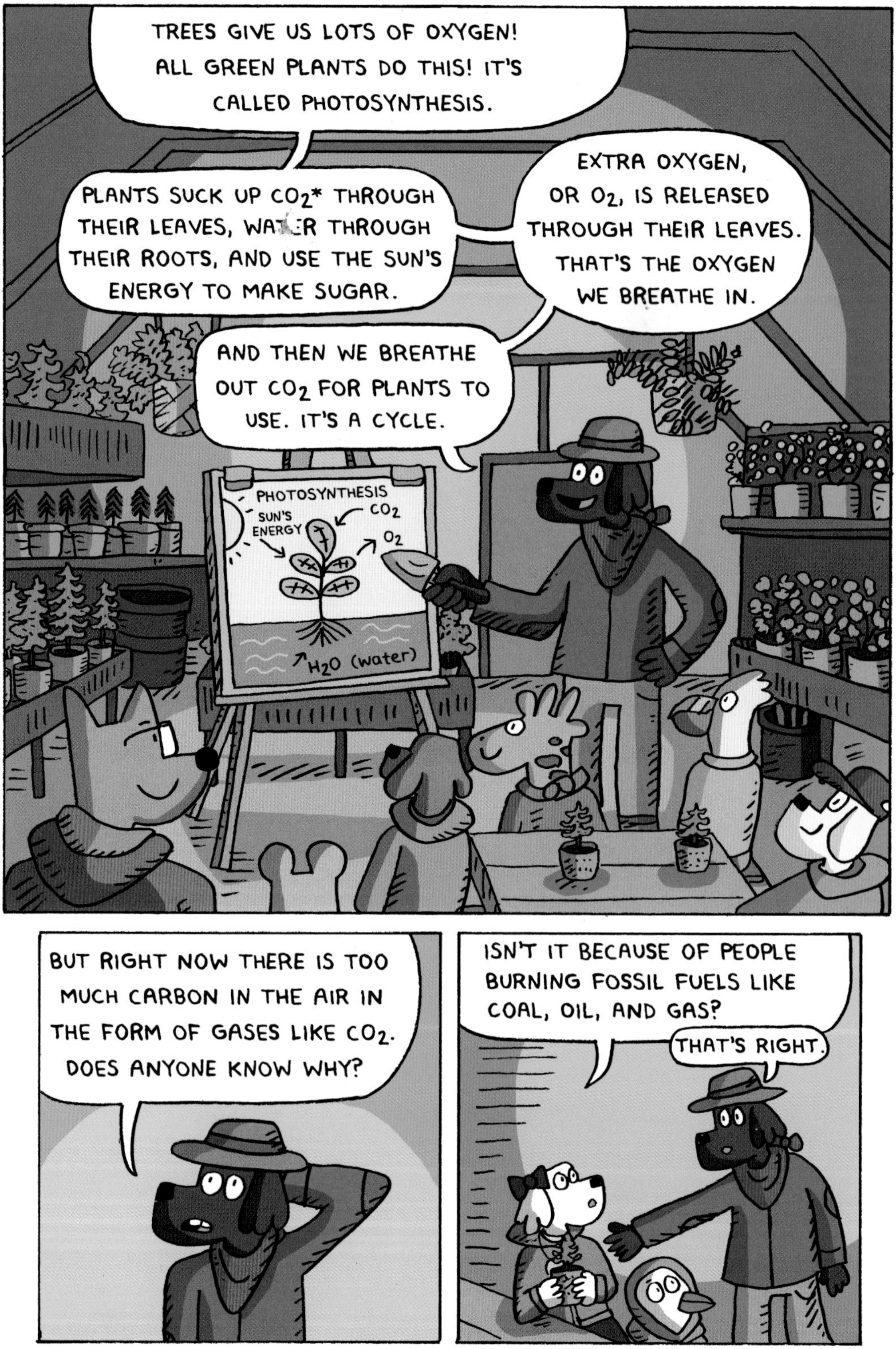
TREES GIVE US LOTS OF OXYGEN! ALL GREEN PLANTS DO THIS! IT'S CALLED PHOTOSYNTHESIS.
PLANTS SUCK UP CO_2* THROUGH THEIR LEAVES, WATER THROUGH THEIR ROOTS, AND USE THE SUN'S ENERGY TO MAKE SUGAR.
EXTRA OXYGEN, OR O_2, IS RELEASED THROUGH THEIR LEAVES. THAT'S THE OXYGEN WE BREATHE IN.
AND THEN WE BREATHE OUT CO_2 FOR PLANTS TO USE. IT'S A CYCLE.
PHOTOSYNTHESIS
SUN'S ENERGY
CO_2
O_2
H_2O (water)
BUT RIGHT NOW THERE IS TOO MUCH CARBON IN THE AIR IN THE FORM OF GASES LIKE CO_2. DOES ANYONE KNOW WHY?
ISN'T IT BECAUSE OF PEOPLE BURNING FOSSIL FUELS LIKE COAL, OIL, AND GAS?
THAT'S RIGHT.

*CARBON DIOXIDE

ALL THAT EXTRA CARBON IN THE ATMOSPHERE IS HEATING UP OUR PLANET AND IT'S MAKING OUR CLIMATE UNSTABLE. THAT'S WHAT WE CALL CLIMATE CHANGE, OR GLOBAL WARMING.

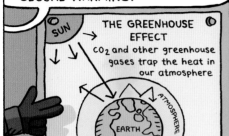

THE GREENHOUSE EFFECT
CO_2 and other greenhouse gases trap the heat in our atmosphere

SUN

ATMOSPHERE

EARTH

BUT WE CAN DO SOMETHING ABOUT IT BY USING LESS FOSSIL FUELS AND PROTECTING OUR FORESTS.

EACH OF YOU HAVE YOUR VERY OWN TOOL TO FIGHT CLIMATE CHANGE. PLANT A TREE TO SAVE OUR FUTURE! RAISE YOUR HAND IF YOU'RE READY TO FIGHT GLOBAL WARMING.

I AM!

YEAH!

I AM!

WE HAVE TO!

FOR SURE!

YES!

OF COURSE!

ME!

AND NOW, EVERYONE, WE'RE GOING TO GET READY FOR OUR NEXT AND FINAL ACTIVITY...A HIKE UP HORSE THIEF MOUNTAIN FOR THE MOST BEAUTIFUL VIEW YOU'VE EVER SEEN.

AND IT'LL BE YOUR LAST CHANCE TO GUESS MY NAME.

YES, BUMBLEBEE?

IS YOUR NAME PHOTOSYNTHESIS?

HA!... TRY AGAIN.

OXYGEN? CO_2?

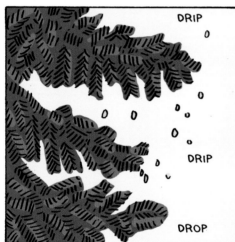

DRIP

DRIP

DROP

SO, ARE YOU GOING TO FINALLY TELL ME WHAT HAPPENED WITH YOU AND AZIZA?

I TOLD YOU WE HAD A LITTLE DISAGREEMENT.

JUST TELL ME, ALREADY.

OKAY, I WILL. WAIT UP.

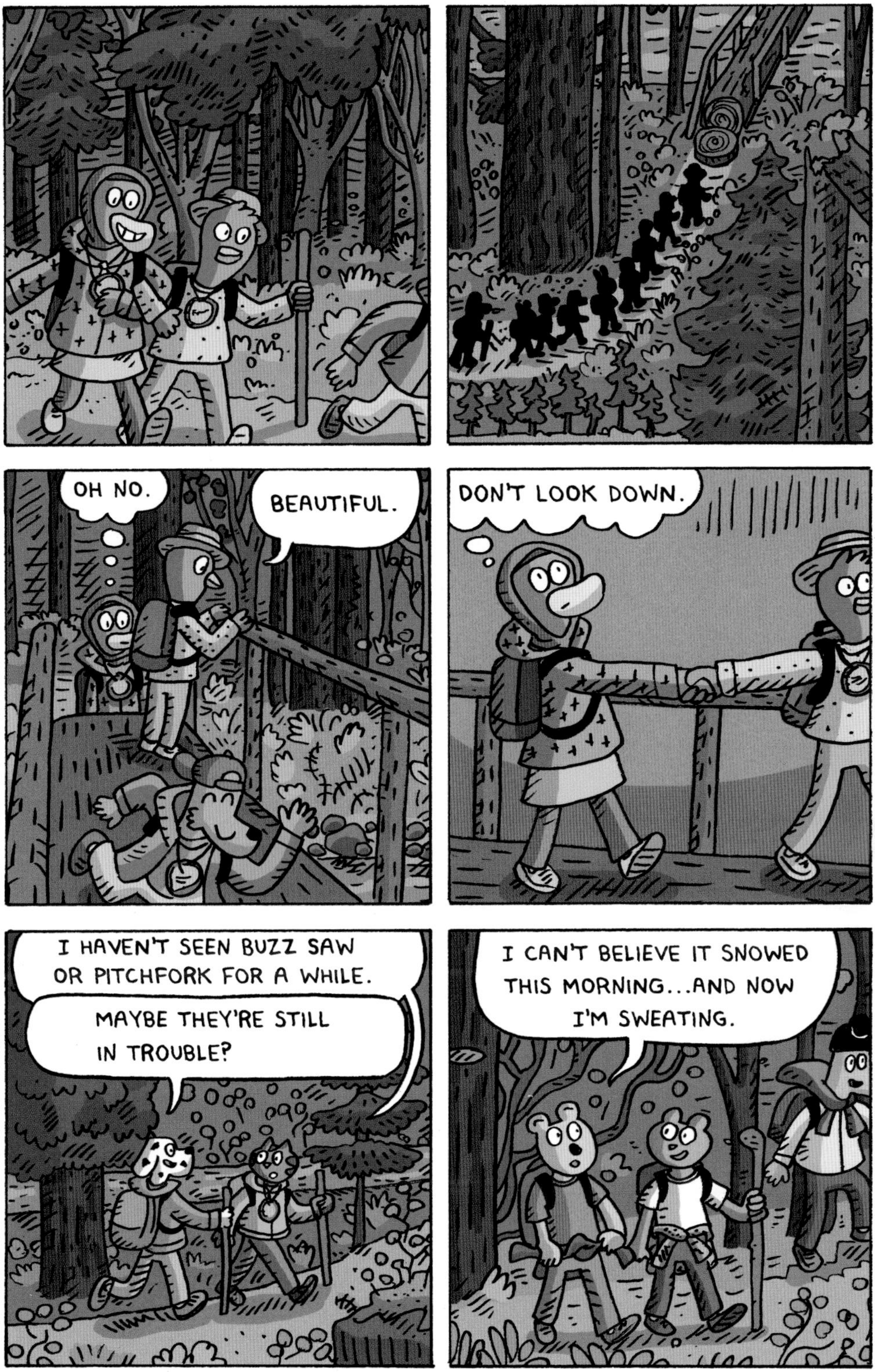
OH NO.
BEAUTIFUL.
DON'T LOOK DOWN.
I HAVEN'T SEEN BUZZ SAW OR PITCHFORK FOR A WHILE.
MAYBE THEY'RE STILL IN TROUBLE?
I CAN'T BELIEVE IT SNOWED THIS MORNING...AND NOW I'M SWEATING.

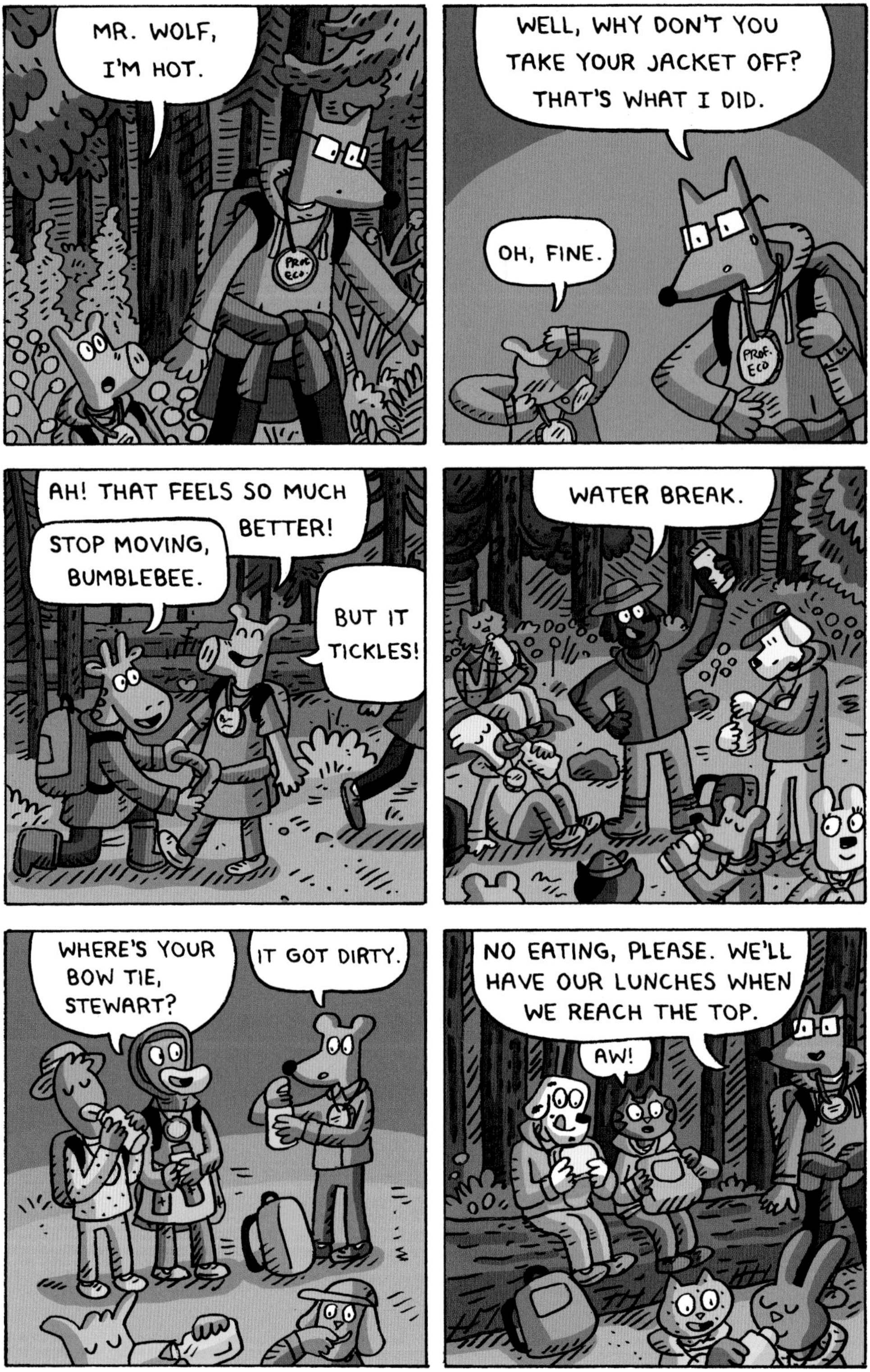
MR. WOLF, I'M HOT.
WELL, WHY DON'T YOU TAKE YOUR JACKET OFF? THAT'S WHAT I DID.
OH, FINE.
PROF. ECO
AH! THAT FEELS SO MUCH BETTER!
STOP MOVING, BUMBLEBEE.
BUT IT TICKLES!
WATER BREAK.
WHERE'S YOUR BOW TIE, STEWART?
IT GOT DIRTY.
NO EATING, PLEASE. WE'LL HAVE OUR LUNCHES WHEN WE REACH THE TOP.
AW!

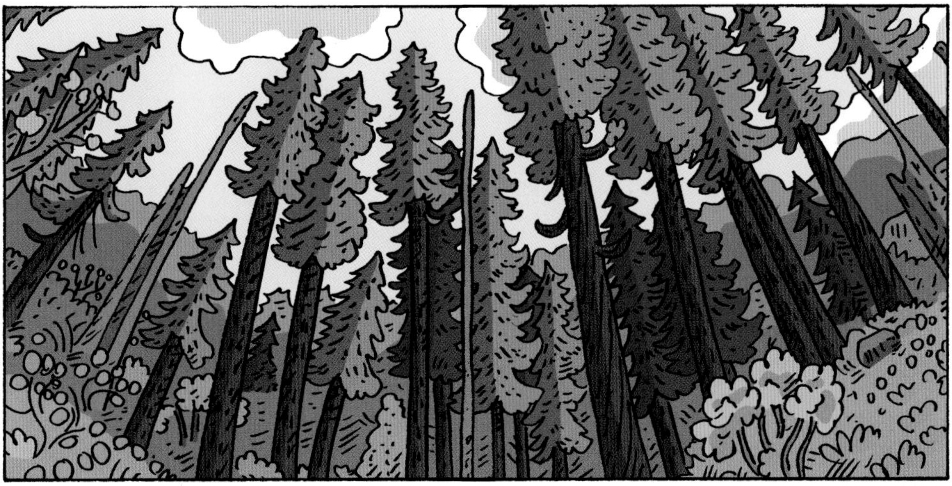

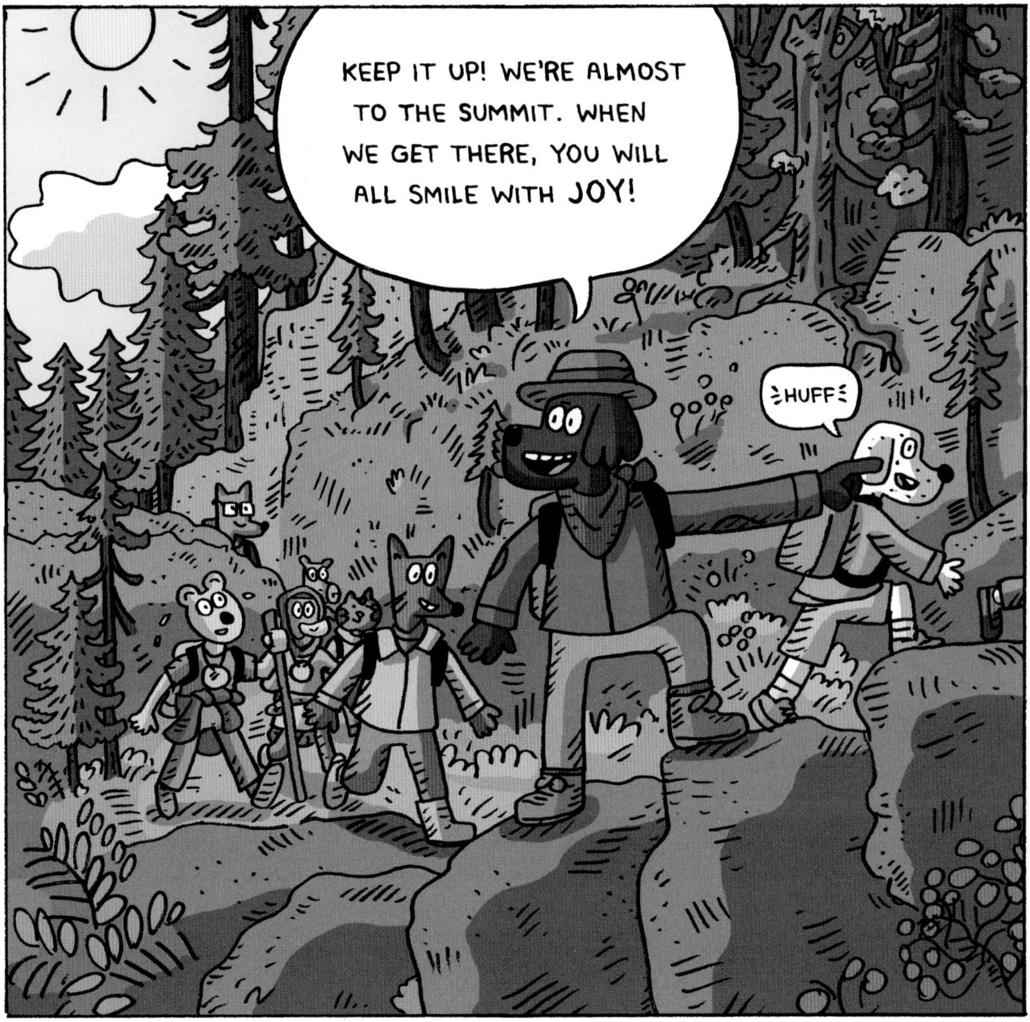
KEEP IT UP! WE'RE ALMOST TO THE SUMMIT. WHEN WE GET THERE, YOU WILL ALL SMILE WITH JOY!
HUFF

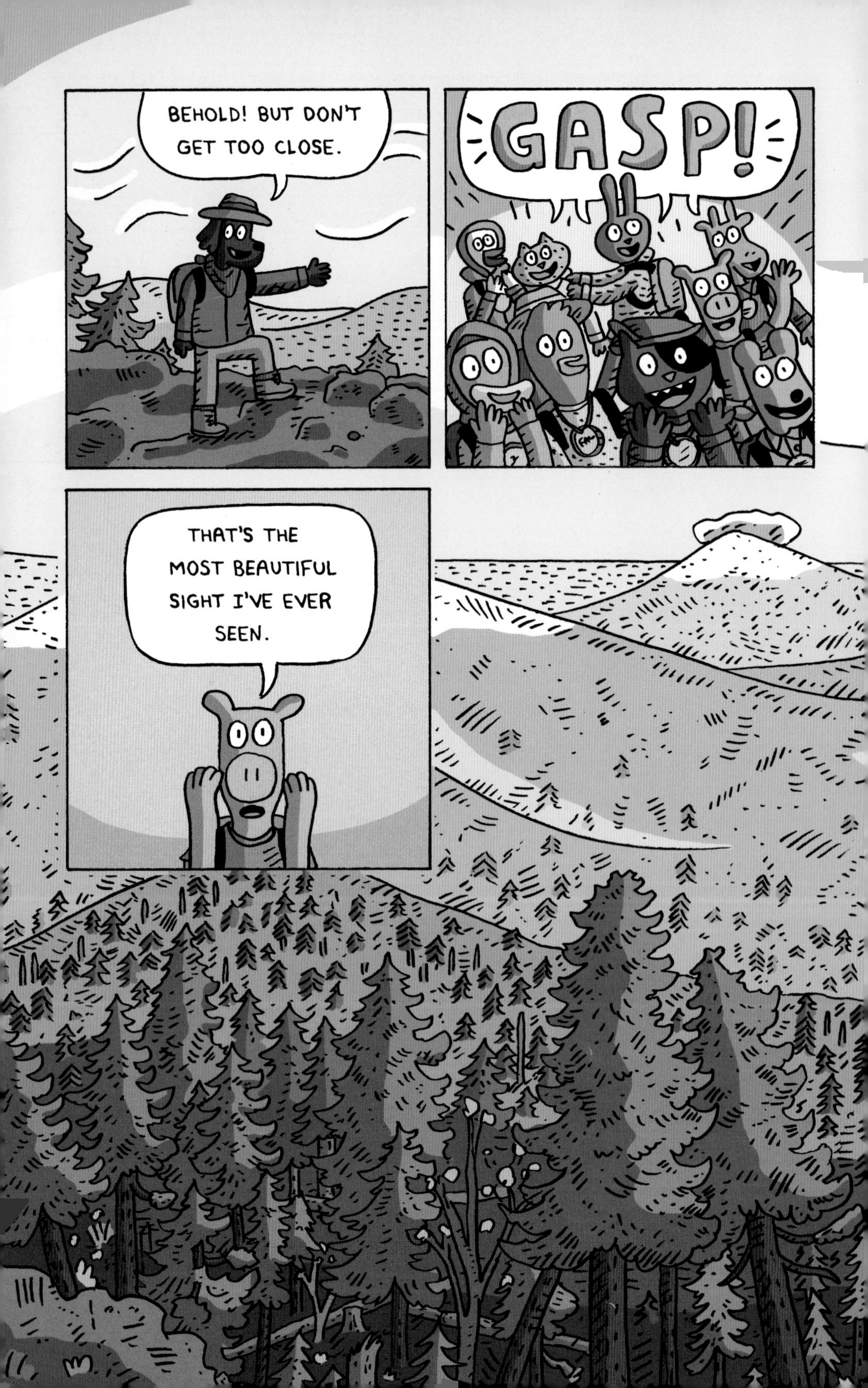
BEHOLD! BUT DON'T GET TOO CLOSE.
GASP!
THAT'S THE MOST BEAUTIFUL SIGHT I'VE EVER SEEN.

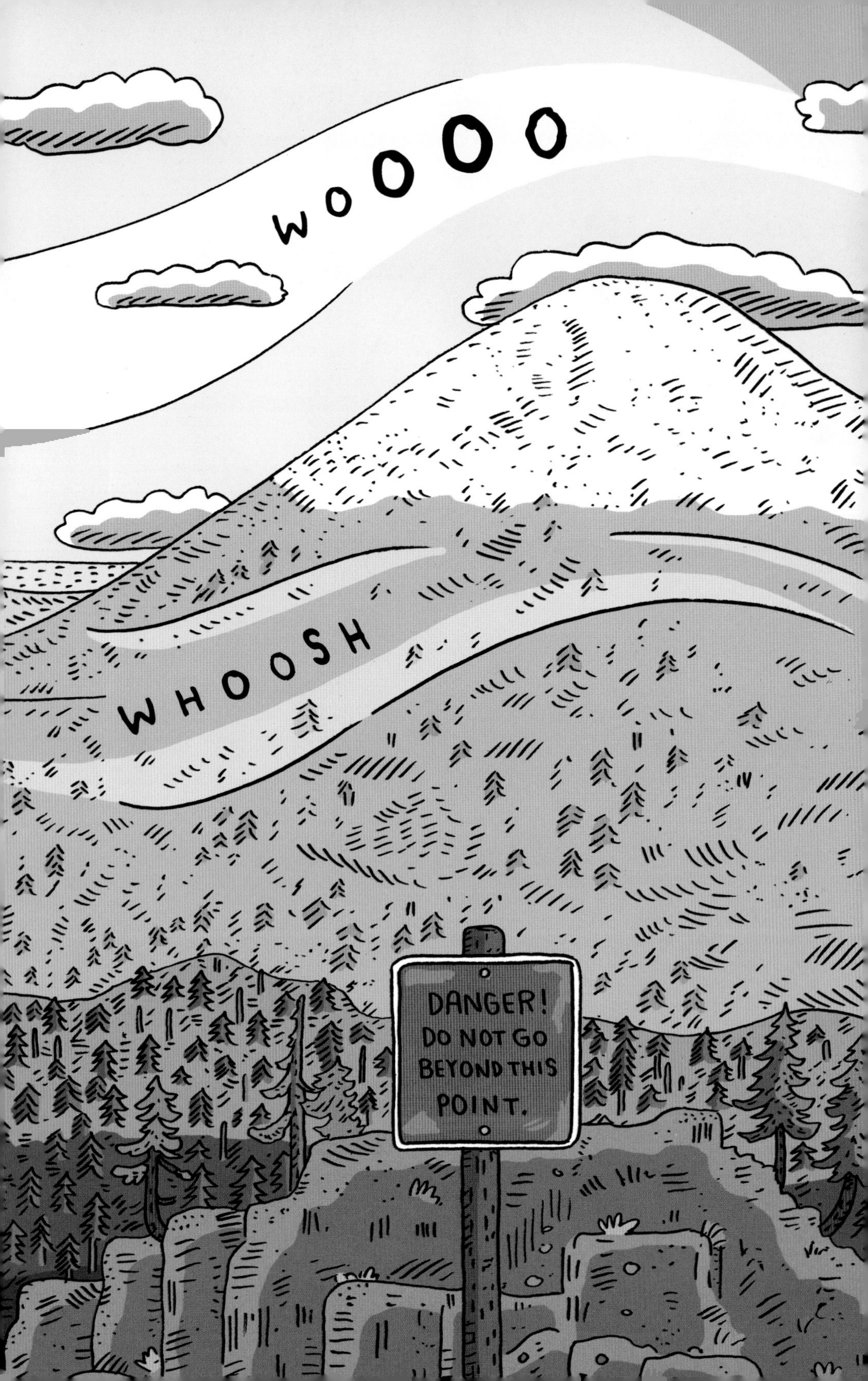
WOOOO
WHOOSH
DANGER! DO NOT GO BEYOND THIS POINT.

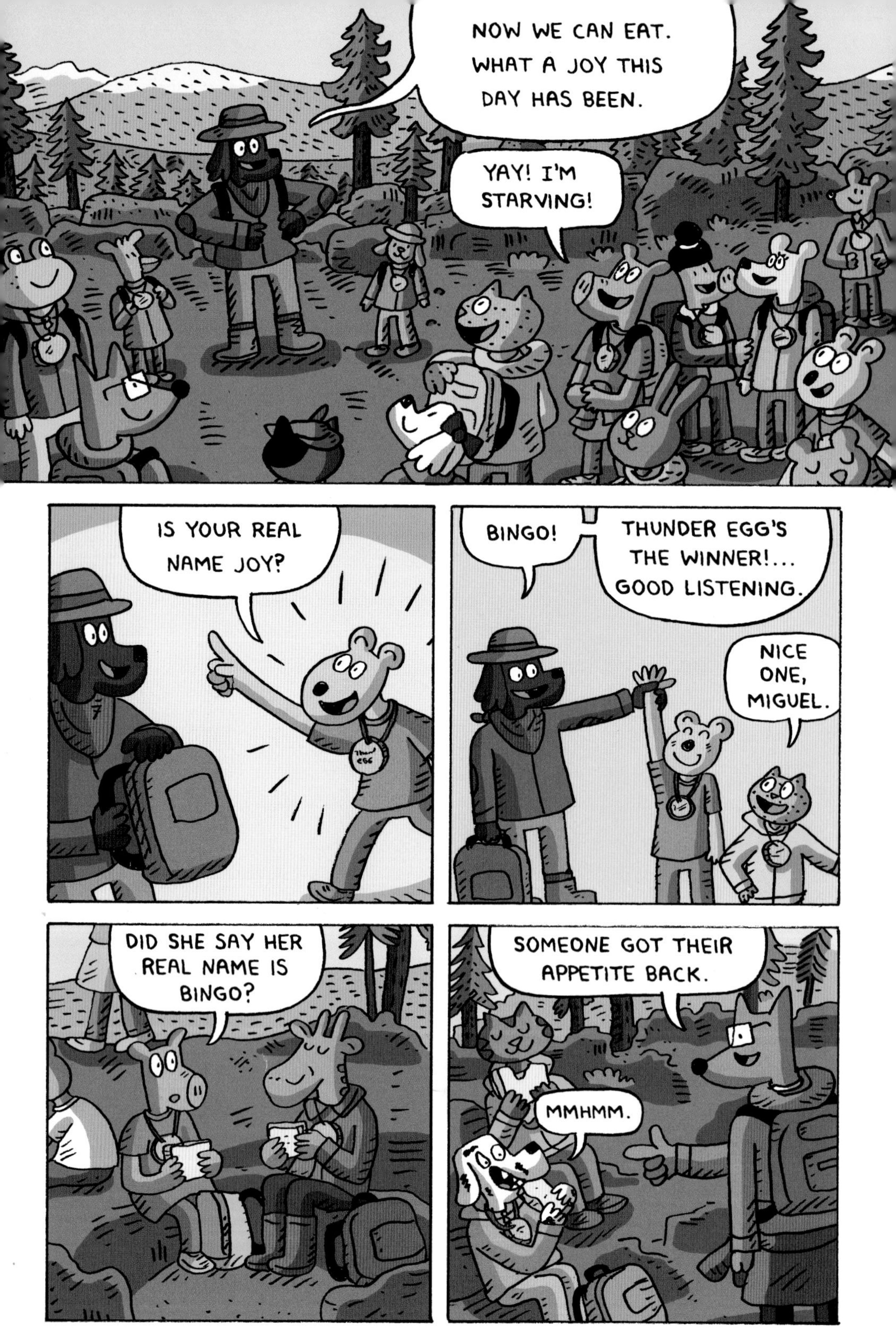
NOW WE CAN EAT. WHAT A JOY THIS DAY HAS BEEN.
YAY! I'M STARVING!
IS YOUR REAL NAME JOY?
BINGO!
THUNDER EGG'S THE WINNER!... GOOD LISTENING.
NICE ONE, MIGUEL.
DID SHE SAY HER REAL NAME IS BINGO?
SOMEONE GOT THEIR APPETITE BACK.
MMHMM.

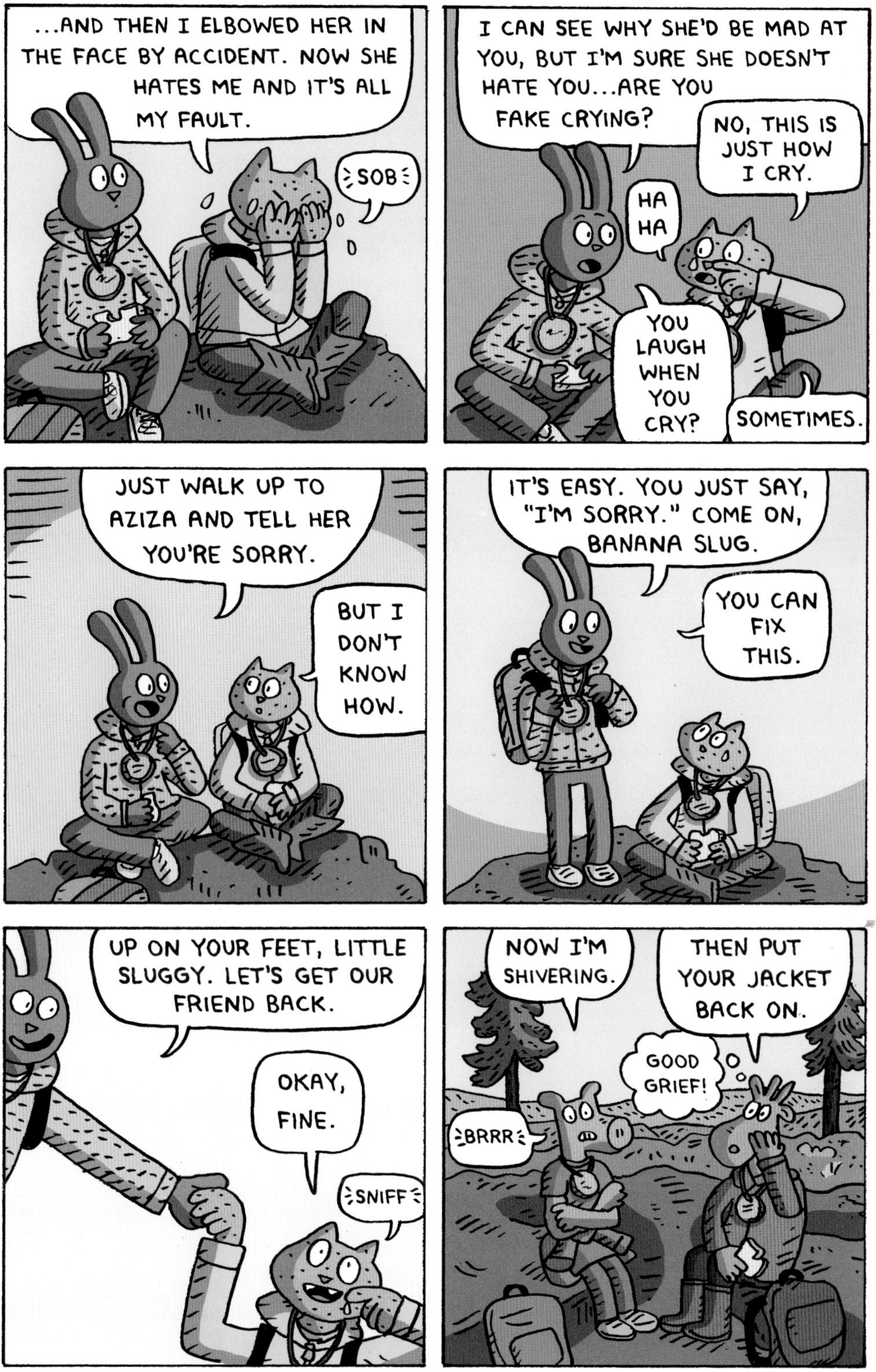
...AND THEN I ELBOWED HER IN THE FACE BY ACCIDENT. NOW SHE HATES ME AND IT'S ALL MY FAULT.
SOB
I CAN SEE WHY SHE'D BE MAD AT YOU, BUT I'M SURE SHE DOESN'T HATE YOU...ARE YOU FAKE CRYING?
NO, THIS IS JUST HOW I CRY.
HA HA
YOU LAUGH WHEN YOU CRY?
SOMETIMES.
JUST WALK UP TO AZIZA AND TELL HER YOU'RE SORRY.
BUT I DON'T KNOW HOW.
IT'S EASY. YOU JUST SAY, "I'M SORRY." COME ON, BANANA SLUG.
YOU CAN FIX THIS.
UP ON YOUR FEET, LITTLE SLUGGY. LET'S GET OUR FRIEND BACK.
OKAY, FINE.
SNIFF
NOW I'M SHIVERING.
THEN PUT YOUR JACKET BACK ON.
GOOD GRIEF!
BRRR

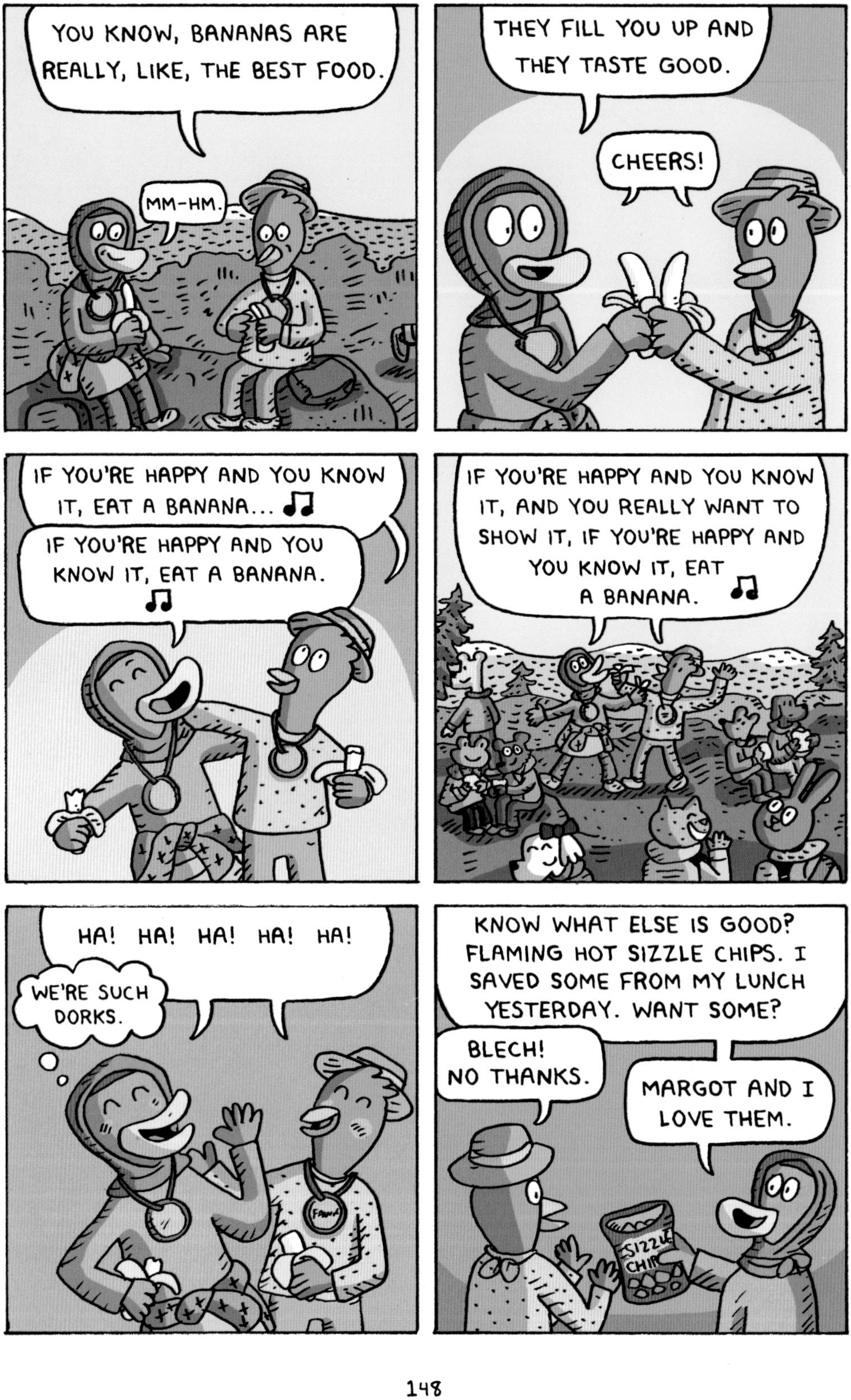
YOU KNOW, BANANAS ARE REALLY, LIKE, THE BEST FOOD.
MM-HM.
THEY FILL YOU UP AND THEY TASTE GOOD.
CHEERS!
IF YOU'RE HAPPY AND YOU KNOW IT, EAT A BANANA... ♫
IF YOU'RE HAPPY AND YOU KNOW IT, EAT A BANANA. ♫
IF YOU'RE HAPPY AND YOU KNOW IT, AND YOU REALLY WANT TO SHOW IT, IF YOU'RE HAPPY AND YOU KNOW IT, EAT A BANANA. ♫
HA! HA! HA! HA! HA!
WE'RE SUCH DORKS.
KNOW WHAT ELSE IS GOOD? FLAMING HOT SIZZLE CHIPS. I SAVED SOME FROM MY LUNCH YESTERDAY. WANT SOME?
BLECH! NO THANKS.
MARGOT AND I LOVE THEM.

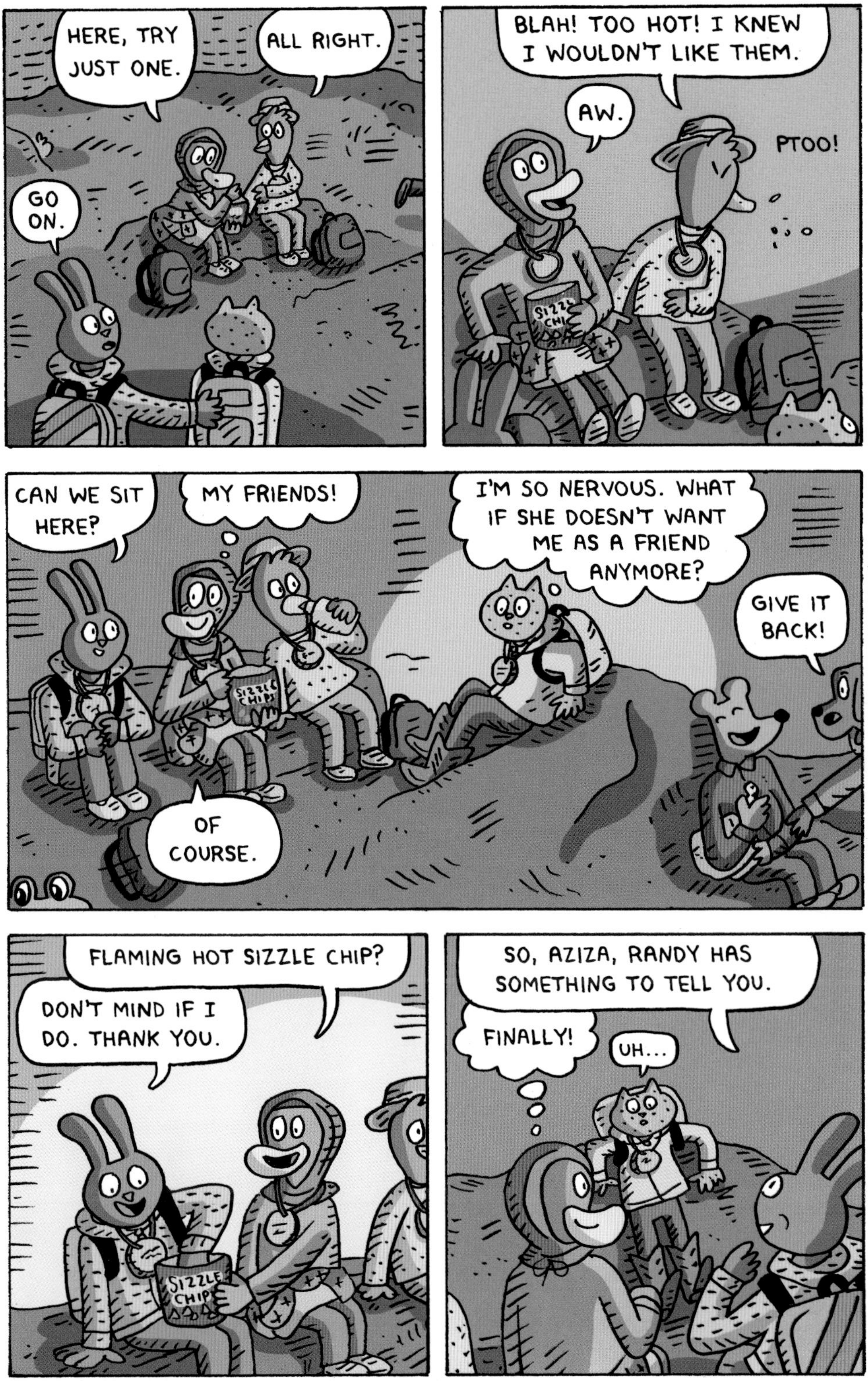
HERE, TRY JUST ONE.
ALL RIGHT.
GO ON.
BLAH! TOO HOT! I KNEW I WOULDN'T LIKE THEM.
AW.
PTOO!
CAN WE SIT HERE?
MY FRIENDS!
OF COURSE.
I'M SO NERVOUS. WHAT IF SHE DOESN'T WANT ME AS A FRIEND ANYMORE?
GIVE IT BACK!
FLAMING HOT SIZZLE CHIP?
DON'T MIND IF I DO. THANK YOU.
SO, AZIZA, RANDY HAS SOMETHING TO TELL YOU.
FINALLY!
UH...

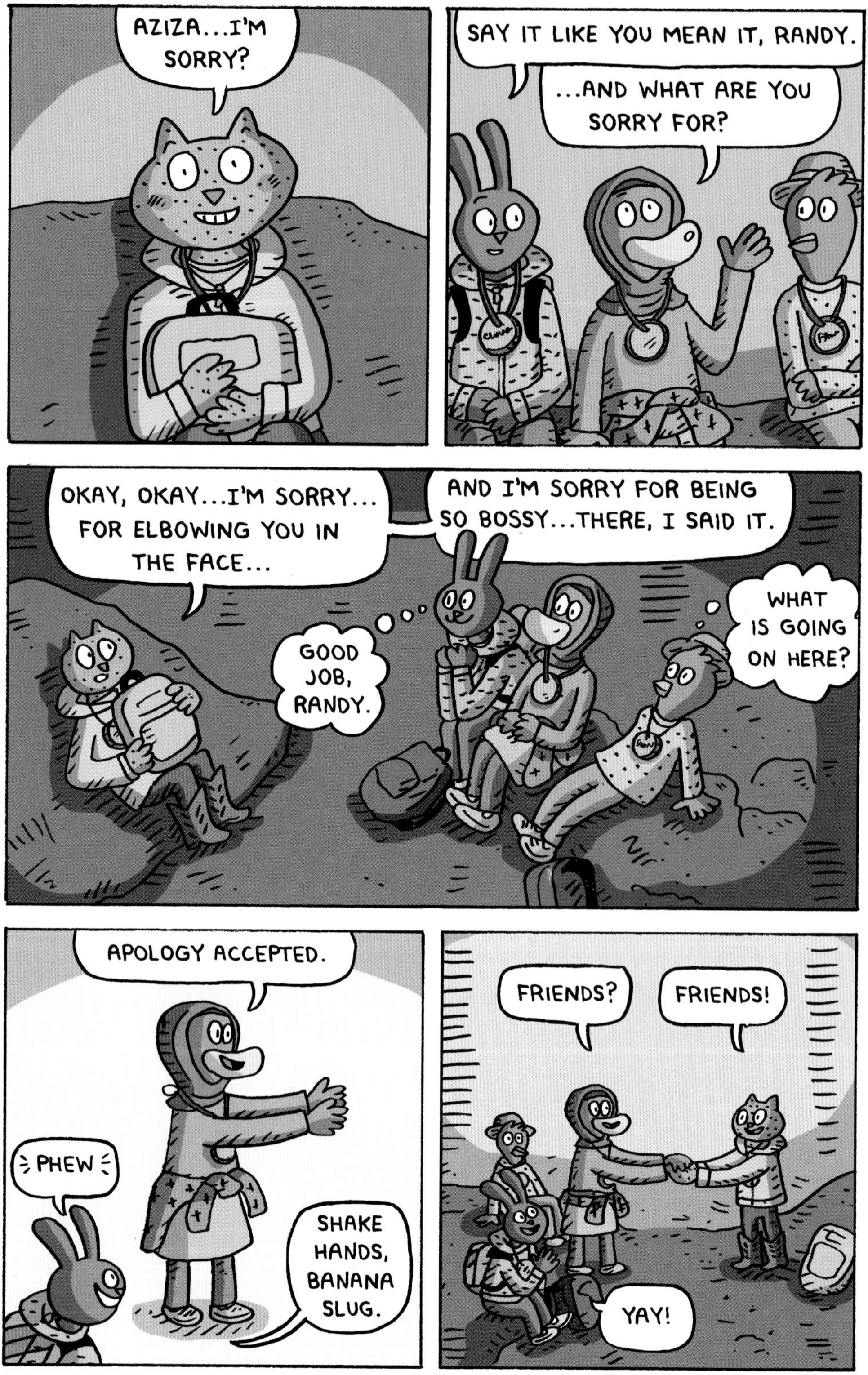
AZIZA...I'M SORRY?
SAY IT LIKE YOU MEAN IT, RANDY.
...AND WHAT ARE YOU SORRY FOR?
OKAY, OKAY...I'M SORRY... FOR ELBOWING YOU IN THE FACE...
AND I'M SORRY FOR BEING SO BOSSY...THERE, I SAID IT.
GOOD JOB, RANDY.
WHAT IS GOING ON HERE?
APOLOGY ACCEPTED.
PHEW
SHAKE HANDS, BANANA SLUG.
FRIENDS?
FRIENDS!
YAY!

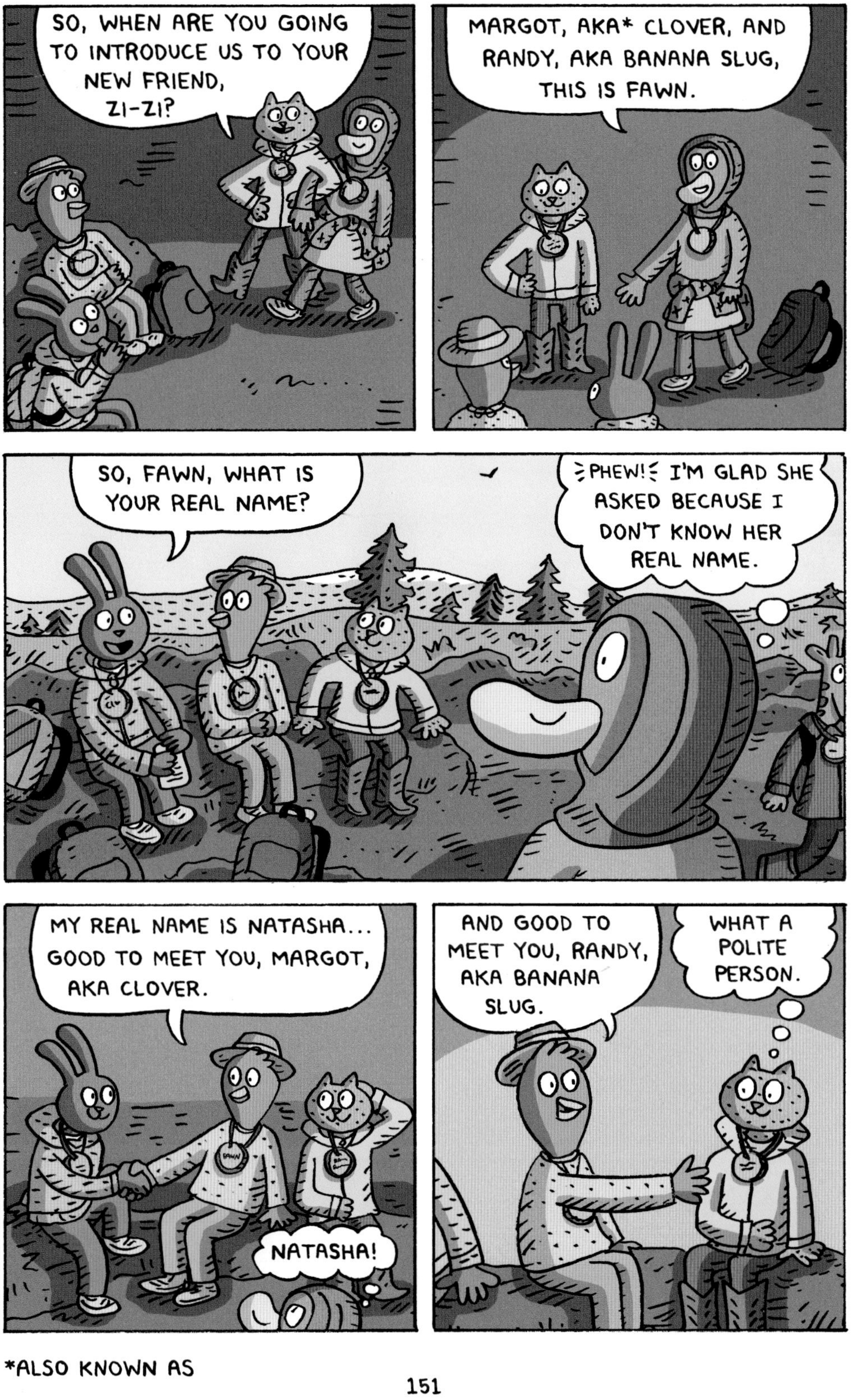
SO, WHEN ARE YOU GOING TO INTRODUCE US TO YOUR NEW FRIEND, ZI-ZI?
MARGOT, AKA* CLOVER, AND RANDY, AKA BANANA SLUG, THIS IS FAWN.
SO, FAWN, WHAT IS YOUR REAL NAME?
PHEW! I'M GLAD SHE ASKED BECAUSE I DON'T KNOW HER REAL NAME.
MY REAL NAME IS NATASHA... GOOD TO MEET YOU, MARGOT, AKA CLOVER.
NATASHA!
AND GOOD TO MEET YOU, RANDY, AKA BANANA SLUG.
WHAT A POLITE PERSON.

*ALSO KNOWN AS

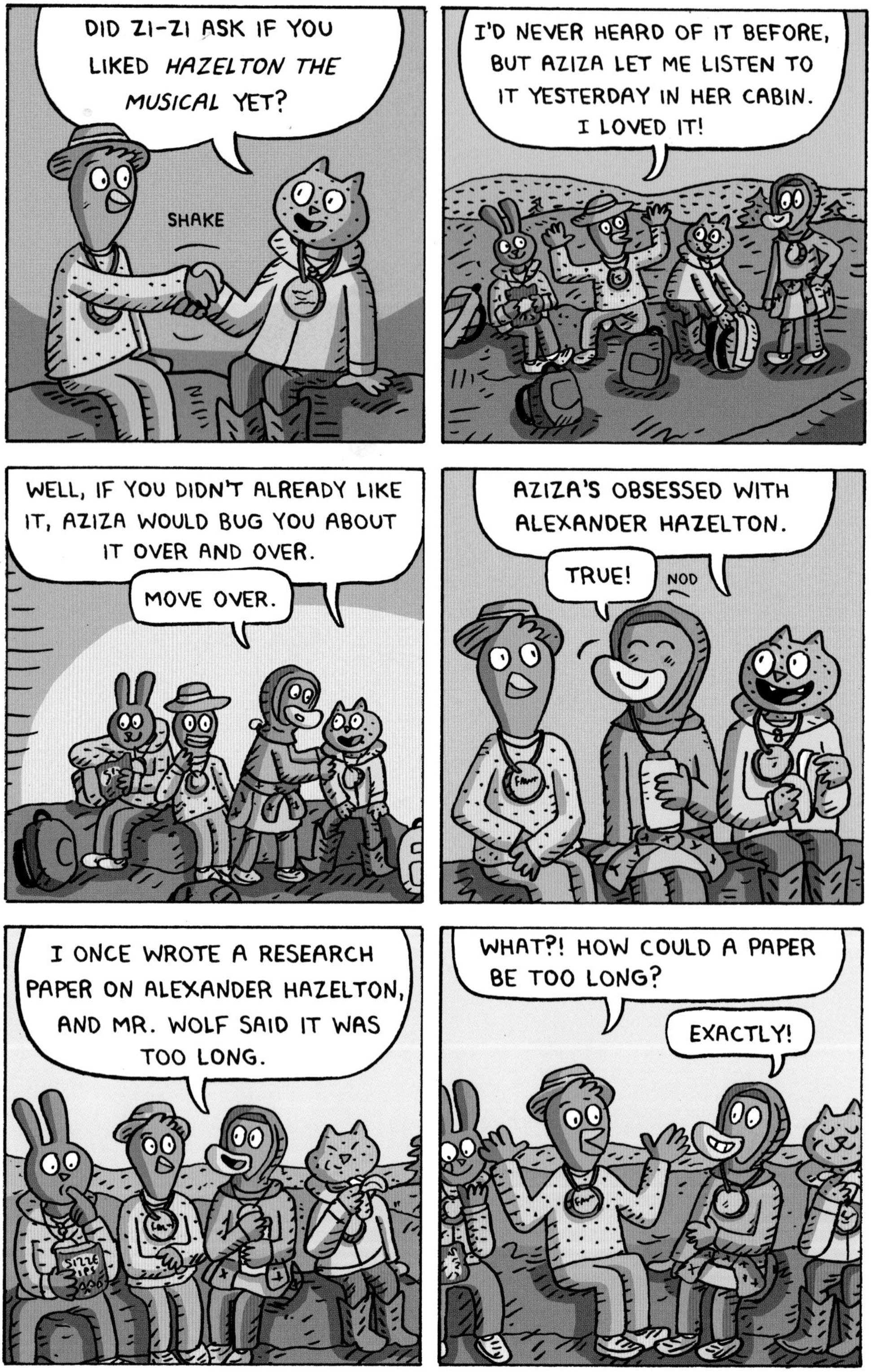
DID ZI-ZI ASK IF YOU LIKED *HAZELTON THE MUSICAL* YET?
SHAKE
I'D NEVER HEARD OF IT BEFORE, BUT AZIZA LET ME LISTEN TO IT YESTERDAY IN HER CABIN. I LOVED IT!
WELL, IF YOU DIDN'T ALREADY LIKE IT, AZIZA WOULD BUG YOU ABOUT IT OVER AND OVER.
MOVE OVER.
AZIZA'S OBSESSED WITH ALEXANDER HAZELTON.
TRUE!
NOD
I ONCE WROTE A RESEARCH PAPER ON ALEXANDER HAZELTON, AND MR. WOLF SAID IT WAS TOO LONG.
WHAT?! HOW COULD A PAPER BE TOO LONG?
EXACTLY!

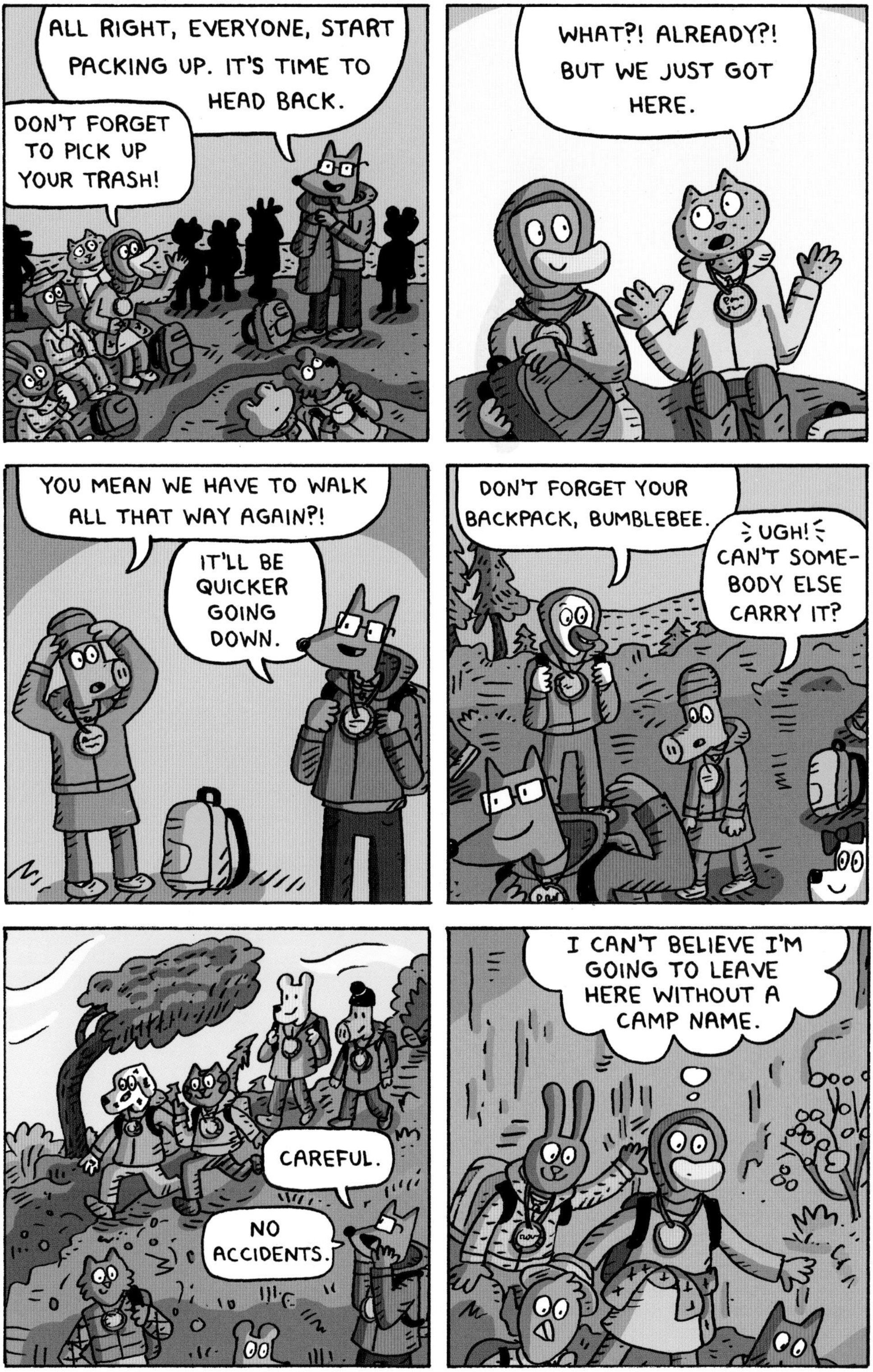
ALL RIGHT, EVERYONE, START PACKING UP. IT'S TIME TO HEAD BACK.
DON'T FORGET TO PICK UP YOUR TRASH!
WHAT?! ALREADY?! BUT WE JUST GOT HERE.
YOU MEAN WE HAVE TO WALK ALL THAT WAY AGAIN?!
IT'LL BE QUICKER GOING DOWN.
DON'T FORGET YOUR BACKPACK, BUMBLEBEE.
UGH! CAN'T SOMEBODY ELSE CARRY IT?
CAREFUL.
NO ACCIDENTS.
I CAN'T BELIEVE I'M GOING TO LEAVE HERE WITHOUT A CAMP NAME.

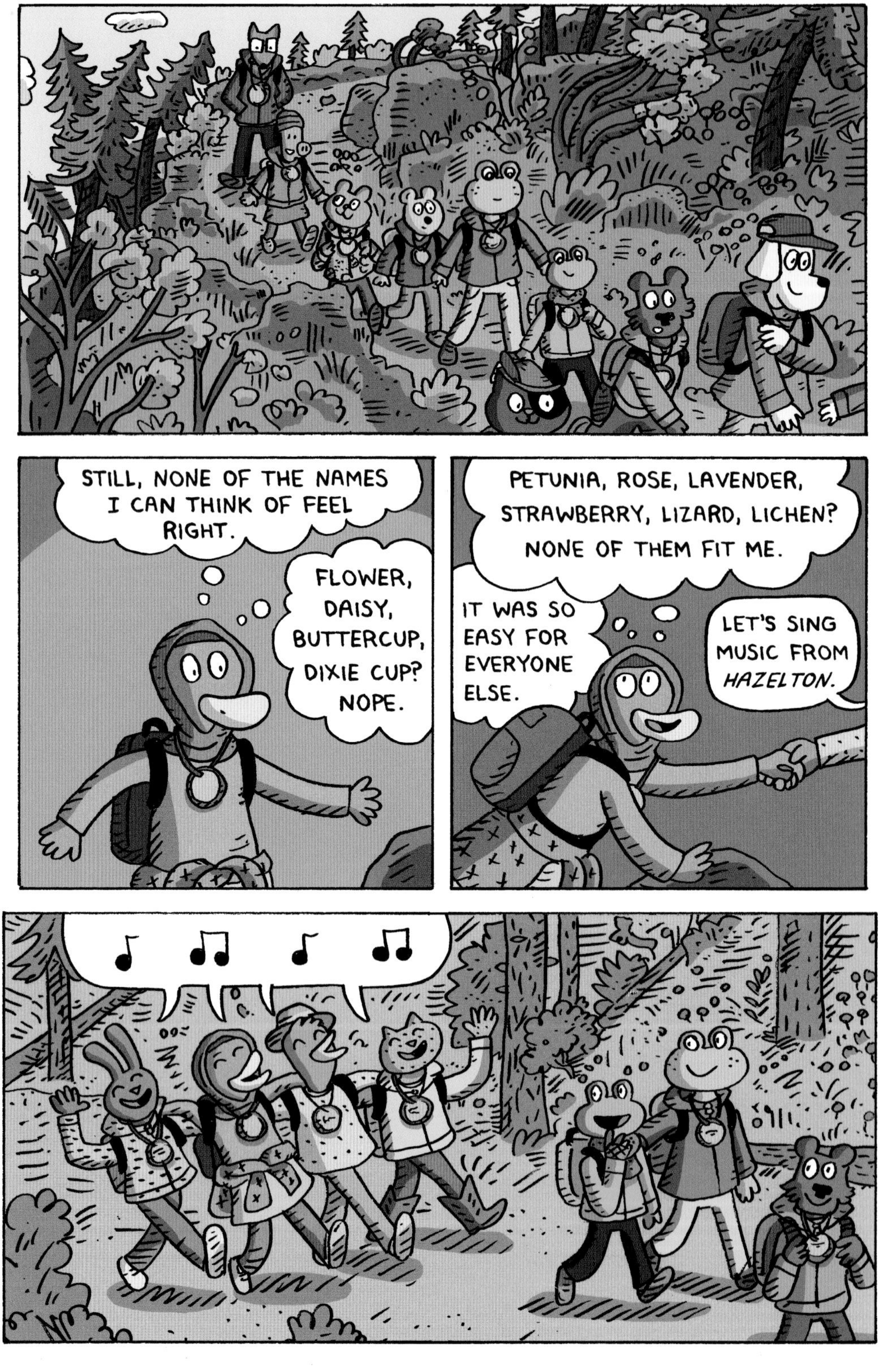
STILL, NONE OF THE NAMES I CAN THINK OF FEEL RIGHT.
FLOWER, DAISY, BUTTERCUP, DIXIE CUP? NOPE.
PETUNIA, ROSE, LAVENDER, STRAWBERRY, LIZARD, LICHEN? NONE OF THEM FIT ME.
IT WAS SO EASY FOR EVERYONE ELSE.
LET'S SING MUSIC FROM *HAZELTON*.

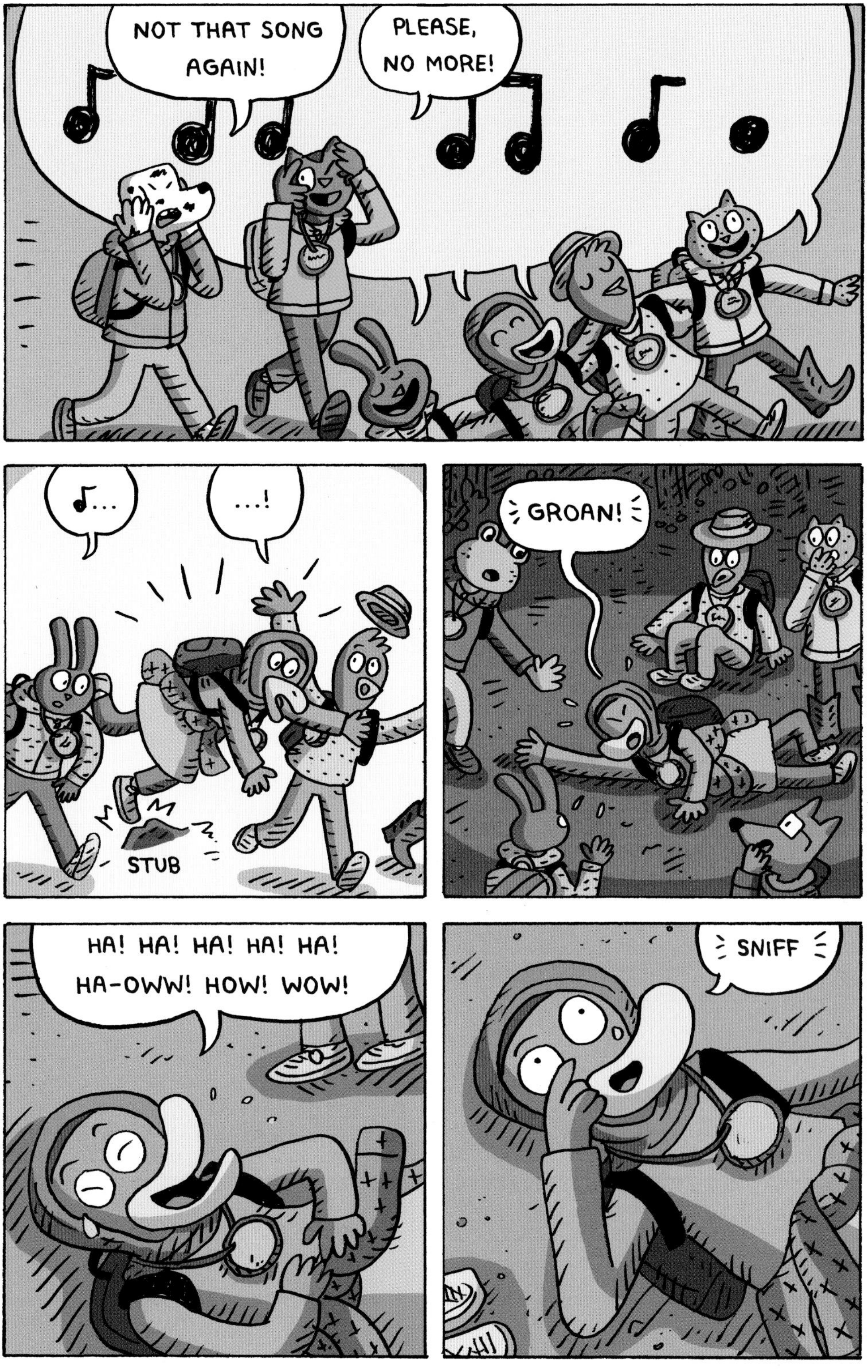
NOT THAT SONG AGAIN!
PLEASE, NO MORE!
♩...
...!
STUB
GROAN!
HA! HA! HA! HA! HA! HA-OWW! HOW! WOW!
SNIFF

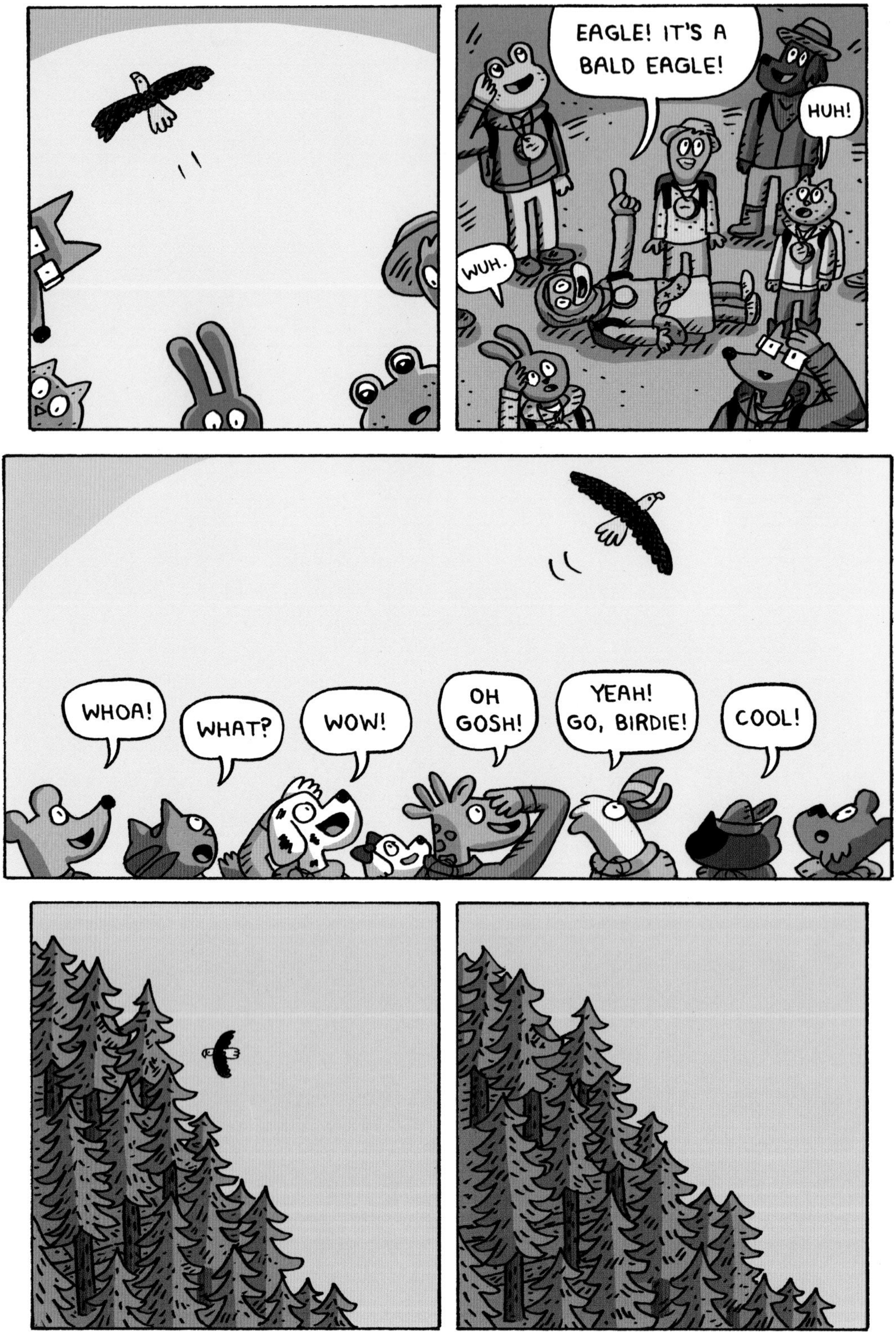
EAGLE! IT'S A BALD EAGLE!
HUH!
WUH.
WHOA!
WHAT?
WOW!
OH GOSH!
YEAH! GO, BIRDIE!
COOL!

CHAPTER TEN
Good-bye

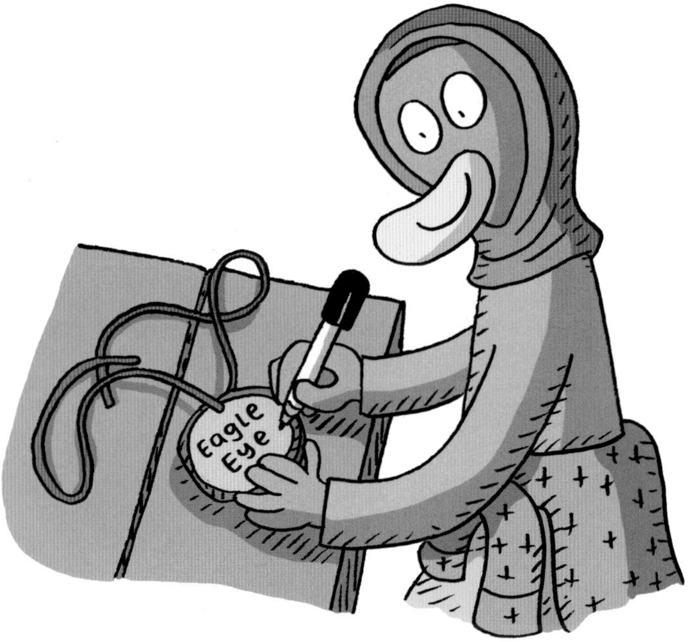
Eagle Eye

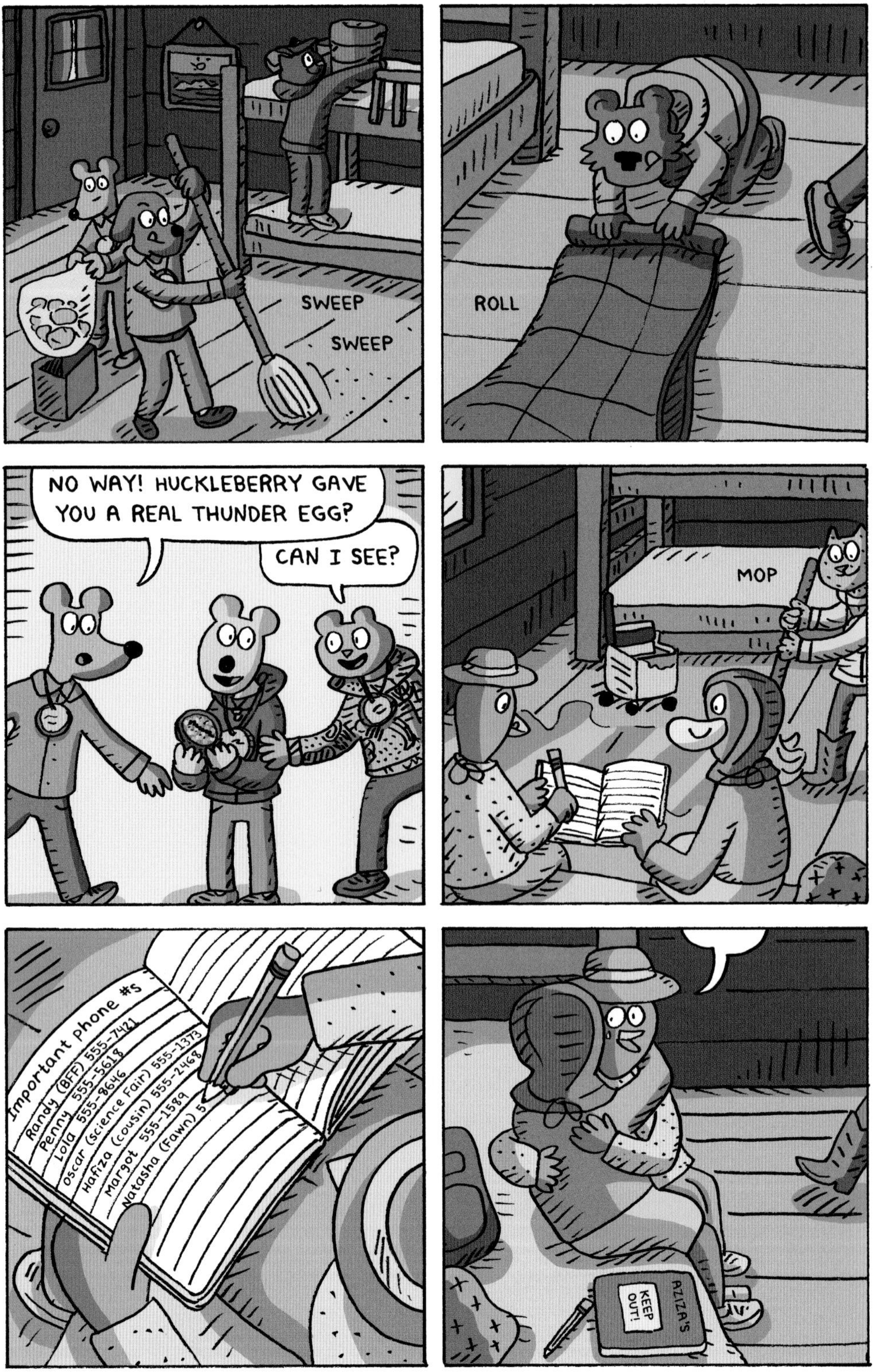
SWEEP
SWEEP
ROLL
NO WAY! HUCKLEBERRY GAVE YOU A REAL THUNDER EGG?
CAN I SEE?
MOP
Important phone #s
Randy (BFF) 555-7421
Penny 555-5618
Lola 555-8646
oscar (science Fair) 555-1373
Hafiza (cousin) 555-2468
Margot 555-1589
Natasha (Fawn) 5
AZIZA'S
KEEP OUT!

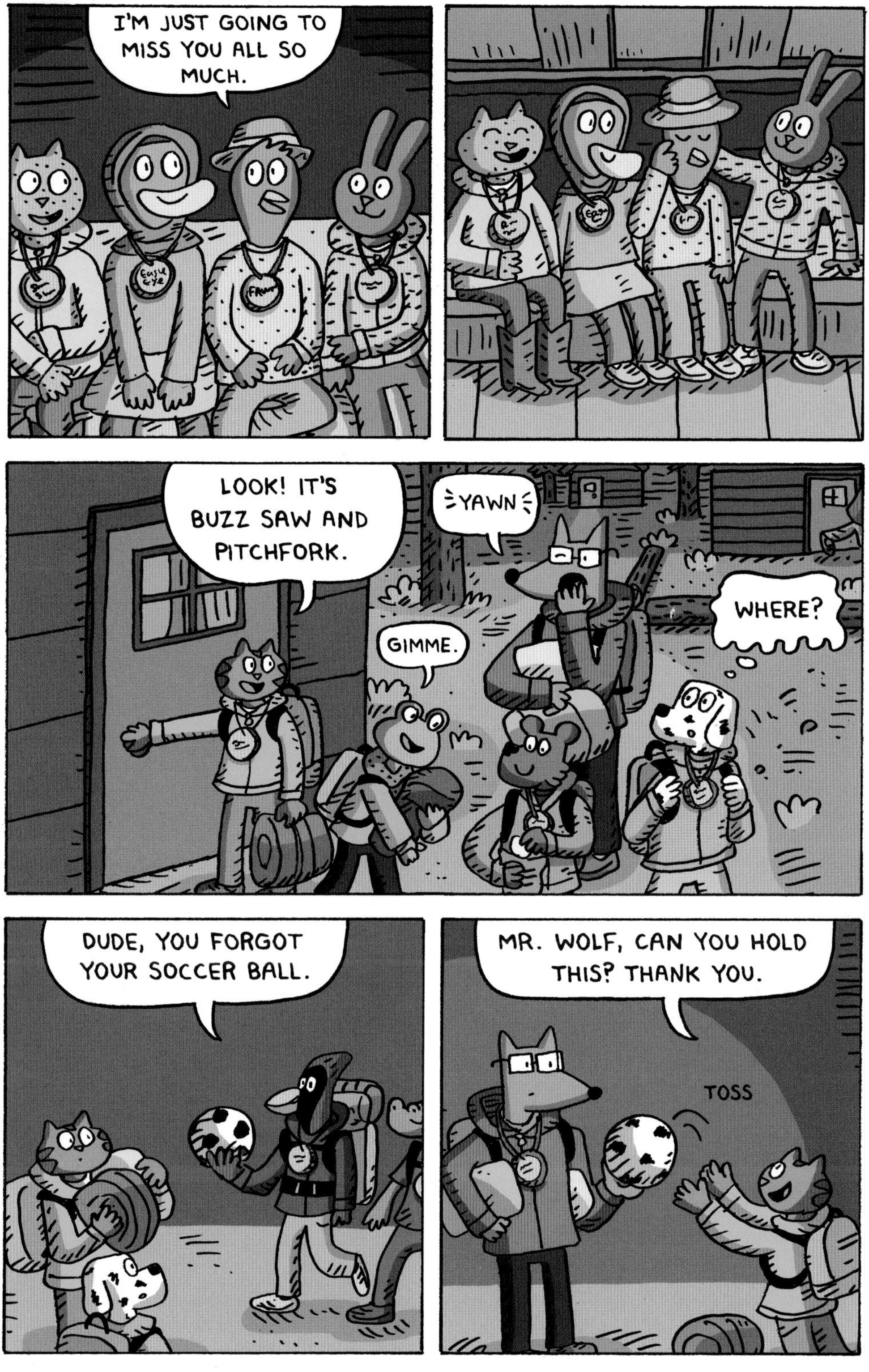
I'M JUST GOING TO MISS YOU ALL SO MUCH.
LOOK! IT'S BUZZ SAW AND PITCHFORK.
YAWN
GIMME.
WHERE?
DUDE, YOU FORGOT YOUR SOCCER BALL.
MR. WOLF, CAN YOU HOLD THIS? THANK YOU.
TOSS

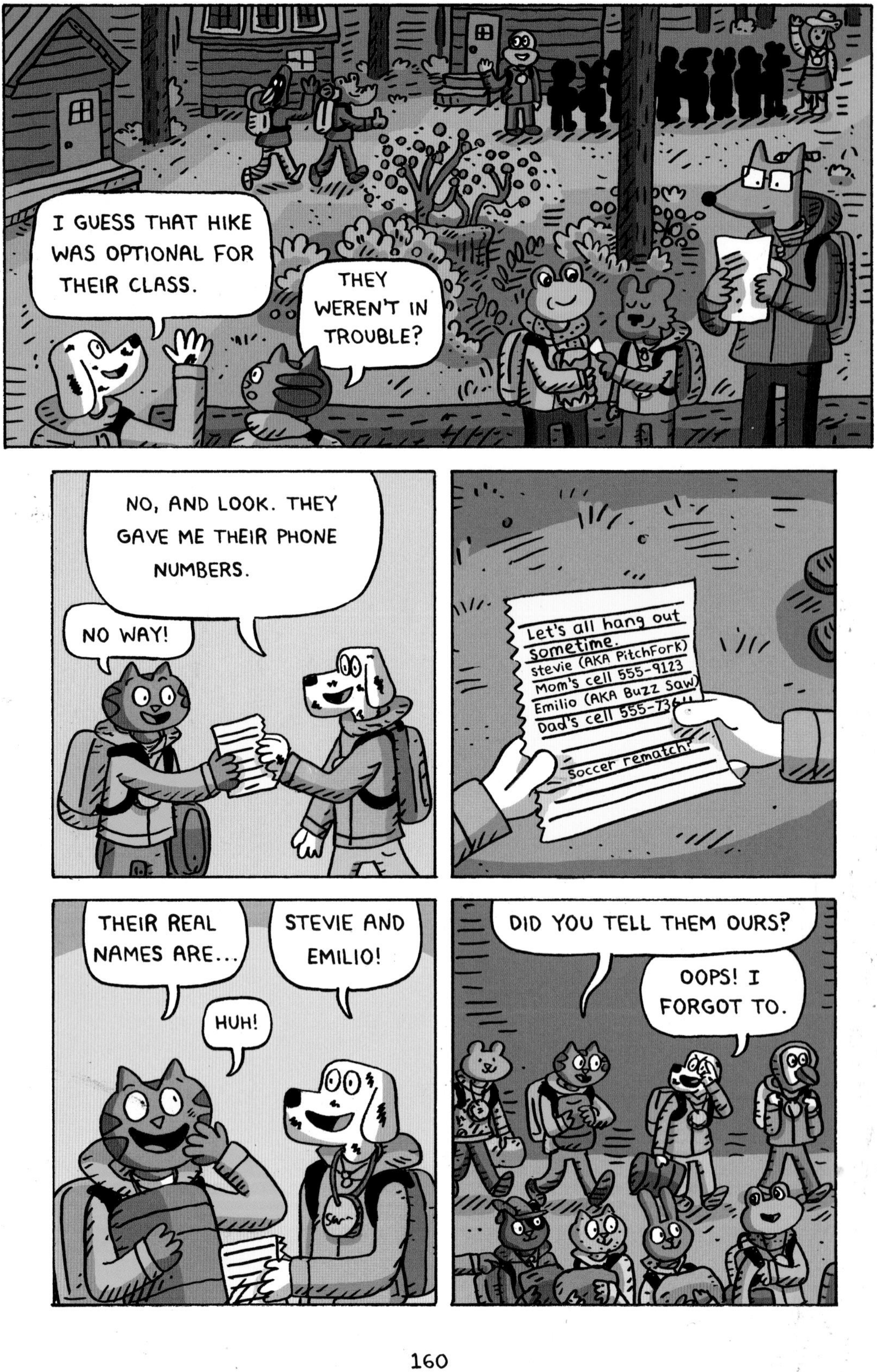
I GUESS THAT HIKE WAS OPTIONAL FOR THEIR CLASS.
THEY WEREN'T IN TROUBLE?
NO, AND LOOK. THEY GAVE ME THEIR PHONE NUMBERS.
NO WAY!
Let's all hang out sometime.
Stevie (AKA PitchFork)
Mom's cell 555-9123
Emilio (AKA Buzz Saw)
Dad's cell 555-73
Soccer rematch?
THEIR REAL NAMES ARE...
STEVIE AND EMILIO!
HUH!
DID YOU TELL THEM OURS?
OOPS! I FORGOT TO.

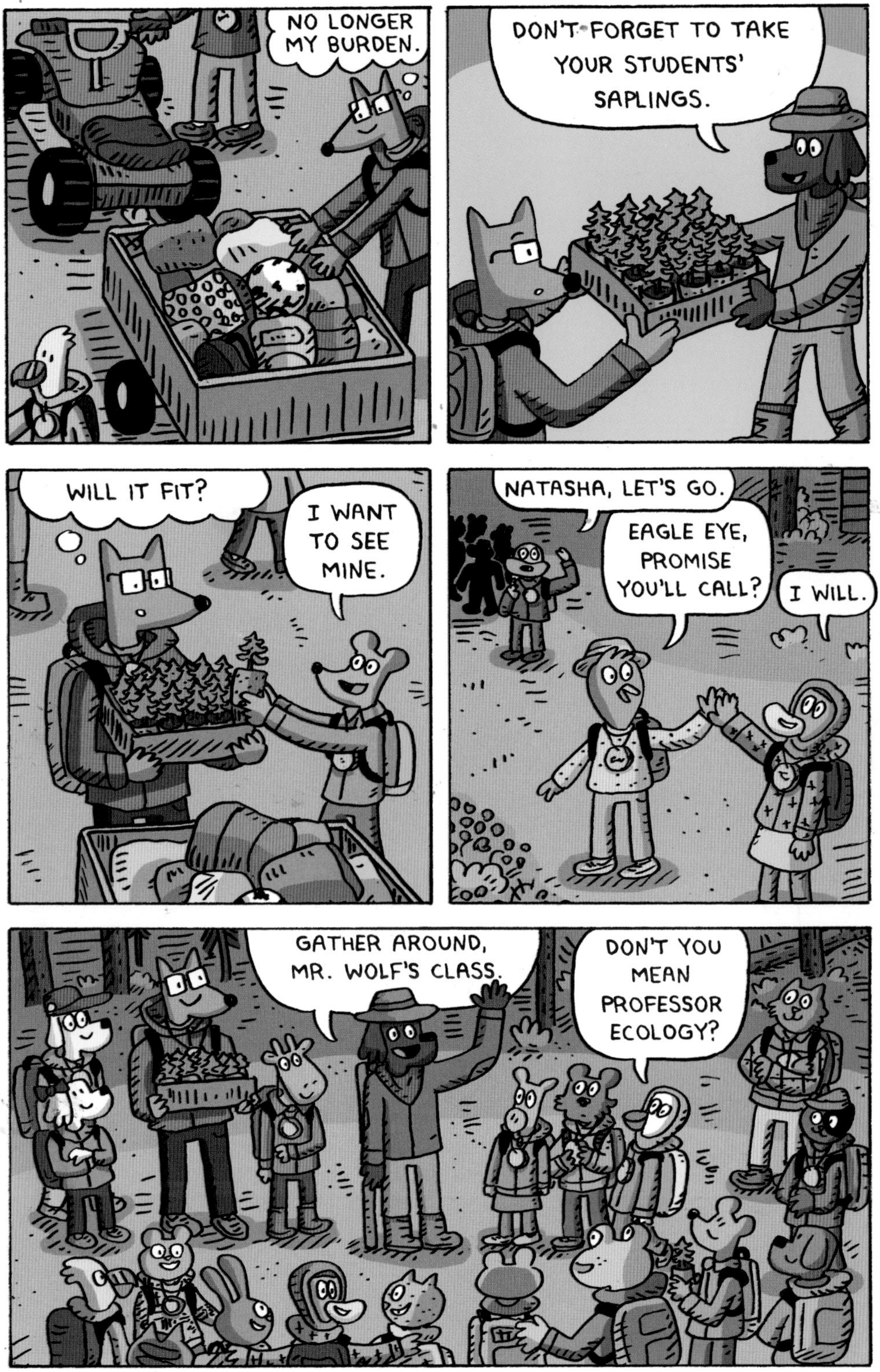
NO LONGER MY BURDEN.
DON'T FORGET TO TAKE YOUR STUDENTS' SAPLINGS.
WILL IT FIT?
I WANT TO SEE MINE.
NATASHA, LET'S GO.
EAGLE EYE, PROMISE YOU'LL CALL?
I WILL.
GATHER AROUND, MR. WOLF'S CLASS.
DON'T YOU MEAN PROFESSOR ECOLOGY?

WHO CAN TELL ME ONE THING YOU LEARNED DURING YOUR STAY AT BATTLE AX CREEK?

YES, BUMBLE-BEE?

I LEARNED THAT PLANTS GIVE US OXYGEN AND MAKE THEIR OWN FOOD FROM THE SUN, CARBON DIOXIDE, AND WATER.

YES, THAT'S PHOTOSYNTHESIS.

WHAT MORE DID WE LEARN? YES?

I LEARNED ABOUT HYDROELECTRICITY.

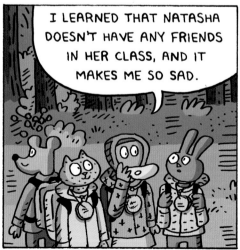

I LEARNED THAT NATASHA DOESN'T HAVE ANY FRIENDS IN HER CLASS, AND IT MAKES ME SO SAD.

YEAH, BUT SHE HAS US NOW. AND WE'LL ALL BE IN THE SAME MIDDLE SCHOOL IN A COUPLE OF YEARS.

BUT THAT'S SO LONG!

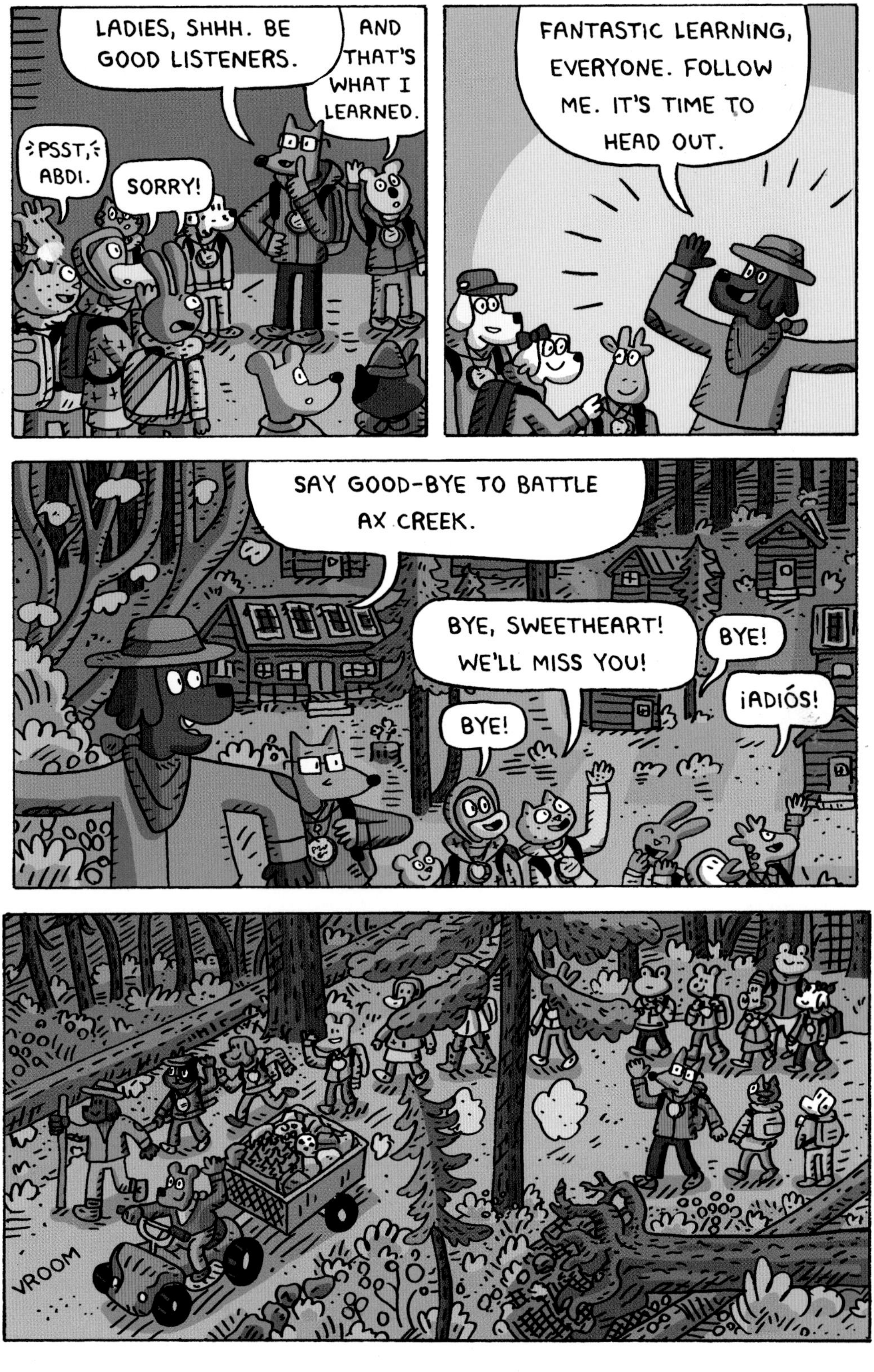
LADIES, SHHH. BE GOOD LISTENERS.
AND THAT'S WHAT I LEARNED.
PSST, ABDI.
SORRY!
FANTASTIC LEARNING, EVERYONE. FOLLOW ME. IT'S TIME TO HEAD OUT.
SAY GOOD-BYE TO BATTLE AX CREEK.
BYE, SWEETHEART! WE'LL MISS YOU!
BYE!
BYE!
¡ADIÓS!
VROOM

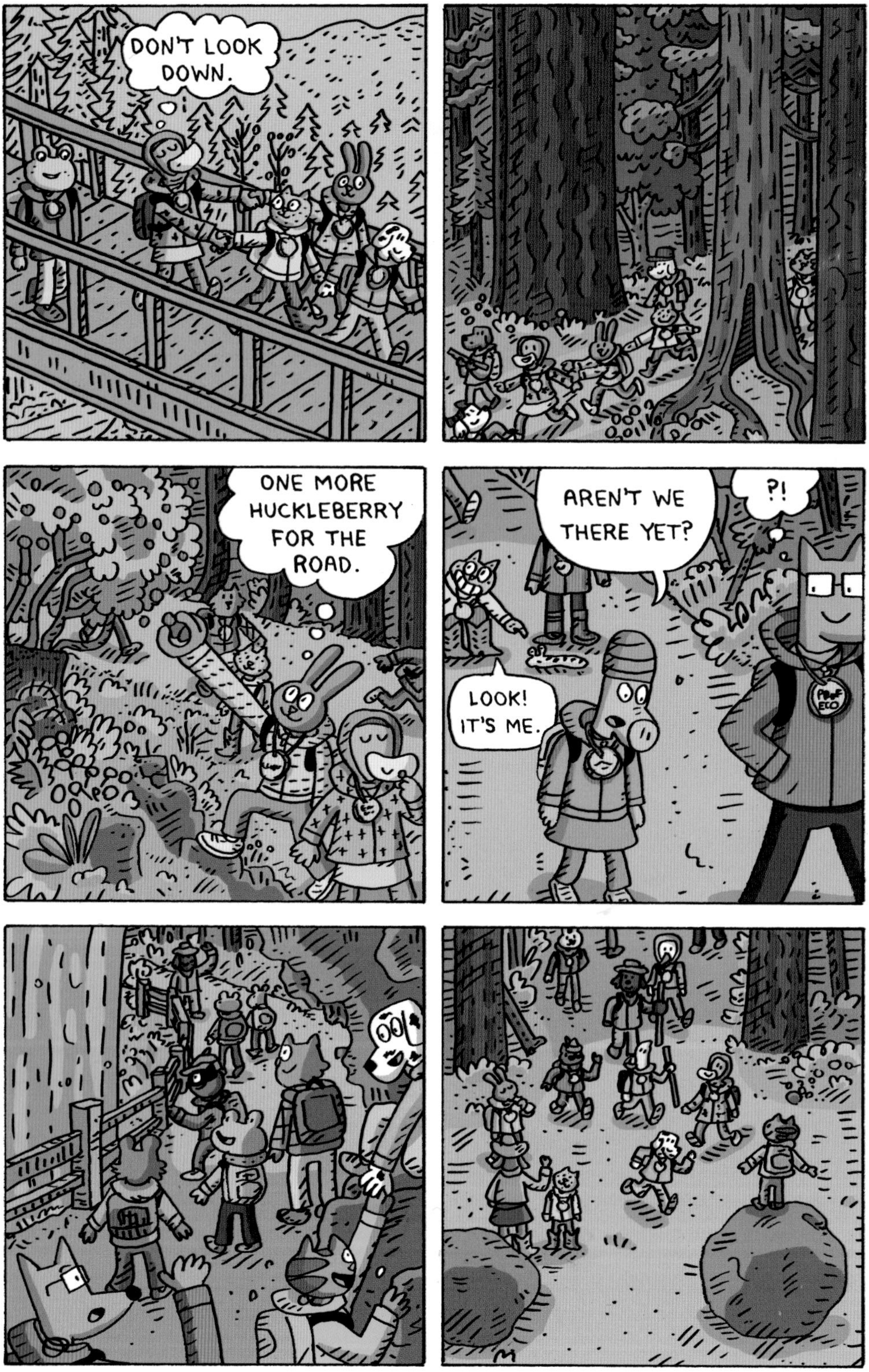
DON'T LOOK DOWN.
ONE MORE HUCKLEBERRY FOR THE ROAD.
AREN'T WE THERE YET?
?!
LOOK! IT'S ME.

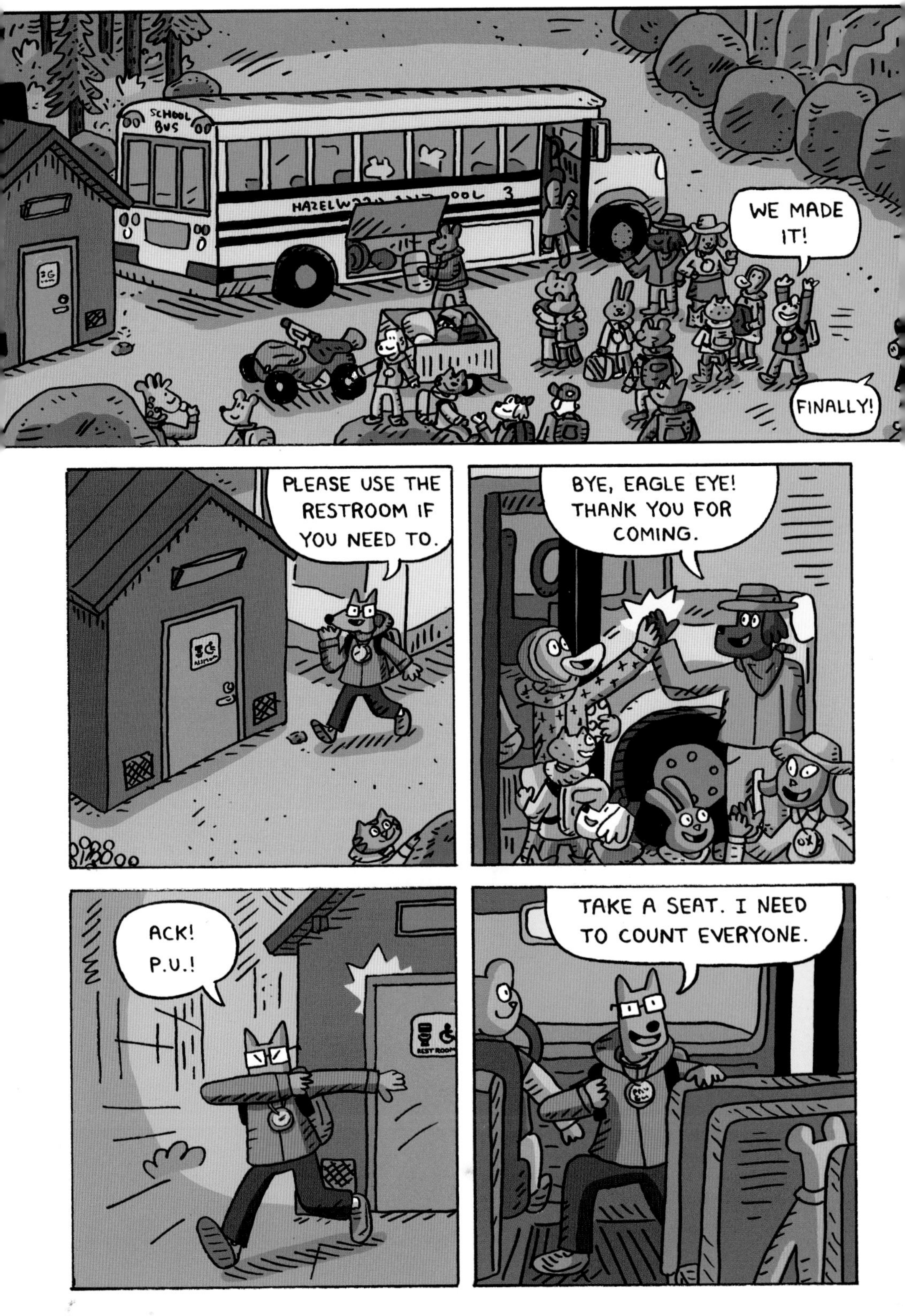

WE MADE IT!
FINALLY!
PLEASE USE THE RESTROOM IF YOU NEED TO.
BYE, EAGLE EYE! THANK YOU FOR COMING.
ACK! P.U.!
TAKE A SEAT. I NEED TO COUNT EVERYONE.

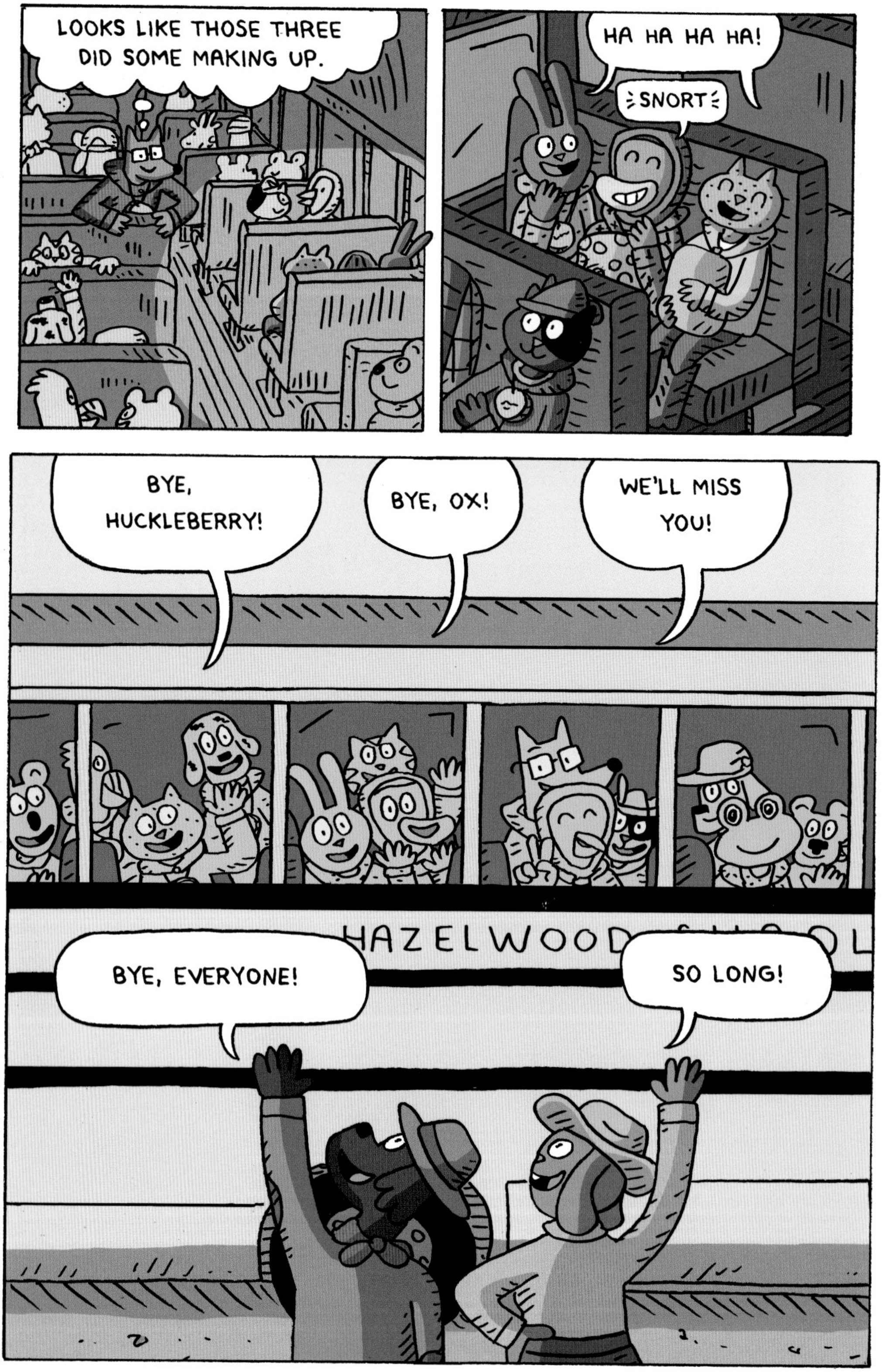
LOOKS LIKE THOSE THREE DID SOME MAKING UP.
HA HA HA HA!
SNORT
BYE, HUCKLEBERRY!
BYE, OX!
WE'LL MISS YOU!
HAZELWOOD SCHOOL
BYE, EVERYONE!
SO LONG!

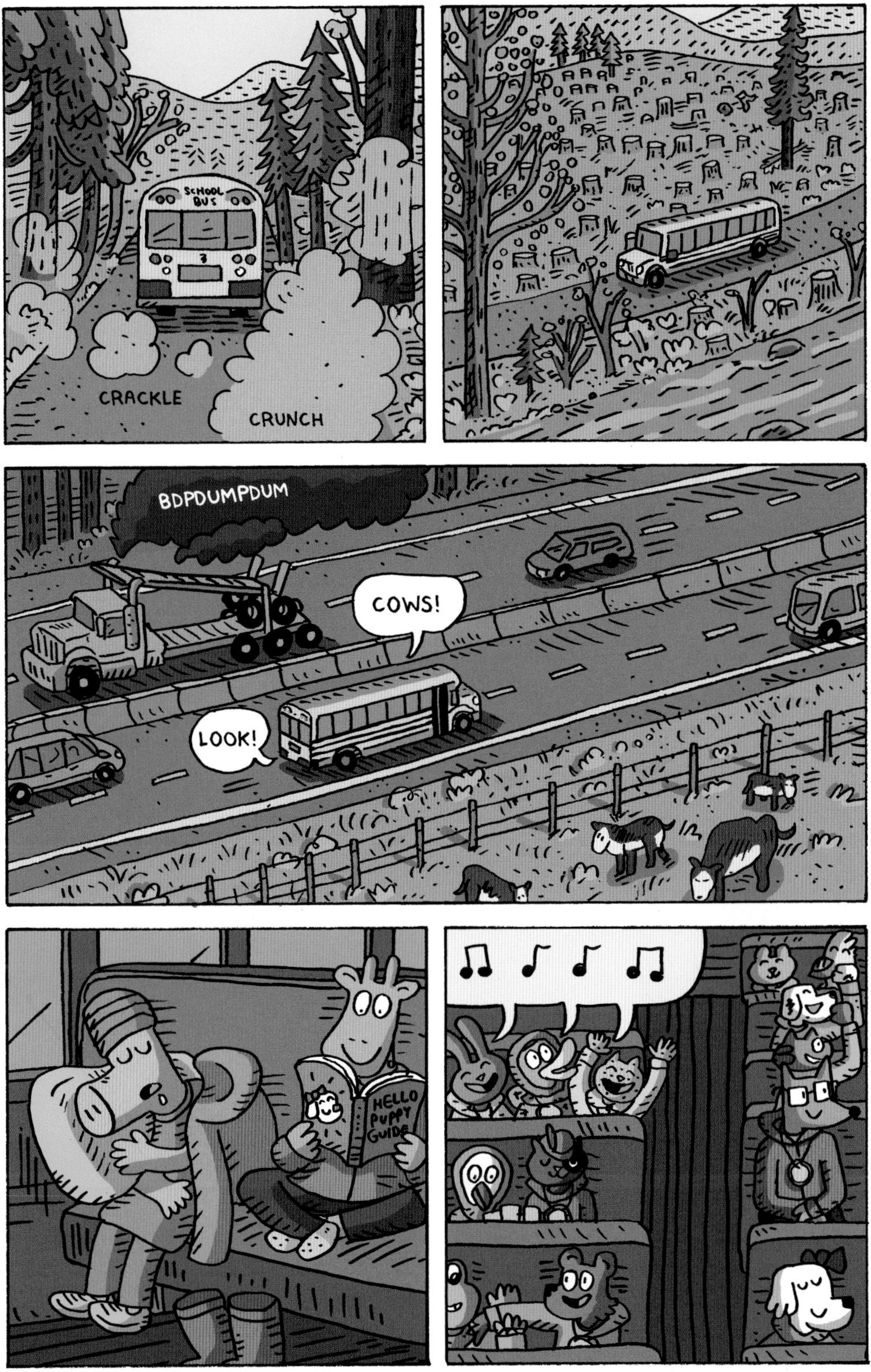
SCHOOL BUS
CRACKLE
CRUNCH
BDPDUMPDUM
COWS!
LOOK!
HELLO PUPPY GUIDE

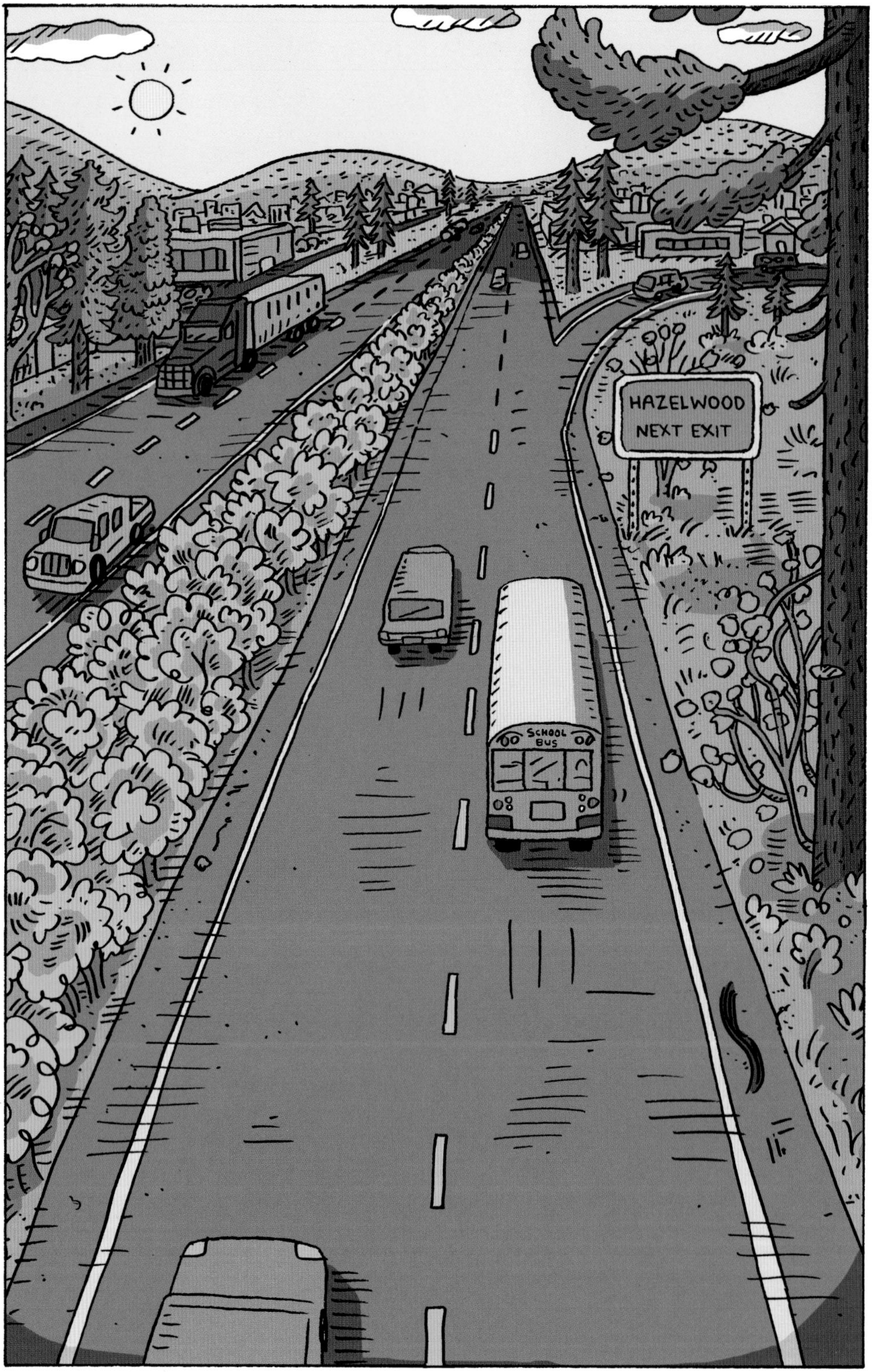
HAZELWOOD
NEXT EXIT
SCHOOL BUS

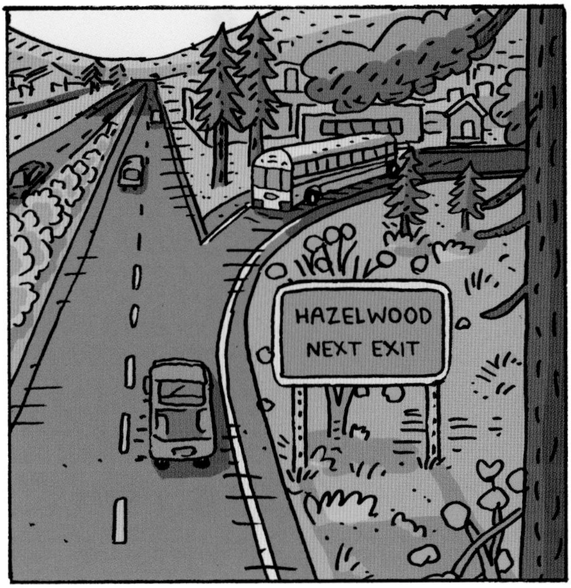
HAZELWOOD
NEXT EXIT

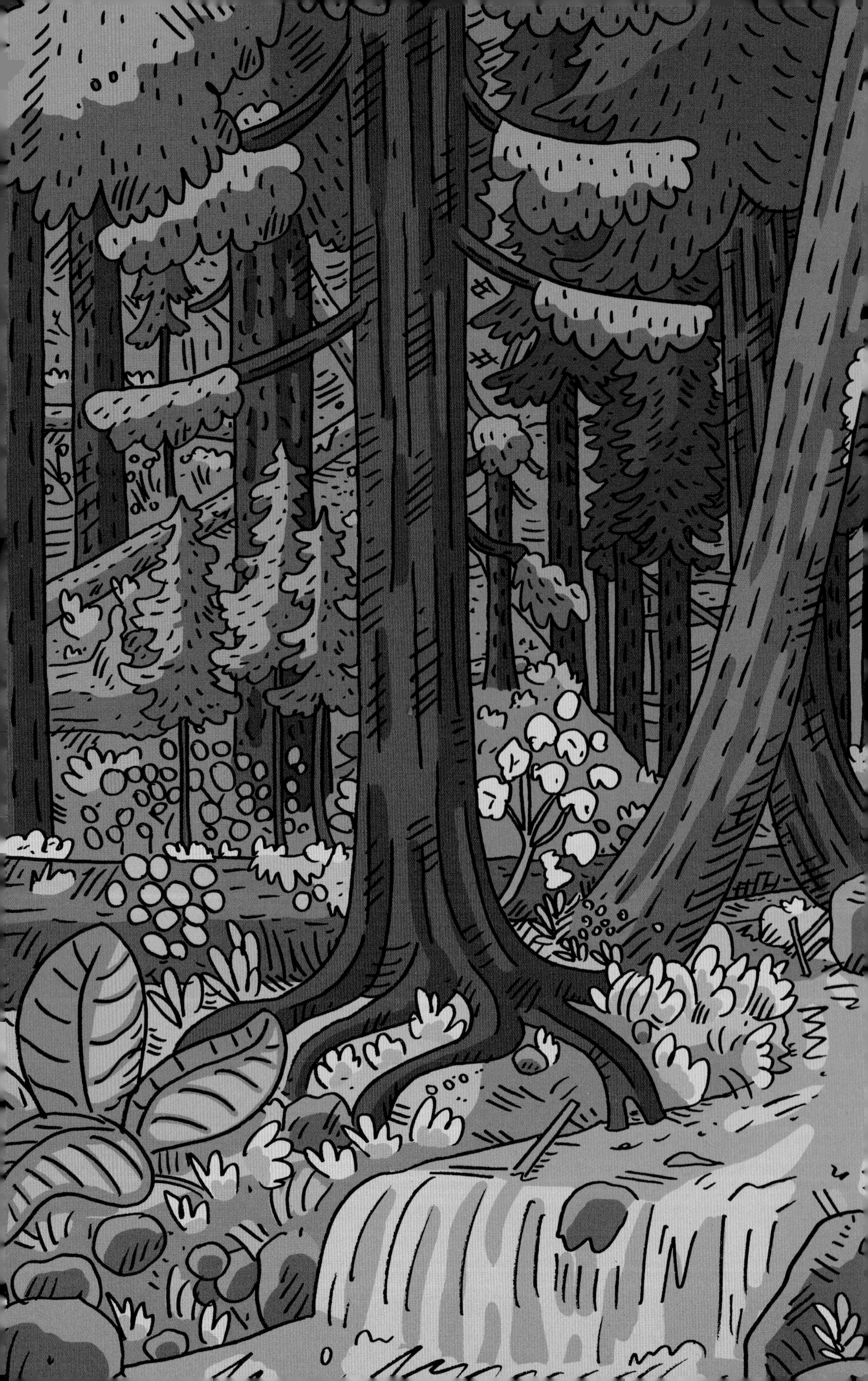

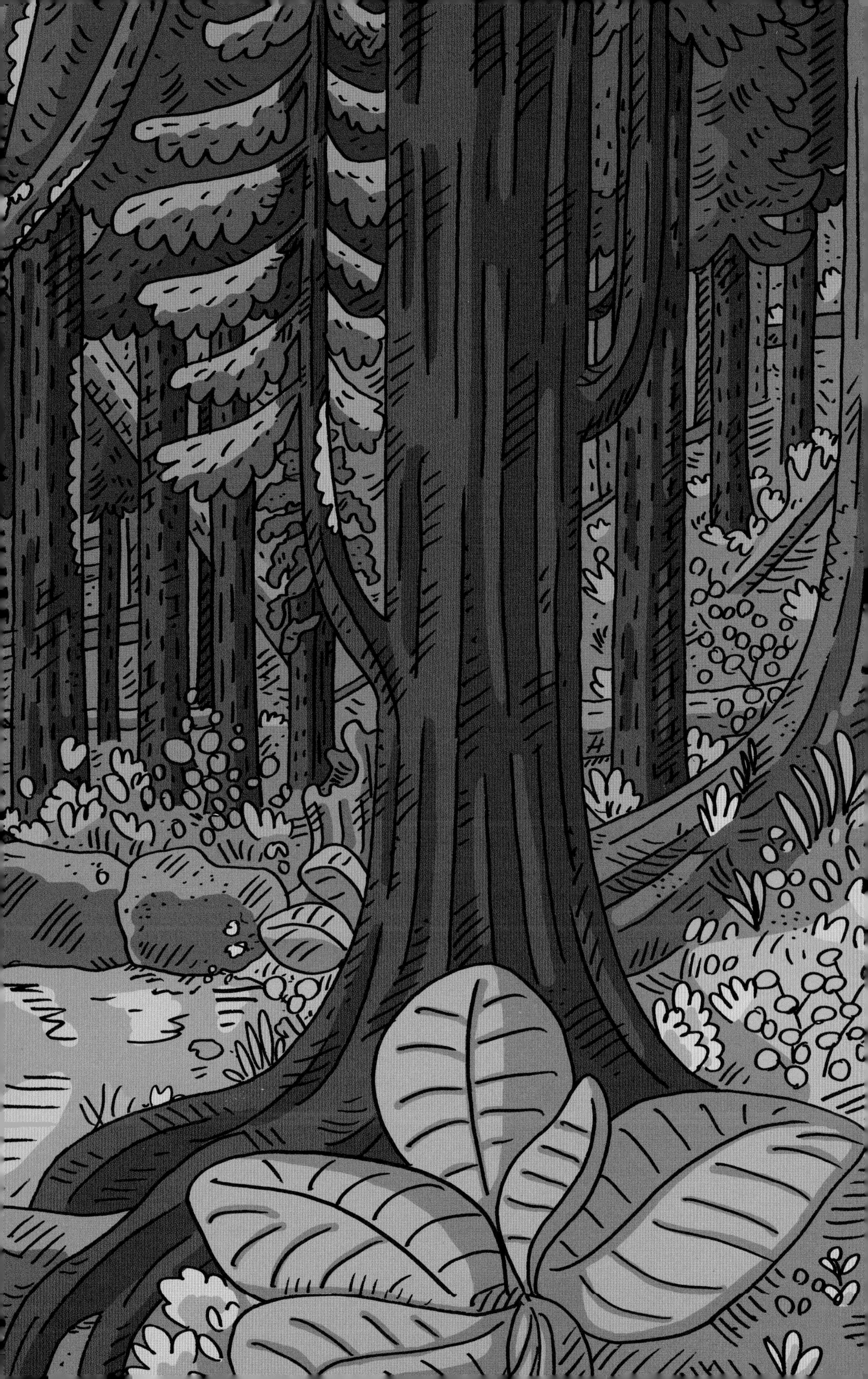

Thank you to . . .

Ariel, Marlen, Don, Alona, Lisa, David, Ed, Jeremy, Anna, Elisha, Theo, Miles, Elliott, Gena, Justin, Elizabeth, Briceton, Benjamin, Derrik, Kristen, Sharon, Joe, and all my extended family.

My agent, Judy Hansen, my editor, Cassandra Pelham Fulton, Jordana Kulak, David Saylor, Phil Falco, Lizette Serrano, Shivana Sookdeo, and everyone at Scholastic who has worked behind the scenes to support Mr. Wolf's Class.

Saadia Faruqi, for reading early drafts and giving me invaluable feedback. Please check out her fantastic Yasmin book series.

Dav Pilkey, Raina Telgemeier, Greg Means, Jonathan Hill, Lark Pien, Jess Keating, Vera Brosgol, Breena Bard, Thien Pham, Gene Luen Yang, Jarrett Lerner, John Schu, Kate Messner, and Jim Di Bartolo for your support.

My students, as always: You inspire me, challenge me, and keep me grounded. You are the future.

Tom Spurgeon and *The Comics Reporter* for building and supporting a community of cartoonists and comics readers. You are missed.

Alec Longstreth for his amazing coloring job and his wife, Claire Sanders, for assisting. Please check out Alec's comics at isleofelsi.com.

And finally, thank you, dear reader, for spending time in Mr. Wolf's class. This book wouldn't exist without you.

Author photo by Renée Lopez

Aron Nels Steinke is the Eisner Award-winning creator of the Mr. Wolf's Class series, and is the illustrator and coauthor, with Ariel Cohn, of *The Zoo Box*. He teaches fourth and fifth grade in Portland, Oregon, to a group of students who are much too competitive at four square. Aron's favorite wild berry is the thimbleberry (*Rubus parviflorus*), and he enjoys foraging for wild plants. The old-growth forest in this story was inspired by many places he likes to visit in the Pacific Northwest, such as the Opal Creek Wilderness area, Breitenbush Hot Springs, Oxbow Regional Park, and the Olympic National Forest. Visit Aron online at mrwolfsclass.com.

Don't stop now! Check out these other exciting adventures in Mr. Wolf's class!

From the Eisner Award-winning author
ARON NELS STEINKE
MR. WOLF'S CLASS

From the Eisner Award-winning author
ARON NELS STEINKE
MR. WOLF'S CLASS
MYSTERY CLUB

From the Eisner Award-winning author
ARON NELS STEINKE
MR. WOLF'S CLASS
LUCKY STARS

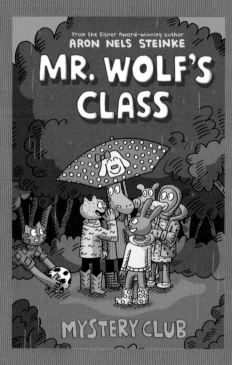